A Spider

ON THE

STAIRS

ALSO BY CASSANDRA CHAN

Trick of the Mind
Village Affairs
The Young Widow

A Spider
ON THE
STAIRS

CASSANDRA CHAN

MINOTAUR BOOKS 🙢 NEW YORK

This is a work of fiction. All of the characters, organizations, and events portrayed in this novel are either products of the author's imagination or are used fictitiously.

To Crissie and Carol Tucker. It's not always easy to live with a writer who hasn't met her deadline, but you two didn't seem to mind at all. In fact, you helped. Or sometimes distracted. Anyway, I'm grateful for it all.

A Spider

ON THE

STAIRS

Spider Lore

Never kill a spider in the afternoon or evening, but always kill the spider unlucky enough to show himself early in the morning, for the old French proverb says:

> *Araignée du matin—chagrin;*
> *Araignée du midi—plaisir;*
> *Araignée du soir—espoir*

(A spider seen in the morning is a sign of grief; a spider seen at noon, of joy; a spider seen in the evening, of hope.)

1

In Which Bethancourt Contemplates the Awfulness of Christmas

*T*he twenty-third of December was a grey, cheerless day, with black clouds scudding across the sky and spatterings of rain. Phillip Bethancourt, looking out the window of his parents' house in Yorkshire, felt it suited his mood exactly. It had been many long years since the exciting scent of the Christmas tree with the brightness of its ornaments and the munificence of the presents spread beneath it had been enough to ameliorate the essential awfulness of the holiday at Wethercross Grange. Attendance, however, was not optional, and every year saw him making his way grudgingly northward, resigned to sacrifice.

It was not that his family did not celebrate the holidays with enthusiasm; quite the contrary, the Grange was decked out for Christmastide. The old manor house was filled with the mixed scents of evergreens, candle wax, and the burning Yule log, along with the fainter aroma of cooking; the mantels were all draped with evergreens and holly, and the Christmas tree in the drawing room was ablaze with lights and colored ornaments. There were even Christmas carols playing softly on the old stereo system. No, it was not that the Grange lacked anything in the way of Christmas cheer, it was Bethancourt's place in it that caused his gloom. On these occasions, there were invariably endless criticisms of his lifestyle, of how he spent his money, of his lack of a proper job or a proper wife. It was no fun, he reflected, being the black sheep, though for the life of him, he had never meant to be. He had taken a first at Oxford, and he had shepherded the money he had inherited carefully, investing wisely and conservatively; he really did not see why he should not now be left alone to do as he liked.

He was in his bedroom at the Grange, dressing for dinner and admittedly dawdling over the process. In the mirror he saw the reflection of a tall, bespectacled young man whose normally shaggy fair hair had been recently trimmed in anticipation of parental criticism, his lean frame dressed in a perfectly tailored dinner jacket made for him by Redwood & Feller. A jacket that he had not worn, to his recollection, since last Christmas.

He was disturbed from the contemplation of his image by the ringing of his mobile phone. Glancing at the caller ID, he recognized the number as that of Scotland Yard and his mood immediately plummeted further. His friend, Detective Sergeant Jack Gibbons, had just come off a long sick leave during which he had continually fretted over his enforced inactivity, and he was now conversely cheery despite having pulled the Christmas holiday shift. In his present mood, the last thing Bethancourt wanted was to talk to someone giddy with joy, but Gibbons was a close friend and he answered the call nonetheless.

"Hullo, Phillip," said Gibbons happily. "How is the weather in the Dales then?"

"Dreadful," answered Bethancourt morosely.

"Raining?"

"Buckets," affirmed Bethancourt.

"Well, maybe it'll clear up," said Gibbons with what Bethancourt viewed as an overly optimistic air. "Or perhaps it'll turn to snow."

4

"Don't say that," begged Bethancourt. "If it starts snowing the way it's raining, it'll block all the roads and I'll never get out of here."

"Oh," said Gibbons. "I hadn't thought of that."

"So," said Bethancourt, endeavoring to change the subject, "what are you up to? Have they given you a case yet?"

This was mere masochism on Bethancourt's part, as he was an avid amateur detective who followed Gibbons's cases closely and would only be disappointed if an interesting case was to come up now, just when he could not take part in it.

"There is a case," affirmed Gibbons sunnily. "I just got the call and I'm on my way over to the Yard in an hour to meet with Superintendent Brumby."

"Splendid," said Bethancourt, although there was a slightly hollow tone to his voice. He sat down in the chair by the window and lit a cigarette.

"I'm to get briefed on the Ashdon killer," said Gibbons. "And then run up to see if this new murder is connected."

Surprise shook Bethancourt momentarily out of his doldrums. "The Ashdon killer?" he repeated. "There's been another victim?"

"Possibly," said Gibbons. "Anyway, another girl's been found dead in a shop."

Bethancourt sighed. "I hate it when they're young and innocent," he said. Then a thought struck him. "Wait a moment," he added. "They're sending you off on a serial-killer case?"

"Just to confirm or rule it out," answered Gibbons. "If I think it really is Ashdon's work, the superintendent will come up and take over. But, Phillip, it's in Yorkshire."

"What?"

"This new murder," explained Gibbons. "It's in Yorkshire."

For the first time since he had arrived in the Dales, a gleam of hope showed in Bethancourt's eye.

"That's brilliant, Jack," he said. "Where in Yorkshire?"

"In York," answered Gibbons. "A body turned up this morning in a little shop called Accessorize in Davygate."

"But York's just up the road," said Bethancourt. "You could drive over for Christmas dinner—won't take you an hour."

"Thanks, Phillip," said Gibbons. "I'd like to do that if I can. I'll have to see how it all goes, though. Will your mother mind a last-minute guest?"

"Not at all," responded Bethancourt. "She's got one of those expandable dining-room tables. Er," he added as another thought occurred to him, "you'd better pack a suit, just in case. We'll be dressing for dinner."

"Oh," said Gibbons, sounding a little nonplussed by this. "Will do, then. I'll ring you again once I'm on my way, although I don't expect I'll know anything till I get there and see the scene for myself."

"Of course," agreed Bethancourt. "Er—are you feeling up to a long trip? I mean, you were only pronounced fit last week, after all."

"I'm tip-top," replied Gibbons. "Never better and all that."

Bethancourt suspected this was not entirely true, but let the remark pass at face value; there would no doubt be time later to remind his friend not to overdo it.

"That's good then," he said.

"I'd best ring off and get changed," said Gibbons. "I'll let you know when I find out my schedule."

"Yes, do," said Bethancourt.

He sat silently for a moment after he had rung off, a slow smile spreading over his face. He looked over at the large borzoi hound curled on the carpet and said, "Well, Cerberus, this mightn't be the worse Christmas ever, after all."

Cerberus thumped his tail in agreement.

Gibbons knew of Detective Superintendent Ian Brumby although he had never met him before. The superintendent was the Yard's authority on serial murders, heading up the division that investigated such crimes, and his expertise was greatly respected. Gibbons was curious to meet him.

Serial killings being fodder for the tabloids, Gibbons had seen Brumby's picture occasionally and knew well enough what the man looked like: a trim forty-five, average height, close-cropped grey hair. But in person the superintendent's face had a drawn look, the lines etched more deeply than forty-five years should account for, and his grey eyes were intense and hollow at the same time.

Gibbons could not help but wonder what Brumby made of him. He knew well enough what the older man saw: a young man with short reddish-brown hair and bright blue eyes, whose recent convalescence had left his normally stocky frame a little pudgy and given his complexion a slightly pasty tinge.

Brumby's manner was quiet and serious.

"These are the photographs they've sent down from York," he said, pushing an open folder across the glossy surface of the conference table. "The body doesn't conform in several instances to what we've come to expect of our Ashdon killer. For contrast, here's his latest work, in the bath shop in Kettering."

He pushed over a second folder, open like the first, and Gibbons bent over the two sets of color photographs. He was by this time tolerably accustomed to the gory scenes such photographs generally depicted, but there was something in these that sent a shiver down his spine.

Both of them portrayed the body of a young woman lying on the floor of a shop: in the first instance, a clothing boutique, and, in the second, a shop specializing in scented soaps and bath salts. Both women had been carefully arranged in coyly suggestive poses, and the fact that they were obviously dead made the positioning grotesque.

"You can see the obvious discrepancies," said Brumby, though in fact Gibbons had not got beyond his initial horror. He hurriedly tried to make a better assessment.

"There's an artistic quality to Ashdon's work," continued Brumby in his even, dispassionate voice, "and a certain care displayed which is lacking in the York murder. Here's another set from the second of Ashdon's killings—I think you can see what I mean."

Another girl, another shop—this time a stationer's—and another deliberately arranged body, the scene for it set with scatterings of brightly colored Post-it notes and a greeting card pressed open against her bosom. Gibbons's eye ranged over the photographs, picking out the details, and he began to have an inkling of what the superintendent meant.

"I'll go over all the fine points with you," said Brumby. "Because although this doesn't look very much like Ashdon's work on the surface, these things are never consistent. His plans for this particular body might have gone awry, or he might have had to hurry for some reason. And," he added, a note of exasperation coming into his tone, "most of the Yorkshire detective force is down with the flu, so I've not been able to contact the detective on duty. But if you get there and have any reason to think this could be another Ashdon murder, don't hesitate to ring me at once."

"Yes, sir," said Gibbons automatically, the larger part of his attention still focused on the photographs before him.

"Let's make a start, then," said Brumby, opening yet a fourth folder.

Bethancourt had finished dressing and was idling in his room, putting off joining the company downstairs for as long as possible, when there was a knock on the door.

"Open up," came a familiar voice. "I've brought you a drink."

Grinning, Bethancourt swung open the door and beheld Daniel Sturridge with a glass in either hand.

"Happy Christmas," he said, taking the proffered glass and adding, "Ta very much."

"Happy Christmas to you," said Daniel, raising his own glass.

The Sturridge family lived in Burnsall, and Bethancourt and Daniel Sturridge had grown up together, attending the same local prep school and then going off to St. Peter's at age eight. They had grown apart thereafter, Bethancourt going on to Oxford while Daniel got a law degree at York University, but they were still on good terms and were accustomed to join forces to withstand their elders at Christmastime.

"Ah," said Bethancourt, setting down his glass on the bureau. "That's just what was needed—I haven't had a drop since the sherry this afternoon."

"God, I hate sherry," said Daniel, collapsing into the armchair as though the very thought of the liquor wore him out. "Scotch for me every time. So what's this I hear about you dating Kate Moss?"

Bethancourt gave him a severe look. "I am not dating Kate Moss. I have never even met Kate Moss."

Daniel shrugged, unrepentant. "To hear my mother tell it, you've been disporting yourself all over London with the most notorious women and have probably taken up heroin as well."

"Dear God," said Bethancourt mildly, and took a drink.

"Yes, but what's all the fuss about then?" asked Daniel. "My mother couldn't have dreamed that up herself—she's not that imaginative."

"The fuss," said Bethancourt, "began because my cousin Neil is apparently going out with some baronet's daughter."

Daniel let loose a whistle. "Neil found someone to date him?" he asked. "Are you sure?"

"As unlikely as it seems, it appears to be true."

"Well, pigs must be flying tonight is all I can say," said Daniel, shaking his head and taking another drink of his whisky. "But where do fashion models come into it? The baronet's daughter isn't one, is she? Because you'll never get me to believe any respectable model would date Neil."

"No," admitted Bethancourt. "So far as I know, the baronet's daughter has no aspirations to a modeling career."

"Probably just as well," muttered Daniel.

"Possibly, although not having seen her, I couldn't say," replied Bethancourt. "Anyway, the model came up because my sister Margaret couldn't stand the thought of having to congratulate Neil on his coup in catching a member of the aristocracy, so she nicely diverted attention from it by announcing that I was dating a fashion model."

"Ah, the light dawns," said Daniel. "Margaret was always very good at diversions."

"Age has only improved her abilities," Bethancourt told him glumly.

"Shall I call her 'Mags' all evening for revenge?" offered Daniel.

Bethancourt sighed. "Let's not provoke her further. I shudder to think what other bits of my personal life she might drag out for public examination."

"Speaking of your personal life," said Daniel, "let's get back to the model. Are you actually dating one then?"

"I was," admitted Bethancourt. "But she's nothing like Kate Moss. She's not notorious or a drug addict or bulimic or anything like that. She's just a very pretty girl from Kent."

"It's probably better that she's not a drug addict," opined Daniel. "And bulimia is so off-putting. Well, my hat's off to you, old man. I always said, if ever anyone of us is going to date a fashion model, it will be Phillip. It was a pity they didn't have that as a category in the yearbook."

Bethancourt laughed. "I like to fulfill my friends' expectations when I can," he said. "But honestly, the entire thing's been blown out of proportion."

"I'll be sure to tell my mother that," said Daniel dryly. "I'm certain she'll see your side of things if I can only get her drunk enough. Oh, by the way, be sure and tell her how nice she's looking, will you?"

"Of course," said Bethancourt, surprised. "Any particular reason?"

"Well, she is looking nice," said Daniel. "She's been on some new diet recently, and she's dropped at least a stone. She'd never admit it, but she's hoping everyone who hasn't seen her for a while will notice and say something."

"I'll be sure to say something then," said Bethancourt. "Coming from a connoisseur of fashion models, possibly it will have some impact. Wait a moment, is this the same diet my aunt Evelyn's been on? She's lost a good bit of weight lately, too."

"Everyone's aunt and mother have been having a go at it," said Daniel. "Well, except your mother, of course—she's kept her figure. It's some new American diet and it's all the rage this year. Anyway, Mum's worked hard at it, so do say something, eh?"

"Will do," promised Bethancourt. He finished his drink and reached for his dinner jacket. "I expect we'd better go down before they come to get us."

As if his words were prescient, there was a knock on the door, and when he opened it, his cousin Bernadette said, "Aunt Ellen says to come down and bring Daniel with you."

"We're coming," said Bethancourt. "Right this moment. You with me, Daniel?"

"Yes," said Daniel, rising from the armchair and buttoning his jacket. "Let's go face the horde together."

Led by Bernadette, the two young men went to join the Christmas festivities.

Gibbons settled into a seat on a train packed with holiday-goers and pulled out his mobile to check the time. The train was already late starting, and it was not due to get into York until half ten even had it been on time. In addition, they had not yet been able to find him any place to stay, York being an extremely popular destination for the holidays. This in Gibbons's opinion did not bode well for wherever he ended up, which was likely to be a rather nasty B&B, if he was any judge. For the first time, he really felt the absence of a Christmas spent with his family in the warmth of the old house in Bedfordshire.

With a sigh, he flicked over to his contact list and scrolled to Bethancourt's number.

His friend, when he answered, sounded rather tipsy.

"Jack!" he said. "Are you here yet?"

"I'm on the train," replied Gibbons, "but God only knows when we'll get into York. I doubt I'll get to view the scene of the crime until morning—I just thought I'd let you know."

"Well, in the fullness of time and all that," said Bethancourt.

"How's your holiday going?" asked Gibbons.

"Oh, well enough I suppose," said Bethancourt. "I can't say I feel very festive, but that would mostly be because each agonizing minute that passes feels like an eternity. I can only speak for myself, of course. My sister Margaret seems happy enough, in her usual humorless way. Not that I want to put you off coming for Christmas dinner."

"Not at all," said Gibbons. "Is your father on about you finding a career again?"

"Hasn't got to that yet," replied Bethancourt. "They're still in an uproar over Marla."

Gibbons frowned, puzzled. "Marla?" he said. "What's she done? I didn't know she was up there with you."

"Good God, of course she's not," said Bethancourt. "But Margaret saw fit to tell everyone at lunch that I was dating a dissipated fashion model—ironic, really, since I'm not anymore."

"What?" Gibbons straightened up in his seat, startling his neighbor. "What do you mean? Have you and Marla broken up again?"

"I forgot you didn't know," said Bethancourt. "It happened at the last minute, before I had to head up here."

"But what happened?" asked Gibbons.

"It was all quite tawdry," said Bethancourt in a weary tone.

"I'll tell you later—I have to get back inside now before I'm missed. I only came out to smoke."

"Are you all right then, Phillip?" asked Gibbons, rather concerned.

"Tip-top," said Bethancourt. "Never better and all that. Ring me when you get here."

"I will," said Gibbons, but Bethancourt had already rung off.

He closed his phone and leaned back in his seat, shaking his head over his friend's many problems, and reflected that for some people the holiday season was simply rife with peril, a time to tread carefully rather than celebrate with abandon.

On occasion, he envied Bethancourt his wealth—it was only natural, after all—but moments like these reminded him that nobody's life was trouble-free, and if you had it easy in one way, there was always something else that you had to struggle with. Gibbons definitely did not envy Bethancourt his family, nor, despite her beauty, did he envy him his relationship with Marla Tate. Like any other man, Gibbons had daydreamed of bedding a woman like Marla, and of showing her off on his arm, but in reality he did not like her much better than she liked him, and months of watching his friend deal with her had convinced him that coping with her mercurial temper could not possibly be worth it. In that regard, he supposed, any difficulties could be said to be Bethancourt's own fault: he had chosen to have such a girlfriend.

"Poor Phillip," he said.

2

In Which Gibbons Gets a
Christmas Surprise

York was decked out for Christmas and awash with holiday makers, of both the local and tourist variety. On Christmas Eve morning, the shops were filled to bursting with last-minute shoppers, and carols sounded from every doorway. It was in very strange contrast, thought Gibbons, to the scene in the small accessory boutique, where he was examining bloodstains on the carpet. It made him feel that the sordid aspects of humanity should not intrude themselves during the Christmas season.

That made him think of Superintendent Brumby, whom he suspected had studied the baser side of human nature for so many years that he no longer could wholly free himself of it, even at Christmas. The superintendent did a very necessary job—and did it well—but the price he paid was high, and Gibbons hoped he himself would be spared that.

The bloodstains in question were soaked into the carpet of Accessorize, and Gibbons was comparing them to the crime-scene photos taken while the body was still present. With a sigh, he dragged his mind back to the subject at hand.

"So the body was disturbed before you ever arrived at the scene," he said.

Detective Constable Redfern, who had been appointed to escort Gibbons around, answered, "That's right. The shop supervisor who opened yesterday morning rather lost her head. She tried to give the corpse CPR. She seemed to feel she had been quite heroic," he added with a grim smile.

Gibbons laughed. "No doubt your superintendent disabused her of that notion."

"He did that," agreed Redfern, grinning. "Anyway, we sent along the crime-scene photos to your people, but then Superintendent MacDonald reconstructed what the scene had originally looked like as best he could, going by what the witnesses said. We took pictures of that, too, and then had our sketch artist come down and do a couple of representations. That's what you're looking at now."

Gibbons nodded, returning his attention to the folder he held and flipping past the glossy photos until he came to the artist's rendering of the scene. He studied it for a moment as a sinking feeling grew in the pit of his stomach, then raised his eyes to compare the drawing with the reality before him.

"I can see why you rang us," he said at last.

Redfern nodded. "It was Superintendent MacDonald twigged it," he said. "None of the rest of us realized what we were looking at, but something about the whole setup rang a bell in his mind."

Gibbons turned back to the crime scene. The shop had a small raised dais at the back where there had been a display of scarves and hats. These had been tossed aside for the most part in order to create a space for the body of a young woman.

"Deborah Selden," read Gibbons from the report Redfern had given him. "She was twenty-two?"

"That's right," said Redfern. "Still living with her parents out in Bishopthorpe."

Gibbons nodded, though he had no idea where Bishopthorpe might be; he was thinking how little he wanted to ring and interrupt Brumby's holiday.

"Will you be our liaison officer?" he asked.

"I don't know," said Redfern, shrugging and spreading his hands. "It's Christmas, after all. And we're shorthanded—the flu's really taken a toll on our manpower this year."

"Yes, I heard it's been bad up north this season," said Gibbons. "Well, if you'll just give me a few minutes to go over all the details here, we can head back to the station and I'll write up my notes for my super."

"You think it's Ashdon then, too?" asked Redfern, a little anxiously.

"I do," answered Gibbons. "But I'm not the expert. The real determination rests with Detective Superintendent Brumby."

"Of course." Redfern nodded his understanding, then turned away to give Gibbons time and space in which to work.

Gibbons took his time over the sketches and the reconstruction photos, noting the details and matching them in his head with the salient features of the Ashdon cases, and taking particular note of the ways in which the scene had been disturbed before either police or paramedics had arrived.

He had never before had anything to do with the investigation of serial killings, but he felt confident of his ability to make a simple determination. All the same, he wanted to have all his ducks in a row when he spoke to Superintendent Brumby. He was well aware that he had been sent to look at this case only because the superintendent believed it was *not* a legitimate Ashdon killing; had Brumby thought otherwise, he would have come himself, Christmas or not. And he was not likely to be best pleased if Gibbons dragged him all the way up to Yorkshire over a red herring.

Nor, to be honest, would Gibbons be any better pleased with

himself. He had been somehow touched by the plight of the superintendent, so haunted by the twisted minds of the criminals he hunted that he was never truly free of his work. The least he could do, Gibbons felt, was not to unnecessarily interrupt the brief break the holidays gave the man.

Once he had finished, Redfern drove him back to the York police station and left him at a borrowed desk while the constable went off to answer yet another urgent call. Gibbons procured a fresh cup of coffee, laid his notes out on the desk in front of him, and rang the superintendent's number.

Brumby answered at once, as if he had been waiting for the call.

"Happy Christmas, sir," said Gibbons after identifying himself.

"Happy Christmas, Sergeant," Brumby replied. "How are you getting on up there?"

"Well," said Gibbons, "there've been some developments, sir. The long and the short of it is that I think this is Ashdon's work after all."

Silence on the other end of the line.

"I know it's not very good news," added Gibbons after a moment.

"No," said Brumby at last, "not what I was hoping for—or expecting, for that matter."

"Shall I go over everything so you can make your own determination?" asked Gibbons. "I've got my notes right here."

Brumby hesitated before replying. "In a moment, Sergeant," he said. "Let me ring you back."

"Of course, sir," said Gibbons, but Brumby had already disconnected.

It did not take long, however, for the superintendent to return the call: Gibbons barely had time to sip his coffee and idly pick up a newspaper before the phone rang again.

"That's better," said Brumby. "We can talk for a bit now. Tell me what you've got, Sergeant."

Gibbons went over the evidence he had gathered, rather expecting to be cross-examined on every point, but Brumby listened for the most part in silence, interjecting a question only once or twice. He let Gibbons finish and then let out the ghost of a sigh.

"That's it then," he said, half to himself. "Very well, Sergeant. I'll start for the north at once. It's a pity it's Christmas Eve—the traffic is sure to be bad, so I don't know how long it will take me. I'll ring your mobile when I arrive."

"Yes, sir," said Gibbons, rather startled to have it settled so quickly. "I'll be waiting."

He rang off and sat silently contemplating how he might fill the next few hours. He did not feel much inclined to join the throngs of last-minute shoppers, and although he had noticed signs advertising a Christmas concert, he doubted tickets would be available at this late date. He could, he supposed, go to a museum or perhaps tour the Minster.

He wondered whether, after Brumby arrived, the superintendent would still want his help, or if he might be sent back to London to await another case. Either way, it did not look like he would be having Christmas dinner at Wethercross Grange. Sighing at his fate, he put his notes back together and wandered off to find someone in the station who could tell him where he might get some lunch.

He was standing at the door, watching the rain come down in torrents and wondering if it might abate, when Brumby rang him back. The superintendent sounded both harried and apologetic.

"I've had words with my sister," he said. "Or, rather, she's had words with me. It seems I am not to be allowed to leave until after dinner tonight, since I won't be here for Christmas dinner tomorrow."

"That makes sense, sir," said Gibbons. "The traffic will have cleared by then, and you'll get here much faster."

"So my sister pointed out," said Brumby wryly. "Still, it will make me at least three hours later than I would have been."

"That's perfectly all right, sir," said Gibbons. "I can't see that the delay will cause any problem."

"Is that your honest opinion, Sergeant?" asked Brumby, almost pleadingly. "Because if you were to feel differently, I want to assure you that I would prefer you to say so."

"Truthfully, no, sir," answered Gibbons. "I can't see that much can be done tonight beyond my filling you in and your going over the crime scene. And that won't hurt for being done a bit later."

Brumby sighed. "That was the argument my sister made," he said. "She also said if I were any kind of decent man, I'd let my team have Christmas Eve with their families before I curtailed their holiday. I suppose she's right."

"I'm sure they'll all appreciate that, sir," said Gibbons.

"Yes, well, I've told her I'm setting out by half eight, dinner or no, so I should be on my way by then."

"That will be fine, sir," Gibbons assured him. "I'll be waiting for your call."

He rang off, feeling rather bemused. Brumby had struck him as such a reserved, disciplined man that this insight into his personal life had surprised him.

He turned back to the door, readying himself to make a dash through the rain, when he saw Redfern returning to the station, trotting through the parking lot with the hood of his parka up.

"There you are, sir," he said as he came in, shedding rivulets of water. "I'm glad I caught you. I've spoken to Superintendent Mac-Donald, and he says I'm to go home for dinner tonight unless there's a major catastrophe. So I wondered if you'd like to come with me, seeing as how you're away from your own family."

Gibbons was touched by this kindness. "Why, thank you, Constable," he said. "That's awfully good of you—if you're sure the rest of your family won't mind?"

Redfern laughed. "Not at all—the more the merrier is how my mum looks at it. And she's got my wife and my sister helping her this year."

"Then I'd be pleased to come," said Gibbons. "Although I may have to eat and run—Superintendent Brumby's starting for York directly after his Christmas Eve dinner and I'll have to meet him whenever he gets here."

"My family's used to that," said Redfern. "I'll tell my mum you'll come then."

Gibbons thanked him again and went out to brave the weather in a much cheerier frame of mind.

Bethancourt had expected to hear from Gibbons that morning, but it was after lunch before his phone rang. By that time he had escaped the rest of the company at the Grange by volunteering to walk the dogs, despite the continuing rain. It was then, as he was climbing up toward Appletreewick Pasture on a very soggy footpath, that his mobile at last began to vibrate.

"Oh, hell," he said, casting about for shelter and finding none apart from a drystone wall. He was at least on the lee side of it, so he scurried through the wet grass to huddle against the stone while he pressed the phone to his ear and tried to shelter it from the rain.

"Are you all right?" asked Gibbons. "There's a funny sound."

"I'm out walking the dogs," said Bethancourt. "And it's windy and raining."

"Oh, I see," said Gibbons. "Well, Happy Christmas."

"Oh, right—Happy Christmas," replied Bethancourt. "Although I don't imagine you're having the best time looking at corpses in York."

"It's not so bad," said Gibbons. "To be quite honest, I feel I've spent more than enough time at my parents' house over the last few weeks. It's a relief to be out on my own, doing a useful job of work. Though of course," he added, lest this seem too callous, "it's rather odd, not being with the family on Christmas."

Bethancourt felt he could do with a bit of oddness, but managed not to voice this sentiment.

20

"So how is it going?" he asked instead.

"There's been an unexpected development," said Gibbons. "It turns out this is another of Ashdon's victims after all. I've called in Brumby—he's arriving later this evening."

"Oh." Bethancourt was not sure how to react. He himself had no interest in the psychopathy of serial killers: their deviation from the norm was too extreme for him to comprehend, and it was always the personalities in a case that interested him. "Well, good job you spotted it," he said.

"It wasn't difficult," said Gibbons. "But I'm afraid it means it's not too likely I'm going to make it out to the Dales for Christmas dinner. I'm sorry."

"Can't be helped," said Bethancourt. "Do cheer my lonely exile with updates on the case, though."

"Of course I will," said Gibbons. "Although I'm not sure exactly what will happen. Brumby may send me home tomorrow—he has his team, after all. I'll ring you and let you know either way."

"Yes, do," said Bethancourt. "One way or another, I'll see you in a couple of days."

Bethancourt straightened up as he returned the phone to his pocket and looked around for the dogs. They were nowhere in sight.

"Bloody hell," he muttered, and began to stride up the path in search of them.

In Which a Complication Arises

ittlesdon's Bookshop was closed on Christmas Day, like everything else, but Mervyn Mittlesdon found reason to visit his shop anyway. His wife was accustomed to say that he preferred the company of his books to that of his family; she meant it as a joke, but there was a kernel of truth to it. The books were always in the back of his mind, calling to him like a siren on the rocks beckoning to a sailor, and he found it impossible to resist their song.

He didn't try very hard, if the truth were told. His little house in Victor Street was a bustle of activity during the holiday, with his daughter and her husband and their new baby arrived for the celebrations, his son home from university, as well as his sister-in-law popping in and out from her own house in North Street. Mittlesdon was very fond of his family—even his sister-in-law—but he disliked having his usual habits interrupted, and during the holidays the bookshop became his haven.

Especially once its doors were closed and the public's frenzied search for presents had faded away, leaving only the calm hush of the books. There was a little space of time between opening presents and eating Christmas dinner, so Mittlesdon quietly absented himself and walked briskly through the rain to his shop. He let himself in by the back door, breathing in the slightly musty smell common to all bookshops like a perfume, and carefully locking the door behind him again. It was very dim inside, but he did not bother with lights, making his way without fuss through the narrow passage until he reached the front room of the shop. It, too, lay in shadow, the light from both the skylight and the windows muted by the inclement weather.

Here he paused, considering the disorder left when he had shooed his employees out the night before. Mittlesdon was by nature a very reserved man who did not possess the knack of easy camaraderie with his staff, but he was also considerate. He knew that the long hours required of retail employees around Christmas curtailed their own celebrations, and he made allowances where he could, like he had yesterday afternoon when he had dismissed his staff without first having them tidy the store as was usual. He himself had collected all the books left laying about by the customers, and this was the disorder he currently confronted: several higgledy-piggledy piles on the counter and an overburdened cart parked nearby. He spent a few minutes sorting the books into their sections, then took up a small stack and made his way to the stairs. There was a bookshelf on the landing, and as he bent over to replace a book there, he saw a spider sitting comfortably in one corner.

"Araignée du matin—chagrin," he murmured, but despite the old proverb, he did not kill it. Instead, he set down the books he carried, shook out his handkerchief, and scooped the spider into it. Then he carried it back down the stairs and released it outside the back door. The spider, a plain British brown, did not seem best pleased to find itself out in the cold drizzle and scuttled away quickly. Mittlesdon was not a superstitious man, but he was to remember this incident later and wonder to himself if there was more to proverbs than he had previously believed.

This chore accomplished, he returned to the staircase and his books, shelving two on the landing and then continuing up the stairs and shelving the rest in the first room there, which held the philosophy section. Then he took out his keys and let himself into the office.

He knew at once that something was wrong, though there was nothing immediately evident. But this was the heart of his domain and he could not mistake any change in its atmosphere. He paused just inside the door, surveying the cramped space filled with desks and stacks of books, but there was nothing apparently amiss. His mind leapt to the one very special book he had in the shop at the moment and he fled to his office, where the safe was kept.

It was a massive, ancient thing at the back of the little room, nearly as big as the old pedestal desk that sat squarely in the opposite corner. Mittlesdon's heart rate eased a little upon seeing that the safe was still closed, but he did not relax entirely until he had opened the heavy door and seen his treasure still sitting securely within.

So great was his relief that he began to think he had been mistaken in his earlier uneasy instinct, his nerves merely prey to the stress of the season. Still, he did not immediately turn to the unfinished work on his desk, but retraced his steps to the outer room.

It was then, from this different angle, that he saw it, on the floor over by the windows. It was so unexpected, so out of place, that at first his mind refused to take it in. He walked slowly over as if in a dream and stood staring down at the dead body, not quite believing it. When at last the reality registered, he nearly swooned, and was forced to sit heavily in the nearest chair for a moment before rising shakily and going downstairs to ring the police.

Gibbons was feeling useless, not a thing he was accustomed to at his job. It was more than a little irksome and—combined with his lack of sleep—was making him irritable, which he tried to hide from his colleagues.

He and Brumby had stayed up into the wee hours, going over the crime-scene and lab reports exhaustively. Brumby had mentioned that the rest of the team would join them in the morning, but considering the season, Gibbons had been unprepared for their arrival before 8:00 A.M.; they had caught him in the midst of his first coffee of the day.

They had driven up with a mobile unit, a quiet, serious group of people who listened expressionlessly to the briefing Brumby gave them, apparently soaking the information up like sponges, and then went about their work without further ado. They were a practiced, well-oiled team, and that did not really leave any place for Gibbons. He rather wished that Brumby would send him back to London, where he might pick up another case, one more suited to his abilities. But until that happened, he was left to kick his heels, watching other people work. It did not sit well with him.

It was midmorning when Brumby got off an extended phone call and, looking around the room, his eyes lit on Gibbons and he beckoned him over.

"I've had another call from Superintendent MacDonald," he said, frowning. "He thinks he may have a second Ashdon killing."

Halfway across the room, Detective Inspector Howard looked around, startled.

"A *second* murder?" he demanded, incredulous.

Brumby's lips thinned as he nodded. "If it's true," he said, "it would be a major breakthrough."

"One that I'm damned if I know what to make of," said Howard, coming over. "Two killings so close together would be a complete deviation from the pattern."

"Would you like me to go over and take a look, sir?" asked Gibbons, trying not to sound too eager.

"Yes," muttered Brumby, clearly disconcerted by this chain of events. "Yes, Sergeant. I'll come with you—Howard, you hold the fort here."

Howard nodded. "Do ring as soon as you know, sir," he urged. "It would really be most extraordinary . . ."

"I know," said Brumby. "I'll ring. Come along, Sergeant. Do you happen to know where Fossgate is?"

Gibbons did.

Superintendent MacDonald was no longer at the address he had given them, as a somewhat sheepish uniformed constable informed them when they arrived.

"He's left Detective Constable Redfern inside with the witness," he offered a little diffidently, as if acknowledging that Redfern was hardly a substitute for a detective superintendent.

Brumby raised a brow, but Gibbons said genially, "Is Redfern the only other detective not down with flu?"

The policeman sighed. "It seems like it, sir," he said.

Mittlesdon's Bookshop was housed in several old buildings that had all been knocked together, little bit by little bit throughout the shop's history, giving it a quaint, cozy air. The storefront was standard enough, if a little wider than most of those on the street, with two display windows on either side of the door and a small counter and cash register at the back of the front room. There was a small Christmas tree on the counter and tinsel was draped along the top shelves in the front room, but beyond that there was not much in the way of holiday decorations.

Immediately beyond the front room was a small area with a skylight, its two solid walls lined with shelves, and two leather armchairs set in the center.

In one of the chairs sat a round-faced, balding man, very neatly dressed, but clearly in distress, his silver-rimmed spectacles discarded in his lap while he dabbed at his face with a white handkerchief. Beside him sat Constable Redfern, looking sympathetic.

The constable looked toward the door as it opened to admit Brumby and Gibbons and then leaned forward to pat the other man's shoulder, saying, "I told you it wouldn't be long. Here's Scotland Yard to sort it all out."

The middle-aged man blinked and fumbled for his glasses while Redfern rose and came to meet them.

"Hello again, Dave," said Gibbons. "This is Detective Superintendent Brumby."

Redfern and Brumby shook hands and Redfern indicated the man behind him.

"This is Mr. Mittlesdon," he said. "He owns the shop and found the body when he came in this morning."

Brumby nodded, glancing around. "I thought the superintendent said he'd leave the body in situ?"

"Oh, he has," Redfern assured him. "The doctor wouldn't be here yet, anyway—he's dealing with a double murder down by the river."

Brumby was frowning. "But then where is the victim?" he asked.

"Upstairs in the office," replied Redfern, pointing to a narrow staircase opposite the counter. "It's kept locked, but I have the key."

"In the *office*?" repeated Brumby incredulously. "But Ashdon's entire MO is to leave the bodies on display."

"Perhaps," suggested Gibbons, "he was interrupted? If he killed her in the office—" he broke off. "But," he finished, "Ashdon doesn't kill them on site."

"He doesn't strike this frequently, either," muttered Brumby. He was still frowning. "Let's get upstairs then and see for ourselves."

He glanced over at their witness, who was leaning back in his chair, clearly trying to regain his composure.

"We'll speak to him once we've seen the body," decided Brumby. "You'd better have the uniform in to keep him company while we're upstairs."

"Yes, sir," said Redfern.

The policeman having been summoned from outside, Redfern led them up an uneven flight of stairs. At the top was a small room with a banister blocking it off from the stairway and a short landing. To their right, the stairs continued, while ahead was a closed door with a quite modern lock on it and a sign saying STAFF ONLY.

"This is apparently always kept locked," said Redfern, fitting a key on a fine silver chain into it, "and Mittlesdon confirms it was locked when he arrived this morning."

The door opened on a larger room with a row of windows along the opposite wall. It was filled with four wooden desks and boxes and stacks of books all over. There were two doors at each end of the room, all of them closed. Redfern threaded his way through the maze toward the windows, stopping just past the edge of the last desk.

"Here we are, sir," he said.

Gibbons, following in Brumby's wake, felt his heart sink as he took in the scene. Unlike the outré setting of the Ashdon killings, this was simply a body, left where it had fallen once the life had been choked out of it.

She had been a tall woman, lanky and lean, with sun-streaked carroty hair. Her face was discolored and bloated, but there were freckles sprinkled across her knuckles, and Gibbons was willing to bet that she had sported a good many on her face as well. From the hands and the lines of her body, he thought she had been young, probably in her twenties.

But even to Gibbons's inexperienced eye, there was no possibility that this crime could be put down to Ashdon's account.

Beside him, he felt Brumby trying to restrain his temper, which he managed rather well once he finally spoke.

"Did Superintendent MacDonald say why he thought this might be one of Ashdon's victims?" he asked.

Redfern looked a little discomfited.

"He didn't say, sir," he answered. "I expect it was mostly because of its being a shop and all." He looked at the body. "It doesn't look much like the other one," he admitted.

"No," said Brumby evenly, "it doesn't."

They stood in silence for several long seconds.

"Right then," said Brumby at last, drawing a deep breath, as if for fortitude. "Constable, would you mind going back and safeguarding our witness? The Sergeant and I will just have a look around and be down directly."

"Yes, sir," said Redfern, sounding relieved.

There was silence again once the constable had left. Gibbons broke it by saying, "Am I wrong, sir, or is this definitely ruled out as a possibility for Ashdon?"

"Oh, you're not wrong, Sergeant," Brumby assured him, shaking his head as he stood over the body. "My preliminary impression is that this is probably a fairly simple case. It doesn't look to me like this murder was premeditated. What do you think?"

"It doesn't seem that way," agreed Gibbons. "It looks almost as if once the killer realized she was dead, he simply panicked and ran out."

"Exactly." Brumby sighed and turned away. "And MacDonald strikes me as far too intelligent an officer to have made such a mistake. I think he's a man with too much on his plate at the moment, and he jumped at the chance to hand this one off."

Gibbons agreed.

"But I've found that it pays to foster goodwill with the locals," continued Brumby. "I mostly end up working on their patches, and they're far more accommodating if one has a good reputation. What would you say to helping out on this one? I can have the med team come over and do the autopsy, and the scene-of-the-crime officers will be done with their first sweep of our site by this afternoon—they might as well make themselves useful and go over this place as well."

Gibbons asked nothing better than to be given this opportunity to investigate on his own.

"I'd like that very much, sir," he said. "To be honest, I think I might be of more use here than over with your team."

Brumby nodded. "You get started here then," he said. "I'll speak to MacDonald and—hell! I forgot poor Howard." He pulled out his mobile and began dialing. "He's probably on tenterhooks waiting to hear if we have an anomaly or not. Carry on, Sergeant—check in with me once you're done here."

Brumby made his way to the door, while Gibbons turned back to the body and pulled out his notebook. He made a preliminary sketch of the scene, taking notes of anything that seemed out of the ordinary. He was a naturally observant man and had always been good at this part of his job, able to pick incongruities out of even apparently chaotic backgrounds.

Here nothing struck him as out of place except for the immediate area around the body, where there had clearly been a struggle. A small hooked rug was rumpled up beneath the body, and a potted plant which had presumably lived on the windowsill had fallen to the floor, cracking open and spilling out half its dirt. To the other side, there were several books on the floor, apparently knocked from the edge of the desk nearest the windows.

But the rest of the room seemed undisturbed. All the desks held papers and files and stacks of books as well as the ubiquitous computers, and it combined to give the impression of a business with not quite enough storage space, but there was nothing else that spoke of violence.

Gibbons inspected the door to the corridor: it had a regular latch, which was set to lock automatically when the door was closed. Gibbons could see no sign of its being forced, though if it had been picked he would not be able to tell just by looking.

He turned to the four doors leading off the room. To the right, nearest the windows, was a private office with a large black safe sitting in one corner and a bookcase standing half empty. The door next to it was the lavatory, and, on the other side of the room, the door opposite led to a cupboard filled with office supplies. The fourth door opened onto a small stockroom, with room enough for a few boxes of books and several tall filing cabinets. Gibbons doubted that all the stock passed through here—it was not big enough for that, nor did there seem any way for deliveries to be made—but clearly some organization was done in the room.

Having given the layout a cursory inspection, Gibbons left the office and went to interview his witness.

Mittlesdon had not gained any composure in the time Gibbons had been gone: he still looked distressed and quite pale. Redfern, hearing Gibbons's footsteps on the stairs, came to meet him at their foot and said in a low voice, "I'm getting a little concerned about him, sir—I think he may be going into shock."

Gibbons eyed the middle-aged man and agreed.

"He could no doubt do with something hot," he said. "I saw a kettle upstairs, but we don't want to disturb anything up there until after forensics has been and gone."

"There's a B and B just down the street, sir," said Redfern. "I could pop in there and ask for a cuppa. I doubt they'd mind."

"Do that then," said Gibbons. "I'll go over what happened with Mr. Mittlesdon while you're gone, and if all's well, we can send him home."

He was eyeing the bookshop proprietor as he spoke, mentally weighing the possibility that a man of that size could have strangled a tall and what looked to be athletic young woman. He didn't think it very likely, but he supposed stranger things had happened.

He introduced himself and sat down with Mittlesdon, who shook his hand automatically whilst peering myopically at him until he remembered the spectacles in his lap. He put them back on, hooking them carefully over his ears, and then dabbed at his forehead with the handkerchief.

"You must forgive me," he said. "It's been a shock, such a very great shock. And it's Christmas, too."

He shook his head, quite lost in his contemplation of the horror he had seen.

"I understand," said Gibbons gently, "that you're the owner of the bookshop?"

"What? Oh, yes, yes. My father started the place and I joined him when I came down from Cambridge."

"Was there any particular reason you came into the shop today?" asked Gibbons. "It being Christmas, I mean."

Mittlesdon looked about blankly. "Well, there's always things to do," he said, raising one hand to indicate a cart full of books standing at one end of the sales counter. "But really, I suppose, I just wanted a few moments of peace and quiet. It's rather crowded at my house over the holidays, you see."

Gibbons nodded in understanding. He himself had five siblings and nearly twice as many cousins; his parents' house was nothing short of bursting at the seams during the holidays.

"So you came in just to tidy up a bit," he said encouragingly.

"Yes, well, I do like to be occupied," said Mittlesdon. "And it's relaxing work for me, I'm so used to it." He hesitated. "I'm afraid," he said apologetically, "I did put away some books before I found—found it. I do hope you're not too upset with me: I know you're supposed to leave everything just as it is at the scene of a crime."

Gibbons smiled; it was quite unusual to find a witness concerned that he might have made the policemen's job harder.

"I'm sure it will be all right," he said. "Some of the books left down here, were they?" He indicated the counter.

"Yes, that's right. Just a small pile of books from—" Mittlesdon broke off, struck by a sudden thought.

"Have you remembered something?" asked Gibbons.

To his surprise, Mittlesdon blushed and looked down at his hands.

"It's nothing," he muttered. "I can't think why such a silly thing should occur to me. It's nonsense, of course."

"I can't tell unless I know what it is," said Gibbons patiently. "Was there something out of place when you came in?"

"No, no." Mittlesdon seemed embarrassed. "I only remembered finding the spider when I was putting away the books. Silly, I know, but I thought of that old proverb—*Araignée du matin—chagrin; Araignée du midi—plaisir; Araignée du soir—espoir,* you know—and, well, I can't help thinking maybe this wouldn't have happened if I'd killed the spider instead of putting it outside. Quite ridiculous, but, well, I can't say I feel entirely myself."

"Of course not," said Gibbons, who did not know many French proverbs. "No one does when they've unexpectedly been faced with a dead body. Let's see, *chagrin,* that's 'sorrow,' isn't it?"

"Oh," said Mittlesdon, looking apologetic again. "I'm sorry. In English it would be—now let me think—yes, it would be, 'A spider seen in the morning is a sign of grief; a spider seen at noon, of joy; a spider seen in the evening, of hope.' Yes, that's it, more or less. I remember as children my sister and I were told never to kill a spider except in the morning."

Gibbons was not at all certain what to make of this speech, except that they were straying very far from the topic of murder.

"Apart from the spider," he said, "did you notice anything else out of the ordinary this morning? Was the door locked just as usual?"

"Oh, yes," said Mittlesdon vaguely. "I would have noticed if it hadn't been—I'm quite careful about such things. No, everything seemed just as we had left it until I went into the office." He swallowed and dabbed his forehead again.

"Did you come in the front door or the back?"

"The back. I always use that way when the shop is closed—it's easier than having to roll up the gate at the front door."

Bit by bit, Gibbons coaxed all the details out of the man, though the story was simple enough.

"Did you know the deceased?" he asked, once Mittlesdon had recounted his finding of the corpse.

Mittlesdon shuddered. "No," he said. "No, indeed. I'd never seen her before in my life."

A sweat had broken out on his brow again, so Gibbons turned the conversation away from the subject to give him time to recover.

"Now what I'd like from you," he said, "is a list of your employees and anyone else who has keys to the shop."

"Oh, we're a very small group," said Mittlesdon. "Although, of course, I haven't everyone's address and phone number in my head." He hesitated. "To get that information, I should have to go back to the office."

He was clearly loath to do any such thing, nor was Gibbons eager to have his crime scene disturbed before the arrival of the SOCKOs.

"Perhaps if you could just give me the names now," he said.

"Oh, but wait," said Mittlesdon, relieved. "I'd forgotten—I have a contact list of them all at home. You know, for emergencies. I could give you that."

"That would be very helpful," said Gibbons. "Oh, look, here comes Constable Redfern with the tea."

Mittlesdon looked up, startled, as Redfern came into the shop cradling a porcelain mug.

"Thought you could do with a cuppa, Mr. Mittlesdon," he said cheerfully. "You have a sip of that and it'll set you right."

"Why, thank you," said Mittlesdon, accepting the mug appreciatively. "That was very kind of you, Constable. I confess, I'm feeling quite stunned by it all."

While Mittlesdon drank his tea, Gibbons took down his address and phone number, ascertained that he had walked to the shop that morning, and made arrangements for a police car to take him home and collect the contact list of his employees.

Having seen the good man off the premises, Gibbons explored the rest of the shop with Redfern in tow.

"I've been in here a time or two," remarked Redfern, as they delved farther back into the shop. "It's a regular rabbits' warren— always a bit more round the corner."

Gibbons had to agree. At the back of the little area where they had been sitting was another steep, narrow staircase lined with books and, to the left of that, another small doorway. Gibbons had assumed that this led to a single back room, but instead he found himself in a long, rather cramped space which widened out at its end into a little room, beyond which was a further doorway and another room with yet another doorway, leading ever on until one ended up at last in a somewhat larger room with two freestanding bookcases in its center and a window with no further egress. All of it, every spare space, was crammed with books.

Gibbons, who was fond of books, was amazed.

"And there's more upstairs," said Redfern. "They've got a wonderful children's section. A lot of very pricey first editions of course—that's Mittlesdon's specialty—but some very fair second-hand copies, too."

Gibbons, examining some shelves of military history, glanced back at him, remembering the baby at dinner the night before.

"Your little girl isn't old enough yet for books, surely," he said.

"No," admitted Redfern with a laugh. "But it's never too early to start thinking about what you'd like to get for her. You'll see, sir, when you have your first—when they're as young as Charlotte, it's more a matter of your own tastes than hers."

"No doubt true," said Gibbons, carefully reshelving the book he had been looking at. "I'm sorry to pull you away from her first Christmas."

"That's all right, sir," said Redfern. "She won't be remembering this one anyway—though I expect my wife will," he added resignedly.

Gibbons smiled in sympathy. "Well," he said, "let's have a look at your daughter's potential library."

They retraced their steps, but before they could start up the stairs, the door to the shop opened to admit Detective Superintendent Freddy MacDonald of the Yorkshire CID.

MacDonald was a big man with a definite presence, dressed

today in an open parka over a brightly striped rugby shirt. Middle age had given him a burgeoning belly and a balding pate, but it had not dulled the sharp gleam in his blue eyes.

"There you are, Redfern," he called out as he strode into the shop. "And you must be Detective Sergeant Gibbons. Freddy MacDonald."

He held out a large hand, which Gibbons shook.

"It's good to meet you, sir," he said.

"Aye, aye," said MacDonald, impatient with these formalities. "Your super says you're to have a look at this case, even though he doesn't think it's Ashdon. What do you think, Sergeant?"

"I don't think it's Ashdon either, sir," answered Gibbons. "But I'm happy to look into it."

MacDonald was eyeing him appraisingly. "I hear you're Scotland Yard's blue-eyed boy," he said. "You seem a bit young for it, but I'm not one to judge on appearances. Has Redfern here been helpful?"

"Very helpful," Gibbons assured him.

MacDonald nodded as if he had expected no less, and Redfern himself seemed unworried by this questioning of his behavior.

"He's generally a helpful sort of lad," said MacDonald, with a glance at Redfern, who grinned back at him. "Helpful enough that I need him back, at least for an hour or two. Can you cope here, Sergeant? I'll leave you Constable Murphy outside, and Brumby says his forensics team should be over shortly."

"That's fine, sir," said Gibbons. "It would be helpful, though, if I could have both Redfern's number and yours in case I should need to contact you."

"By all means," said MacDonald. "Sync up your phones, will you, Redfern? And I'll be sending him back to you, Sergeant, but I'm desperate short of men."

"What happened to Detective Inspector Curtis?" asked Redfern, pulling out his mobile.

"Had to send him home," answered MacDonald. "The DI was

36

running a fever of one hundred three and couldn't think his way out of a paper bag. Have you got that sorted then? Fine—let's get on. Sergeant, I'll check back with you later, as soon as we've dealt with this little matter over by the river."

And, with Redfern in tow, MacDonald swept back out.

A little bemused by the encounter, Gibbons tucked his mobile away, then turned toward the stairs to continue his exploration of the shop. He paused to examine a series of framed photographs that were grouped on the sides of the doorjamb. These depicted author signings the shop had hosted, with various members of the staff grinning from positions on either side of the celebrity. Some were faces Gibbons did not recognize, but others were impressive: there was Jeffrey Archer, Brian Jacques, and Reginald Hill. Mittlesdon, Gibbons noticed, was present in nearly all the photos, but the other members of the staff varied considerably. Reflecting that he might have just seen a picture of the murderer, Gibbons turned away to climb the stairs and inspect the children's department.

He had rather expected to be interrupted in his tour by the arrival of either the medical team or the SOCKOs, but he finished his inspection of the children's department—as well as the rest of the shop on the floors above the office—unimpeded. It was the kind of shop where it would be difficult to tell if anything was out of place, particularly in view of the crowds that must have been milling about, disrupting things, just before Christmas, but Gibbons saw nothing obviously amiss. So he returned again to the office to give it a more thorough going-over while he waited.

He again approached the body, this time pulling on a pair of rubber gloves from a ready supply he kept in his coat pocket. The victim was dressed in a full skirt, its colors muted reds and browns, with a turtleneck worn under a brown jumper. Over all was a lined trench coat, but nowhere did Gibbons see any sign of a handbag.

He knelt down and delicately, disturbing everything as little as possible, searched the coat's pockets. He turned up a single latch key, a crumpled bit of paper with a shopping list and a telephone number jotted down on it, a pencil and a torn piece of newspaper that proved to be *The Times* crossword puzzle from three days ago, a tube of lipstick from Boots, and, pieced together from various pockets, a total of about fifty pounds in coins and small notes.

There was not a single credit card or a driver's license, nothing that might have been used to identify her. Gibbons sat back on his heels, frowning a little. Then he stood, letting his eye rove over the room once more. Perhaps he had simply missed her bag; sometimes, he had noticed, women carried very small bags that hardly looked like handbags at all.

He began a meticulous search of the room.

In Which a Deluge Occurs and Grants Bethancourt a Reprieve

The scene inside the Grange on Christmas morning was traditional, with family and guests grouped about the tall Christmas tree in the drawing room, watching the younger members tear open their Christmas packages. Bethancourt was fighting a hangover, the result of tying one on with Daniel Sturridge the night before. He stood at the back of the assembled company, clutching a large mug of coffee and reflecting on Christmases past, when snow was a regular part of the holiday instead of the current grey drizzle. Or was it that he remembered only the snowy Christmases? Impossible to tell, at this remove.

He had put his mobile in his pocket when dressing that morning out of habit rather than any expectation of hearing from Gibbons, and so was caught off guard when it began to vibrate. He started, spilling some of his coffee.

"Oh, dear," he said. "I'll just run and grab a towel."

And he slipped out hastily, pulling his phone out as he went.

"Hullo," he said, keeping his voice down and retreating farther from the drawing-room door. "I thought you'd be knee deep in serial killers by now."

Gibbons chuckled. "Actually," he said, "I'm doing something altogether different. There's been another unexpected development."

"Good God, another one?" asked Bethancourt. "Are you still in York?"

"Oh, yes," replied Gibbons. "Do you know a bookshop called Mittlesdon's?"

"Of course I do," answered Bethancourt. "I used to go round there quite regularly in my school days. And I believe my father still buys the occasional book there. But I thought you said the Ashdon victim was found in a shop called Accessorize."

"So she was," agreed Gibbons. "But there's been another murder, not connected to Ashdon. It's a young woman found strangled in the back office of Mittlesdon's Bookshop. I'm helping the local CID out with the case."

"That sounds interesting," said Bethancourt hopefully. "Was the shop broken into?"

"It doesn't look like it," said Gibbons, "but I don't know a lot yet—I'm still waiting for forensics."

"I expect it's probably Mittlesdon," said Bethancourt. "I remember him as being very prim and proper—it's always that sort who have a monomania about something. Or someone."

"I thought I'd wait and at least find out who the victim is before I arrested anybody," said Gibbons dryly. "Very cautious of me, I know."

"Well, if you must be sensible, I suppose you must," said Bethancourt good-naturedly. "I'll come by when I get let out of here, shall I?"

"I thought you might like to," said Gibbons. "When are you leaving, by the way?"

Bethancourt sighed. "Not till tomorrow afternoon—I'm stuck till after lunch. I should be able to get away then, though."

"Well, I'll ring you later then and let you know where I've got to," said Gibbons. "I've got to go—I think I hear the SOCKOs arriving."

"All right," said Bethancourt, and rang off.

Gibbons had rather thought the medical examiner would arrive first, but instead it was the forensics team, led by a lean, older man with very sharp eyes named Bert Mason.

"This is a change," Mason said cheerfully as he ushered his team into the shop, all carrying heavy cases. He looked about him, seeming to take in everything with a single glance.

"The body's upstairs," said Gibbons. "I'd like you to take a look at the locks on both the front and back doors, though, as well as the lock to the office."

"Right," said Mason. "Jim, did you hear? Good man. Lead the way then, Sergeant, and we'll get started."

Upstairs, Mason paused on the threshold of the office for a moment, his brown eyes flickering over everything, while the rest of the SOCKOs peered at the room from behind him, like greyhounds waiting to be unleashed.

"Right then," said Mason, drawing a deep breath. "There's going to be a lot of trace here, so let's go carefully and collect as much as we can."

"One thing I haven't found is her handbag, if she had one," said Gibbons.

"Murderer might have taken it away with him," said one of the female SOCKOs, kneeling to unlatch her case.

"Or she mightn't have carried one," added another. "Don't worry, sir, we'll keep an eye out for it."

Gibbons stood back, out of their way, watching their quiet efficiency at work and turning things over in his mind until he was interrupted by Constable Murphy peering in at the door in search of him.

"They're back from dropping Mr. Mittlesdon off, sir," he announced. "And I've got that contact list for you."

"Thank you, Constable," said Gibbons, moving to take it. "The doctor's not come yet then?"

"No, sir, but I'll show him up as soon as he does," answered Murphy, and Gibbons nodded.

Murphy withdrew while Gibbons ran his eye down the sheet. There were more names than he had thought there would be, which, he thought, just went to prove that he knew very little about running a bookshop.

Jim, the locks man, tramped up the stairs, breathing a little heavily as he reached the top. He saw Gibbons standing in the doorway and headed for him.

"I've had a good look at the locks downstairs," he reported, "and I can't see any signs of tampering on them. If you ask me, our killer had a key, or else a door was left open for him."

Gibbons nodded; it was what he had expected to hear. "Check this one out, too, will you?" he asked. "It's apparently kept locked all the time, and the owner says it was locked when he let himself in this morning."

He moved out of the way so Jim could have room to work, and returned his attention to the list of names in his hand. Next to some of them Mittlesdon had placed asterisks, and at the bottom of the page he had written, in a very neat hand, "*keyholders."

"Well, well, well," murmured Gibbons. "I wonder what you lot were doing last night or thereabouts."

"Would you mind if I stopped at the house in York for a bit?" Bethancourt asked his father. "It's no bother if you were planning to use it."

Robert Bethancourt looked up in surprise.

"I didn't know you were planning on visiting York," he said. "I thought you were off back to London tomorrow."

"If you did go," put in his mother practically, "you could check on the place and make sure it hasn't flooded again—Carter's away for the holidays, so he won't be checking in until the end of the week."

Bethancourt nodded. The family's townhouse in York had had problems in the past with water in the basement when there had been heavy rains.

"I was going to head home," Bethancourt answered his father, "but something's come up. Jack's in York, looking into a murder, and I thought I might join him there and have a look in."

"Oh," said Robert. He eyed his son speculatively.

When Bethancourt had first shown an interest in criminal cases, Robert had prevailed upon his old school chum, currently the chief commissioner of New Scotland Yard, to allow Bethancourt access to official investigations, in the hope that his son would be inspired to take up a career with the police. But that had been some time ago, and Bethancourt did not seem any nearer to collecting a policeman's salary than he had been at the beginning.

"Certainly," said Robert now. "The house is empty at the moment, there's no reason you shouldn't use it. Have Jack in to stay, too, if you like. It's sure to be more comfortable than wherever he's billeted."

"There's not much available in York at the last minute," agreed Ellen. "Not during Christmas at any rate. The poor lad's probably stuck in some grotty B and B."

Bethancourt had not thought of that. "I didn't think to ask," he admitted.

"What kind of case is it?" asked Robert.

"He came up on the trail of a serial killer," answered Bethancourt, "but I think now he's helping the Yorkshire CID with something else—half the force is apparently down with the flu."

"I heard about that," said Robert. "The Ashdon killer, isn't it? The first time he's struck this far north."

"That's right," said Bethancourt. "I don't actually know too

43

much about the case—Jack got put onto it after I left town. I'll drive over tomorrow after lunch then."

"Do let us know whether or not the house is all right," said Ellen.

"Of course," said Bethancourt. "Thanks."

But his luck seemed to have turned. A fresh squall swept over the Dales during dinner and heavy flooding was predicted as a result. The guests who were not staying at the Grange left soon after the meal in order to make sure they would reach their homes before the rivers rose.

Bethancourt's father, having seen the last of them out, remarked, "You might want to leave tonight, Phillip, instead of tomorrow. I doubt any of us will be getting out of Wharfedale by morning."

Margaret looked up from her seat by the fire. "But tomorrow's Boxing Day," she said. "Aren't we taking the donations down to Harrogate in the morning?"

"I doubt it," answered Robert. "If they're right about the rain keeping up, I imagine the road will be flooded at either end by morning. Half your mother's luncheon guests won't be able to make it here, either."

"Well," said Bethancourt, doing his best to control his eagerness, "if we're not going to make it to Harrogate anyway, I might as well go to York tonight."

"I don't see why not," said his father. "You could be stuck here for days otherwise, depending on the weather. I swear, I've never seen such a holiday season."

"I'll just go pack my things then," said Bethancourt happily.

He drove into York just after midnight under a pitch-black sky with not a star to be seen. He had left most of the rain behind him in the Dales, however; in York it had been reduced to a steady drizzle.

Gibbons was waiting for him at the back gate, having been alerted to his friend's imminent arrival by phone.

"Hello, Cerberus," he said, bending down to scratch the big

dog's ears as Bethancourt let him out of the car. "Happy Christmas, Phillip."

"If you say so," replied Bethancourt ungraciously. "Let's get in, shall we? I'm not dressed for this weather."

He led the way up the garden, fishing in his jacket pocket for the keys.

"It's good of you to ask me to stay," said Gibbons, slinging his duffel over one shoulder. "That place they had me staying in was positively depressing."

"Are the rest of the Scotland Yard team still there?" asked Bethancourt. "Damn this lock—oh, wait, I've got the wrong key."

"No," answered Gibbons. "Mine was the last room open at that B and B, and besides, they had to come up with something better than that for a detective superintendent. Someone high up pulled strings and got him a suite at the Best Western. They didn't have anything else open, so I understand the rest of the team is camping out in the sitting room."

"I'd really rather not invite them here unless you think it necessary," said Bethancourt, finally succeeding with the door.

"Why the devil should you?" said Gibbons ruthlessly. "You're my friend, not theirs."

"Thank God," said Bethancourt mildly. "I don't know what my mother would have said if I had turned the place into a police headquarters. Here we are then—doesn't look like it flooded."

"Carpet's dry," agreed Gibbons, maneuvering with his duffel a little awkwardly in the narrow hallway in order to close the door. "Does it flood often?"

"You have no idea," said Bethancourt darkly. "Here, let's leave the luggage till later and search out a drink. It's Christmas—you'd think my father would have the bar fully stocked, just in case. Let me get a light on. . . . There we go."

"Can I put the electric fire on?" asked Gibbons as they entered the drawing room. "It's chilly."

"By all means," replied Bethancourt, making for the drinks

cabinet standing in one corner. "As I thought," he said, opening the doors, "the pater stocked up. What will you have?"

"Is there scotch?" asked Gibbons, who from previous experience knew that the Bethancourts' taste in whisky ran to expensive single malts.

"There's a twenty-five-year-old bottle of Bowmore," said Bethancourt. "Will that do?"

Gibbons sighed in pleasure. "Very nicely," he said, sinking into a very comfortable armchair and stretching his feet toward the glow of the electric fire. The drawing room was very elegant, meant for entertaining, but it was comfortable, too, and infinitely preferable to the B&B he had come from, which had smelled like cabbage.

"I think I'll join you," said Bethancourt, pulling out a couple of crystal glasses. "So how's this new murder shaping?"

"I haven't got very far yet," answered Gibbons. "There was no identification on the body, so we're not even sure who the victim was. The medical examiner confirms that she was strangled and puts the time of death at sometime after seven on Christmas Eve."

"Quite a nasty Christmas present," remarked Bethancourt, handing him a glass and collapsing into a second armchair. "Cheers."

"Cheers. Ah, that's good," said Gibbons, savoring the taste of the liquor on his tongue. "Where was I?"

"The medical examiner," prompted Bethancourt.

"Right," said Gibbons. "Well, he puts her age at about twenty-five, and she was apparently in perfect health before she was murdered. She struggled with her attacker, so we're looking for a reasonably strong specimen—our victim was a tall woman. She took a couple of punches to the head before she was killed, so it's possible she was unconscious when she was strangled. Anyway, the murderer used something—possibly a scarf or a cloth belt, the doctor said."

"It sounds fairly straightforward," said Bethancourt, disappointed. "A quarrel of some kind, and things get out of hand."

"Ah, but here's where it gets interesting," said Gibbons. "How did she and her killer get into the bookshop in the first place?"

Bethancourt shrugged and lit a cigarette. "The killer's probably someone who works there and has a set of keys," he answered.

"Possibly," conceded Gibbons. "But why were they in the bookshop on Christmas Eve?"

"Stealing something, most likely," suggested Bethancourt. "Old Mittlesdon has some very nice editions, some of them worth thousands. Christmas would certainly be an excellent opportunity to loot the place—it's probably the one time you could be certain Mittlesdon wouldn't be there."

"Yes." Gibbons sighed. "I'd thought of that, but Mittlesdon says his most valuable items were in the safe, and were all accounted for. Moreover, no one except him has the combination."

Bethancourt shrugged. "It still doesn't strike me as very interesting," he said. "No doubt they had a plan for getting into the safe, but argued before they got to that part of the program. When the argument ended in murder, our killer got the wind up and fled."

"A very plausible scenario," agreed Gibbons. "But things might have a different interpretation put on them. Anyway, I'll know better once I've managed to talk to all of the key-holders."

"I take it you didn't have time to track any of them down today?" asked Bethancourt.

"No." Gibbons shook his head. "By the time I was done at the scene and with the autopsy, I only had time to follow up with Mittlesdon. He was still quite shaken up, but he managed to give me a few details about his employees."

"Anything interesting?" asked Bethancourt.

"No, just clearing up who's in charge of what. Unfortunately, the one piece of real information I got from him was not encouraging." Gibbons frowned at his glass and then sighed and drank.

"Well, what was it?" asked Bethancourt impatiently.

"Oh—sorry," said Gibbons. "I think I must be tired. Well, it's about the keys. All employees have the key to the office door, but only four of them have the keys to the store itself."

"That would seem to narrow it down nicely," said Bethancourt. "And yet I see from your expression that for some reason it doesn't."

"It doesn't because people are quite cavalier with their keys," said Gibbons. "So far as I can tell, nearly any of the employees could have made off with a set of keys for long enough to have copies made. For example, the back door is always kept locked, but the smokers go out that way to have a cigarette, and it's common for them to borrow a set of keys from one of the managers, or even the spare set that's kept in the office."

"Oh dear," said Bethancourt.

"Mr. Mittlesdon earnestly assured me that all of his employees were very trustworthy," said Gibbons dryly.

"Except perhaps for the one who's a murderer?" suggested Bethancourt.

"He hasn't got that far," said Gibbons. "He's still in the 'it must be an outsider' phase."

"It really can't have been, can it?" asked Bethancourt. "I mean, quite apart from the matter of the keys, there must have been some reason for your killer and victim to have been at a bookshop at Christmas—it's not like they could have wandered in there by accident."

"No, most certainly not," agreed Gibbons. "Well, we'll see what comes out tomorrow." He yawned. "That drink's gone straight to my head. I'm sorry, Phillip, I think I had better go to bed."

"Don't be sorry," responded Bethancourt. "It's after midnight, after all."

"Yes, but I meant to ask about Marla," said Gibbons.

Bethancourt's face shuttered at once.

"That can wait," he said shortly. "There's really nothing to tell in any case. Here, let's get you set up upstairs. What's the agenda for tomorrow, by the way?"

He had risen and was leading the way out of the room; Gibbons had little choice but to follow.

"The shop's set to open at ten," he said, bending to pick up his duffel and swing it onto his shoulder. "Mittlesdon's manager is scheduled to open tomorrow, along with four of the sales people. Mittlesdon says they usually show up about fifteen minutes early, although the manager might be there as early as half nine. I reckon that means I should be there by nine or a little earlier."

Bethancourt nodded as he tramped up the stairs. "Breakfast at eight then?" he suggested.

"That sounds about right," agreed Gibbons.

"We'll have to go out for it," warned Bethancourt, opening one of the bedroom doors. "There won't be anything perishable in the house. Here you are—the best room at Bethancourt's B and B."

It looked like heaven to Gibbons, a well-appointed guest room with a very comfortable-looking double bed complete with a thick, silk-covered duvet and four feather pillows.

"Perfect," he said. "Thanks again, old man."

"Not at all," replied Bethancourt automatically, checking to make sure the bed was made up. "The WC's at the end of the hall; there should be towels in the armoire here. . . . Yes, there they are. Do you need anything else?"

He looked around the room as if checking to make sure he had missed nothing.

"No," answered Gibbons. "I'm fine. I take it you'll come with me in the morning?"

"If that's all right, I will," said Bethancourt. "You never know—it might not be as simple as it appears." He smiled a little sheepishly.

Gibbons laughed at him.

"You just want to make my job harder," he said. "Yes, you can come, though I'd appreciate it if you'd fade into the background if Brumby or MacDonald show up."

"Not a problem," said Bethancourt. "I'll leave you to get some sleep, then. Good night, Jack."

"Good night," echoed Gibbons.

Bethancourt went back out into the hall, closing the door firmly behind him and picking up his bag, which he hefted along to the next door down. The room inside was much like the room he had just left Gibbons in. Bethancourt deposited the bag on the bed and went back downstairs. There he topped up the whisky in his glass, which he sipped while he carried Gibbons's empty glass back to the kitchen. He checked the refrigerator and cupboards there for supplies, and found that though—as he had expected—there was no milk or other perishables, there was a stock of coffee.

"Wonderful," he murmured, and proceeded to set the coffee-pot ready for the morning.

He finished his whisky and left the glass in the sink before putting out all the lights on the ground floor and wandering back upstairs to his room, followed this time by Cerberus, who immediately lay down on the hearth rug to continue his nap. His master, however, was restless, and rather wished Gibbons had not brought up Marla just at bedtime. Nevertheless, in view of the early hour at which he would have to rise in the morning, he prepared for bed and settled in, lying wakeful in the dark, the specter of a slim, redheaded woman appearing against all desire in his mind's eye. He was, he decided, still considerably angry, but he could see no help for that. He closed his eyes tightly and tried to think about the dead woman in the bookshop.

5

In Which Bethancourt Encounters
a Flash from the Past

*I*t was not actually raining when they set out the next morning, though the skies were dark and threatening and the air was raw. Cerberus gamboled along beside them, being by far the most awake of the party and the only one who did not seem to mind the cold.

"We'll warm up as we go," said Bethancourt, starting off at a good pace. He was still feeling very fortunate to have escaped his parents' house a day early. "It's not far in any case."

"Oh," said Gibbons, stifling a yawn. Despite copious amounts of coffee, he was not feeling very alert.

"Not that way," said Bethancourt, catching him by the arm. "We can cut through here and go down along Straker's Passage. Haven't you ever heard of a snickelway?"

"No," answered Gibbons grumpily.

"Oh," said Bethancourt, correctly interpreting this monosyllabic response as a lack of interest. "Well, York's full of them. In this case, it's a shortcut."

Gibbons let himself be steered off the sidewalk and along a

path apparently leading into a garden. It did not seem to him a very likely way to get to Fossgate, but he trusted Bethancourt to know all the highways and byways of the city in which he had grown up. And in fact a passage that Gibbons would have called an alleyway and that Bethancourt persisted in calling a snickelway brought them up to the back side of the bookshop, and then along its side to Fossgate. Gibbons fished out the keys and, after taking down the police tape, let them in the front door.

"My," said Bethancourt, stepping over the threshold, "this brings back memories."

"Were you really here that much when you were a schoolboy?" asked Gibbons, hunting for the light switch.

"Yes; it was an approved place to visit," answered Bethancourt. "Not only that, but old Mr. Mittlesdon would often let us trade in old books for new ones, which saved on pocket money. Besides, I like bookshops."

While Bethancourt began a leisurely inspection of Mittlesdon's current stock, Gibbons went to check the back door. When he returned, he found PC Murphy in the front room with Bethancourt.

"Ah," said Bethancourt, sounding relieved. "Here he is. Constable Murphy was looking for you, Sergeant."

Murphy looked hopefully at Gibbons. "Very good to see you, sir," he said with a slight emphasis.

"Sorry about the confusion, Constable," said Gibbons. "This is a colleague of mine, Phillip Bethancourt. He's in York for the holidays, so I asked him to stop by—purely unofficial, of course."

Murphy seemed more than willing to accept this explanation.

"DC Redfern will be coming," he told Gibbons. "Superintendent MacDonald sent him round to follow up with a witness in that double-murder case, but then he should be over this way. I'm to help in any way I can until he gets here."

"Thank you, Constable," said Gibbons. "Actually, your presence will be very helpful—I imagine it will be reassuring to the arriving employees to see a man in uniform. And if you could keep an eye on things here, I'll be able to interview them one by one."

"Yes, sir," said Murphy. "I can do that easily enough."

"Good man," said Gibbons. "I think the best plan will be for me to conduct the interviews in the larger room at the very back—that should keep the conversations private enough, and will also enable us to have an eye on that back door."

"That makes sense," agreed Bethancourt.

"Let's just have a look at the setup back there then," said Gibbons.

He led the way through the warren of narrow rooms and into the open space at the back. Here they switched on the lights and shifted the chairs about to make a conversational grouping rather than one set up for reading and blocking out one's fellow man.

That accomplished, they returned to the front room to await the arrival of their witnesses.

They did not have to wait long. In another ten minutes or so a tall, lanky man with long brown hair and glasses came up to the door, looking considerably startled to find the shop open. He was about thirty, with a slight stoop to his shoulders, and was attractive in a bookish sort of way.

As Gibbons had predicted, he looked somewhat relieved to see a policeman present as he entered the shop and addressed them anxiously, saying, "Hello, is something wrong? I'm Gareth Rhys-Jones, the manager here."

Gibbons exhibited his ID, moving forward to offer his hand.

"I'm Detective Sergeant Gibbons, sir," he said. "This is Constable Murphy, and a colleague, Phillip Bethancourt. I'm afraid there was an incident here over the holidays."

Rhys-Jones shook their hands automatically, looking bewildered.

"An incident?" he asked. "Was the shop robbed? I should really notify the owner, Mr. Mittlesdon. . . ."

"We've spoken with Mr. Mittlesdon," Gibbons assured him. "In fact, it was he who rang us. Perhaps if you could come this way, we could talk."

"Yes, yes, of course," said Rhys-Jones, letting himself be ushered forward.

Gibbons led the way through the myriad of book-clogged little rooms, emerging at last into the larger room. Without comment, Rhys-Jones sat in the chair Gibbons indicated.

"Now, Mr. Rhys-Jones," said Gibbons, taking his own seat. "I understand you must have a lot of questions—"

"Yes," said Rhys-Jones, making an effort to collect himself. "Can I ask exactly what was taken?"

"But the shop wasn't robbed, Mr. Rhys-Jones," said Gibbons. "We were called in to investigate the body of a young woman, found here on Christmas morning."

Rhys-Jones looked even more baffled. "A body?" he repeated. "But . . . whose body? Was it one of our employees?"

"Mr. Mittlesdon did not recognize the deceased," said Gibbons.

"Oh." Rhys-Jones appeared at a loss for a moment. Then he frowned. "Wait a moment," he said. "Did you say Christmas Day? But the shop wasn't open then."

"No," agreed Gibbons. "We believe the victim was killed the night before, on Christmas Eve. I understand that you closed the shop with Mr. Mittlesdon on Christmas Eve?"

"That's right," said Rhys-Jones. "But we check, you know, before we lock up, to make sure no one's left in the shop. There couldn't have been a body here then."

"What time did you close on Christmas Eve?" asked Gibbons.

"Well, it was supposed to be early closing, but we were late—we always are on Christmas Eve. Let's see, we let everyone go home as soon as the last customers were out, and Mr. Mittlesdon and I just put the cash in the safe before we left ourselves. It must have been almost teatime by then."

"Did you actually lock the doors, or was that Mr. Mittlesdon?" asked Gibbons.

Rhys-Jones frowned, trying to remember. "I'm not entirely certain," he admitted. "I think it was Mr. Mittlesdon, but we've closed the shop so often together, I can't be sure."

Gibbons nodded. "And how did you spend the holiday?" he asked.

"Oh, I was invited to the Mittlesdons' for Christmas Eve dinner," said Rhys-Jones. "And I went to another friend's for Christmas Day. My family's in Wales, you see—too far to travel for just the day."

"I see," said Gibbons. "I'd also like to ask about your set of keys to the shop—do you keep them with your house keys or separately?"

"Separately," said Rhys-Jones, looking bewildered. "I usually leave the shop keys on my desk at home when I'm not at work."

"Do you live alone?" asked Gibbons.

"No," answered Rhys-Jones. "My girlfriend moved in with me a few months ago. She was gone over the holidays, though, if that's what you mean. Her family's from Essex, and she spent the holiday there."

"Oh?" Gibbons asked. "Not with you?"

Rhys-Jones shook his head ruefully. "Anyone who works in retail isn't around much during the holidays," he said. "And there's certainly no time to plan anything or decorate."

Gibbons nodded understanding and asked for the girlfriend's name.

Rhys-Jones flushed. "Her name's Laurel Brooks," he answered, "but you can't possibly imagine she had anything to do with this."

"Probably not," said Gibbons soothingly. "At the moment, I'm just trying to track down all the shop keys to eliminate them."

Rhys-Jones did not seem much appeased by this, but he nodded.

"Now," said Gibbons, "I'd like to ask you to look at a picture of the victim. I must warn you, however, that it was taken at the autopsy and is rather graphic."

"You mean you want to know if I can identify her," said Rhys-Jones.

"Yes," said Gibbons. "Though I'll admit, her face is not in the best shape—I'm hoping to have a sketch of how she might have looked while alive to show people later today, but all I've got right now is the autopsy photograph."

Rhys-Jones swallowed but nodded. "I'll have a look," he said.

"Excellent, thank you," said Gibbons, turning to his briefcase. He withdrew a glossy color photo and passed it over to Rhys-Jones.

"Good Lord," he said mildly, drawing back a little. Then he frowned and, resettling his glasses more firmly on his nose, bent over the picture.

In the next moment, a sick look came over his face and he sat back, looking a little pale.

"I think it's Jody," he whispered.

"Jody?" asked Gibbons. He did not remember the name from the employee list Mittlesdon had given him.

"I think so," replied Rhys-Jones, clearly shocked. "Like you said, it's hard to tell, but, well, that carroty hair—there's no mistaking that, is there? Dear God, how did this happen?"

"Is Jody a friend?" asked Gibbons gently.

"What? Oh, yes. Yes, she is—or was, at any rate."

Rhys-Jones pushed his hair impatiently back from his face and Gibbons waited for him to collect himself.

"She used to work here," he said in a moment. "Jody Farraday. She left almost a year ago, just after Christmas."

"Have you kept in touch?" asked Gibbons.

Rhys-Jones shook his head. "No, Jody wasn't like that. She moved away from York when she left the bookshop, no forwarding address or anything, just moving on, as she put it. God, I can't believe she's dead." He glanced down again at the picture laying in his lap and shuddered. "It might not be her," he said, but not as if he believed it. "The face is—very disfigured."

"I know," said Gibbons, taking back the photograph. "Thank you for taking the trouble to look at it. We'll investigate the possibility."

"Will you let me know, one way or the other?" asked Rhys-Jones.

"Certainly," replied Gibbons, tucking the photo away. "We usually release the identity of the deceased as soon as their people have been informed. Tell me, had you seen Miss Farraday since she left York last year?"

"No. No, I hadn't." Rhys-Jones shook his head as if to clear it. "I still can't quite believe . . . I mean, if it wasn't for the hair . . ."

"It must come as a very great shock," said Gibbons sympathetically.

"Yes," agreed Rhys-Jones simply.

"While she was here," continued Gibbons, "did she make any enemies? Or perhaps leave someone in the lurch when she went?"

Rhys-Jones was shaking his head before Gibbons finished the question. There was a faint, reminiscent smile on his thin lips.

"You don't understand," he said. "You wouldn't, of course, not having known her. Jody was everybody's friend, and even when she said or did something that would ordinarily irk you, well, with Jody one just laughed. Not," he added, "that I mean to paint her as any kind of angel. She was very eccentric, very much her own person."

"I see," said Gibbons, taking this at face value. "So you can think of no reason someone might want to kill her?"

Rhys-Jones sighed. "Not specifically," he said. "But Jody was very inventive—she came up with quite wild schemes sometimes. If anyone wanted to kill her, I can only think it had to do with one of her schemes gone wrong."

But when Gibbons asked for an example of such a scheme, Rhys-Jones could not come up with one, though he appeared to be thoroughly ransacking his memory.

"I'm sorry," he said at last. "I just can't remember—I never paid much attention to any of them, you see. They were so unrealistic."

Gibbons nodded and let him go then, requesting that he not contact his fellow employees until after Gibbons had spoken to them all.

Rhys-Jones seemed a little startled when asked to leave by the back door.

"But—" he said, and then, "Oh! I didn't—I mean, I suppose the shop will have to remain closed today?"

"I'm afraid so," answered Gibbons. "We'll be in contact with Mr. Mittlesdon as to when he can reopen. Hopefully that will be very soon."

He had been ushering Rhys-Jones to the door as he spoke and now he held it open, politely but firmly. Clearly confounded by events, Rhys-Jones stepped through without further objection and walked off into the cold.

Bethancourt was eyeing the rows of shelves in the room.

"Do you know," he said, "a bookshop would be an excellent place to hide something. You'd have practically no chance of finding it unless you knew where it was."

"Somebody might happen on it accidentally, though," replied Gibbons. "That would make me think twice about hiding anything I valued here."

"Well, I don't know," said Bethancourt. "I expect there would be certain sections where it would be worth the risk." He turned back to Gibbons, abruptly abandoning the subject. "I thought," he said, "that Mittlesdon didn't recognize the body?"

"He claimed not to," agreed Gibbons placidly.

"It seems a little odd, since she was one of his employees at one time."

"Very odd indeed," said Gibbons. "Let's see what the others have to say before we reach any conclusions, though."

"I've already got lots of conclusions," volunteered Bethancourt, following his friend back towards the front room. "I'm trying to narrow them down, but they just keep proliferating."

"Let me know if one of them starts to stand out from the pack," said Gibbons dryly.

Under the watchful eye of PC Murphy, two more employees were sitting in the little reading area, chatting animatedly with each other.

One was a heavy woman in her mid-to-late twenties with golden hair and pendulous breasts, her face revealing a certain prettiness beneath the fat. The other was much younger, perhaps eighteen, a thin whip of a boy with soft brown hair that fell into his eyes, an aura of geekiness about him.

They seemed a slightly odd pair, but there was no doubt they were getting on famously. The boy saw Gibbons and Bethancourt first, and broke off the conversation to say, "Look, Alice, here they come."

Alice turned round in her chair and her blue eyes widened in surprise.

"Phillip!" she exclaimed delightedly. "Is that you?"

Bethancourt looked startled, but in the next instant realization dawned and he said, "Alice, how wonderful to see you again."

His expression somewhat belied his words as she embraced him enthusiastically and he patted her back in response.

"Heavens, I'd no idea you were here," she said, giving him a last squeeze and then drawing back to look at him. "You look splendid," she continued. "Hardly changed at all."

"You're looking grand yourself," said Bethancourt, but his eye had strayed self-consciously toward Gibbons.

"Are you a policeman, then?" asked Alice brightly. "I hadn't heard that."

"Er, no," said Bethancourt, intensely aware of Murphy's scrutiny. "I'm here quite unofficially, just as a favor to a friend. Jack," he continued, turning hastily to Gibbons, "This is Alice Reynolds, an old school friend."

Gibbons, no less taken aback than Bethancourt, was frowning, but before he could say anything, Alice interrupted.

"Not Reynolds anymore, I'm afraid," she said. "It's Alice Knowles now. How do you do, Inspector."

"Ah," said Bethancourt, looking unaccountably relieved. "I didn't know."

"Detective Sergeant Gibbons, ma'am," said Gibbons, shaking hands. "And this is . . . ?"

"Oh, excuse me," said Alice, turning back to her companion. "Rod Bemis, Sergeant Gibbons and Phillip Bethancourt. Rod works here part-time, like me. He's a student at York University."

Rod rose silently and shook hands with both men, muttering something like "hello" in an undertone.

"Well," said Bethancourt with false brightness, "this is unexpected. I think—"

He was interrupted by a knock on the door, and they all turned to see Redfern peering through the glass at them.

"I locked it after Mrs. Knowles and Mr. Bemis arrived," said Murphy apologetically, moving to let Redfern in.

Gibbons smiled at his witnesses. "That's Detective Constable Redfern," he told them. "He was delayed with another case, but he'll be helping with my interviews. Good morning, Constable," he added to Redfern as the young man came in, tugging off his gloves.

"Morning, sir," said Redfern. "Chilly out there today, isn't it?"

He was taking stock of everyone as he came forward, smiling genially at Alice, nodding at Bethancourt, and endeavoring to make eye contact with Bemis, who was staring at his feet.

Gibbons introduced everyone, ending with Bethancourt and mentioning his status as a colleague.

"I'm very glad you've come, Constable," he continued, addressing himself to Redfern, "as we've just run into an unexpected glitch. It seems that Mrs. Knowles here," he bestowed a smile on her, "actually went to school with Mr. Bethancourt."

"Yes, so obviously I must recuse myself," said Bethancourt rapidly, before anyone else could point it out. "I leave it all in your competent hands, gentlemen." He nodded a good-bye at the policemen. "Good to have met you both."

"We must get together and catch up," interposed Alice before Bethancourt could make his escape.

"Yes, we must," agreed Bethancourt without a scintilla of sincerity. "I'll speak to you later, Sergeant."

He beamed at them all and, motioning his dog to his side, swept out.

"Good grief," he groaned once he was outside. "I might have known any case in York was bound to turn on me. Hell, I might as well go and get some groceries in."

He strode up the street with his dog at his heels, huddling into his jacket against the cold, and muttering imprecations against York, Yorkshire, and the Christmas season. *And what on earth,* he thought, *possessed Alice to let herself go in that fashion?* He remembered her distinctly from their days at school: a lithe, pretty girl with long, shapely legs and dancing blue eyes. He found he rather resented not being able to remember her that way anymore.

Still fuming, he emerged onto the Stonebow and suddenly realized the shop he was making for was one that he had been accustomed to stop at on his way back to St. Peter's from the bookshop and which had ceased to exist several years ago.

"Damn," he said, and had to stop and think for a moment about where the nearest grocer's was.

"Phillip!" said a female voice behind him. "Is that you?"

He really could not believe it. Surely fate had given him enough blasts from the past to deal with this season.

Pasting a smile on his face, he turned and beheld not some old girlfriend, nor yet some ghost from his childhood past, but Trudy Fielding, one of Marla's model friends from London. But she was smiling as if pleased to see him, so perhaps she had not yet heard of the breakup.

"Trudy," he said, greeting her as cheerfully as he could. "What the devil are you doing in this godforsaken town?"

She laughed at him. "I think York's a wonderful place to spend Christmas," she said. "I may make a habit of it—I've been having a brilliant time. But I'm only here because of Jake—the band's playing The Duchess this weekend."

"Oh, of course," said Bethancourt, remembering that Trudy's current boyfriend was Jake Torrington, lead singer for the Idle Toads.

"A better question is what you're doing here, and why you think the place is the ninth circle of hell," said Trudy.

Bethancourt smiled sheepishly. "I went to school here," he answered. "My family has a house in the Dales."

"Oh, I didn't know that," said Trudy. "I never go home for the holidays myself—way too much water under that bridge."

She wrinkled her nose, while Bethancourt stared at her, struck by the beautiful simplicity of her plan. But then he shook his head.

"If I didn't show up for Christmas," he said, "I would have extra grief every day for the ensuing year. I think I prefer to get all the misery done with in one go."

"There's something to that," she agreed. "But I get grief no matter what I do—divorced parents, you see."

"Ah, I see," he said. "Yes, there's no good answer to that, is there?"

"I avoid the whole situation," she said firmly. "Look, I've got to run, but do come by and visit—we're here all week, staying at the Dean Court Hotel. Do you know it?"

"Yes," answered Bethancourt.

"Oh, of course, if you grew up here, you would, wouldn't you?" Trudy laughed at herself, and then leaned forward to air kiss his cheek. "See you later then?"

"Absolutely," promised Bethancourt. "I'll look you up."

He watched as she went on toward The Duchess, wondering how long it would be before Trudy spoke to Marla again, and what would be her attitude toward him once she did. It was, in her own words, a situation best avoided.

Sighing, he turned in the opposite direction to seek out a grocery store.

Gibbons meanwhile was manfully restraining himself from eliciting stories of Bethancourt's youth from Alice Knowles. She had spent a blameless holiday with her children at her parents' house in Scarborough, returning early this morning to hand the boys over to their father for the rest of the week.

The first sight of the autopsy photograph had nearly made her faint, so it was hardly surprising that she'd failed to identify the victim. When asked if she remembered Jody Farraday, however, she looked thoughtful.

"Is that who you think it is?" she asked. "Because of the hair, I suppose?"

She looked a little nauseated at the recollection of those bright tresses surrounding the swollen, discolored face.

"I don't know," answered Gibbons. "It's been suggested that it might be."

Alice sighed. "I do remember her, of course," she said. "But I really couldn't tell you if that photograph was of her or not."

"What did you think of Miss Farraday?" asked Gibbons.

"Oh, she was a one." Alice smiled. "Really, the oddest creature, and yet there was something very appealing about her. One couldn't help but like her. I do hope it isn't her."

There was not much more to be got out of Alice Knowles, who

explained that she worked part-time at the bookshop just to keep herself busy while the boys were at nursery school.

"I always loved this place," she said, looking around at the orderly rows of books on their shelves. "And I felt a bit at loose ends after the divorce—you know how it is. It's better to be useful."

Gibbons felt relieved. As long as her story checked out, there was no reason to exclude Bethancourt from the investigation, since Alice could not possibly be a suspect; Scarborough was just far enough away to make it impossible for her to have murdered anyone in York on Christmas Eve.

Rod was a harder nut to crack. He was painfully shy and awkward in his manner. There was no doubt an intellect of some merit hiding beneath his mop of hair, but the boy seemed intent on hiding all vestiges of it. He had been hired on at the bookshop only in October, so he could not be expected to recognize Jody Farraday, if indeed she was the victim.

Bemis came from a family of Jehovah's Witnesses in Lincolnshire and had not previously lived in York before arriving that fall to study at the university. Since his family did not celebrate Christmas, he had elected to remain in York over the holiday and earn extra money working at Mittlesdon's. He had spent Christmas night alone in his dorm room, playing a video game.

"He could have murdered half-a-dozen people," remarked Redfern, after they had let Bemis go, "but why should he?"

"Yes, he strikes me as quite harmless," agreed Gibbons. "But time will tell. Let's see—we still have four key-holders to interview." He looked up from his notebook with a rueful smile. "Although everyone is so careless with their keys, nearly any of the employees might have copies of them. Rod there," he jerked his head in the direction of the doorway through which Bemis had exited, "is probably the least likely, given his short tenure here."

Redfern nodded. "Still," he said, "we've got to start somewhere—it might as well be with the official key-holders."

"Right," said Gibbons, returning to his notes. "According to Mittlesdon, Catherine Stockton is visiting her family in Cornwall and is not expected back until the weekend."

"Do you really think a woman could be our killer, sir?" asked Redfern a little hesitantly, as if reluctant to pour cold water on Gibbons's theories.

"Not unless she was uncommonly large and strong," answered Gibbons, unruffled by the criticism. "But since I've no idea what our victim was doing here in the first place, or why someone wanted to murder her, I'm not ruling out the possibility that more than one of the people who work here know something about this crime."

Redfern was nodding. "I see," he said. He glanced around the quiet shop, the orderly rows of books marching from one end of the room to the other, disappearing into the shadows at the back of the shop. "It does seem a most unlikely place for a murder," he said.

"I thought so, too," said Gibbons, his eyes following Redfern's. "It's almost a pity to have to dig beneath the surface and bring up all the ugliness. But something led to that young woman's death." He sighed. "Let's go look up Mr. Tony Grandidge, shall we? His family lives in York, so presumably he spent the holiday here."

"All right, sir," said Redfern, gathering up his things. "Where's this Grandidge live then?"

Gibbons squinted at his notes. "St. Mary's, off Bootham," he answered. "Know where that is?"

Redfern grinned at him. "That's an easy one," he said. "Won't take us but a minute to walk over there—and you'll get to see some of the sights along the way."

The route Redfern took led them directly through the city center, so there were indeed plenty of sights, as well as plenty of crowds.

"Have you ever heard of a snickelway, Constable?" asked Gibbons as they walked, dodging around the shoppers and gawkers.

Redfern cast him a slightly startled glance. "Certainly," he replied. "Did you want to go by the snickelways? It'll take a bit longer—"

"No, no," said Gibbons hastily. He was faintly annoyed to find that Bethancourt had not been making the word up. "Just an idle question, that's all."

They passed beneath Bootham Bar and walked for a little way along the busy thoroughfare. St. Mary's proved to be a narrow residential street leading off the main street with rows of terraced houses; number 20 was about halfway down. Grandidge had the third-floor flat, and was at home when they rang his bell. He was a thin, wiry young man, not much over twenty, with a shock of dark hair and an attractive, if somewhat dissipated, mien. He looked as if he had not been up for very long.

"What's up then?" he asked as he gave a cursory glance at their IDs and motioned them into the sitting room.

"We're investigating a crime that took place over the holiday, at Mittlesdon's Bookshop," Gibbons told him.

Grandidge looked alarmed. "At the bookshop?" he repeated. "What happened?"

"A murder was committed there," said Gibbons.

It seemed not to be the answer Grandidge had been expecting. He looked from one to the other of the policemen as if waiting for one of them to tell him it was a joke.

"A murder?" he said incredulously. "In the *bookshop*?"

"Yes," said Gibbons. "I understand you work there, in inventory?"

Grandidge shoved his hair out of his eyes with an impatient motion and sat down abruptly. "You could say that," he agreed. "In fact, you could say I am the receiving department—it would be nearer the truth."

"And in that capacity, you have the keys to the shop?"

"Well, yes," said Grandidge, looking a little puzzled.

"Can you account for your keys?" asked Gibbons.

"Of course," said Grandidge. His tone was confident, but the glance he gave round the flat was uncertain. "I think they must be in the bedroom," he added, rising and heading for a door on the far side of the room. But he paused on the way, to inspect a side table, and then stopped again to go through a small pile of things on the kitchen counter. "Ah, here they are," he said triumphantly, turning to hold up three keys on a plain ring. He tossed them to Gibbons, who caught them effortlessly.

"Thank you, sir," he said, giving them a brief glance before tucking them into his pocket. "Now, if you could just tell me how you spent Christmas?"

"I was at my uncle's house in Upper Poppleton," Grandidge answered, swiping at his hair again as he rejoined them. "I went out there on Christmas Eve and didn't get back here till yesterday. Or no, wait—I did just run over on Christmas Day for a moment. I'd forgotten my dress shoes, you see. And of course we were all in to midnight service at the Minster."

"Of course," said Gibbons, slightly amused by these exceptions. "If I could just have your uncle's name and address?"

"Brian Sanderson, the Old Farm, Upper Poppleton," Grandidge rattled off.

Gibbons nodded, making note of the information in his notebook. Then, after giving his usual warning, he asked Grandidge to look at the autopsy picture of the victim.

Grandidge paled when he got his first eyeful of it, but he studied it intently nonetheless, finally handing it back with a little shudder and the words, "I don't think it's anyone I know."

Gibbons accepted this statement, but asked, "Do you remember a woman called Jody Farraday?"

"Jody? Oh, yes, I remember her—" Grandidge broke off, frowning. "It is like her hair in the picture," he said slowly. "It might—yes, I think it could be her. But . . ."

Gibbons raised a brow. "But?" he asked.

"Well, it's just that Jody hasn't been around for months,"

explained Grandidge. "She left York about this time last year, and I haven't seen her since. I can't imagine what she'd be doing back at the bookshop."

"Well, the identification isn't certain yet," said Gibbons. "You said you hadn't seen her since she left—would you have expected her to get in touch with you if she were back in town?"

"We were friends," admitted Grandidge. "I don't say I would have been her first call, but if she was here for any length of time, I think I'd hear from her. For that matter, I'd expect her to stop by the bookshop, too. We all liked her there and she was fond of the place."

"But she hadn't done so lately?"

Grandidge shook his head.

They took their leave of him after that.

"I wonder if our victim really is this Jody Farraday," said Gibbons as they emerged once again into the cold. "No one except the shop manager has come up with the identification on their own."

"On the other hand," said Redfern, "none of the others have had anything else to suggest."

"True," said Gibbons. "I wonder—"

He broke off as Redfern's mobile began to ring, and the constable, glancing at it, said, "It's the super," and answered it.

The conversation was brief: on Redfern's end it consisted of saying, "Yes, sir," twice and then sighing as he rang off.

"I'm awfully sorry, sir," he said to Gibbons, "but I've got to go. A bit of trouble has broken out over at Coppergate, and the super says I'm to go get it sorted—he's still on that double-murder himself."

"That's fine, Constable," said Gibbons, who really did not mind. "I've got your number if I need anything badly, and anyway I wanted some lunch about now."

Redfern looked as if he would have appreciated some lunch as well, but he only sighed again and took himself off at a rapid pace.

Gibbons, following more slowly, pulled out his mobile and dialed Bethancourt's number.

"I want some lunch," he announced when Bethancourt answered.

"Really?" said Bethancourt. "I was planning on drinking mine."

"Have lunch with me instead," suggested Gibbons. "Afterward you could take me round to Libby Alston's place in—let me see here—Holgate."

Silence.

"I thought I was off the case," said Bethancourt, a cautious note in his voice, as if he did not want to raise his hopes.

"I can't see why," replied Gibbons. "It's true that I have yet to confirm Mrs. Knowles' alibi, but it seems unlikely that it won't hold up."

"Alice has an alibi?" asked Bethancourt, brightening. "That's a piece of luck. What was she doing?"

"I don't know exactly, but whatever it was, she was doing it in Scarborough."

"That's right," said Bethancourt thoughtfully. "Her people are from Scarborough. I'd forgotten that."

"So do you want to meet me for lunch?" asked Gibbons.

"Yes," answered Bethancourt. "Where are you?"

"On Bootham, headed back toward Bootham Bar."

"All right. Just continue on as you are, past the Bar, and The Dean Court Hotel will be down the street to your right. I'll meet you there."

"Right," said Gibbons. "I'll find it."

It was not a long walk, but the wind had picked up and he was very glad to reach the hotel and get in out of the cold. Bethancourt had not yet arrived, and upon inspection he found that there were two restaurants, so he sat down in the lobby to wait. Bethancourt was picky about his meals, and it wouldn't do to choose the wrong place.

In about ten more minutes Bethancourt appeared, pausing just inside the door to remove his glasses, which had fogged up.

"There you are," said Gibbons, tucking away his notebook and rising from his seat.

Bethancourt blinked at him. "Didn't you get a table?" he asked, polishing his glasses against his sleeve. "I thought you were hungry."

"I'm near starving, but I didn't know which restaurant you meant to eat at," replied Gibbons.

"Oh, the bistro," said Bethancourt, as if there could hardly be any doubt. "Here, let's go in."

The restaurant was crowded, but it was a large enough establishment to still have a few tables free, and the two young men were soon settled comfortably. They sipped hot coffee while Gibbons brought Bethancourt up-to-date.

"I want to interview all the employees that I can today," he finished. "A few of them aren't back from their holiday yet and will have to wait."

"How many more are there?" asked Bethancourt.

"Only three, I think," said Gibbons, pulling out his notebook and consulting a list. "Well, four if you count the assistant manager I want to talk to next."

"The one in Holgate," said Bethancourt.

"That's right. Where is that, anyway?"

"Not too far," answered Bethancourt. "West of the city center."

Gibbons nodded, sipped his coffee, and then, meeting his friend's eyes, he rested his chin in his hand and said, "So, it's full-disclosure time. Who is Alice Knowles and what is she to you?"

"Nothing anymore," replied Bethancourt. "She was my girlfriend at St. Peter's my last two years there. She was very pretty then," he added, looking a little depressed over Alice's fall from grace in that regard.

"You didn't continue to see each other after you left for Oxford?" asked Gibbons.

"Well, as I recollect, we meant to," said Bethancourt. "Best intentions and all that. But of course it didn't work out. I was soon head over heels for somebody else and feeling horribly guilty every time I came home. Until I found out Alice was seeing another chap, of course." He smiled in recollection.

Gibbons shook his head. "I don't know why your personal life is always so complicated," he said.

Bethancourt looked mildly affronted. "That's not complicated," he said. "That's perfectly normal. Hardly anybody actually ends up with their girlfriend from school."

"I suppose not," admitted Gibbons, "but your affairs always seem to be rife with drama."

Bethancourt opened his mouth to retort, but remembered in time that Gibbons's own tragic love affair was a little too fresh to be casually remarked upon.

"Well, anyway, I haven't seen Alice since my first year at Oxford," he said. "I didn't even know she was living in York."

Gibbons grinned at him. "And judging by looks, you wish you'd never found out."

"Well, I like the past to stay in the past," said Bethancourt. "I don't see what's wrong with that."

"Nothing, I suppose," said Gibbons with a shrug.

The food arrived then and they dug in with a good appetite, their conversation turning to York and its history and Bethancourt's history in the old city.

When the plates had been cleared away and they were sipping coffee, Bethancourt's mobile rang; looking at the ID, he frowned and switched it off, looking somewhat discomfited.

Gibbons raised an eyebrow.

"Marla," said Bethancourt. "She's got a bloody nerve."

"Ah, yes," said Gibbons. "You never did tell me what happened. I take it this is a more serious breakup than usual?"

"What?" Bethancourt frowned. "What on earth do you mean by that? We've never broken up before."

Gibbons winced in the manner of a man who has committed a faux pas. Marla Tate was as renowned for her mercurial temper as she was for her beauty, and she and Bethancourt were always rowing, and almost as frequently claiming to break up. It never lasted.

"I meant, a more serious row than usual," Gibbons amended hastily.

"Oh, yes," said Bethancourt glumly. "It's definitely over. I accused her of infidelity, you see, and she's not about to forgive me."

"Infidelity?" asked Gibbons, thinking that this did not sound much like his friend. "Why did you think she'd been unfaithful?"

"Well, she was," said Bethancourt defensively. "And I didn't so much accuse her of that as I did accuse her of having no discretion at all. Which is true, damn it all."

Gibbons felt as though his head were spinning. "So Marla was having a bit on the side and when you confronted her she broke up with you?" he asked. "Is she in love with this other chap?"

"Oh, I don't think so," said Bethancourt. "At least, I don't imagine so. Damn it all, that never occurred to me."

"Sorry," said Gibbons, who was still largely confused. "I'm trying to work it out is all. You're not being very clear, you know."

"I can't see what you think there is to work out," replied Bethancourt. "It's simple enough: Marla had an affair with the photographer on that shoot she did in Aruba last week and in consequence I've broken it off with her."

"I'm very sorry to hear it," said Gibbons sincerely. "But, well, it just seems to me that you're being a bit draconian about it all. I mean, not to be rude or anything, but you haven't always been faithful yourself, you know."

Bethancourt sighed. "I know," he answered. "And it's not the first time I've suspected that she was mixing pleasure with business when she's been off on those location shoots. It's not that so much as it's the lack of discretion, and consequently the lack of consideration for my feelings. I mean, if I have occasionally strayed from the straight and narrow, at least I made sure that all her friends weren't discussing it behind her back."

"I see," said Gibbons. He was silent for a moment. "I think," he said, "that you're trying to tell me that there are rules for infidelity. Well, Phillip, I believe infidelity itself is against the rules."

"Don't preach, Jack," said Bethancourt wearily. "I really can't take being preached at just now. All I'm saying is that when one commits an indiscretion, one should make certain that no one else ends up bearing the consequences."

And Gibbons could not disagree with that. It was a kind of morality, if not the one he had been brought up with.

"Well, I'm sorry about it all," he said. In his mind he was still far from certain that the death knell had been sounded for the relationship, but he could not very well tell Bethancourt that. Still, it would do no harm to inquire.

"You don't think you could forgive her, then?"

"She doesn't want to be forgiven," said Bethancourt in a grim tone. "She apparently feels it was quite rude of me to bring the subject up and broke up with me on the spot."

"I thought you broke up with her?" asked Gibbons, feeling confused again.

"I did, directly after she refused to apologize for putting me in the embarrassing position of hearing about the affair in a club from a passing acquaintance. It was really very awkward."

"I can see it would be," agreed Gibbons. "Er, are you trying to say that Marla broke up with you because you found out she's been unfaithful to you?"

"Well, it sounds silly when you put it like that," said Bethancourt. "Although I suppose that was more or less the sequence of events."

"It's not silly, it's completely mad," said Gibbons firmly.

"Well, it is what it is," muttered Bethancourt. "Oh, look, here's the bill. We'd better get on, don't you think?"

Gibbons readily agreed.

"Who are we going to see?" asked Bethancourt, reading over the bill before placing his credit card in the folder with it.

"Libby Alston," said Gibbons. "She's the assistant manager of the bookshop." He plucked out the contact sheet on which he had made various notes. "She's been with the store for the last seven years, and lives in Holgate."

"Yes, I remember you said that," answered Bethancourt. "It shouldn't take us long to get there."

The walk out to Holgate was longer than Gibbons had anticipated, and the rain started up again about halfway through the trek. Bethancourt seemed not to feel the distance, but Gibbons was aware that he was more tired than he should have been at the end of it. He made an effort to pull himself together as they approached the address.

Libby Alston's house was a modern one on Beech Avenue, a modest, two-story brick affair. She answered the door herself, a big woman of about forty with color-tinted auburn hair and intelligent, light blue eyes. The detectives were rather surprised: as she was the assistant manager to Rhys-Jones, they had both expected her to be younger than he, but in fact she was the oldest employee of the bookshop. She was wearing a patterned dress, and a small, tow-headed child was peering round her skirts.

"Hello," she said, smiling but with a certain reserve in her eyes. "Can I help you?"

"Yes, ma'am," said Gibbons. "We're looking for Libby Alston?"

"That's me," she answered readily. "What can I do for you?"

Gibbons held up his ID card. "I'm Detective Sergeant Gibbons," he said. "And this is my colleague, Phillip Bethancourt. We'd like a word about Mittlesdon's Bookshop."

Libby was clearly startled, as well as instantly curious.

"The bookshop?" she asked. "Here, do come in—Jonathan, sweetie, move out of the way. Amanda," she raised her voice, "come take your little brother, please."

From the back hallway Alice in Wonderland appeared, complete with hair band and a blue dress, though without a pinafore. She regarded the two men with wide eyes while she came forward and reached for her brother's hand.

"You two go along to your father," said Libby. "I'll be back in in a few moments."

The little girl nodded and, with one last glance at the intimidating strangers, led her brother off.

"Come into the sitting room," said Libby, beckoning them toward the front room on the right. "Do sit down."

She took one end of the sofa with the air of assuming her accustomed place, while Bethancourt and Gibbons distributed themselves in two of the armchairs.

"Now do tell me what's happened," said Libby, looking more curious than worried.

Gibbons went through the usual explanation and inquiry about the shop keys. Unlike the youthful Tony Grandidge, Libby knew exactly where her keys were: in her purse, which she kept on the hall table. Asked to identify the autopsy picture, she looked at it carefully, biting her lip but otherwise not showing any sign of distress. At first nothing particular seemed to register with her, but then she suddenly cocked her head and frowned.

"Did you say this was a young woman?" she asked.

"That's right," answered Gibbons. "The medical examiner estimates her age at between twenty-five and thirty. He says she was a very fit woman—not, perhaps, an athlete, but someone who might go hiking or bicycle riding."

Libby nodded slowly. "It could be someone who used to work at the shop," she said, and for the first time the facts of the case seemed to hit home for her as a certain uneasiness appeared in her eyes. "There was a girl named Jody Farraday—she was a tall, rangy girl in her twenties. But to be perfectly honest," and she lifted her eyes from the photograph to look at Gibbons, "I'm mostly reminded of her because of this woman's hair. Jody's was like that, and about that length."

Gibbons was excited, though he did not show it; having a second person independently identify the victim as Jody Farraday was a great help.

"In fact," continued Libby thoughtfully, "I believe I have a picture of Jody somewhere . . . yes, I think I do."

She rose and went to a chest in one corner of the room and opened the drawer, while Gibbons said, "A photograph would be wonderful, Mrs. Alston. It might enable us to identify the victim without waiting for the artist's sketch."

"Well, I'm not sure it's her," said Libby, shuffling through a batch of snapshots. "Like I said, it's the hair made me think of it. Right, here we are."

She turned back to them and proffered a photo, which Gibbons took eagerly. It depicted a group of people standing in the office at Mittlesdon's, including all the employees Gibbons had already interviewed. They were gathered about a birthday cake placed on one of the desks, with Mittlesdon himself in the center, smiling self-consciously. In the back was a tall woman with bright red hair and an infectious grin. Gibbons—and Bethancourt, who had risen to look over his friend's shoulder—peered intensely at the small image.

"I think it might be her," said Gibbons.

"She's got distinctive bone structure," said Bethancourt. "That ought to help."

"You can keep it if you like," said Libby.

"Thank you very much, Mrs. Alston," said Gibbons, tucking the photo away. "This will prove very useful."

"Pleased to be of help," she answered.

For the rest, Libby Alston had no alibi other than being at her in-laws with her family on Christmas Day, and she had no notion what might have brought Jody Farraday back to Mittlesdon's, if indeed the corpse was hers.

When they emerged from the house, the short winter day was already drawing to a close, the sun rapidly sinking below the rooftops and casting the street into deep shadow. Bethancourt shivered and turned up the collar of his coat.

"What's next?" he asked.

"It rather depends," answered Gibbons, consulting his notebook. "I'd like to get this photograph back to the station to see if it will help at all with identification. But there's one more employee, another sales assistant let's see—he lives in Heworth."

He looked up at Bethancourt questioningly.

"Nothing's very far out of the way in York," said Bethancourt. "But let's get a taxi, shall we? I think the wind's picking up and it's a bit of a tramp to Heworth."

Dominic Bartlett was wearing a bow tie and a sleeveless pullover when he opened the door of his flat to them. He was a tall, heavyset man of about thirty, who looked down his nose at them through round spectacles that seemed constantly to be sliding down from the bridge of his nose, ensuring that their wearer was always tilting his head back in order to see through the lenses. He had the appearance of an intellectual snob, but in fact was quite pleasant in his manner, if somewhat nonplussed to find the police on his doorstep.

"My family lives in Bristol now," he told them as they settled into chairs in his sitting room. "Not really much sense in making the trip just for one day, even if it is Christmas. I stayed in York over the holiday. Excuse me, did you say someone had died in the shop?"

"Yes, sir," said Gibbons. "A woman was killed there. So you were alone here on Christmas Eve?"

Bartlett was still frowning over the death.

"What?" he said. "Oh, no, I went to a dinner party at a friend's house. But I don't understand—how did anyone get into the shop after it was closed?"

"We're still investigating that aspect of the matter," said Gibbons. He produced the autopsy photo again, but Bartlett failed to recognize the victim. Bethancourt, watching him silently, thought he did not try very hard; he seemed principally disturbed to be confronted with the evidence of violence. But he did remember Jody Farraday.

"Oh, yes, I knew Jody," he said, his eyes lighting up. "She had a wonderful wit. And she was so brave."

"Brave?" asked Gibbons.

Bartlett waved a hand. "Perhaps that's the wrong word," he said. "She was just—very confident, I suppose. Not afraid of being out on her own, or of trying new things, new places. I found her very refreshing." He paused, sobering. "Do you really think it's her?" he asked anxiously.

"We don't know as yet," answered Gibbons. "At this time, it's only a possibility."

"I see, I see," Bartlett muttered. "This is very disturbing. I don't like to think—well, of course not."

This was said half to himself, but despite its incoherence, his listeners understood his feelings very well.

"It's an unnerving situation," said Gibbons sympathetically.

Bartlett bobbed his head in agreement and pushed his glasses back up on his nose. Behind the lenses, his eyes looked at them blankly, a man at a loss for how to deal with such an unexpected state of affairs.

"So those are our suspects?" asked Bethancourt as they left Bartlett's flat, turning their backs to the wind and walking southward, toward police headquarters. "I missed meeting this Tony Grandidge chap, but I can't say they seem a likely bunch to me. Didn't you say there were a couple of others, who were out of town?"

"Exactly," responded Gibbons dryly. "Out of town, as in out of town for the holidays."

"Oh," said Bethancourt. "As in out of town during the murder. That is a bit difficult. Fairly far out of town, I take it?"

"As I recollect," answered Gibbons, tugging on his gloves, "one is on a cruise in the Mediterranean, and the other is visiting her family in Cornwall."

"Well, that puts paid to that," said Bethancourt.

"On the other hand," said Gibbons, "the key-holders are not our only suspects."

"They're not?" asked Bethancourt, and then, before Gibbons could answer, he added, "Oh! I'd forgotten about the proliferation of keys."

"Which widens the field considerably," said Gibbons.

"Yes," said Bethancourt thoughtfully. "In fact, if nearly any employee could have had a copy made, then it follows that Jody Farraday herself might have had a set. In which case, she could have let both herself and her murderer into the bookshop."

Gibbons nodded. "Always assuming that our corpse really is Jody Farraday. That's the first thing to nail down. I don't think the photo Libby Alston gave us is good enough on its own to give us a positive ID, but it ought to help. And meanwhile we can be finding out about Miss Farraday in case it is her."

"Yes, surely someone has seen the woman in the last year," said Bethancourt. "And yet, I rather thought our witnesses were telling the truth when they said they hadn't."

Gibbons shrugged. "Murderers are often very good liars," he said. "I've noticed that."

And Bethancourt had to agree.

6

In Which Bethancourt Goes A-Wassailing and Wee Willie Winkie Chases Gibbons Down

*G*ibbons frowned at the computer screen. He was back at police headquarters, in the conference room Detective Superintendent Brumby's team had taken over, doing a basic background search on Jody Farraday. Normally, this would turn up all sorts of information, but he was finding next to nothing on the mysterious Miss Farraday. There was a birth certificate on file, indicating that she had turned twenty-eight last October, and a driver's license had been issued to her eight years ago in Northumberland. Other than that, nothing. No credit cards or bank accounts, no address beyond the one given eight years ago in Northumberland, and no telephone number or even an electricity bill in her name. Gibbons was beginning to think he had input something wrong.

Thoughtfully, he rose and looked around for Detective Sergeant Andrew Rowett, Brumby's expert in electronic records.

Rowett, a dour-faced man of thirty-five or so, grinned at Gibbons when he saw him.

"Thought you might come looking for me sooner or later," he said.

His tone was a little smug, but Gibbons did not begrudge it him. He grinned back good-naturedly and said, "So you've already had a look at Jody Farraday, have you?"

"Brumby mentioned she might be your victim," said Rowett, "so I just thought I'd run her through the system. You know, at least find out if she were missing or no."

"I didn't see her in the missing-persons database," said Gibbons. "But then, I didn't see anyone there who could be our victim. Did you find something I missed?"

Rowett shook his head. "I started with the same check," he answered, "and came up with nothing. So I ran a few others, but our Miss Farraday doesn't show up anywhere. I think what we have here is someone living under the radar, probably deliberately so. I didn't go a lot further, since I didn't think we were sure yet she was our victim?" He raised an eyebrow in question.

"No," admitted Gibbons, "we're not. They're still working on identification, and I've contributed a bad snapshot of Jody to help, but it's possible the victim is someone else altogether."

"Not someone recently reported as missing," Rowett assured him. "I ran that search first, locally and then nationally, but the only possible matches I came up with were obviously wrong." He paused and stroked his chin. "I didn't look very far back," he said. "I could do that, if you think it worth the time?"

Gibbons considered. "I have a kind of feeling," he confessed, "that it is Jody Farraday. I think I'd like to go a little further in that direction before you spend a lot of time slogging through cold cases. But I've never come across anyone off the grid before. I take it that means she was engaged in some kind of criminal activity?"

"Not necessarily," said Rowett. "You'd think so, but there are a lot of odd people about. Some of them just don't like the idea of the government knowing too much about them. Career criminals, on the other hand, tend to have lots and lots of identifying information—sometimes in triplicate, if you take my meaning." He grinned again.

"I see," said Gibbons, with a smile to show he appreciated the humor. "But sometimes there are criminals who live off the grid?"

"Sometimes," said Rowett. "They tend to be either very low-ranking or else they're very dangerous characters indeed. Spies and assassins or, just once in a while, serial killers." He sighed.

Gibbons fervently hoped he was not dealing with a dead spy.

"I'll keep on with the research," added Rowett. "A titbit or two will turn up eventually, if experience is any guide. Let me know what more you find out—anything could turn out to be helpful."

Gibbons thanked him and went off to pay another visit to Mr. Mittlesdon.

Bethancourt had not accompanied Gibbons to the police station, knowing he would merely be left to kick his heels there while Gibbons worked.

Left therefore to his own devices, he decided the most he could hope to contribute was to get in touch with some of his parents' friends and bring himself up-to-date on York gossip. It was still, he reflected, Christmastide, which meant the Heywoods would be holding open house.

Accordingly, he turned his steps toward the Heywoods' home in Monkgate, ruminating on what kind of reception he might receive. Among his parents' friends the Heywoods were known for their bonhomie, considered an oddity as it was not a quality generally found in his parents' acquaintances. It perhaps explained, however, why Bethancourt had always been on good terms with them, even during his school days, when he had frequently run into them about the city, ofttimes when he should have been in his dormitory.

There was only a glimmer of twilight left in the sky when he turned into Monkgate and found, as he had expected, the Heywood house lit up and obviously ready to welcome visitors. He stepped up to the door and heard the unmistakable sounds of a cocktail party in full swing. Smiling to himself, he lifted and then let fall the heavy brass knocker.

Donald Heywood himself answered the door. He looked blank for a moment and then, before Bethancourt could say anything, exclaimed, "By all that's holy, if it isn't young Bethancourt! Come in, lad, come in. It's a good few years since we've seen you—and how are your parents keeping this season?"

Bethancourt was swept into the house, divested of his coat while he made polite responses to Heywood's inquiries, and introduced to the rest of the gathering. He knew about half of them, though he was not surprised to find so many new faces: the Heywoods' circle was an ever-expanding one. Bethancourt, having had a large, mulled wine pressed into his hand, joined the party happily, renewing old acquaintances and making new ones.

A great deal of the conversation centered around the recent flooding, and Bethancourt was inundated with questions about the situation in the Dales. Eventually, however, he managed to work his way round to introducing the topic of murder.

No one had yet heard of the death at Mittlesdon's, though there was some mention of the serial killing.

"All these killers want is publicity," opined one man, a large, robust figure in an unfortunate plaid vest. "If the media would stop playing up to them and making a cause célèbre out of all their nasty perversions, why, they'd stop killing, I warrant."

Bethancourt regarded him bemusedly while Peter, the Heywoods' eldest son, refuted this view.

"Do you know Brian Sanderson?" asked a voice in his ear, and Bethancourt turned to see another of his parents' friends, Daphne Stearn. She nodded toward the plaid vest.

"Happy Christmas, Mrs. Stearn," he said. "No, I don't think I know him. Is he connected with those Sanderson's Carveries one sees around town?"

"That's right," said Daphne. "He's the man himself. He's made a fortune out of the business, and is very proud of it." Her tone indicated that in her view it was nothing much to be proud of.

"I see," said Bethancourt neutrally. "He seems to fancy himself a student of criminal psychology."

Daphne snorted.

"Well, Phillip here should know," Peter Heywood said, turning to him. "Didn't I hear you had taken an interest in police work? Do you know any of the Scotland Yard people who've come up to investigate the serial killing?"

"One of them is a friend of mine," admitted Bethancourt. "But he's been spending most of his time on this Mittlesdon's murder."

"Mittlesdon?" asked Daphne, surprised. "The bookshop?"

"That's right," said Bethancourt. "A young woman was murdered there over the holidays."

"Good God," said Peter. "At Mittlesdon's Bookshop? That must be some kind of sacrilege."

"Had you heard about that, Brian?" asked Daphne. "Doesn't your nephew work there?"

"He does, he does," said Sanderson, frowning. "He didn't say anything about it over the holidays, though."

"They didn't find her until Christmas morning," said Bethancourt.

"Ah, well, that'll account for it," said Sanderson. "I haven't seen Tony since Christmas Day. I'm sorry to hear there's been a crime there, though—I'm quite an aficionado of Mittlesdon's. Always popping in to see what new things he's got."

"Brian thinks it makes him look intellectual," whispered Daphne in Bethancourt's ear.

Bethancourt repressed a smile and answered Sanderson. "I understand Mr. Mittlesdon was quite distressed over it."

"But what happened?" asked Peter. "Surely the shop was shut."

"Nobody's sure yet," said Bethancourt. "I believe the working theory is that an ex-employee somehow gained access. But whether she was killed by someone currently working at the shop or by someone she brought with her is unknown."

Other people were being drawn in by the conversation, no doubt attracted by the mention of murder. It resulted, as Bethancourt had hoped, in a general discussion of crime in York and of Mittlesdon's Bookshop. He fell back into a listening mode, while Daphne Stearn continued to enliven the observations of the rest of the party with her peppery commentary in his ear.

All in all, he quite enjoyed himself, although at the end of the evening he was not sure how much useful information he had gathered. Thanks to Daphne, he could now identify several other matrons who had lost weight on his aunt Evelyn's diet, and knew rather more than he wanted to about the indiscretions of some of York's leading citizens. But he hadn't really discovered much that would help the case. As in his school days, Mittlesdon's was still looked on as a reliable place to purchase both rare manuscripts and used books. If anything, the wealthier class of York seemed to feel the bookshop's reputation had grown, and there was talk of how Mervyn Mittlesdon had done very well for himself. In any case, there had certainly not been any scandals recently associated with the shop or its employees.

But, reflected Bethancourt as he at length emerged from the party feeling rather tipsy, it was very difficult to tell exactly which aspect of the bookshop needed investigating. Had the murder in fact had anything to do with the business of bookselling? Or was it entirely to do with Jody Farraday's personal life?

Gibbons was currently involved in trying to work out the same question. He had found Mittlesdon at home in his house in Victor Street, but he seemed to know little about any of his employees' personal lives.

The house was in a quiet, pleasant neighborhood, one in a row of midsized Victorian terraces. In the normal way of things, it would have ample room for Mittlesdon, his wife, and his son when the latter was home from university, but at the moment it had a crowded feel. Or at least that was the impression Gibbons had, when he arrived to find a bustle of activity going on in the kitchen while a more sedate party occupied the drawing room, occasionally interrupted by the babysitters and their charges from upstairs.

Mittlesdon made introductions in a slightly flustered manner and then ushered Gibbons into a small office.

"There," he said, closing the door behind them and seating himself behind the desk. "That's better, I think?"

He looked anxiously at Gibbons, as if the detective might have some objection to this arrangement.

"Yes, indeed," said Gibbons, sitting in the only other chair, a straight-backed one by the door. "I'm sorry to interrupt your holiday party, sir."

"Not at all, not at all." Mittlesdon waved a hand. "This sad business must come first, of course." He hesitated. "Might I ask how things are coming along?"

"Well," said Gibbons, "we've made a very tentative identification of the body. There's still plenty of room for error there, but my working theory is that she was an ex-employee of yours named Jody Farraday."

Mittlesdon looked considerably surprised.

"Jody?" he echoed. "Oh, I don't think it could be she, Sergeant. As I understood it, she left York altogether when she left the bookshop. Indeed," he added, "I should be very sad to hear anything had happened to her—she was a very lively young lady, very well liked among the staff."

"It may not be her," said Gibbons. "On the other hand, it's not impossible that she had returned to York recently. And I understand there is a considerable physical resemblance."

Mittlesdon thought that over, looking a little bewildered.

"Jody was a very tall girl," he said. "I suppose her most striking feature was her hair—it was a bright red. But natural, not dyed. Or at least so the other women at the shop said—I know little about such things myself."

"Just so," said Gibbons, hiding a smile. "In the event it is her, I should like to know anything you can tell me about her background or her family."

"Well, well," said Mittlesdon, clearly still startled by the idea that the victim might be a onetime employee. "Let me see. I believe Jody was with us for two or three years. And a very good worker she was, too." He adjusted his spectacles and directed his gaze to Gibbons. "Most people think there's not much to do at a bookshop," he said. "They think we spend all our time sitting about and reading. But that's not the case at all, not at all. In fact, there's a great deal of work to be done, quite apart from the special orders. I'm always grateful when we take on someone who's willing to work hard."

Gibbons nodded patiently. "And how did you come to hire Miss Farraday?" he asked.

Mittlesdon frowned in thought. "I seem to remember that she started early in the autumn," he said slowly, working it out. "Yes, I believe it was that September, or just possibly October, when she joined the staff. It was after Kennedy left us at any rate."

"Kennedy?" said Gibbons.

"Yes, Broderick Kennedy, a very intelligent young man," answered Mittlesdon. "He was at university here, and stayed the summer in York after he graduated. But then he went on to a new job in Leeds in his field—computer science, it was."

"Which meant you had an opening at the shop," prompted Gibbons, trying to steer the conversation back to Jody Farraday.

"That's right," agreed Mittlesdon. "I believe Gareth found her. At least, he had me interview her."

"Gareth," repeated Gibbons. "That would be Mr. Rhys-Jones,

the shop manager?" When Mittlesdon nodded, he continued, "So as manager, he would vet job applications before passing them on to you, would he?" he asked.

"Yes, yes—and he's much better at it than I am," said Mittlesdon. "Picking them out, I mean. He seems to have a knack for it."

"So you wouldn't know exactly how he came to choose her?" said Gibbons, refusing to be diverted from the point.

"Well, no," admitted Mittlesdon.

"What about her family?" asked Gibbons. "Did she come from York originally?"

But here Mittlesdon was of no help at all. He did not remember Jody ever referring to any family in the area, although she seemed familiar with the city.

"Of course," he added, "we would have an emergency contact on file for her, but I don't remember now who that might have been."

He seemed aware that he was failing to provide any useful information, because he suddenly sat up straighter and said, "But perhaps my son could help us—I've noticed the younger people seem to pick up all kinds of information about each other. I'll just call him in, shall I?"

"By all means," said Gibbons. "Did he know Miss Farraday well?"

"Better than I did, at any rate, although she was somewhat older than he. Still, several of the younger members of the staff sometimes go for a drink after we close up the shop."

"Does your son work at the shop, then?" asked Gibbons, annoyed that he had overlooked someone with such obvious access to the shop keys.

"He helps out in the summer," answered Mittlesdon. "He's away at Cambridge most of the time these days, but of course he's worked at the shop ever since he was old enough." He opened the door and called out, "Matthew! Matthew, could you come into the office for a moment?"

In a minute, Matthew Mittlesdon appeared, looking very much like a typical college student. He took after his mother rather than his father, being leaner and browner than Mittlesdon and with a luxuriant mop of wavy hair.

"Jody?" he said, sounding shocked when told the news. "That's very sad. I liked her—everybody did. I do hope you find whoever did it."

"Do you remember anything about her family?" asked his father.

Matthew shrugged. "I don't think she ever mentioned anyone to me," he answered. "I'm fairly certain, at least, that she didn't have family hereabouts."

"Was she from the area originally, do you know?" asked Gibbons. "Or do you recollect how she came to be taken on at the shop?"

Matthew perched himself on the edge of his father's desk, looking thoughtful. "I think she was a friend of Tony's," he said. "At least, I seem to remember that he put her up for the job. But it's Gareth you should be talking to—it was an open secret that they were seeing each other."

"It was?" demanded Mittlesdon. "I never knew that. It doesn't seem like Gareth at all."

"No, he's usually more circumspect," agreed Matthew with another shrug. "But Jody was like that—she brought things out in people you never knew were there."

Which, thought Gibbons, was a very interesting observation, given the circumstances.

By the time Gibbons made his way from Victor Street back to the other side of the Ouse it was getting late, but he thought he could still fit in one more call. The temperature had dropped and he shivered a bit as he waited to cross the street.

"And where the devil has Phillip got to?" he muttered to

himself. As if in answer to this plaint, his mobile began to vibrate agitatedly in his pocket and he pulled off his glove to dig it out.

"Hello," said Bethancourt cheerfully. "Are you still at the station?"

"No," answered Gibbons. "I'm on my way to Rhys-Jones' flat—it's over on Granville Terrace, which is somewhere off of Lawrence Street, or so I was told."

"I know Lawrence Street," said Bethancourt. "It's actually just a continuation of Walmgate. I'll meet you there, shall I, and we'll ferret out Granville Terrace together."

"All right," said Gibbons. "I'll wait for you before I ring the bell."

But he found Bethancourt waiting for him instead when at last he reached the place. In truth, Gibbons, normally accustomed to working long hours without a break, was finding his return from the sick list more arduous than he had anticipated. He was also beginning to want his dinner, and to think it would have been wiser to have stopped for a meal before conducting this interview.

"There you are," said Bethancourt, pitching his cigarette into the gutter. "I was just beginning to wonder if you'd got lost along the way. I've found the house—it's just up the street there."

"Good man," said Gibbons. "Let's get this over with."

Rhys-Jones had changed from the flannels and dress shirt he had worn that morning to a pair of jeans and a rugby shirt. The casual clothes looked better on his lanky frame, and caused Gibbons to upgrade his opinion of Rhys-Jones's looks from "bookishly attractive" to simply "attractive."

He seemed surprised to see them, but did not demur at Gibbons's request for another interview.

"Of course, of course," he said, motioning them in.

The door opened directly into the sitting room of a modest flat, furnished with one or two good pieces and filled out with functional, inexpensive stuff. There were, as might be expected, a great many books: one entire wall had been shelved right up to the ceiling, and was filled to capacity with books of every description, from lavish art books to dog-eared mass-market paperbacks. In addition, there was a pile of books on one end table and another on a corner of the dining table.

Sitting on the sofa was a slender, dark-haired woman, who threw a questioning glance at Rhys-Jones as he shut the door and hurried forward to perform introductions.

"These are the police detectives," he told the woman. "This is Sergeant Gibbons and Mr. Bethancourt. This," he added, turning to the two young men, "is Laurel Brooks, my fiancée."

Laurel rose to shake hands with them, saying, "Gareth has been telling me about the trouble over the holidays—I've only just come back into town this evening."

"Ah, yes," said Gibbons. "I believe Mr. Rhys-Jones mentioned you were away. Having Christmas with the family, was it?"

"Yes," she answered. "We all do our best to get home for the holidays."

"That's nice," said Gibbons genially. "And where's home?"

"Essex." She smiled as she said it, but it did not reach her eyes; she clearly understood that this was an inquiry into her movements, no more and no less.

"Well, do sit down," said Rhys-Jones.

"Thank you, sir," said Gibbons, but he turned back to Laurel. "Could I ask you to excuse us, miss?" he said politely. "We have a few questions to ask Mr. Rhys-Jones involving details of the crime, which we would prefer to keep as confidential as possible. I'm sure you understand."

Both Rhys-Jones and his fiancée looked alarmed, but Laurel had little choice but to acquiesce.

"Of course," she said uncertainly. "I'll just go into the study."

She and Rhys-Jones exchanged worried looks as she made her way out of the room, but Bethancourt thought he could detect a slight expression of relief on Rhys-Jones's face as he watched her go.

"Please," he said, turning back to the detectives and gesturing toward the sofa and chairs.

This time Gibbons took the seat offered. He was still wearing a pleasant smile, but Bethancourt, knowing him as he did, could see the cold calculation in his friend's eyes.

"I thought," Gibbons began, "we might talk a little more freely without Miss Brooks. I'd like you to tell us everything you know about Jody Farraday."

A sick look came over Rhys-Jones and he swallowed before asking, "It's her, then? The—the body in the shop?"

"We don't have a certain identification yet," answered Gibbons. "But so far, we've found no one else missing who fits the description. Unfortunately, we can't find Miss Farraday, either."

Rhys-Jones passed a hand over his face; he looked shaken, and his voice when he spoke was broken.

"I—I don't know what to say."

Gibbons was gentle. "Let's not jump to any conclusions," he said. "Tell me about Jody. The two of you were close?"

Rhys-Jones nodded. "At least," he said, "I thought we were. Now, well, I have to say I don't think I ever understood her, not really. She was unlike anyone I've ever known."

"How did she come to work at Mittlesdon's?"

"Tony brought her in," said Rhys-Jones. "Tony Grandidge, our stock man. I don't know where he'd met her, but I remember interviewing her and hiring her on the spot, and saying it was a good job he'd found her."

"Mr. Mittlesdon said she was a good worker," put in Bethancourt.

"That's right," agreed Rhys-Jones. "And a fast learner. She was a godsend that Christmas season—the customers liked her, and by then she seemed to know the stock as well as any of us."

Gibbons nodded. "And when did you begin seeing each other?"   .

Rhys-Jones was startled by the question, and he cast a swift glance toward the staircase before saying, in a low voice, "Laurel doesn't know about that."

"Ah," said Gibbons. "So you were involved with both of them at the same time?"

"No!" Rhys-Jones said indignantly. "I would never do anything like that. No, I quite liked Jody—I suppose you could say I was fascinated by her—but I was dating Laurel and that was that. And then, well, Laurel got a job offer at the University of Bedfordshire, down south."

He paused, as if searching for words.

"Had you been dating long?" asked Bethancourt, to help him over the hump.

"For about a year," said Rhys-Jones. "I—well, I don't expect that's true, not really." He looked up and met Gibbons's eyes. "I'm trying to be honest," he said, rather awkwardly.

"I appreciate that," said Gibbons. "And I quite understand that it's uncomfortable to talk about these things with strangers. But there's no help for it, and it's really in your best interest in the end."

"Yes, yes, of course." Rhys-Jones drew a deep breath. "Laurel wanted to take the post, but obviously I couldn't leave my job, nor did I want to."

"People have endured long-distance relationships before," pointed out Gibbons.

"Well, yes, and I suppose that's what I expected," said Rhys-Jones. "But I wasn't very happy about it, while on her side Laurel seemed to feel that if I wasn't ready to marry her, well, then there wasn't much point in her staying. The upshot was that we had a terrific row and broke up. Laurel went to Bedfordshire, and I took up with Jody." He sighed. "In retrospect, the feelings I was beginning to have for Jody probably contributed to the breakup, but I didn't see it that way at the time."

"No, one never does," murmured Bethancourt, half to himself.

"Surely," said Gibbons, "it must have been rather awkward, since you were Miss Farraday's boss."

"With anyone else but Jody, it would have been," agreed Rhys-Jones. "But she was different. She—well, she took things in stride, sort of encompassing them all and sorting everything into its proper place so that it all worked together."

He looked at his audience, as if hoping they would understand, but found only polite attention. He tried again.

"I can't explain it, because I don't understand it myself," he said. "But somehow Jody made it work. It's not that we tried to hide our relationship at the shop, or that she tried to treat me just as her boss. But she never read anything personal into any instruction I had to give her at work, and she was always just as respectful of my position as she had been before."

"And outside of work?" asked Bethancourt.

"Well, you know—" Rhys-Jones gestured, looking embarrassed.

Gibbons glanced at Bethancourt, who remained intent on Rhys-Jones.

"Yes," said Bethancourt, "I expect we've all been there: the first flush of romance and all that. But then things settle down, just as they did with you and Miss Brooks. Day-to-day life begins sticking its nose in, so to speak."

Rhys-Jones was nodding. "That's putting it very well," he said. "It is always like that, isn't it?" He paused, running a hand through his hair. "Jody and I got on marvelously, but after things settled down, as you say, I, well, I don't know. I guess I began to miss something—an indefinable something. It was almost as if Jody, as affectionate as she was, always held a part of herself back. And," he admitted, his voice lowering, "I began to miss Laurel."

"Natural enough," said Bethancourt. "And I expect some of Miss Farraday's more unique qualities began to seem a little less charming?"

Rhys-Jones looked sheepish. "A bit," he admitted.

Bethancourt smiled. "Don't look so ashamed—we've all done it. And so, I might add, has the other half of the equation."

Once again, Rhys-Jones glanced toward the stairs. "I suppose they do at that," he said thoughtfully.

"Tell us a little more about Jody," said Gibbons. "I'm interested in anything you can remember about her background, her interests, even her hopes and dreams. Because if we're to solve this crime, we must come to understand her."

Rhys-Jones leaned back and let out a breath. "That's a tall order," he said, "but all right. Look here, would you like a coffee or something? Laurel and I were just about to have our after-dinner mug. And would you mind if I took her up a cup and let her know we're likely to be a little while over this?"

"Of course," said Gibbons. "And I'd love a cup. I'm sure Phillip here would as well."

"Yes, thanks," replied Bethancourt automatically.

Rhys-Jones bustled off in the direction of the kitchen, while Bethancourt leaned toward Gibbons and muttered, "What I could really use is dinner."

"Shush," replied Gibbons. "We're getting worthwhile information here. Why were you so interested in his relationship with Jody?"

Bethancourt shrugged. "I wanted to see how intense it had been," he answered. "A tumultuous, passionate affair has been known to result in murder before now. But I don't think that's what we have here, do you?"

"No," agreed Gibbons. "He could be lying, of course, but it all fits so very well. And Rhys-Jones doesn't strike me as that sort anyway; in fact, I think he's exceptionally self-aware."

"And almost obnoxiously fair," added Bethancourt. "It's positively annoying, the effort he goes to in order to be objective about his own feelings."

Gibbons was amused. "Seeing a lack in yourself, are you?" he asked.

"Certainly not," replied Bethancourt with offended dignity. "My mind was entirely occupied with the case. And my stomach."

"You get very cross when you're hungry, did you know that?" said Gibbons.

"I am not—wait, here he is," said Bethancourt, breaking off as Rhys-Jones reentered the room, bearing a tray full of coffee mugs.

"I'll just run this up to Laurel," said Rhys-Jones, setting down the tray and selecting a mug already mixed with milk. "I won't be a minute."

He was as good as his word, returning quickly, although he sighed as he resumed his seat and picked up a mug for himself.

"She's settled in," he said. "But I'm going to have to explain all this to her—I'm not looking forward to it."

"It doesn't sound like she has much to be upset about really," said Gibbons.

Bethancourt gave him an incredulous look.

"The man dated someone else for months and never told her," he said. "Of course she's going to be upset."

Rhys-Jones sighed again. "It's worse than that, actually," he said. "I told her I'd spent the entire time she was away missing her."

"Did you really?" Bethancourt raised a brow.

"It seemed like the right thing to say at the time," said Rhys-Jones defensively. "I was trying to get her back, you see."

"How did you end things with Miss Farraday?" asked Gibbons.

"I didn't," said Rhys-Jones. "It all happened rather suddenly, really. As I told you, I had begun to have second thoughts, and it was just about then that Jody began talking about relocating somewhere else. At first it was just the kind of daydreaming we all do from time to time—you know, wouldn't it be nice to have a cottage in Cornwall and so on. But gradually it dawned on me that she really wanted to go. And then I heard that Laurel was back in town."

"Bedfordshire University didn't work out?" asked Gibbons.

"No, it didn't," said Rhys-Jones. "Laurel said it hadn't gone well from the start, but she finished out her term and then made arrangements to come back to York. Anyway, I was rather taken aback by the sudden turn of events, and to be honest, I hadn't quite screwed my courage to the sticking point to tell Jody I didn't think we were going to make it together. But I knew when I heard about Laurel being back in town that I wanted to ask her if we could try again. And then, while I was stewing around about it all, Jody came to me and said she understood I didn't want to leave York, but it was time for her to go and she hoped we could still be friends."

"So everything was wrapped up nicely," said Bethancourt, a hint of envy in his tone.

"Well, yes, I reckon you could say that."

"Except," put in Gibbons, "the part about explaining it all to Miss Brooks."

"Yes," said Rhys-Jones gloomily. "Except for that."

"In any case," said Gibbons, "if you could give us a few details about Miss Farraday? Where was she born, for instance?"

Rhys-Jones frowned. "I don't know that she ever mentioned it," he said. "I have the impression that it was somewhere hereabouts, I mean somewhere in Yorkshire. I do know that she talked about moving round a lot as a child. It was just she and her mother, no siblings or father."

"Did she mentioned any schools?" asked Gibbons.

"I expect she told one or two stories about things that happened in school, but you know how that is—no one ever mentions the name of the school. Well, not unless they're boasting about attending Eton or something."

Gibbons accepted this and was about to ask another question when Rhys-Jones suddenly said, "Wait a bit, though, didn't she say something . . ." He frowned in concentration, trying to bring back the memory. "Yes, she was talking about living at a campgrounds one winter when she and her mother were going through a thin time. And she said her mother was teaching her at home." He looked back at the detectives.

"So she was homeschooled as a child?" asked Gibbons, trying not to sound disappointed; homeschooled children had no old school friends to give insights into their character and relationships.

"I don't know if that was always the case, if she was entirely homeschooled or not," answered Rhys-Jones. "Although I did get the impression that a great deal of her higher learning was self-taught. She never went to university, at least not officially."

"What does 'not officially' mean?"

Rhys-Jones smiled. "I gathered she would sometimes sneak into lectures and sit at the back. She had a very inquiring mind—she liked learning. When she first came to the bookshop we got into a discussion about economics and I gave her a copy of *Wealth of Nations*. She devoured it in a single night, and was full of nothing else for the next week."

"So she was particularly intelligent," said Bethancourt.

"Oh, yes," said Rhys-Jones. "Yes, very much so. Jody was very quick."

"Was she pursuing some kind of career?" asked Gibbons.

"No," said Rhys-Jones with a shrug. "She just liked to learn." He considered for a moment. "Jody was very much in the here and now," he said. "And she moved about a lot—said she began to feel stifled if she stayed in one place too long."

"So where did she go when she left here?" asked Gibbons.

But Rhys-Jones didn't know. "I don't think she had a particular destination in mind," he said. "She headed south, and that was all I ever knew."

"What about other friends?" asked Bethancourt. "I mean, aside from the bookshop. Did she know anyone else in town?"

"There was Rachel," answered Rhys-Jones. "I can't recall her surname, but she and Jody were childhood friends. Or at least that's the impression I had."

"She lives here in York?" asked Gibbons.

Rhys-Jones nodded. "Over by the hospital, in Ratcliffe Street. I was at her flat several times with Jody. And Rachel was in the shop not so very long ago, so I think she's still in town."

Gibbons noted these particulars down while Rhys-Jones continued.

"There were some other people—friends of Rachel's, I believe— a couple named Dave and Marlene, and another woman . . ." He paused for a moment, frowning in thought before snapping his fingers as his expression cleared. "Donna, that was her name. And then there was that odd chap—I only met him the once—Will something-or-other—he was another childhood friend."

"And where did Jody herself live?" asked Gibbons.

"Mostly in a flat in George Street," answered Rhys-Jones. "She was subletting it whilst the owner was gone, on condition she would take care of his cats. After that, I believe she found a room to rent out near the university. I never went there, but I remember the other place well enough."

Gibbons noted down these addresses.

"Now, I want you to think carefully about this next question," he said. "We've heard from several different sources that it would not be too difficult for an employee to come by a set of keys to the bookshop. Would you say Jody might have had such an opportunity?"

Rhys-Jones looked stunned. For a long moment, he simply stared at Gibbons.

"Mr. Rhys-Jones?" prompted Gibbons.

"I . . ." began Rhys-Jones. "It's just that I can't believe I didn't see it before now." He reddened. "I know you'll think me an awful dolt, but it never even occurred to me at the time, although it seems perfectly obvious now."

"What seems obvious?" asked Gibbons impatiently.

"Well, Jody and her keys. She had a huge collection of them, you see—some kind of odd security blanket, I always thought. I used to tease her about them sometimes. But I swear it never occurred to me that she might have added the keys to the bookshop to her collection—I can't think why. But of course she must have, because, as you say, it wouldn't be at all difficult to do."

Gibbons was frowning a bit. "What exactly do you mean by a huge collection?" he asked.

"She had a big ring," said Rhys-Jones, sketching a five-inch diameter in the air. "It was jammed with keys of all descriptions. Some of them were clearly useless—she even admitted as much, said she just liked the look of them—but most of them were ordinary enough. And then she had a couple of shoe boxes with more keys in them."

"But how did she keep track of which key opened what?" asked Gibbons.

"Oh, in most cases she didn't know, or had forgotten," said Rhys-Jones. "Although," he added, "I always thought she knew well enough what some of them were to—and there were a few master keys amongst them. Not that she would ever have used them to trespass or anything—she just liked knowing she could if she wanted to."

Gibbons's expression said that this was past all understanding, but Bethancourt's hazel eyes had narrowed and he was nodding.

"Freedom," he said. "The freedom to come and go as one pleases. Yes, I can see that."

"I suppose," said Rhys-Jones.

"But you're wrong about her never using them," continued Bethancourt.

"I don't see how you make that out," objected Rhys-Jones.

"Because in all probability, she used them to let herself and her killer into Mittlesdon's on Christmas Eve," answered Bethancourt.

Once they left Rhys-Jones, Gibbons was all for continuing on to interview Jody's friend Rachel, but he was clearly not up to it, and Bethancourt put his foot down.

"Dinner first," he said firmly. "You won't be any better pleased if you rush the interview because you're hungry. Besides, everyone thinks better on a full stomach—it's been scientifically proven."

Gibbons argued this last point, but he allowed himself to be led to a restaurant while he argued, and Bethancourt was relieved. He thought his friend was looking rather pale, and Gibbons shifted about in his chair in a way that indicated to Bethancourt that his newly healed injuries were paining him.

"So what did you make of what Rhys-Jones told us?" asked Bethancourt after they had settled in at their table and ordered.

"That he should have told us all this before," replied Gibbons crossly. He took a sip of the wine Bethancourt had ordered. "And our victim was a nutcase."

"Really now," protested Bethancourt. "Surely *nonconformist* would be a better word. I don't think she was crazy."

"Whatever. This wine's very good—I think I needed a drink."

"So did I," said Bethancourt, also sampling the wine. "Not bad, not bad at all," he said. "But what I meant to ask was, do you think Rhys-Jones could have done it? Because it strikes me as unlikely on the face of it."

"Me too," agreed Gibbons. "But 'unlikely' isn't 'impossible.' And at least we now have a better sense of who Jody Farraday was. Not," he added, "that it helps."

"More information always helps," said Bethancourt.

"Not when it tells you that your victim was the kind of person who was up for anything and had keys to the place where she died," said Gibbons. "We still haven't the slightest idea why she was here in York or where the devil she was staying."

"You don't think she was staying with Rhys-Jones then?" asked Bethancourt. "His girlfriend was away, after all."

Gibbons considered this, shifting unconsciously in his chair. "It's possible," he admitted. "Did I ever ask him directly?"

"I don't believe so," replied Bethancourt, searching through his memory.

"Then she could have been," said Gibbons. "He would never

have volunteered the information. Although if she did, and if he's got her things somewhere, I'm going to kill him. Or," he added, remembering that murder was unbecoming to Her Majesty's officers of the law, "at least have Brumby charge him with obstructing a police investigation."

"Good idea," said Bethancourt. "What the man needs is to have the fear of God put into him. Look, here's the soup. Drink up, old man—you're looking a bit frayed about the edges."

"I'm fine," said Gibbons, but he nevertheless devoted his attention to the soup.

Bethancourt had hoped that this would serve to revive his friend, but instead the warm liquid seemed to make Gibbons realize how tired he was, and by the time they had finished their meal he was flagging noticeably.

"I think that wine went right to my head," he said, standing and struggling with his coat. "I feel a bit dizzy."

"You only had a couple of glasses," said Bethancourt, putting out a hand to steady him.

"Yes, well, that appears to have been enough," said Gibbons.

"You've probably overdone it," said Bethancourt. "Don't forget you're still recovering—you can't expect to bounce back all at once."

Gibbons clearly did expect it, but after he had to pause to catch his balance twice more on the way to the door, even he had to admit he was in no shape to conduct another interview.

"Better in the morning anyway," said Bethancourt. "People are always more vulnerable in the morning."

Gibbons cast him a dubious look.

"I mean," said Bethancourt, "they've got their set routines in the morning, all designed to get them to work on time or whatever. You come in and upset that and then they don't know where they're at. Thus the vulnerability."

In fact, he would have said anything that would have resulted in Gibbons's forgoing another interview that night in favor of going home to bed, but this line of reasoning seemed to strike Gibbons.

"But not Jody," he said, letting Bethancourt lead him toward a taxi. "She doesn't seem to have liked routines. Most people depend on them. Routines make their life seem safe." He squinted up at Bethancourt. "You don't like them either."

"Yes, I do," said Bethancourt. "Just because I don't need to be anywhere particular in the mornings doesn't mean I don't have a routine. I am quite addicted to the quiet hour spent with coffee, cigarettes, and the morning paper."

"Half the time you're not even up in the morning," said Gibbons, dropping heavily into the backseat of the taxi.

"I like my quiet hour whenever I get up," retorted Bethancourt. "And you needn't make it sound as if I'm slothful. I sleep late because I stay up late."

Gibbons, unable to think of a suitable reply to this, fell silent, while Bethancourt gave directions to the taxi driver.

"You're right about Jody, though," said Bethancourt, leaning back and lighting a cigarette. "She doesn't seem to have liked a regular pace to her life. I'll be quite interested to see what sort of picture Rachel paints of her."

"We really should talk to her tonight," said Gibbons. "I think I'm feeling better."

"That's because you're sitting down," answered Bethancourt tartly. "When you need to have a taxi called to transport you a scant mile, then you're not fit for anything but bed."

"I could have walked," muttered Gibbons, but in so low a tone that Bethancourt didn't catch it.

Back at the house, the near prospect of his bed seemed to take the fight out of Gibbons, who laboriously climbed the stairs without further argument. Bethancourt gave him half an hour to perform his ablutions and get undressed before he went to ask if anything was wanted. But by that time Gibbons was nicely tucked up and sound asleep.

Left to himself for the evening, Bethancourt took his dog out for a long ramble along the river, but still found himself restless when they returned.

"What the hell," he said to himself. "Marla's not even due back from Kent yet—ten to one Trudy hasn't heard from her. I'll risk it anyway."

And he went off to The Duchess, where the Idle Toads were playing.

7

In Which Bethancourt and Gibbons Discover Two Many Obligations and the Spectre of Aunt Evelyn Arises

*G*ibbons woke early the next morning with the sun shining in at his window and feeling much better. Indeed, he was inclined to chastise himself for not having continued with his program the evening before; after all, he couldn't have been feeling that bad. He stalwartly ignored the twinge of pain in his abdomen that tried to belie this point of view.

The house was quiet, but he easily found the coffee and the makings of breakfast and busied himself in the kitchen, rather hoping Bethancourt would emerge before he was done.

But his host had evidently had a late night, because he had still not appeared by the time Gibbons had eaten and dressed. Loath to wake his friend, but eager to be off about the morning's business, Gibbons was just deciding to leave Bethancourt a note when he heard the ringing of his mobile phone, left on the kitchen table. He had just sat down on the stairs to put on his boots, and, with one shoe on and one off, he hobbled hastily into the kitchen, snatching up the phone just before it sent the call to voice mail.

"Independent bugger, aren't you?" asked Superintendent Mac-Donald cheerfully. "I was thinking I would hear from you last night, but there was never a peep out of you. You're not feeling miffed that I had to take Constable Redfern away from you, are you?"

"Not at all, sir," said Gibbons, catching his breath. "And I'm sorry I didn't report in last night. I did mean to stop by the station, but it got late before I had realized the time."

"Never bother about that, lad," said MacDonald. "You just ring my mobile whenever you have a mind to, whether it's dawn or midnight. Everyone else does, I don't know why you shouldn't, too."

"I'll remember that, sir," said Gibbons. "In any case, there's less to report than I would have liked. I've got a better picture of our victim, but very little in the way of hard facts."

He was about to go into detail when he was interrupted by the chimes alerting him to a second call. The ID read BRUMBY.

"Er, excuse me, sir," he said to MacDonald. "That's Superintendent Brumby on the other line. Could you hold for a moment?"

"Nay, lad," said MacDonald. "I'm on my way into the station this minute—you come along once you've dealt with your super, and we'll go over things there."

And he rang off without waiting for a reply.

Sighing, Gibbons flashed over to the other line.

"Good morning, Sergeant," said Brumby. "I was wondering if you were planning to report in this morning."

"Yes, sir," said Gibbons. "In fact, I was just on my way over to you. I meant to speak to you last night, but time got away from me."

"It always does," said Brumby. "I'll see you shortly then, Sergeant."

Gibbons rang off and looked up to find a tousle-headed Bethancourt blinking sleepily at him and carrying the boot he had left on the stairs.

"Sorry I slept in," he said, offering the boot.

"Thanks," said Gibbons, taking it and dropping into a chair to tug it on.

Bethancourt yawned. "So what's up?" he asked. "Are you off to interview Rachel?"

"No," answered Gibbons. "That was MacDonald and Brumby, both wanting me to report in. I think my morning's pretty well spoken for."

"Then I might as well go back to bed," said Bethancourt. "I haven't had much sleep."

"Where did you go last night?" asked Gibbons.

"Out to a club," replied Bethancourt. "I stayed later than I meant to."

Gibbons raised an eyebrow.

Bethancourt pushed his tousled hair out of his eyes, looking rather sheepish. "There was a girl," he confessed.

"You are incorrigible," said Gibbons, shaking his head.

"And I had rather a lot to drink," admitted Bethancourt. "As best I can remember, so did she. Anyway, ring me when you're done with all the officials. I should be up and about by then."

"Very well," said Gibbons, rising and reaching for his coat. "If I escape unscathed from both superintendents, I'll let you know."

"Good luck," said Bethancourt solemnly.

On the wall of the incident room at the station a map of England had appeared, with the sites and dates of Ashdon's murders marked on it in red. It was impossible not to try to find a pattern in the red dots, but squint as he might, no pattern emerged for Gibbons as he awaited Brumby's pleasure.

"You seem very intent, Sergeant." Detective Inspector Howard paused, rifling through a sheaf of papers. "Going to put us all to shame by figuring it out?"

Gibbons flushed. "No, sir," he answered. "I was only looking— he's struck over a very wide area, hasn't he?"

Howard lifted his eyes to the map. "But nothing north of the Midlands," he said. "Not, at least, until now."

Together they tracked the invisible line from Kettering north to York.

"Perhaps on account of Christmas?" ventured Gibbons, voicing the stray thought before he could stop himself.

Howard snorted a laugh. "God knows, it brings out the worst in a lot of people," he said. "Ah, here's Superintendent Brumby. I've got those lists you wanted, sir."

Brumby nodded, preoccupied. "I'll be right there," he said. "I just need a word with Gibbons here."

"Yes, sir."

Brumby's sober grey eyes rested on Gibbons for a long moment, making some kind of assessment.

"So," he said at last, unbuttoning his overcoat and tugging at the scarf around his neck to loosen it, "how are you coming with the Mittlesdon case? Here, let's have a seat."

A couple of the conference-table chairs had been pushed to one side, out of the way; they shifted them to face each other, giving Gibbons a moment to marshal his thoughts before he launched into a report of his meager findings. Brumby took it all in silently, sipping occasionally at the takeaway coffee he had brought in with him.

"You've made a good start," he said when Gibbons was done. "The lack of records to trace her by makes it difficult. As does the fact that she may have had her own keys."

"Yes, sir," agreed Gibbons.

"MacDonald treating you all right?"

"I haven't seen much of him, to tell the truth," answered Gibbons. "I'm off to report to him once I'm done here, but otherwise he's been pretty busy with other business."

Brumby nodded. "The whole point of putting you on the case, I suppose," he said. "Well, carry on, Sergeant. Let me know if there are any problems, or if you need any help."

"Thank you, sir." Gibbons hesitated. "Can I ask how the Ashdon case is going?"

"We, too, have our work cut out for us," said Brumby. "Still, every piece of information we gain brings us closer to catching him. Just at the moment, we're waiting on lab reports and going through endless footage from both the CCTV cameras on the street, since the shop didn't have a security camera." He did not look enthusiastic at this prospect.

"Are there any theories as to why he's strayed so far out of his territory?" asked Gibbons.

Brumby gave him a small, weary smile. "As many theories as we have detectives," he said. "The most reasonable ones to date revolve around the idea that Ashdon is up here for the holidays, or that he's recently moved. But until we find something to go on, it's all just castles in the air."

"It must be very frustrating, sir," said Gibbons sympathetically.

"You have no idea, Sergeant." Brumby's expression turned grim. "The more so as we know perfectly well he's out there somewhere, planning his next murder. . . ." He sighed. "Well, that kind of thinking never gets one anywhere. Carry on, Sergeant. And," he added as Gibbons rose, "do remember to report in occasionally, eh?"

"Yes, sir," said Gibbons.

His interview with MacDonald was in marked contrast to his conversation with Brumby. He found MacDonald at his desk, rummaging through a pile of papers and case files and being periodically interrupted by the telephone. None of this activity ceased while Gibbons made his report.

"You haven't got far, have you?" demanded MacDonald when Gibbons had finished. The superintendent ran his eyes down a page of figures, tossed it aside, and selected another paper from the heap on his desk. "You don't know who she was, you don't know why she was there, and you don't know if the bookshop people are suspects. Most importantly, you don't know who killed her."

Gibbons had learned long ago not to dissemble in the face of this kind of tactic.

"All that is true, sir," he replied evenly.

MacDonald shot him a sharp look before returning his attention to the report in his hand.

"And what are you aiming to do about it all?" he asked.

"I was going to start by interviewing Miss Farraday's friend Rachel," answered Gibbons. "I'm hoping she can shed some light on Miss Farraday's latest activities, and possibly identify the body."

"Killing two birds with one stone there," remarked Mac-Donald, dropping the sheaf of papers he was reading into the wastebasket. The phone rang as he was about to expand on this, and he signaled Gibbons to wait while he answered it. He listened intently for a moment, a frown growing as he did so, and then said, "Well, arrest him, for God's sake. You can sort it all out once you've got him in nick. What? . . . No, DI Curtis isn't coming back, he's gone into hospital. . . . Yes, that's right. So get on with it!"

He swore under his breath as he hung up the phone, and focused an irate eye on Gibbons. "You're feeling all right, are you, Sergeant?" he asked. "No sniffles or anything?"

"No, sir," said Gibbons. "I feel fine."

"Thank God," muttered MacDonald, picking up a case file. "Be off with you then," he said. "And if you do manage to catch the murderer, I'd appreciate it if you'd let me know."

"I do apologize for not checking in last night," said Gibbons, who did not wish to be taken as an arrogant Scotland Yard know-it-all. "I honestly did intend to."

MacDonald looked back at him. "Was there a girl or summat?" he asked.

"No, sir," said Gibbons. "To be honest, I simply fell asleep."

MacDonald opened his mouth, closed it again as a thought

struck him, and pursed his lips. "I remember hearing," he said, "that you had just recently come off sick leave. Is that true?"

Gibbons nodded.

"And what were you off for?"

"Recovering from gunshot wounds," answered Gibbons. "But I'm quite fit now, sir."

"Good God," said MacDonald. "Well, I'd like to hear the story behind that, but I haven't time. Very well, I'll make allowances for your stamina. Bloody hell, does that phone never stop?"

And this time he waved Gibbons away as he reached for the receiver.

Bethancourt did not sleep as late as he had planned. He burrowed under the covers upon returning to bed and dozed a bit, but found himself unable to get back to a sound sleep. Instead, he found himself thinking up various reasons for Jody Farraday to have returned to Mittlesdon's on Christmas Eve, and trying to determine if there was any way of investigating any of them. His mind, if not his body, was firmly awake.

So when the house phone rang some twenty minutes after Gibbons had left, he decided he might as well answer it as not and rolled out of bed.

There was an extension in the master bedroom across the hall, and he reached it by the fourth ring.

"Hello," said a well-bred female voice. "Is that Phillip Bethancourt?"

"Yes," answered Bethancourt, searching in his dressing-gown pocket for his cigarettes. "Speaking."

"It's Alice, Phillip," said the voice, and for a moment he could not think who that was.

Then, "Alice?" he repeated, a little dazed. "Alice Reynolds? I mean, Knowles?"

"That's right." She gave a little laugh. "I thought you might be there, and I was right. How are you?"

"Fine, fine," replied Bethancourt, sinking down on the bed. He found his cigarettes and lit one. "And how are you?"

"Oh, I'm doing very well, thanks."

There was a slight pause.

"So nice to run into you the other day," said Bethancourt. "Difficult circumstances, of course."

"Yes, so very sad. I find—well, it's very odd, knowing someone who's been murdered, however distant the connection."

"I imagine so," replied Bethancourt.

"I'd really no idea you had become interested in criminal work," continued Alice.

"Yes, well, I hadn't planned to," said Bethancourt, who was beginning to come fully awake and to wonder why she had rung. "Happened quite by accident, you know, through having met Jack at Oxford."

"Jack—oh, that would be that nice Sergeant Gibbons, would it?"

"That's right. We were both up at the same time."

"I see."

There was another pause.

"Well," said Alice, "I was thinking—if you liked—I thought it might be nice to get together and catch up."

"Er," said Bethancourt, caught off guard.

His first instinct was to say no. He was not a man who dwelled much on the past, and he had no present interest in Alice Knowles at all. He was ready to admit to himself that had she preserved her face and figure he might not have said no to renewing the relationship—at least on a temporary basis—but as it was, he would refuse that honor.

But then it occurred to him that, regardless of his personal feelings, Alice was his one legitimate tie to the Mittlesdon murder.

"I'd love to," he said. "Are you free for lunch today by any chance?"

"Why, yes," said Alice, sounding a little surprised at the promptness of his invitation. "Yes, that would be fine."

"I don't know how much longer I'll be in town, you see," said Bethancourt.

"Oh! Oh, of course."

"And I'm afraid I'll have to depend on you to suggest somewhere to meet," he continued. "I'm quite out of touch with things here nowadays."

"Naturally," she answered. "Let me think a moment. . . . Well, why not Loch Fyne? They've got a quite pleasant bar. And it's just down the street from the bookshop, so you can't miss it."

"I think I know the place you mean," said Bethancourt. "Just past the bridge, isn't it?"

"That's right. Will that do?"

"Perfectly," said Bethancourt. "Shall we meet there at one?"

"Half past would be better for me, if it's not too late?" said Alice.

"Not at all. Half one it is. I'll see you then."

"I look forward to it."

He rang off and turned to find that Cerberus had followed him and was sitting patiently by the bed.

"I have no idea what I just got myself into," Bethancourt told him.

An hour later, he had showered, shaved, and, seeing that the rain had stopped and the sun was out, given his dog a good walk instead of just letting the animal out into the garden. They had returned and he was consuming his third cup of coffee when Gibbons rang.

"All serene?" asked Bethancourt.

"There was some sticky going, but all's well," replied Gibbons. "I'm on my way to call at Rachel's house now."

Bethancourt checked his watch. "She'll have left for work by now, won't she?" he said.

"Only if she has a regular office job," said Gibbons. "I'm feeling lucky—I think she works nights."

"That sounds indecent," said Bethancourt, "but I'm on—at least, I assume I can come with you?"

"Certainly," said Gibbons. "I'll meet you there. You remember the address?"

"Yes," said Bethancourt. "It'll take me ten minutes or so to walk over."

"I'll meet you on the corner then," said Gibbons and rang off.

Bethancourt finished his coffee while he donned his boots and coat, and he was on the verge of leaving the house when his mobile rang again. It was not a number he recognized, but he answered it anyway.

"This is Catherine," said a languid voice. "I think you must be that charming man I met at the club last night?"

"I certainly hope I am," responded Bethancourt, a smile playing about his lips.

"Tall? Blond? Glasses?"

"That sounds like me," said Bethancourt. "As I remember, you are a heavenly creature with long hair in a green dress."

"Alas, I took the dress off," said Catherine. "Does that disqualify me?"

"It depends," he said. "Are your eyes still green?"

Her laughter was a soft trill. "Do you know," she said, "I believe they are."

"Then we're all set. My, that's a relief."

"Isn't it? I thought, since you were so interesting last night, you might want to come by Club Salvation tonight and give a reprise. Only, of course, if you felt up to it."

"Well, well," said Bethancourt. "All that interesting stuff does take it out of a chap, I'll admit."

"Does it? I rather thought it came naturally."

"No, not at all. Still, I think I might be able to pull it off once more. Actually, now that I think about it, I believe I'm feeling particularly interesting this season. I might be good for a week."

Catherine laughed again. "Then I'll look forward to it. Till tonight."

"Till tonight," echoed Bethancourt.

He rang off with a broad grin on his face, and was whistling as he locked the front door and went off to meet Gibbons.

Gibbons's luck was holding. Rachel Morrison, as it turned out, was a nurse who worked at the hospital and today was her off-shift. They met her on her doorstep as she was returning from the grocer's.

She was a thin, sharp-featured woman, but with a wide, warm smile. Bethancourt responded with one of his own, which caused her a moment's self-consciousness, expressed in a flustered patting of her hair.

"We were hoping," continued Gibbons, "that you could give us some information about Jody Farraday."

"I know her, of course," Rachel answered, looking from one to the other of the men and taking in their somber expressions. "I'm surprised to hear she's come to the law's attention," she added. "Here, come inside where we can talk properly."

"Thank you," said Gibbons. "We'd prefer to have a private conversation."

"Though I'll warn you," she said, allowing Bethancourt to take her bag of groceries while she unlocked the front door, "I haven't heard from Jody recently, and the last I did hear, she was down south."

"She keeps in touch with you, then?" asked Gibbons.

"In a manner of speaking," answered Rachel with a laugh. "Here, I'll show you."

She let them into the front hall and led the way back to the kitchen. Just inside the door was a small drop-front desk, and above it hung a cork board filled with various notes, cards, and newspaper cuttings. Rachel reached up and unpinned a postcard from one corner and handed it to Gibbons.

The picture was of a coastal village. On the reverse was scrawled: "R—I'm settled here at last and think I'll stay the summer. Got an interesting job at the marina. You know how to reach me if you want to. Or I'll turn up again. Love, yr. bp."

It was dated last April.

Gibbons read it carefully with Bethancourt peering over his shoulder.

"How did you reach her?" he asked, looking up.

"Message on MySpace," Rachel answered cheerfully. "Jody doesn't always have a computer, but she finds a place somewhere to check my page once a week or so."

Gibbons looked hopeful. "Then she had an e-mail address? How about a MySpace page of her own?"

"She's got both," Rachel confirmed. "But she doesn't use either one much. She's funny that way—doesn't like to be tied down." She shrugged. "She used to say she was an analog spirit living in a digital age. Really, she's just eccentric."

Bethancourt was still looking at the postcard.

"What's 'bp'?" he asked.

"'Bp'?" repeated Rachel, looking puzzled.

"Yes, she signs herself here as 'yr. bp.'"

"Oh, that means 'bad penny.' You know, a reference to turning up again?"

"Oh, yes, I see."

"And this card was the last you heard from her?" asked Gibbons, handing it back.

"No," answered Rachel, pinning it once again to the board and moving to deal with the bag of groceries Bethancourt had set on the counter. "She rang on my birthday in June. She was still in Port Isaac then." She paused to face them, a jug of milk in her hand. "Has she got herself into trouble, then?" she asked, a worried frown on her face.

"In a manner of speaking," said Gibbons carefully.

Bethancourt, who had come forward to help with the grocery unpacking, saw the expression in her eyes change. He reached out to take the jug of milk from her hand and said, "Yes, it's bad news. Perhaps you'd like to sit down?"

Numbly, she let him take the milk while she stared, frozen, at Gibbons.

"Dead?" she asked at last. And when Gibbons nodded she turned away, putting her hands to her face.

Gibbons gave her a moment while Bethancourt deposited the milk in the refrigerator, and then caught his friend's eyes, jerking his head toward their witness.

Bethancourt nodded and went to put a hand on Rachel's shoulder.

"Come and sit down," he said, moving her gently to the kitchen table. "Would you like anything? A glass of water or some tea?"

Rachel dragged a hand across her face, wiping away tears.

"I think I'd rather have a drink," she said. "There's a bottle of Bell's in that cupboard over there."

Bethancourt nodded and fetched it together with a glass from the dish drainer while Gibbons settled himself opposite Rachel at the table. She sniffed, took the drink Bethancourt handed her, and had a healthy swallow of it.

"There," she said, making an effort to pull herself together. "All right. Tell me what happened."

"Miss Farraday was killed on Christmas Eve," said Gibbons.

"But how?" asked Rachel. To Bethancourt's ear, her tone betrayed bewilderment. He slid into the chair on the other side of her, leaning an elbow on the table so that he could see her face.

"She was the victim of an attack," replied Gibbons. "We believe she had an altercation with whomever she was meeting that night, during the course of which she was struck. The blow may or may not have knocked her out, but it disabled her enough for her attacker to strangle her."

While he spoke, Rachel's hand sought her throat, and her eyes, now full of shock, brimmed with tears.

"That's horrible," she whispered. "Poor Jody."

"Yes," said Gibbons. "It was a very violent crime. Do you know of anyone who might have wanted to harm Miss Farraday?"

Rachel shook her head at once. "Everyone always liked Jody," she said. "There's no denying she was an oddbod, but nobody ever seemed to mind. I can't imagine anyone wanting to kill her. It wasn't," she added, "just a mugging then?"

"No, ma'am," said Gibbons. "I'm afraid there's no chance of that."

"How long had you known Miss Farraday?" asked Bethancourt. "Were the two of you close?"

Rachel hesitated for a moment before replying, "I think, actually, I was her closest friend. At least I was the oldest—we met at school in Haxby when we were eight."

Gibbons raised an eyebrow. "At school?" he asked. "We understood from Mr. Rhys-Jones that Miss Farraday was homeschooled."

"Part of the time," agreed Rachel. "Although I think that had more to do with where she and her mother found themselves— they moved around a lot. Anyway, she was only at my school for three years. But that's an eternity when you're eight."

"True," said Bethancourt. "Still, it's a long time to keep up with someone, particularly if you don't live in the same place." He was mentally riffling through a list of his acquaintances, but could not think of anyone from the second form with whom he still kept in touch.

"Well, yes," agreed Rachel slowly, as if she had never really thought about it before. Then she shrugged. "But things are never the way they usually are if Jody's involved. It's like she's a jinx on anything normal." She gave a half laugh, which turned into a hiccup, and she ended by sniffling and sipping the whisky Bethancourt had poured for her.

"Being such an old friend," said Gibbons, "would you know of any family Miss Farraday might have? I understand her mother passed on some years ago."

"Yes," affirmed Rachel. "I went to the funeral. But there aren't any other relatives—there never have been. It was always only her mother and Jody."

"Her mother had no other family?" asked Gibbons.

"She may have had," said Rachel, "but she never spoke of them. The story I heard was that she had been abused as a child, and had run away when she was fourteen. So far as I know, all contact was broken off. At least, Jody never met any of them. And," she continued, forestalling Gibbons's next question, "I don't know anything about Jody's father and I'm not sure she did either."

"He was never around?" asked Gibbons.

"Jody never even met him," said Rachel. "Her mother always maintained he had died shortly after Jody was born—it was a rather romantic story, really. But later on, after I grew up, I did begin to wonder how true it all was. I wouldn't be surprised to learn he simply deserted Doris when he found out she was pregnant. But I don't really know."

Gibbons absorbed this silently. "In that case," he said at last, "would you be willing to identify the body?"

Rachel looked considerably startled by this request, and Gibbons added, "We believe our victim is Miss Farraday, but positive identification has thus far been difficult. We've only one rather bad snapshot of her, and have been unable to find dental records or DNA samples. In fact, so far as we can determine, she's not even been reported missing."

"I could certainly identify her," said Rachel, recovering herself. "But it's difficult, just now, to get any time away from the hospital. Is she still down in Cornwall?"

"No," answered Gibbons. "She was killed here in York. Did you not know she was in town?"

Rachel sat back, all grief apparently forgotten in her amazement. "Jody was *here*?" she demanded.

"Yes," said Gibbons. "She didn't let you know of her plans?"

Rachel shook her head emphatically, but then paused as a thought struck her.

"Yes?" prompted Gibbons hopefully.

"I wasn't here," she said. She spoke half to herself and her tone was one of sorrow and regret. "My family always spends Christmas at my grandmother's in the Lake District. Jody knew that, of course. And she probably came up on the spur of the moment—it was the way she did most things. In fact . . ."

Her voice trailed off as she looked about the room. Gibbons waited patiently until at last she looked back at him.

"I'm just wondering," she said, "if she was here after all. She had keys and she would have known I was away. There were a few things out of place when I came back, but my neighbors had been in to feed the cat so I didn't think anything of it. But it could have been Jody."

The mention of keys struck a chord in Gibbons's mind. "Rhys-Jones said Jody kept a collection of keys. . . ."

"True enough," agreed Rachel. "It was totally pointless to try and prevent her from adding your house keys to her collection." She sighed. "I always wondered what a psychiatrist would have made of those keys."

"Keys or no, she couldn't have still been staying here on Christmas Eve," put in Bethancourt practically. "We haven't found any of her things, and surely you would have noticed if she had left a bag here."

Rachel frowned and nodded. "That's true," she said. "No, there was nothing left here. But I can't think where else she would have stayed."

"But you would have expected her to come to you if she had arrived before you left for the Lake District?" asked Gibbons.

"Oh, yes, certainly."

"And when did you leave?"

"On the twenty-third," Rachel answered. "Jody couldn't have been in York before then."

"What about Rhys-Jones?" asked Bethancourt. "Might she have stayed with him?"

"I don't think so," said Rachel. "They were still on friendly terms, but he had gone back to his old girlfriend and Jody knew that. I don't think she would have intruded."

"There wasn't a lot of animosity over the breakup then?" asked Gibbons.

"Not on Jody's part," said Rachel. "She liked him, but she never thought it would work out for the long term. Jody, well, she had trouble trusting people very far—you had to prove yourself over time."

Gibbons nodded. "Can you think of any other friends here she might have rung up? Mr. Rhys-Jones mentioned some other people. . . ."

He consulted his notebook and read off the names Rhys-Jones had given them. Rachel identified them readily as people she had introduced Jody to and supplied surnames and phone numbers.

"And Wilfrid," she said with a laugh, "that would be Wilfrid Jenks. He's another one from our school days. But I don't think he lives around here anymore—he was probably visiting when Gareth met him. I don't know, he was never a particular friend of mine, but he was someone Jody kept up with sporadically."

She paused for a moment, thinking, and then added a couple of others, including Tony Grandidge, the young man who single-handedly managed Mittlesdon's stock room.

"That was how Jody got the job at Mittlesdon's," she said. "She ran into Tony at a café and the two of them got talking. I think they went out once or twice, though it was never anything serious."

Gibbons noted this down and then asked, "You've said that both Miss Farraday and her mother moved around a lot. Was there any reason for that? I mean, did you ever have the impression they were running from something or someone?"

"No." Rachel shook her head. "They were just very odd people. Jody always seemed to me to be afraid of getting tied down, of having anything regular in her life." She looked wistful. "Although when I last spoke to her, I thought she might be mellowing a little. She talked about maybe getting a dog, and that's definitely a responsibility."

"Yes, indeed," agreed Bethancourt.

"And you can't think of anyone who might have had a grudge against Miss Farraday?" asked Gibbons. "Sometimes even a small thing will lead to murder."

Rachel began to shake her head, but then paused.

"Have you thought of someone?" asked Gibbons as the silence lengthened.

"Not someone," said Rachel slowly. "But Jody liked to know things, including other people's secrets. She never told," she added hastily. "But she did find out things—she'd surprise me sometimes with something that she had known but never mentioned."

"So if I follow you," said Gibbons, "you're thinking somebody found out she knew a secret she shouldn't have. And they decided not to trust her discretion."

Rachel nodded. "It's all I can think of," she said. "Just hearing about her and how eccentric and independent she was, you might think that would have made her enemies. But it never did. I couldn't tell you why, but people always accepted Jody—her odd bents just made them chuckle and shake their heads."

Which, thought Bethancourt, seemed an appropriate epitaph.

Gibbons was excited to find some trace of Jody before her arrival in York and headed off to the police station to pursue this lead. Bethancourt, who had no patience for that kind of research, left him to it and went to keep his luncheon appointment with Alice Knowles.

The warming weather together with the cessation of the endless winter rain had brought the holiday crowds out in force, and he dodged impatiently around them, making his way through the busy streets. He paused once, when his mobile rang, and moved out of the stream of foot traffic to answer it, thinking it must be Gibbons. But when he looked at the caller ID, he saw it was Marla.

"Hell," he said, pressing the End button and returning the phone to his pocket.

He endeavored to dismiss the call from his mind as he hurried on. He had been brought up always to arrive before his date, and he strove to meet this goal, though in fact he rarely achieved it.

Nor did he in this case. Loch Fyne was a large establishment with a broad bar at the back of the high-ceilinged room. Alice was waiting for him there, seated in one of the high bar chairs with her legs crossed, nursing a glass of white wine. She had clearly dressed with some care, discarding the tweed skirt and comfortable flat boots she had worn to the bookshop the day before in favor of heels and a dress in a flattering shade of blue.

She smiled at him as he came up, slightly breathless and tugging his coat open in the sudden heat of the restaurant.

"Sorry to be late," he said, smiling back. "I see you've got yourself a drink."

"I don't usually indulge so early," she said with a little laugh. "But this is sort of a special occasion, isn't it? I hope you're going to join me."

Bethancourt, looking down at her, thought that a drink—or perhaps several—was an excellent idea, and said so.

"But let's get a table, eh?" he said, holding up a hand to attract the bartender's attention. "I'd like to have a look at the menu, per-haps order a bottle of wine, if that's all right with you?"

They got themselves settled at a quiet table off to one side. Dis-cussion of the meal to come and the wine offerings got them through the initial stages, but it was not long before the first remi-niscence of their school days was introduced. Bethancourt was exceedingly relieved when the bottle of wine arrived.

It was not that he particularly wished to avoid discussion of his years at St. Peter's, or even that he disliked reliving anecdotes from that time; it was only painting the period in rosier colors than it deserved that he objected to. In his view, there had been good times and bad times, and he had moved on from both.

"So how long have you been working at Mittlesdon's?" he asked, in an effort to stem the tide.

"Oh . . ." Alice waved a plump, bejeweled hand. "Soon after I got married. I had quit my job, you see, but I found I needed something to do. I was never one to act the lady of leisure, you know."

"Of course not," said Bethancourt, smiling to show his intent to compliment.

Alice took it as such, simpering through her lashes at him.

His smile faltered in consequence as a sudden qualm assailed him: was he leading her on?

"So you're quite the fixture there these days?" he said.

"Yes, I expect you could put it that way," she replied. "I always liked the place, as you know. Do you remember that day we were snogging in the back room and got surprised by Mr. Mittlesdon himself? Do you know, he never in all this time twigged it was me, not until I happened to mention it recently. And then he blushed bright red!"

Bethancourt joined her laughter, a trifle more heartily than was called for, but he was feeling increasingly awkward. Virtually all her reminiscences had referred to the more intimate moments of their former relationship, and Bethancourt was slowly becoming convinced that she was expecting far more from this encounter than luncheon. He was not unaccustomed to advances from the opposite sex, but he had never before had to deal with his own ulterior motives. He looked back at Alice and wondered if there was really anything she could tell him about the case.

As if divining his thought, she rested her chin on her hand and looked pensive, saying, "I have to admit I never thought I'd see the day when anything like this would happen at Mittlesdon's. Even when we heard of Veronica's death, well, it was at a remove, as they say. Murder just seems so very—very inappropriate."

She grinned sheepishly when Bethancourt laughed.

"That did come out sounding foolish, didn't it?" she said.

"No, no," said Bethancourt, "I know exactly what you mean. I don't think my friend Sergeant Gibbons quite grasps the idea, but I feel just the way you do. Mittlesdon's is such a staid, solid sort of place, a kind of bulwark against just this sort of thing, it's outrageous that murder should rear its ugly head there."

Alice nodded in satisfaction with this sentiment.

"You've put it very well," she said.

"Actually," said Bethancourt, "the more we find out about Jody Farraday, the more she seems anomalous. To Mittlesdon's, I mean."

"Oh, no." Alice shook her head. "A proper bookshop is always full of characters. Jody fit the bill quite nicely. I don't think it so much matters," she added thoughtfully, "how odd you are, provided you have a curious mind."

"But you're not odd," protested Bethancourt.

"Well, no," Alice admitted. "I'm not saying oddity is a prerequisite, mind you. Most of us are, well—perhaps not altogether ordinary—but quite mainstream. I still find it difficult to believe any one of us killed Jody."

She looked at him hopefully.

"It's not certain that any of you did," said Bethancourt, reckoning that this was safe enough territory. "It's perfectly possible that Jody still had keys to the shop and let herself and her murderer in."

Alice seemed surprised. "But Jody wouldn't have had keys," she said earnestly. "Only the managers have those."

"Very true," agreed Bethancourt. "But I understand it would not be difficult to come by a copy."

"Well, no," said Alice, picking at her salad thoughtfully. "When you put it that way, no, it wouldn't. But why on earth should Jody have wanted to go to the bookshop on Christmas Eve?"

Bethancourt shrugged. "That's what we would all like to know," he said.

The conversation was interrupted by the arrival of their meal, and when it resumed they fell into a catching-up mode free of reminiscences, to Bethancourt's great relief. From time to time he caught a glimmer of the old Alice, who had so entranced him in their school days, but for the most part the bold, lively girl he had known then seemed to have disappeared along with her figure. She still had a curious mind, as she had said, but the duties of life and motherhood had changed her outlook and tempered her desires. He was slightly surprised to find that, even had she remained slim and taut, he would not now be interested in her as anything but a casual dalliance.

And yet, if he was fair, the traits Alice exhibited in the present had been evident even in their school days, although back then they had been dominated by youthful enthusiasms. He could not with honesty say that he was surprised by the way she had turned out.

Which led him to wonder if he would be at all interested in the Marla of ten years on. She, even more than the youthful Alice, was the epitome of a man's sexual desire, which had certainly been the basis of Bethancourt's initial interest in her. The relationship on his part had flourished largely because he enjoyed her boundless energy and found circumventing her mercurial temper mentally challenging. But he had never given any thought as to how he might feel a few years on; he had been content to take each day as it came.

Well, he decided, it was all moot now.

Gibbons spent the lunch hour on the phone with various members of the Cornwall constabulary, while nearby Sergeant Rowett worked his magic on the computer. At some point, another member of Brumby's team delivered sandwiches and coffee; these were consumed silently, in between answering the phone and tapping on the keyboard. Periodically, the two men compared notes until at last, late in the afternoon, Gibbons tucked his mobile away, slapped Rowett on the shoulder in a gesture of thanks, and went to find Superintendent Brumby.

Brumby, it developed, had stepped outside to smoke, and Gibbons found him there, leaning back against the brick of the police station and watching the rain fall with a pensive air.

"Have you got news, Sergeant?" he asked as Gibbons came up to join him.

"A bit of news on the Mittlesdon case, yes, sir," replied Gibbons. "We've discovered that our victim had been living in Cornwall for most of the past year. Sergeant Rowett is still searching the Cornwall records for some sign of her, but I've got hold of a Detective Sergeant Ogburn in Cornwall, who's managed to track down her employer for me. I'd like permission to go down there and investigate further."

Brumby nodded. "Good work, Sergeant," he said. "What does MacDonald say?"

"I don't know yet," said Gibbons. "I came to you first, sir. After all, my going to Cornwall may be of some help to MacDonald, but it's no use to you at all, and you are my immediate superior."

"Very well reasoned, Sergeant," said Brumby dryly. "Well, if MacDonald agrees, I'm all for it. We might as well clear any case we can, because I don't think York is destined to be a breakthrough in the Ashdon matter. Let's leave MacDonald with fond thoughts of us—tell him the Yard'll bear the cost of the trip."

"Thank you, sir," said Gibbons.

"Yes, all right. Off you go, Sergeant. Let me know what you find out."

MacDonald was considerably more difficult to find than Brumby had been. He was not in his office and did not answer his mobile. Gibbons tried Constable Redfern's number and got an answer almost at once.

"The super?" asked Redfern, sounding preoccupied. "Try down in interrogation—I believe he brought in a couple of suspects in the Deanery robbery."

"Thanks, Dave," said Gibbons. "I'll check there."

"Are you getting anywhere with the Mittlesdon case, then?" asked Redfern.

"There's a couple of things have turned up," answered Gibbons. "Nothing substantive yet, but I'm hoping."

"I'd like to hear about it," said Redfern, "but I'm full up right now. Perhaps a pint later in the week?"

This, Gibbons agreed to happily. He thanked the constable and rang off to make his way down to the interrogation rooms.

MacDonald was indeed ensconced in one of the rooms, but Gibbons had no intention of interrupting him in the middle of an interview. Resigned, he kicked his heels in the hallway for half an hour before MacDonald at last emerged. He looked well satisfied, from which Gibbons deduced that the interview had gone well.

"Well enough," agreed MacDonald. "These blighters can't keep their story straight. One of them," and he began to chuckle, "had the gall to blame it all on his girlfriend. A real charmer, eh?"

"Yes, sir," said Gibbons, laughing.

"So how are you getting on, Sergeant?" asked MacDonald. "I take it there's been some developments? Or have you only come to tell me you're flummoxed?"

"Not yet," said Gibbons, and gave him the details of what he'd found.

"It'd be useful to know what our Jody was up to and with whom," admitted MacDonald when Gibbons had done. "Aye, fly off to Cornwall by all means, particularly if the Yard's paying."

After his lunch with Alice, Bethancourt found himself reflecting on his past relationships with women. Ordinarily he would have said that he enjoyed very good relations with the women in his life, but for some reason on this afternoon he found the whole topic depressing. As an anodyne, he fetched his dog from the house and went shopping, joining the crowds looking for after-Christmas bargains. Cerberus was much pleased with this activity; he was a beautiful dog and garnered many compliments—as well as petting and treats—when he was out in public. His feathered tail waved gently as his master wandered from store to store in search of something he wanted to buy. When at length Bethancourt found himself absently admiring a pair of jade earrings and wondering whether or not he should pick them up for Marla, he abruptly tired of his shopping expedition and returned to the house.

He was surprised to find Gibbons already there, packing a bag.

"What's up?" he asked. "Is the case solved or something?"

"No," replied Gibbons, stuffing a pair of socks into his duffel. "But I'm off to Cornwall to follow up on Jody's life there. I tried to ring you, but your mobile's off."

"It is?" Bethancourt dug the phone out of his pocket and stared at it. "So it is," he said. "I wonder when I did that." He thumbed it back on and was immediately alerted that he had messages.

"See?" said Gibbons. "One of those is from me, asking if you want to come along to Cornwall. Do you?"

Bethancourt raised his eyes from his phone and thought for a moment.

"I don't see how I can," he answered. "I've got Cerberus, you see, and I take it you're flying?"

"That's right," said Gibbons. He paused, hands on his hips, and surveyed the room to see if there was anything else he needed. "It won't be a long trip," he added. "I'll be back tomorrow evening."

"That's all right then," said Bethancourt. "Shall I take you to the airport and you can tell me all about it on the way?"

"I'd appreciate that," said Gibbons. Satisfied that he had forgotten nothing, he bent and zipped the duffel closed.

Bethancourt had returned his attention to his phone. He was staring down at it in a perplexed manner, his lips tightened together.

"What is it?" asked Gibbons.

"Nothing," answered Bethancourt. "Marla apparently left a message."

"Did she?" said Gibbons. "Maybe she rang to apologize."

Bethancourt shot him an incredulous look. "You must be mad," he said. "Marla never apologizes."

"Well, what did she say, then?" asked Gibbons practically.

"I don't know," said Bethancourt. "I'm debating whether or not I should listen to it. On the whole, I think not."

"But—" began Gibbons, but Bethancourt had already deleted the message. "Are you really sure that was a good idea?" he asked.

"Quite sure. Now, here's one we had better pay attention to: my father's rung up about something."

He set the phone on speaker and in a moment Robert Bethancourt's clipped tones were heard.

"Glad to hear the cellar's still dry," he said. "Will you let me know if you plan to leave? There's no hurry—your aunt will be bringing the children back to school in a few days, but there's plenty of room for you all. And your mother says to tell you that Mrs. Carter will be coming in to clean on the third. Hope your case is coming well."

Bethancourt erased the message and made a face. "I forgot about my aunt Evelyn," he said.

"Will she not want us here?" asked Gibbons.

"She won't mind," replied Bethancourt. "It's me that doesn't want her here. My father may think there's plenty of room, but I'm not convinced that there's enough room in all England for my aunt and I to coexist comfortably together."

Gibbons laughed.

8

In Which Gibbons Looks to the Past, and Bethancourt Has An Awkward Morning

*D*etective Sergeant Benny Ogburn of the Devon and Cornwall constabulary was older than Gibbons by almost a decade, but that did not prevent their hitting it off from the moment they met at the airport. Gibbons was relieved: he was on the young side for his rank, and he had previously encountered some prejudice on the part of older sergeants. Ogburn, however, greeted him as an equal, took him off to a pub for a beer, and ran down a list of interviews he had arranged for Gibbons on the morrow. It was surprisingly comprehensive for something done on such short notice, but Ogburn shrugged it off when Gibbons complimented him on it.

"It wasn't hard," he said. "You gave me the employer, and he and her co-workers gave me the boyfriend, who gave me the other friends. And her neighbor gave me the landlord—though, truth to tell, he doesn't know much beyond the fact that she paid her rent regularly."

"I don't suppose my landlord knows much more about me,"

said Gibbons. "So what time tomorrow do we start the interviews?"

"Eight o'clock do you?" asked Ogburn. "I thought we'd best begin early so as to make sure we had enough time—you never know what's going to crop up as you go."

Gibbons agreed: it was a rare investigation that did not turn up the unexpected.

But as they worked through the schedule the next day, they found no cause to deviate from Ogburn's original program. Bit by bit, Gibbons garnered a picture of Jody's life in Cornwall that bore a remarkable resemblance to her life in York: a wide circle of friends, but few if any of them close ones; well liked at her work and casual friends with several of her co-workers; a boyfriend who, like Rhys-Jones, seemed more a convenience than a deep emotional bond.

The one surprise that emerged was that, according to everyone, she had left Cornwall for good and was moving permanently back to Yorkshire. None of her acquaintances seemed to know why, or at least not until Gibbons's last interview of the day, with Jody's erstwhile neighbor, Irene Haddam.

Mrs. Haddam was a divorced woman of forty-five or so, living alone with her dog. She was attractive for her age, with good bones in her face and sun-streaked, flyaway hair. Gibbons did not expect to gain much from the interview; it had struck him as unlikely that such a woman would have much in common with a twenty-seven-year-old from Yorkshire. But in this he was wrong.

"I was very fond of Jody," she told him, in an attractive, husky voice. "We got to be quite close while she was here, and I was sorry to see her go."

"When she left, did you see her off yourself?" asked Gibbons on a sudden hunch.

"Oh, yes. Barney and I drove her to the station and saw her onto her train."

"Barney?" repeated Gibbons, thinking this must be Mrs. Haddam's boyfriend.

"My dog," said Mrs. Haddam, gesturing toward the golden retriever curled up on a pillow in the corner.

"Oh!" said Gibbons. "Of course. Tell me, did she talk to you at all about why she was going back?"

Mrs. Haddam smiled. "We had long conversations about it," she said. "It was the culmination of a great deal of thinking she had been doing about herself and her situation over the time she was here." She paused for a moment. "I expect you've already realized that Jody was an unusual person?"

"Yes indeed," said Gibbons wryly.

Mrs. Haddam nodded. "Then it will make sense to you when I say that over the last year or so Jody was coming to a realization that settling down in one place might not be the hell on earth she had always envisioned."

"It makes a great deal of sense," said Gibbons encouragingly.

"There's one conversation we had that stands out in my mind," continued Mrs. Haddam. "She was telling me some anecdote from her days at the bookshop in York, and I remarked that she always referred to York as 'home.' That made her stop and think a bit, and then she said—as if it were just dawning on her—that she'd never been happier than when she was in York, either during this last stint or during her childhood. So I asked her why, if that was the case, she kept leaving the place and her friends there. And she said, 'Reflex, I suppose.' And then she laughed and said, 'Not a very good reason, is it?' It was after that conversation that I noticed she began to talk of possibly returning to York for good."

"And when was it she definitely made up her mind to do so?" asked Gibbons.

"Oh, not until shortly before she left," answered Mrs. Haddam with a laugh. "Jody was very impulsive—she rarely planned anything out. But, let's see, she began talking of it sometime in November. Yes, it was after she'd heard from one of her old friends up there."

Gibbons noted it down, though he was not sure how much help it would be. Another thought struck him.

"Do you know where she was planning to stay in York?" he asked.

"She had a friend named Rachel," said Mrs. Haddam. "Jody said she would take her in until she could find a place of her own."

"I see," said Gibbons, as neutrally as he could, though he was in fact rather disappointed.

But Mrs. Haddam had not finished.

"That would be after the holiday, of course," she said. "She was going to spend Christmas with another friend—the one she'd heard from in November. He'd just bought a bungalow in a village near York, and he invited her up to spend the holidays there. I think perhaps she took the invitation as some kind of sign, because it was after that, as I said, that she decided to go back."

"He?" asked Gibbons, wondering if this could be Rhys-Jones after all.

"Just a friend," said Mrs. Haddam hastily. "I think they had gone to school together when they were young."

"Ah," said Gibbons, mentally dismissing Rhys-Jones again. "Do you remember his name?"

"Not really," admitted Mrs. Haddam. "Jody very often talked about her friends in York, but never having met any of them, I'm afraid I tended to get them mixed up. Rachel I remember because Jody referred to her more than anyone else, and even suggested she might come to visit at one time, though I gather it never worked out."

Gibbons looked so obviously disappointed that Mrs. Haddam added, "But let me think a moment—perhaps I can remember something else."

They sat silently for several moments while Mrs. Haddam

struggled with her memory and Gibbons awaited the results anxiously. But finally she shook her head.

"The name's gone," she said. "It might have been Bill, but I don't think that's right. But the village had a two-word name, something to do with apples."

"The village where this fellow had bought a home?" clarified Gibbons.

"Yes, that's right. I remember I asked if it was in the Dales and Jody said no, it was only a bit south of York. But I'm afraid that's the best I can do."

"That's very helpful indeed," said Gibbons, thinking to himself that there could not be so very many villages with apples in their names. "In fact, you've given me more information than anyone else I've talked to all day. Now I'd just like to note down the particular dates. Do you remember what day Miss Farraday left? And did she have much luggage with her, by the way?"

"No," answered Mrs. Haddam. "She had a couple of largish bags and that was it. She didn't leave anything behind, either. Jody believed in traveling light, and she knew how to go about it."

But that still, thought Gibbons, left two sizable cases unaccounted for.

"She took the train to London on the twenty-second," continued Mrs. Haddam. "She was going to stay the night there because she wanted to do some shopping in town—she fancied bringing Rachel a Christmas present from Harrods. So she fixed up to stay the night at some dreary little B and B, but I don't remember where it was now."

And that painted its own little picture in Gibbons's mind. It was such an ordinary kind of thing to do, the first really ordinary thing he had heard about Jody Farraday.

"So she would have taken the train north the next day, on the twenty-third?" he asked.

"That's right. She was getting in that evening, I believe."

Gibbons wrote down the twenty-third and suddenly realized

that was the day Rachel Morrison had left for the Lake District. That, he thought, was rather sad: the two friends had probably missed each other by a matter of hours. No doubt Jody had planned to surprise her friend on her return after the holiday.

Mrs. Haddam did not have much more to add. Gibbons thanked her for her help, urged her to ring him if she thought of anything else, and took his leave.

"Should have started with her," remarked Ogburn as they re-traced their steps down the street. "But I never thought she would know so much."

"If we'd started with her, she wouldn't have," replied Gibbons. "Murphy's Law, you know."

Ogburn laughed. "True enough," he said. "Here, we've just time for a pint and a bite to eat before your flight leaves. I know a little place down this way."

"Today's great thought," said Gibbons and followed him happily, feeling that the trip to Cornwall had definitely been worth it.

The day had dawned fair in York, but by eleven o'clock the wind had risen and the clouds were gathering again. By noon, the York plain was engulfed in a steady, drenching downpour that showed no sign of letting up, while water slowly crept up over berms all across the country, spreading in deepening pools along the low places and taking back whole stretches of road. The tarmac at Bradford-Leeds Airport, however, remained navigable through-out the day and into the night; Gibbons's flight in from Cornwall was late because of delays in Newquay, not on account of the weather in Yorkshire.

That was not to say that the drive from York had gone smoothly. Bethancourt, driving a Land Rover borrowed from one of his parents' friends, had had to be quite creative in order to find a way through, but he had managed it at last and now waited just outside the terminal, smoking a cigarette and watching Cerberus nose about on the pavement. He had not heard much from Gibbons during the course of the day and was impatient to see his friend and hear all the news.

When at last the flight landed and Gibbons emerged, Bethancourt thought his friend looked as if he had spent the brief flight soundly asleep and would like to have stayed that way. Gibbons greeted him with a smile that turned into a yawn.

"Good morning," responded Bethancourt, grinning at him. "Had a good sleep?"

"It was a long day," admitted Gibbons, making a valiant effort to stifle another yawn and only partially succeeding. "What time is it?"

Bethancourt clicked on his mobile. "Twelve past ten," he answered. "And we should get back on the road if we're to have any hope of reaching York tonight—the roads are bad and getting worse."

"By all means," said Gibbons. "I can fill you in on the way—not that there's much to tell."

"There isn't?" asked Bethancourt, disappointed. He gestured and began to lead the way back to the car.

"It's raining a lot worse here than in Cornwall," observed Gibbons, quickening his stride.

"It's raining more here than it ever has anywhere," said Bethancourt gloomily. "At least I got a spot close to the terminal—here's the car."

Gibbons looked askance at the muddy Land Rover. "What happened to the Jaguar?" he asked.

"Nothing," replied Bethancourt. "I just didn't fancy getting bogged down in the floods. Throw your kit in the back."

Gibbons obeyed and then scrambled into the passenger seat while Bethancourt, having let Cerberus into the backseat, settled himself behind the wheel. He took off his glasses to wipe them dry and asked, "So did you find out anything at all?"

"Oh, yes," answered Gibbons. "Benny Ogburn—the Devon and Cornwall sergeant—was incredibly helpful. He had nearly everyone lined up for me and we went through them one after another like a dose of salts. Employer, co-workers, landlord, boyfriend."

"Boyfriend?" asked Bethancourt, a little surprised. He replaced his glasses and looked at Gibbons.

"Well, in a manner of speaking," said Gibbons. "More of a casual liaison—an affair of convenience, you might say. This chap—Dick Smale—didn't seem too upset that Jody had decided to go back to Yorkshire and certainly never considered going with her. He looked positively startled when I suggested it."

"She was moving back here?" said Bethancourt, sounding surprised as he started up the car. "This wasn't just a visit?"

"That's right," answered Gibbons. He had pulled out his notebook and was riffling through the pages by the dim lights of the dashboard. "Here we are," he said, and read off the gist of his interview with Irene Haddam.

"There's a map in the glove box," said Bethancourt when he had finished. "I seem to remember there being a pair of villages, Appleton-this and Appleton-that."

"I thought you might know," said Gibbons, leaning forward to dig out the map. "South of York, like Mrs. Haddam said?"

"Yes, and not too far south, if memory serves," answered Bethancourt.

Gibbons unfolded the map, spreading it in his lap, and studied it for a moment.

"Here we are," he said, marking the spot with his finger. "Appleton Roebuck and Nun Appleton. Look like quite small places."

"They probably are," said Bethancourt. "All the same, it will be quite a job to go knocking on all the doors until we find a fellow who knew Jody."

"Not a bit of it," said Gibbons. "Mrs. Haddam said he bought a house there in November. All I have to do is have Andy Rowett look up the home sales for both villages—I doubt there were that many in the relevant time period."

"Aren't you clever," said Bethancourt admiringly. "It helps to be associated with the police, I must say."

"In fact," said Gibbons, ignoring this jibe, "Andy is most likely still at his computer at this hour—if I ring him now, he'll have it ready for me in the morning."

He pulled out his mobile and began scrolling through the contacts while Bethancourt merged into the traffic on the A road and accelerated cautiously into the rain.

"There we are," said Gibbons, pressing TALK. "Andy? It's Jack Gibbons. . . . No, I'm back. On the way in from Leeds . . . Yes, that's right. Look here, Andy, do you have time to do me a favor? . . . Oh, good. I just need the records of the home sales in a couple of villages for the last two months. Appleton Roebuck and Nun Appleton— they're both about ten miles south of York. Can you e-mail me the results when you're done? . . . Perfect. Ta very much." He rang off and looked back at Bethancourt. "Andy says it won't take any time at all," he announced.

"So we can be off bright and early tomorrow to see this chap," said Bethancourt. "If he did kill her, I still wonder why they were in Mittlesdon's on Christmas Eve."

Gibbon shrugged. "There's a lot we don't know," he said. "I think the killer is someone with a secret, and so far we haven't found many secrets in this case."

"Perhaps Mittlesdon was having an affair," suggested Bethancourt. "Or perhaps his son was cooking the books."

"Or that clerk—what's his name, Dominic Bartlett—has a dark past."

"If he does, it's well hidden," remarked Gibbons, settling himself more comfortably in his seat. "Sergeant Rowett has already run background checks on all the Mittlesdon employees, even those who weren't present over the holidays. They're all perfectly blameless individuals. But of course," he added, "it needn't have been anyone who works at Mittlesdon's."

Bethancourt considered this for a moment as he guided the car through the rain.

"Jody seems to have been a rather solitary person," he said at last. "She had friends, but few who were very close to her, and she doesn't seem to have belonged to any particular group, either here in York or in Cornwall."

"But she was welcome in several," said Gibbons. "Rachel's group of friends in York, the bookshop's little coterie, and there's the set Dick Smale hangs out with in Cornwall. And from what we've gathered of her character, she probably knew secrets about people in all of them."

"And about their friends and relations," said Bethancourt gloomily. "It makes for a very wide field of suspects."

"Ah, well, we'll narrow it down in time," said Gibbons.

"I can't see what you're so bloody optimistic about," said Bethancourt. "Half of York could have had reason to murder the woman."

"But not that many people have secrets worth killing to protect," pointed out Gibbons. "Tomorrow we'll have a go at the fellow she was staying with—it all may end right there. But if not, I think I shall begin to dig a little deeper into everybody's closets, starting with Rachel and the Mittlesdon lot. By the way, have you heard anything more from Alice?"

"Aside from the fact that she still fancies me?" asked Bethancourt, and, when Gibbons laughed, he added, "Well, it's damned awkward, Jack. I don't know how I got out of lunch alive yesterday, and this morning was a minor disaster."

"This morning?" asked Gibbons, still amused. "Don't tell me you actually slept with her to get information. Phillip, how devoted of you!"

"Of course I didn't," said Bethancourt with an air of wounded dignity. "I asked her to ring me if she thought of any little piece of gossip or anything about her co-workers. So she rang this morning to tell me—of all things—that she thought Dominic Bartlett might be gay."

Gibbons laughed outright. "Figured that out all on her own, did she?"

"Apparently," replied Bethancourt. "Really, I don't know how the woman became so parochial—I swear she wasn't like that at school."

"So," said Gibbons, "her theory of the case is that Bartlett murdered Jody to keep her from spreading the word about his homosexuality? That's rich, that is."

Bethancourt laughed, too. "I don't think Alice took it quite that far. She was just obeying instructions to pass on any little thing she could think of. And, of course, to woo me further."

"Oh, yes," said Gibbons. "You left out the bit about the minor disaster."

"Well, you remember that girl I met at the club the other night?" said Bethancourt. "I happened to meet up with her again last night after you'd gone. And her number is rather similar to Alice's, so when Alice rang this morning, I thought it was Catherine and answered accordingly."

"Catherine, eh?" Gibbons shot his friend a sharp glance. "That's quick work, I must say. How long has it been since you and Marla broke it off?"

"Nearly a fortnight," replied Bethancourt indignantly. "And I don't see how an innocent bit of flirting is cause for indictment on that account."

"Your flirting is never innocent," said Gibbons, dismissing this argument out of hand. "Has Marla rung you again?"

"Several times," admitted Bethancourt.

"But you haven't spoken to her?"

"There is absolutely nothing to say," replied Bethancourt.

"She doesn't seem to feel that way," pointed out Gibbons.

And to this Bethancourt had no reply.

It was still raining in the morning. Bethancourt and Gibbons were up early, Gibbons quite chipper, having slept most of the way home from the airport; Bethancourt was far less so, as it had been left to him to spend two hours finding an unflooded route back to York. They sat at the breakfast table, Gibbons wolfing down eggs and toast, Bethancourt with only coffee, both with their attention fixed on Gibbons's laptop. Andy Rowett had been as good as his word, and the home-sale records from Appleton Roebuck and Nun Appleton had been in Gibbons's e-mail when he woke up.

"There's not much here," said Gibbons, taking a mouthful of eggs while he ran his eyes down the list.

"We're probably not looking for anything too expensive," said Bethancourt, adjusting his glasses. "Mrs. Haddam referred to it as a 'bungalow,' and in general people's first houses aren't big ones."

"Mmm," said Gibbons.

They were both silent while they scanned the list.

"Look here," said Gibbons suddenly, putting down his fork. "Wilfrid Jenks," he read. "Wasn't that the name of Jody's friend whom Rhys-Jones mentioned and Rachel said wasn't in the area any longer?"

"I believe so," said Bethancourt, finding the place on the screen. "Well, that's very satisfactory, isn't it?"

"He purchased a bungalow in Appleton Roebuck for two hundred forty-three thousand pounds on November twenty-fourth," Gibbons read off the list. "As you thought, it's a small property—a two-bedroom bungalow it sounds like." He looked up, his blue eyes bright. "Let's get on the road, shall we?"

The Land Rover had been returned the night before, so they took the Jaguar by default. Bethancourt, normally a rather erratic driver, was cautious and attentive on this occasion, particularly once they had left the A road and were creeping along a series of country lanes. These were set amidst fallow fields and were frequently full of water, but he managed to maneuver the low-slung car through. In half an hour or so they had arrived and with a little trouble found the bungalow, a cozy-looking brick-built building standing apart from its neighbors in a small field. There was a light in the front window and a white Volkswagen Transporter van parked in the drive. Bethancourt pulled in behind it and they got out, following a flagged path up to the front door.

A thin man of about thirty answered their knock. He was a little stoop-shouldered, a rather average-looking man except for his eyes, which were large with long, thick lashes. He seemed more curious than alarmed by their visit and readily invited them in out of the rain. He did not, however, go so far as to usher them into the sitting room, whence the sound of a television came, so they remained standing in the little entrance hall.

"We've come about Jody Farraday," began Gibbons.

"Oh, Jody," said Jenks, smiling and revealing two deep dimples. "I've been wondering when she'd turn up again. Did she give me as a reference or something?"

"Not exactly, sir," said Gibbons. "She was a friend of yours, then?"

"Oh, yes," answered Jenks. "I've known her for years. We were at school together in York when we were kids."

"Then I'm afraid I have some sad news for you, Mr. Jenks," said Gibbons. "Miss Farraday was found murdered on Christmas day."

Jenks's eyes narrowed, as if he suspected them of some monstrous practical joke, and then, when Gibbons's sympathetic expression did not waver, he drew in a sharp breath and passed a hand over his face.

"That's—that's dreadful," he said in a low voice. "I—I had just seen her, for the first time in months."

"It must come as a great shock," said Bethancourt.

"Yes. Yes, it does." Jenks took a deep breath and looked back at Gibbons. "What happened?" he asked. "Where was she?"

"In York," answered Gibbons. "She was found at Mittlesdon's Bookshop, where I understand she was once employed."

"Yes, she was there for a while," said Jenks. "She only left a year or so ago. God, this is awful news, just awful."

"We understood," said Gibbons, "that she had planned to spend the holidays here with you."

"That's right." Jenks brushed impatiently at his eyes. "I'd invited her up from Cornwall, where she'd been staying. She arrived a couple of days before Christmas, but then she went off on Christmas Eve—I wasn't sure where."

"Isn't that rather odd, when she was planning on being here with you for Christmas?" asked Gibbons.

Jenks shrugged. "Well, it is odd, but not for Jody," he said. "She was terribly impulsive. One got used to it over the years. I was a bit disappointed, but I didn't think anything more about it."

"So there was no argument between you?" asked Gibbons.

"God, no." Jenks had been replying automatically, the larger part of his attention occupied with dealing with the blow he had just been dealt, but this suggestion seemed to rouse him. He looked at Gibbons, distressed. "I never thought . . ." He shook his head. "I can see it doesn't look very good," he said, "but you must believe me—we were on the best of terms when we parted."

Gibbons nodded neutrally.

"And she gave you no notion of where she might be going or with whom?" he asked.

"Not really," answered Jenks. "But I definitely expected her back at some point—I mean, I didn't think she had given up the idea of moving back here or anything. She said something about a lead on a job, but she didn't give me any details. I rather thought," he added, "that she had decided to go to Rachel's—another friend from school. She lives right in York, you see, and it would be more convenient for job hunting."

Gibbons nodded. "But she gave you the impression she wouldn't be back the next day?"

"No; then I should have worried when she didn't turn up," said Jenks. "And she took her bags, so I never thought she'd be gone less than a few days."

"So you knew," said Bethancourt, "that Miss Farraday was planning a permanent move back to York?"

"Yes, we talked about it." Jenks sounded sad. "I thought it was a wonderful idea. I haven't been back in the area all that long myself, and I liked the idea that we were both coming back to our roots."

"I see," said Gibbons. "Were you the reason she was returning here, then?"

Jenks looked confused. "I'm sorry?" he asked.

"Was Miss Farraday moving to York in order to be with you?" clarified Gibbons.

Jenks seemed to find this idea distasteful; he drew back a little from them, frowning.

"You mean in a romantic sense?" he said. "Certainly not. Jody and I were never like that—we were just childhood friends, more like brother and sister than anything else. Frankly, I didn't fancy her in that way, and I'd be astonished if she'd harbored any sexual feelings towards me."

His tone was very firm, almost as if they had indeed been siblings and Gibbons had accused him of incest.

"I understand, sir," Gibbons said, interjecting a soothing note into his voice.

"We had heard," said Bethancourt, "that although Miss Farraday had been talking of a return to York, she hadn't definitely decided on it until she heard you were here, you see."

"But she knew I was here," said Jenks. "I contacted her as soon as I came back—she was still at Mittlesdon's then."

It was the detectives' turn to be confused. "Ah," said Gibbons, "I think we've misunderstood. You only recently purchased this house, but you've been living in the area for some time, is that right, sir?"

"Yes," said Jenks. "I moved up here almost two years ago when I took a job in Leeds."

His tone had gone flat again, his righteous indignation appeased.

Gibbons nodded. "To return to Miss Farraday's movements," he said, "do you recollect what time she left here on Christmas Eve?"

"Oh, I don't know." Jenks drew a deep breath and tried to concentrate. "Sometime after lunch. I had one or two things I wanted to pick up, so we drove in that afternoon. I let her off at Coppergate, she said she'd see me soon and we parted. . . ." He paused for a moment and when he spoke again, his voice was rough. "I didn't know it would be the last time I would ever see her," he said.

"You spent the evening alone then?" asked Gibbons.

"That's right," said Jenks. "I went to the midnight service at the Minster and then came back here."

There seemed nothing more to learn from him and he had begun to have to fight to keep his composure, so Gibbons brought the interview to a close and they took their leave. As they left the bungalow and scurried back to the car through the rain, they heard the volume of the television inside turned up high.

"Making sure we can't hear him cry," muttered Gibbons as he slid into the passenger seat and closed the door.

"Poor sod," agreed Bethancourt. "Unless you think he killed her?"

Gibbons considered this question while Bethancourt reversed out of the drive and started back toward the A64.

"Might have done," he conceded at last. "If he was lying about his feelings for Jody, that is. Do you think he was?"

Bethancourt frowned. "He seemed genuinely repulsed at the idea of their being a couple," he said. "But perhaps he's a very good actor. It does add up, you know. He invites her for the holidays, intending to propose to her, only she rejects him out of hand. She leaves for York, he follows her, words are exchanged, she tells him he's a disgusting toad, and he strangles her."

"Very pretty," said Gibbons. "But how did they end up in the bookshop?"

Bethancourt waved a hand. "Happenstance. They were arguing in the street and Jody didn't want to make a scene, so she said, 'Here, let's get inside—I can let us into this place.'"

"I suppose," said Gibbons rather doubtfully. "It's not out of the realm of possibility anyway. But wouldn't Rachel have known if Jody and Jenks were involved?"

"Well, Jody didn't tell her she was moving back here," pointed out Bethancourt. He paused, and then said, "Oh, God."

Gibbons had been gazing out his window at the rain, but this jerked his attention back to his companion.

"What?" he demanded as the car slowed and then came to a halt.

"It's a puddle," said Bethancourt in a discouraged tone, and Gibbons peered out the windscreen to see a small pond of water in their path, its surface puckered by the falling rain.

"That looks a lot deeper than when we came through," said Gibbons.

"So it does," said Bethancourt. "The question is: is it too deep for the car to get through it? On the other hand, I can't think of any other way we could take, so I suppose we might as well try."

"Go very slow," advised Gibbons. "And steadily."

"Right," said Bethancourt, letting in the clutch. "You'd better look out and give a shout if the water looks too deep."

"I knew you were going to say that," said Gibbons resignedly.

He rolled down his window and stuck his head out into the rain as Bethancourt eased the Jaguar into the water.

"You're all right," he called, shaking the water out of his eyes. "It's not even up to the middle of the tire yet."

Bethancourt continued their slow progress while Gibbons watched the water rise and then, at last, watched it begin to retreat.

"I do hope we don't have to do that again," he said, rolling his window back up as they cleared the flooded roadway. "It was most uncomfortable and I am now quite depressingly wet."

"I hope your police friends are going to rescue us if we get stuck. Otherwise, it's a very long tramp back to York."

But as they crept along the sodden roads, he found himself playing lookout more than once again, and by the time they drove into York he badly needed a change of clothes.

It was still early in the day when at length they reemerged from the house in St. Saviourgate and made a dash through the rain along the snickelways to Mittlesdon's.

The shop had been allowed to reopen its doors that morning, an event noted in the local media but not overwhelmingly attended by the public, most of whom were worrying about their cellars flooding as the rain continued to fall. Bethancourt and Gibbons had intended to turn out for it, but the Jenks interview put them behindhand, and the bookshop had been open for the better part of an hour when they arrived.

Most of the staff was present, including an unctuous Alice, who seemed to have recovered from Bethancourt's morning faux pas. His smile became more brittle with each encounter with her.

Fortunately, she was mostly kept busy. The staff in general seemed to be throwing themselves into their work with an air of relief, tidying away the detritus left over from the Christmas shoppers and straightening up the shelves. There was much coming and going between the sales floor and the office, whilst behind the counter Libby Alston, the oldest member of the staff, made telephone calls to patrons, checking them off on a long list.

There was a sprinkling of customers, though not many of them showed much interest in books; they mostly wandered about, surreptitiously looking for the site of the murder. One tourist actually came in with a camera and asked outright; Rhys-Jones informed him with chilly politeness that access to the office was limited to staff.

Gibbons's goal was unobtrusive observation, which in a bookshop was not difficult: he simply browsed. Bethancourt, joining him in this, paused in front of a display of bestsellers.

"That looks interesting," said Gibbons, indicating a book titled *Bad Science*. "I like his columns in *The Guardian*."

"I've read it," answered Bethancourt. "It was fascinating."

He reached for the book, but volume next to it caught his eye, and he picked that up instead.

"I wonder if this is that diet everyone's been talking about," he said.

Gibbons peered at the cover, which portrayed a smiling woman in her forties with perfectly tinted honey-blonde hair and beautifully applied makeup, showing a respectable amount of cleavage.

"Isn't that that American telly star?" he asked. "Yes, there's her name—Dana Dugan."

"Right," said Bethancourt. "I think my aunt said something about it coming from America." He adjusted his glasses to look at the cover photograph. "My, she's well preserved, isn't she?"

"Just what I was thinking," said Gibbons. "Anyway, what do you want a diet book for? You can't possibly think you need to lose weight."

"No, no," said Bethancourt, "nothing like that. I was just curious, that's all. Apparently this thing is the talk of the town—or at least the middle-aged-women's part of town. My aunt's lost nearly a stone on it."

He opened the book and was flipping randomly through it when a female voice exclaimed, "Good Lord. What are you doing here?"

Both men turned to regard a willowy blond woman with sleepy green eyes. She did not look pleased to see Bethancourt.

"Catherine," he said gallantly. "What a delightful surprise. Do let me introduce you to my friend Jack Gibbons. Jack, this is Catherine, the lady I mentioned to you last night."

Catherine shook hands with Gibbons automatically, her eyes returning immediately to Bethancourt.

"How did you find out where I work?" she demanded.

"Work?" repeated Bethancourt blankly, as though he had never heard of the concept. "You don't mean . . . oh, dear."

Gibbons's eyes lit up. "Oh, are you Catherine Stockton?"

She nodded stiffly, but before things could be sorted, they were interrupted by a large man in a regrettable striped waistcoat.

"Catherine, my dear," he said heartily, swooping in to put an arm around her and plant a kiss on her cheek, all of which she received with a marked air of reserve. "Good to see you—I wanted to tell you that my little niece was bowled over with that lovely edition of *The Wizard of Oz* you found for me. Nothing like the classics, eh?"

"Mr. Sanderson," said Catherine, smiling, but also removing herself from the circle of his arm. "I'm so glad little Anna was pleased."

Sanderson's eyes had lit upon Bethancourt. "Well, if it isn't Mr. Bethancourt," he said. "That's right, isn't it? We met the other night at the Heywoods', didn't we?"

"We did," said Bethancourt, reaching to shake hands. "Very pleased to see you again, sir. This is my friend Jack Gibbons."

"Good to meet you," said Sanderson. "Stop a minute—you aren't the police chap investigating the murder here, are you?"

"That's me," said Gibbons, his blue eyes suddenly regarding Sanderson with more than ordinary interest. "Detective Sergeant Gibbons of New Scotland Yard." His smile was bland.

Catherine was looking from one to the other of them with an

almost dazed expression. Then her eyes narrowed as she looked back at Bethancourt.

"Oh my God," she said.

"So is there any news?" Sanderson was asking Gibbons. "I do hope you manage to clear this nasty business up quickly—not the sort of thing Mittlesdon wants hanging over his head."

He had the air of the Man in Charge, and Gibbons raised an eyebrow.

"Certainly not," he agreed genially.

Bethancourt had the unpleasant sensation that the situation was rapidly getting away from him. He smiled weakly at Catherine.

"Perhaps—" he began, only to be interrupted once again, this time by Mittlesdon.

"There you are, Catherine," he said, bustling up. "I've got a list of messages a mile long waiting for you in your office. And Mrs. Broadley has rung up three times already this morning."

"I'd better ring her back," said Catherine. "Has anything come in for me?"

Mittlesdon waved his hand. "Tony's still sorting through everything in the back. Oh, hello, Brian," he added, catching sight of Sanderson. "Anything I can do for you, or were you just browsing today?"

Catherine was moving off toward the stairs, but not before looking daggers at Bethancourt, who smiled bravely and called after her, "See you later, then?"

She did not reply.

"I just wanted to see if you'd got that copy of Burke in for me," Sanderson told Mittlesdon.

Mittlesdon shook his head. "I'm afraid I haven't had a chance to look yet," he said. "But come along to the stockroom and see if Tony's come across it."

They moved off, leaving Bethancourt and Gibbons alone. Gibbons eyed his friend with a bemused expression on his face.

"Catherine," he said.

"Yes," replied Bethancourt, wretchedly. "That was Catherine."

"The girl at the nightclub."

"Yes," said Bethancourt in a very small voice.

"Let's see," said Gibbons. "Your ex-girlfriend from school works here, and just as we've eliminated her as a suspect, you go and hook up with the children's-literature expert."

"Well, I didn't know she was the children's-literature expert," protested Bethancourt. "She certainly doesn't look like one."

"I'll give you that," agreed Gibbons, sighing.

"And now," said Bethancourt, "she thinks I was chatting her up just to get information about Mittlesdon's."

"Oh," said Gibbons, enlightened. "Is that what she was on about?"

"I'm afraid so," said Bethancourt.

"Really," said Gibbons, with a mock air of admiration, "your life is very complicated, isn't it? Who on earth was that Sanderson man, and why did you tell him about me?"

"I didn't, not exactly," answered Bethancourt. "I ran across him at that cocktail party I went to—I told you about it. He's Sanderson Carveries." Something came back to him. "I think Tony Grandidge is his nephew or cousin or some such. At least, I'm almost certain that's what he said that night."

Gibbons nodded. "It explains why Mittlesdon is so ready to let him into the back." He raised a brow. "Any other personal connections with my murder investigation that you've forgotten to tell me about?"

Bethancourt sighed. "I'll go, shall I?" he said resignedly.

"No, stay," decided Gibbons. "There's nothing to say you shouldn't shop here, and I have to run off in any case to speak to Mittlesdon's accountants. Do try not to get further involved in anyone's personal life, if you can manage it."

"I won't," said Bethancourt, rather lamely.

He watched Gibbons go and then looked down at the book in

his hands, surprised to find he was still holding it. Feeling much chastened, and wondering if there was any way he could set things right, he plonked himself down in one of the easy chairs and began to read about the latest American diet craze.

9

In Which Bethancourt and Gibbons Receive a Late-Night Summons

*I*t was past one o'clock in the morning and the rain made a steady patter against the darkened windows. Gibbons sat at the kitchen table with his laptop open before him and an array of case files and notes spread out all around it. He had been hard at work in the two days since he had returned from Cornwall, but no matter how he added it up, he did not seem to be much farther forward.

He looked up as a door across the room opened and Bethancourt came up the stairs from the cellar. His appearance was slightly disheveled and there was a muddy streak across his cheek.

"There's a bit of damp," he said, "but no flooding yet. I think we may make it through."

"But it's still raining," Gibbons reminded him.

"Well, yes, there is that," admitted Bethancourt, coming to join his friend at the table. "I can't do anything about it, however."

Gibbons grunted, having returned his attention to his computer. Bethancourt eyed him, lit a cigarette, and inspected the cold remains of the cocoa in the mug he had left on the table.

Sighing, he rose to reheat it in the microwave on the worktop, and then, having given Gibbons those few moments of quiet, he asked, "Anything interesting?"

"No," said Gibbons with a sigh, pushing back from the table and rubbing his head with both hands. "Constable Redfern's been rummaging around, but he hasn't come up with much more than I have. This," he waved at the computer, "is to say that rumor has it your Catherine slept with her superior to get her assistant professorship at York University. Which in turn led to her getting the job at Mittlesdon's, out of which she has done quite well."

"She's not my Catherine," replied Bethancourt automatically. "Alice," he added, "told me the same thing, but I put it down to jealousy. Sorry."

Gibbons shrugged. "It's not as if it makes a very compelling motive for murder, even if it's true," he said. He paused and then asked curiously, "Does Alice know you've been dallying with Catherine?"

"I think she's figured it out," said Bethancourt resignedly. "There's definitely an edge to her conversation lately. Although that might be because I've been leading her on to the point of leaving myself open to a breach-of-promise suit."

"Her information has been very helpful," said Gibbons.

"But it hasn't really got us anywhere." Bethancourt slumped back in his chair and held up a finger. "Item: we've found out that Tony Grandidge was a scamp at university and was actually arrested for trespass, and that he's carrying more debt than he probably should be. He has been pursuing Catherine Stockton for some time, but she has remained cool to his advances, as she likes to keep a firm line between business and pleasure."

"Still not talking to you, eh?" asked Gibbons.

"No," replied Bethancourt, and held up a second finger. "Item two: we have discovered that Catherine Stockton leads rather a more risqué life than her co-workers and employer are aware of, which might, in the case of the true sociopath, be a cause for murder. Unfortunately, she was verifiably in Avon on Christmas night."

Gibbons raised a brow. "Unfortunately?" he asked. "Do I detect a trace of bitterness?"

Bethancourt ignored him and raised another finger. "Item three: Libby Alston's husband had an affair a couple of years ago. She appears ignorant of this fact, but you never can tell."

"She might have flown into a rage upon learning of his infidelity," said Gibbons. "I could see it happening—in fact, I've known such things to happen before, and there's no doubt she's very protective of her family. But I can't seem to find a plausible scenario in which Jody, on returning to York to finally settle down, decides it's a good first move to inform Libby of her husband's affair."

"Even if she did," put in Bethancourt, "it's even less likely that she would do it on Christmas Eve at the bookshop. I mean, *why*, for God's sake?"

"No," agreed Gibbons, "it doesn't make sense."

"Item four," continued Bethancourt, and then paused. "Are we counting the Dominic Bartlett thing?" he asked.

"We can count it," said Gibbons, "but I don't see that it will do us any good. He's obviously very embarrassed about being scammed by the youthful object of his affections, but I can't see him having the gumption to kill Jody. And that's assuming she would ever have told anyone about it—Rachel Morrison says not."

"It does seem out of character," agreed Bethancourt. "Very well, item four can be that friend of Rachel's who got arrested for possession of cocaine."

"And again we run up against a reason for Jody to have threatened him with revealing it," said Gibbons. "After all, it was several years ago, and he got off with parole, which is long since over. There seems no earthly reason for Jody to have brought it up."

"True," said Bethancourt, who was becoming discouraged.

"So long as we're taking stock," said Gibbons, "we really ought to count Rhys-Jones in, too. He could easily have done it, and he does have motive."

"Mark him down as item five," said Bethancourt. He paused to sip his cocoa and consider. "That's it, isn't it?" he said. "It's not much for two days' work."

"There's also Jenks," said Gibbons. "It remains perfectly possible that he lied about the nature of his relationship with Jody, and killed her in a fit of jealous rage. Only I still can't account for their being at the bookshop."

"There's not an iota of proof either," pointed out Bethancourt. "And if he lied about their relationship, well, so did Jody. She told your Mrs. Haddam he was just an old friend. Still, we can have him as item six if you like."

"We have ruled out a few things," said Gibbons, trying to stay positive. "Mittlesdon's accountants swear there's never been even a hint of irregularity in the bookshop's accounts, and if Mittlesdon himself has a secret vice, I certainly haven't been able to uncover it. Rod Bemis—the nerdy student fellow—leads a life free from any complication greater than being a bit late with his assignments sometimes. And we've confirmed all alibis, for those who have them."

"And you've tracked down most of Jody's old friends here," said Bethancourt.

"I haven't looked at them as closely," said Gibbons, "so there might still be something there, although thus far they all deny knowing she had returned to York. I should probably just let Rowett look into them for me, but I don't want to pile extra work on Brumby's team."

"They don't seem to mind," said Bethancourt.

Gibbons started to reply, but was interrupted by his mobile phone, which was buried somewhere on the table beneath the case files and notes.

"Damn," he said, leaning forward to shift the papers around in search of it.

"Who could be ringing now?" asked Bethancourt uneasily. "It's past one A.M."

"I don't know." Gibbons was frowning as he patted the various piles in search of the phone. "There!" he exclaimed at last. He swept away a stack of crime-scene photos and seized the phone, snapping it open and bringing it to his ear in one motion.

"Still up then, Gibbons?" came MacDonald's voice. "Good lad. There's been an odd sort of development at one of my crime scenes. Thought you might want to take a look."

"Of course, if you think it worthwhile, sir," replied Gibbons, inwardly quite bewildered. "Are you there now?"

"Have been since half eleven," answered MacDonald. "But the complication has just come to light. I've held up everything, pending. You just buzz round and tell me what you think, and I'll be grateful for it."

Gibbons badly wanted to ask exactly what things were pending on, but held his peace and took down the address, which proved to be somewhere called Upper Poppleton.

"Do you know where Upper Poppleton is?" he asked Bethancourt.

Bethancourt, who was listening avidly to Gibbons's side of the conversation, nodded. "Certainly," he said.

"I'll be there shortly, sir," Gibbons told MacDonald. "The friend I'm staying with will probably drive me out, if that's all right with you?"

"The more the merrier," said MacDonald absently, and Gibbons could tell that his attention was already elsewhere. "See you soon, Sergeant."

He rang off.

"What's happened?" demanded Bethancourt.

"That was MacDonald," said Gibbons, putting down the phone

thoughtfully, "and I don't quite know. He wants me at another crime scene, but he didn't say why. Just that there had been an odd development. I wonder . . . Well, the quickest way to find out is to go there. How long will it take?"

"Ten minutes or so, unless the road's flooded out," answered Bethancourt, downing the last of his cocoa. "What the devil is in Upper Poppleton?"

"I haven't the slightest idea," retorted Gibbons, "except that a crime happened at this address." He waved the piece of paper he had jotted it down on. "Is it a village?" he asked as they made their way out to the hall.

"Upper Poppleton?" responded Bethancourt. "That's right— it's northeast of the city center. None of the bookshop people live up there, so I can't imagine what the connection is."

"Are there shops?" asked Gibbons.

"I expect there are," said Bethancourt, zipping up his coat. "Why?"

"I was only thinking," said Gibbons, "that perhaps it was to do with Ashdon and not with the Mittlesdon case. Although," he added, "another killing so close to his last would be quite out of character."

"Oh." Bethancourt called Cerberus to heel and opened the door, wrinkling his nose at the rain. "Let's run for it, shall we?"

Gibbons agreed and they dashed down the length of the garden, through the gate, and then around to where the Jaguar was parked. They were very damp by the time they slid into the car, and Bethancourt flipped the heat on.

"Let's get over the river here, where we know we can," he said. "I think we should be all right after that. At least, there's only one dicey bit up by Clifton Ings and Water End. But after that, the road draws away from the river onto higher ground."

"Whatever you say," replied Gibbons, fastening his safety belt.

They set off into a dark and very wet night, but Bethancourt's prediction held true. The water on the roads slowed them down, but they encountered no serious flooding. The address Mac-Donald had given them led to a large property on the outskirts of the village, where an old grange had been renovated and added to in order to make a modern country home for a well-to-do man. The drive was currently choked with police cars and vans, but there seemed not to be much movement among them. Bethancourt nosed the Jaguar as close to the house as he could get before drawing over to the side and parking beneath an old beech tree.

"Can I come in?" he asked as he shut off the engine.

"Come along," answered Gibbons. "I told MacDonald you'd be with me. We'd better leave Cerberus, though."

Cerberus, who had gone to sleep in the backseat, did not appear to mind this arrangement overmuch, and they left him there while they jogged through the rain to the front door.

MacDonald awaited them in the front hall, sitting with his coat open on a bench amidst his forensics team. Beside him was a small, balding man with black-framed glasses, and on a chair opposite sat Constable Redfern.

"Ah, here they are," said MacDonald, looking round as Gibbons and Bethancourt came in. "We'll soon be set to rights now, lads. And who's this sterling addition to my investigation team?"

"Phillip Bethancourt, sir," said Gibbons. "He was kind enough to drive me up here."

Bethancourt smiled engagingly and held out a hand. "I doubt your team really needs a chauffeur, sir," he said, "but I was curious, and Jack didn't think you'd mind my having a look-in."

MacDonald shook his hand, giving him an appraising glance. "Nay," he said, "you may as well come and see the show. Have you met Biddulph here, Sergeant? He's my genius electronics man."

Biddulph appeared unimpressed by this praise. He rose to his feet, revealing distinctly bowed legs, and shook hands with a nod, but very little change in expression.

"It was Biddulph called my attention to this little conundrum," said MacDonald. "Tell Sergeant Gibbons, Biddy."

"It were a professional job, that's all," said Biddulph. "Don't get much of that." He eyed Gibbons. "I can describe how it was done if you want."

"God, no, Biddy," interrupted MacDonald before Gibbons could reply. "He's a detective, not an electrician—he doesn't want all your gobbledygook. Just get to the point."

Biddulph gave a much-tried sigh. "The *point*," he said, "is that the last time I saw an alarm system buggered this way was at Accessorize when we found the Ashdon victim."

Gibbons just stared at him for a long moment. Then he turned to MacDonald and asked, "Who was killed here, sir?"

"That's just it," said MacDonald. "It wasn't a young lady at all. In fact, it was one of our leading citizens—a middle-aged chap named Brian Sanderson."

Both Gibbons and Bethancourt started in surprise.

"Ah," said MacDonald, "I see you'd already encountered our local guiding light. Well, there's no denying he got around. Where did you find him?"

"He was a regular customer at Mittlesdon's," answered Gibbons, his mind racing.

"I met him at a cocktail party," offered Bethancourt.

MacDonald raised a brow but said nothing in reply to this.

"There are some other similarities," he said. "Come have a look at the body."

Bethancourt followed the two detectives down the hallway with some trepidation. Normally he did not see the scene of the crime until long after the body had been removed, and he was not particularly eager to see this one now. But it seemed to be assumed that he would accompany them, so he did, hoping it would not be too gruesome.

The door to a large room at the back of the house stood open, and as they approached, the brilliant flash of a camera blazed out into the corridor. Inside, the room was fitted out as a kind of study-cum-lounge, with a desk and file cabinets in one corner and

162

a large couch and television on the other side. Sanderson's body was sprawled on the floor by the couch, looking to Bethancourt's eye oddly unlike a corpse: he was certainly pale, and very still, but he might have been merely unconscious. There was, however, the faintest smell of blood, a trickle of which ran down Sanderson's face from his ear, with a much larger stain appearing on his trousers. He was dressed in an unfortunate paisley waistcoat, and this somehow struck Bethancourt as sad and rather poignant.

An older man whom MacDonald introduced as Dr. Somersby, the medical examiner, came forward to meet them, while his younger assistant hovered in the background and the cameraman continued to snap pictures of everything in the room from every possible angle.

Somersby briskly shook hands with both Gibbons and Bethancourt, then turned impatiently back to MacDonald. "I've done all I can here," he announced. "Am I taking the body or not?"

MacDonald shrugged. "That's what Sergeant Gibbons is here to determine," he answered. "Tell him what you've found so far."

"He was killed this evening, between six and nine o'clock," Somersby recited. "His wrists and ankles were bound whilst he was still alive, and it looks like he was beaten, though I can't be sure of that until I get him stripped and on the table. His genitals were cut into with a very sharp knife, and afterwards he was killed by the insertion of a sharp, serrated knife into the left ear, where it probably penetrated the brain stem."

Bethancourt found that he had inadvertently dropped his hands to cover his nether regions, and firmly returned them to his pockets while Gibbons drew a sharp breath.

"That sounds like Ashdon, all right," he said. He looked at MacDonald. "But there are differences, too. Do you think we're dealing with a copycat killer?"

"It was my first thought," admitted MacDonald. "But then I thought Brumby might like to make that call himself. What do you think, Sergeant? Would he be interested in my little country-house murder?"

"Yes, sir," said Gibbons decidedly. "Without a doubt. Whatever's going on here, the superintendent will want to see it." His eyes swept the room before he looked back at MacDonald. "Would you like me to ring him?"

"That would be very good of you, lad," said MacDonald. "Somersby, you'll have to hold off till Superintendent Brumby gets here."

"Really, Freddie," said Somersby, "it's getting on for two A.M. You could at least hazard a guess as to how likely it is this Brumby will want my services."

Gibbons had turned aside to make his phone call, and Bethancourt found himself suddenly very much in the way. He edged away from the burgeoning argument between MacDonald and the doctor, and, not wanting to eavesdrop on Gibbons's conversation, retreated to the doorway, there to observe the scene more discreetly and wonder what it was all about. After all, how many coincidences could one case have?

Gibbons rang off and paced over to the body, kneeling to inspect the dead man more carefully. Bethancourt shuddered: though not as gruesome as he had feared, he had no desire for a closer view. Gibbons showed no such delicacy, however, pulling a pair of latex gloves from his pocket and slipping them on before reaching out to lift the paisley vest away from the torso.

"Have you got anything there, Sergeant?" asked MacDonald, clearly looking for an excuse to get away from his dispute with Somersby.

"I'm off home," announced the doctor to MacDonald's back. "Young Stephens here can get the body back to the morgue once Scotland Yard's had their say."

MacDonald sighed. "Fine, fine, Neil," he said. "I'll ring you in the morning. What did you say, Sergeant?"

Gibbons had not, in fact, said anything, but Somersby let his prey go, grumbling under his breath as he turned to his assistant and began to give him instructions. MacDonald joined Gibbons by the corpse and they conferred together in low voices, while the officer with the camera moved on to another portion of the room.

Bethancourt, still leaning against the doorjamb, let his eyes roam over the room. He was unpracticed at picking the salient details out from a crime scene, but he was a naturally observant man, and as long as he was there, he reckoned he might as well have a go. He could not help thinking, however, that it was ever so much more convenient when Gibbons did the gleaning and came to him with the facts already established.

The wait was not a short one. Bethancourt gave up on observation, wandered out in the rain to smoke and check on his dog, and finally joined the medical examiner's assistant, who had gone to sit in the hall. They struck up a conversation, and passed the time in discussion of murder, Yorkshire, and the merits versus the drawbacks of the medical profession, while nearby a uniformed officer chatted with a couple of idle forensics-team members, and in a chair on the other side Biddulph tilted his head back and fell asleep.

At last the door swung open to admit Brumby and Detective Inspector Howard. Both men bore the rumpled appearance of people who have been woken from a sound sleep and made to dress while only half awake.

All conversation ceased in the hall with their entrance, and all eyes turned in their direction while the two men shook the rain off and looked about, taking stock.

"Can someone show me where Superintendent MacDonald is at?" asked Brumby in a mild tone when no one came forward.

The uniformed man started, looked at his cohorts, who shrugged, and said, "I can, sir. It's just this way."

"Thank you, Constable," said Brumby, falling in behind.

Stephens, the medical examiner's assistant, looked after them and then shifted in his seat, saying to Bethancourt, "I suppose I'd better follow along in case they want me."

"I'll come with you," said Bethancourt.

Gibbons and MacDonald had moved on from the body and were examining marks in the carpet. They looked up at the sound of purposeful footsteps, and Gibbons rose to his feet. MacDonald, however, merely grinned up from where he was squatting on his haunches.

"Ah, there you are, Superintendent," he said. "Come to join our little party, have you?"

"I'll never say you didn't do your best to keep me occupied while I was here," replied Brumby dryly. "What's happened then? Give me the details, if you please."

MacDonald rose laboriously to his feet while Gibbons led his superiors over to the body, speaking rapidly as they went. Stephens followed them, cutting around the group to stand in a proprietary way at the foot of the body, but nobody paid any attention to him, apart from Brumby's automatic polite nod.

Bethancourt hovered just inside the doorway, trying to listen in on the discussion discreetly, without attracting attention. He was not convinced that there was much here to occupy him: the psychopathic behavior of serial killers did not much interest him, and he could not see any tie to the Mittlesdon murder, aside from the fact that Sanderson had been a very good customer of the shop. Certainly, in Gibbons's exhaustive search of Jody Farraday's contacts, Sanderson's name had never surfaced. The one firm connection he possessed was his relation to Tony Grandidge, but it seemed hardly likely that Jody's murderer had begun killing random relatives of her onetime co-workers.

Eventually, as the police conferred about the crime-scene details, bringing in instances from the mysterious Ashdon's past crimes, Bethancourt gave up and returned to the hallway, where at least he did not have to look at dead bodies and it was only a step to the front porch, where he could smoke.

Gibbons was intensely aware that this could be the big break-through in the Ashdon case, yet at the same time he could not make up his mind if it was indeed that, or merely the work of a clever copycat killer. He kept returning, time and again, to the fact that the victim was a middle-aged man, not a young woman, and had been murdered in a country house rather than a shop. Was it possible that such a wildly variant crime had been commit-ted by someone aping Ashdon's modus operandi?

Brumby and Howard seemed equally perplexed, and although Brumby had agreed almost at once to take over the case from MacDonald, it was clear that he was doing so as a precautionary measure. They were therefore awaiting the arrival of the Scotland Yard forensics team, but Gibbons noticed that MacDonald had not yet left or sent home his own men, signaling that there was some doubt in the Yorkshire detective's mind.

"But it must be Ashdon," said Howard, sounding uncertain despite his words. "No copycat could possibly think we'd assume this was Ashdon's work, not when the victim and setting are so different."

"That's true," said Brumby reflectively.

"But," put in Gibbons, "perhaps the killer wasn't trying to pass this off as Ashdon's work. What if he was only copying Ashdon in an attempt to get away with the murder?"

Brumby and Howard looked at him, apparently startled by this train of thought, but MacDonald nodded immediately.

"You've got the nub of it there, Sergeant," he said. "Say I'm a fellow with a desire to rid the world of Sanderson here—and be-lieve me, there's no shortage of such folk about. Only I've never taken to killing before and I'm feeling a bit intimidated by the ef-ficiency of the Yorkshire constabulary. And then there's a murder at Accessorize, and the papers are full of this serial killer, and how he's got away with a half-dozen murders or more. If I'm a bright lad, mightn't I just take a page out of Ashdon's book with the idea that if he can bring it off, so can I?"

"I've never known it to happen before," said Brumby thoughtfully. "On the other hand, there's a first time for everything. Is that your reading of the matter, then, Superintendent?"

But MacDonald shook his head. "Nay," he said. "It's just a thing that occurred to me. To my mind, there's nothing yet to say it's one or the other. Ashdon might have had some personal grudge against Sanderson and decided to do away with him."

"That's what I was thinking," admitted Howard, with a glance around the room. "If it *is* Ashdon, there's no denying this isn't a typical crime for him."

"Let's say for the moment that this is Ashdon's work," said Brumby. "That puts the Accesorize murder in an entirely different light. It was already singular in occurring so far north, but this makes it look as though Yorkshire is actually Ashdon's home ground."

Howard was nodding. "And it indicates an escalation. At long last, may I say."

"And by 'escalation,'" asked MacDonald, "do you mean more frequent killings?"

"That's right," said Brumby. "It's a stage in a serial killer's pathology. There are exceptions, of course, but generally over time a killer will need to kill more frequently to satisfy his cravings. It's an unfortunate fact of life that we don't catch most of them before they reach that stage." His eyes, as he said this, were bleak.

"A lot of the time," said Howard, "we don't even know there's a serial killer out there until he reaches the escalation point—the murders are too scattered, and often the killer is still developing a recognizable modus operandi, so that the crimes aren't connected with each other at once."

"I see," said MacDonald. "And in this Ashdon's case?"

"He's been a challenge from the first," admitted Brumby. "We've not been able to connect any earlier crimes to him before the murder at the antique shop in Ashdon—earlier crimes can give us additional information to build a profile with. Usually, serial killers operate in one area, but Ashdon's killings are all over the map, and that makes it extremely difficult to profile his next possible victim."

"We can profile her," corrected Howard, "but without a geographic area in which to identify women who fit the profile, well, we can't have an eye on every woman in Britain who fits the description."

MacDonald rubbed his jaw. "Nay," he agreed. "I can see how that might not work so very well."

Brumby's eyes wandered back to the body. "But if this murder is what it seems, then we might at last have more to go on," he said. Abruptly, he turned back to Gibbons. "You say you'd met the victim, Sergeant?" he asked.

"That's right," answered Gibbons. "He was a regular customer at Mittlesdon's and turned up the other day when the shop reopened. The friend I'm staying with had met him at a party and they remembered each other from that."

MacDonald had raised his eyebrows. "Well connected is he, this friend of yours?" he asked.

"I suppose you could say that," replied Gibbons, a little uncomfortable with this line of inquiry.

"Why do you ask that, Superintendent?" said Brumby alertly.

"Because Sanderson was a social climber," said MacDonald bluntly. "The only party he'd deign to be seen at would be a posh one." He turned back to Gibbons. "This is the friend who brought you tonight?"

"Yes, sir," answered Gibbons, looking round and finding, somewhat to his surprise, that Bethancourt was not in sight. "He must have gone outside."

"Let's have him in," said Brumby. "I'd rather like to hear about this party."

Gibbons nodded and went in search of his friend, whom he

found outside on the porch, sheltering from the rain while he smoked a cigarette in company with two men from MacDonald's forensics team.

"Brumby'd like to speak with you," Gibbons told him.

Bethancourt raised an eyebrow. "With me?" he asked.

"I told him you'd met Sanderson once," said Gibbons.

"So did you," retorted Bethancourt, but he held his cigarette out into the rain to douse it, and then handed it to one of the forensics men, who deposited it into a plastic evidence bag. "Cheers," he said, and followed Gibbons back inside.

He went without any real trepidation, having had enough experience of police procedures to know that talking to anyone with a scintilla of knowledge about the case was de rigueur. But he had yet to meet Superintendent Brumby, and the sharp glance of the detective, along with the sober atmosphere at the scene of the crime, combined to immediately make him feel as though he were facing a tutor whose lecture he had failed to attend.

In the face of this, he smiled amiably, held out a hand, and, as Gibbons pronounced his name, said, "Good to meet you, sir."

Gibbons continued with the introductions, and Bethancourt dutifully shook hands with Howard while MacDonald eyed him narrowly.

"Bethancourt, eh?" he said. "Seems to me there's a magistrate who goes by that name out in Skipton."

"That would be my father," replied Bethancourt.

"Skipton," repeated Brumby thoughtfully. "Is that out in the Dales?"

"Right you are," said MacDonald. "It's one of the many 'gateways to the Dales.'" He was running his eyes up and down Bethancourt's figure. "So where does your family hail from then?"

"The family house is in Appletreewick," answered Bethancourt evenly.

"Hmm," said MacDonald. "Wharfedale, isn't it?"

"Yes, sir," said Bethancourt.

"And you live here in York?"

"No, I live in London."

"But I thought," interrupted Howard, "that Sergeant Gibbons was staying with you?"

"I am," said Gibbons, thinking it was time to intervene. "The Bethancourts also own a house here in York, in St. Saviourgate."

"My, my," murmured MacDonald.

Bethancourt grinned at him.

"If you've finished placing our witness?" said Brumby.

"Oh, aye, I'm done," said MacDonald. "Just like to have firm ground underfoot."

Brumby turned to Bethancourt. "Where and when did you meet the deceased?" he asked.

"Just the other night," said Bethancourt. "I attended a cocktail party at the Heywoods' house. In Monkgate," he added to Mac-Donald, who smiled in acknowledgment. "Mr. Sanderson was present, and I was introduced to him there."

"Do you know these Heywoods well?" asked Brumby.

"I've known them a long time," said Bethancourt. "They're friends of the family, and I saw them regularly while I was at school here, but I haven't kept up since I left the area. But they're very sociable people—they tend to hold open house during the holidays."

Brumby glanced at MacDonald, who nodded and said, "Donald and Mary Heywood are leading citizens hereabouts, well known for their philanthropy and for their parties. A cocktail party of theirs would be an event Sanderson would have aspired to. I hear," and he raised an inquiring eyebrow in Bethancourt's direction, "that if you're generous in your donations to certain causes, it's not too hard to come by an invitation to the Heywoods', though it's far more difficult to breach the inner circle. But Sanderson likely wouldn't have known the difference."

"It's true enough," agreed Bethancourt.

Brumby was nodding as he absorbed this information. "And what did you make of Mr. Sanderson?" he asked.

Bethancourt thought for a moment before replying. "I took him for a self-made man," he answered, "and one who thought quite a lot of himself. He was commenting," he added, "on the Ashdon case when we were introduced, in fact."

"And?" asked Brumby.

Bethancourt smiled. "He was of the opinion that if only the media would stop covering such things, then the killer would give up murdering people."

"God, if only it were that easy," muttered Howard.

"Indeed," said Brumby. "Very well, Mr. Bethancourt, you've been very helpful. If you think of anything else, do let Sergeant Gibbons know."

"Certainly," said Bethancourt, recognizing a dismissal when he heard one and retreating toward the doorway. This time, however, he stopped in the hallway, hoping to catch Gibbons's eye. In a moment he succeeded, and his friend came out to him.

"What's up?" he asked. "Have you thought of something else?"

"No," answered Bethancourt, a trifle impatiently. "I just wanted to ask if you can get a ride home from somebody."

Gibbons was surprised. "You're leaving?" he asked.

Bethancourt gestured. "There's really nothing for me to do here," he said. "I don't know anything about serial killers, and I'm hardly likely to be helpful at a crime scene. And it'll be hours yet before you've got more information to share."

"True," said Gibbons, who had not thought of it in that light. "Yes, I expect anyone here will give me a lift back. You go ahead, and I'll let you know if anything exciting comes up."

"Thanks," said Bethancourt. "I'll see you later then."

Before Gibbons could turn back to the crime scene, he saw Brumby's forensics team arriving, led by Dave Mason carrying a formidable case, and went to meet them while Bethancourt made his escape.

"Sergeant Gibbons," said Mason, nodding a greeting. "Are we back there, then?"

"That's right," said Gibbons, gesturing. "Jim, you might want to talk to that gentleman napping there in the hall—he's the local electronics genius, and he's the one first spotted Ashdon's signature here."

"Good, good," said Jim, glancing back over his shoulder. "What's his name?"

"Biddulph," answered Gibbons. "Here, come along and I'll introduce you."

Gibbons was thoughtful as he returned to the crime scene, and he looked at the room with fresh eyes. It had never occurred to him before to think what an outsider would make of the slow progress of police procedure at a scene. To him, the room was burgeoning with hidden information that had to be carefully collected, and he knew as well as any trained detective that a foot put wrong at the crime scene could result in an unsolved or at least untriable case. But there was, he had now to admit, a certain tedium that accompanied all the details that had to be attended to.

Brumby, Howard, and MacDonald were still discussing the case, now having moved on to a scenario in which Ashdon had *not* committed this murder, and MacDonald was expounding on the wide range of suspects they would then have.

Gibbons moved up and asked, "Do you think there might be anything to the Mittlesdon connection in that case?"

MacDonald shrugged. "Doesn't seem likely, not at least from the point of view of motive. Sanderson made a lot of enemies on his way up, and he was known to be a rather abrasive sort. So far as I know, his only connection with Mittlesdon's was that he bought books there—hardly a motive for murdering the poor sod."

"And his nephew works there," said Gibbons.

MacDonald raised a brow. "Does he now?"

"Obviously," said Brumby, "our first step must be to either rule in or out the Ashdon angle. But if we conclude this *is* Ashdon's work, then, well, we'll have to look at people in Sanderson's life who fit our serial killer's profile."

He looked almost hopefully at MacDonald, as if this suggestion might prod the Yorkshireman into a sudden remembrance of a homicidal associate of Sanderson's. But MacDonald merely nodded thoughtfully.

"What's the setup here, by the way?" asked Howard. "I mean, who lives here besides the victim, who found him, all that kind of thing."

Automatically, MacDonald recited, "Sanderson lived here with his wife, Amy. Youngest daughter is currently in residence, though mostly she's away at university. There was a large party here for the holidays, but the last of them left for home yesterday. Tonight's the servants' night out, and Mrs. Sanderson and her daughter went out to a show in town. Because of the rain, they were planning to spend the night at the Sandersons' flat in York, but when Mrs. Sanderson couldn't get her husband on the phone, she became concerned and drove home after all. She's been sedated," he added. "She was quite overcome."

"It would be a disturbing sight for anyone," agreed Brumby, though Gibbons noted that Brumby himself did not appear to find it disturbing in the least. Nor, to be honest, had Gibbons, and he wondered at his own reaction. That made him think of Bethancourt again, and he was curious as to what his friend's feelings about it had been.

But his thoughts were interrupted by one of the forensics team, who rather pointedly began vacuuming for trace evidence on the carpet near their feet.

"Sorry, Syms," said Brumby. "Are we in your way?"

"It would be helpful if you could move into the hallway, sir," said Syms respectfully but firmly.

Brumby smiled at MacDonald. "Run off from my own crime scene," he said. "Let's adjourn, shall we?"

"Right," said MacDonald, pushing away from the chair back he had been leaning on. "If you're all finished here, I'll just give my lads the word they can take themselves off."

"Of course," said Brumby, leading the way out. "And naturally all our findings will be available to your people."

MacDonald bustled off back to the front of the house and his waiting team, while Brumby and Howard stopped just outside the door, ready to be called in if anything interesting turned up. But as the hours passed, not much that was worthy of note appeared. And Ashdon was notorious for leaving a very clean crime scene.

10

In Which Bethancourt Is Rudely Awakened, Gibbons Reaches the End of His Endurance, and They Both Take Naps

*B*ethancourt had indeed found the crime scene disturbing. Quite apart from the dead man himself, the whole room bore the stink of an unclean mind, and he had found the contact disquieting. He felt he had been somehow contaminated by the exposure, which was evidenced by the fact that, though it was close on 5:00 A.M. when he returned home and he was undeniably tired, he still felt it necessary to shower before seeking his bed. He was weary enough that, once there, he fell asleep almost instantly, but his dreams were restless and permeated with a vaguely threatening atmosphere.

All things being considered, it was not so very surprising that when his aunt stormed into his bedroom at eight the next morning, he was not only considerably startled, but also disoriented.

"I can't imagine what's wrong with you," she said.

Bethancourt started awake, heart pounding, and half sat up. He peered myopically at the figure marching into his room.

"Aunt Evelyn?"

"This is really unconscionable, Phillip," she continued, brandishing a sheet of paper in her fist. "How could you leave this kind of thing out for the children to find?"

Bethancourt was looking blearily about, trying to ascertain his place in the space-time continuum. "Aunt Evelyn?" he said again. "What are you doing here?"

This seemed to enrage her further. "You had better get yourself out of bed this instant," she said, "and get yourself downstairs to clean your mess up, young man."

"Yes, all right," said Bethancourt, hoping that agreement would make her go away.

"I never heard of such a thing," she fumed. "Leaving that kind of graphic display out where anybody could find it, much less impressionable children. I want it out of the kitchen at once."

And she stuck out the paper she held.

Bethancourt reached an arm out from under the covers and took it, squinting at it uncertainly. Without his glasses, he could not make out much, and all that he could think of was that he had certainly not been looking at pornography in the kitchen.

"I'll be right down," he said.

She did not seem in the least appeased, but the sight of his naked arm had brought her to the realization that her nephew had no clothes on and thus was hardly likely to get out of bed while she was in the room.

"I'll be waiting," she said, and abruptly turned and left.

Bethancourt sank back into the pillows, trying to force his brain into action and make sense of it all. A phone conversation with his father came back to him, and he cursed loudly. He had completely forgotten that his aunt was due in to take her daughter and friend back to school.

That just left the question of what all the fuss was about. He groped for his glasses on the nightstand, then refocused his eyes on the photograph he held. He was prepared, as unlikely as it seemed, to be faced with a graphic image of a naked woman, but what met his gaze was infinitely worse. It was the graphic photo-graph of a dead woman.

"Christ," he swore, flinging out of bed and grabbing his dress-ing gown. "The case files!"

He shoved his feet into slippers and went dashing downstairs, still tying up his belt as he went.

"So sorry, Aunt Evelyn," he said, making a beeline for the kitchen. "There was another murder last night, and Jack and I ran out without a thought. I'm afraid I didn't even remember it was today you were coming."

His aunt had never been one for excuses, though the apology seemed to count for something.

"Surely," she said, following him, "these files are confidential in any case. You shouldn't be leaving them about where anyone can find them."

"I didn't," replied Bethancourt shortly. "I left them in a locked private house."

"Where there were children," said his aunt indignantly.

"There weren't any when I went to bed," muttered Bethancourt, swinging off the last stair and moving rapidly down the passage to the kitchen door. Out of the corner of his eye he saw two heads peering out from the dining-room door and he stopped abruptly, startled, which caused his aunt to barrel into him.

"Phillip!" she protested.

"That's not Bernadette and her friend," he said, staring blankly at the now empty dining-room doorway.

Evelyn glanced back over her shoulder and frowned. "It must be the boys," she said. "I told them to go upstairs."

She took a step toward the dining room, but stopped as Bethan-court, now thoroughly bewildered, asked, "Boys? What boys? I thought you were bringing Bernadette and her little friend back for school."

"And Jeremy and Arthur," said Evelyn, and, when Bethancourt

looked blank, she added impatiently, "Humphrey's youngest sister, Denise's, children. You've met them."

"Oh, right," said Bethancourt, who dimly remembered a Christmas visit some years ago and two very small tow-headed boys. "They're that old already?"

Evelyn rolled her eyes at him and proceeded down the hall, calling sharply, "Jeremy! Arthur! Have you been back in the kitchen again?"

Bethancourt, momentarily reprieved, continued on to the kitchen, and swore when he opened the door and beheld the broad oak table.

Gibbons had, as he recollected, left a good half of it covered with notes and reports from the various case files, but there had been a kind of order to it, which he was certain they had not disturbed in the course of their hurried departure the night before.

It had been disturbed now. The reports had been tossed aside in the search to uncover the photographs of the bodies. There were, of course, other photographs as well, but it was naturally the ones of the corpses that intrigued the boys, and they had made a thorough mess of things to get to them.

"Dear God," said Bethancourt, stooping to pick up an errant lab report that had landed on the floor. "And all before coffee," he added, detouring to collect a sprawl of papers that had slid off one of the chairs.

He carried them over to add to the mess on the table, surveying the damage there and realizing with a sinking heart that all the files had been mixed together like shuffled playing cards. He was going to have to go through every sheet and determine which case it belonged to. He stared at it all for a long moment and then said firmly, "Not without a coffee first."

He was adding coffee to the pot and waiting for the kettle to boil when Evelyn came in through the butler's pantry, saying with a decided air, "That's the boys sorted—good Lord, Phillip, you haven't made a start at all."

Bethancourt regarded her with a baleful eye. "I was at a crime scene until five o'clock this morning," he said.

"That hardly means you can't clear away some papers," Evelyn retorted, moving to make the required start herself. "Really, Phillip, you may have become quite accustomed to this sort of thing, but you should remember most of us aren't so jaded."

"I am not accustomed to it," contradicted Bethancourt, who had set the coffee brewing and now went to help her. "This stuff gives me nightmares—or it would, if I'd had any sleep. No, just put it all in a pile and I'll take it upstairs to sort."

He made good his escape as quickly as he could, piling case files and coffeepot on a large tray and carting the whole thing up to the bedroom. He darted back out for a moment to peek into Gibbons's room, but, as he'd suspected, his friend was not there. He fled back to his own bedroom with a sigh of relief, closing the door firmly behind him. Cerberus, who had not moved from his bed in the corner, opened an eye.

"And a great lot of help you were," Bethancourt told the dog. "You might have warned me she was coming in."

Cerberus closed his eye again, and settled his nose under his tail. Bethancourt looked at his bed longingly, but decided he had better get Gibbons's files and notes back in order before the detective returned and wanted them. Resigned, he poured himself some of the coffee and then sat down on the floor with the stack of case files.

It took quite some time to sort them all out, and he could only hope that the boys had not absconded with any of the photographs. He decided, upon consideration, to leave the pictures till last, judging them to be too much for his newly opened eyes. He sipped his coffee and selected a forensics report from the pile: at the top of the page was a lengthy file number. He placed it on the carpet to his right, and next picked up several sheets stapled together. They bore a different number, so he set it to the left of the first page. And so on, and so forth, through the entire stack.

He did not read the reports, although he did not think Gibbons would have minded if he had. Still, a line here and there jumped out at him: "... body was arranged like a display ..."; "upon arriving at the crime scene ..."; "... chemical analysis of the stains found that ..."; "The victim was identified as Veronica Matthews, of number 4 Privet Drive ..."

Bethancourt frowned at that last one; the name struck a chord, but he could not remember where he'd heard it before. He skimmed over the sheet in his hand, discovering that Veronica Matthews had been Ashdon's first victim, her body found in the window of an antiques shop in Essex. So, very likely he had read about the murder in the papers. And yet, it seemed to him that he had heard it more recently than that.

"Jack probably mentioned it," he muttered, laying the report aside and reaching for the next one.

By the time he had got it all sorted, he had finished the pot of coffee he had brought up with him and was beginning to feel hungry. He dressed and went cautiously downstairs, finding to his relief that Evelyn had apparently taken the children out somewhere. He let Cerberus out into the rain in the back garden and found Gibbons just coming home, looking pale and tired.

"You're up," said Gibbons, surprised, as he bent to greet Cerberus and then hurried to join his friend in the shelter of the porch. "I thought you'd still be asleep or I would have rung."

"By all rights I should be asleep," said Bethancourt. "But we were invaded this morning by my aunt Evelyn, come to take the children back to school. Are you just coming back from Upper Poppleton?"

Gibbons shook his head. "We've been at the incident room for the last couple of hours, going over everything with London."

"Do they still think it's Ashdon?" asked Bethancourt.

"No one knows." Gibbons spread his hands. "It seems as if it must be, but it's so very unusual a development that nobody knows what to make of it. Brumby and his entire team are completely flummoxed."

"And what about the Mittlesdon case?" asked Bethancourt. "Do you think there's any connection?"

"Not likely, is it?" said Gibbons, staring out at the rain. "And yet . . ." He looked back at Bethancourt with a shrug. "Nobody else thinks so."

They looked at each other for a moment, then Bethancourt said slowly, "Still, it's a bit odd, you know, that they should both be connected to Mittlesdon's."

"I know." Gibbons sighed. "I keep thinking the same thing. But I'm damned if I can see *how* they're connected."

"I can't either," admitted Bethancourt.

"Well, it's on the back burner now, in any case," Gibbons said. "I've apparently been elected liaison between Brumby and Mac-Donald, and I've got to get back to it. I only came by to pick up my notes and computer. And," he added, "a change of clothes."

Bethancourt looked at him with some concern. "Are you going to be all right?" he asked. "You've only just come off the sick list, you know."

Gibbons brushed this aside. "I'll manage," he said. "A wash'll put me right."

"I'll put on some coffee whilst you change," said Bethancourt. "And I'm just about to make some breakfast—do you have time to eat?"

"It would be heaven," said Gibbons appreciatively.

Bethancourt whistled for Cerberus, and they turned to go inside, where Bethancourt got to work in the kitchen while Gibbons repaired upstairs. Bethancourt was not usually much of a breakfast eater, but little sleep and early rising had made him hungry and he thought Gibbons could probably do with a large meal. He was a good cook, and busied himself quietly, and when Gibbons came down he found a traditional English breakfast spread upon the kitchen table.

They were mostly silent as they ate, Gibbons because he was wolfing down his meal at a great rate, with one eye on the clock, and Bethancourt because he did not want to distract him.

"Thanks," said Gibbons at last, drinking off the last of his coffee and rising from the table. "That was marvelous. I'll ring you whenever I get a free moment and let you know how it's going."

"Right," said Bethancourt. "I'll see you later, then."

And Gibbons ran back out into the rain.

Left to himself, Bethancourt could not help but poke at the idea that Jody's murder and Sanderson's were connected. As he cleared away the breakfast dishes, he mulled over both cases, trying to determine if there was anything other than Mittlesdon's Bookshop to connect them. Not, he decided, if Sanderson's death was the work of Ashdon; in that case, Jody's murder stood out as an anomaly. But if Sanderson's was a more prosaic murder, perhaps there might be some tie between the two cases. It was then that he remembered that it was Sanderson's nephew, Tony Grandidge, who had introduced Jody to Mittlesdon's in the first place. It did not seem to be much of a connection, but it was worth looking into, he thought. So, when he had finished with the dishes, he rang the bookshop and asked for Alice.

"Did Tony Grandidge come in to work this morning?" he asked her.

"His uncle was killed last night," said Alice, sounding shocked. "Murdered."

"Yes, I know," said Bethancourt patiently. "It's why I was asking if he had come in."

"Oh!" said Alice. "Of course you would know, wouldn't you? I'm sorry—we're all feeling a little stunned here this morning. Yes, Tony came in. He said he'd rather keep his mind occupied."

"Perfectly natural," said Bethancourt. "I think I'll drop round—I have a quick question for him."

"Well, then, I'll see you when you get here," said Alice. She sounded as though she was anticipating a long discussion of this latest event.

"Er, yes," said Bethancourt. "Till then."

He rang off, shaking his head over Alice, and went to pull on a pair of Wellies and a coat before calling to his dog and leaving for the bookshop.

Bethancourt found Tony Grandidge working in the stock room amid stacks of boxes and carts half full of books. It seemed, at first glance, utterly chaotic, but as Bethancourt took it all in, he realized there was an order to it after all. Smaller and odd-size boxes, representing the special orders and rare books, were stacked by the door, ready to be taken up to the office, and were separated by addressee, while the larger boxes were divided between the used stock and the new.

Grandidge was sorting the books out of the boxes and onto carts, but he paused and looked up as Bethancourt came in, a puzzled frown on his face.

"Hullo," said Bethancourt. "They said I could come back and talk to you."

"I remember you now," said Grandidge, straightening and pushing a dark lock of hair out of his eyes. "You were in with that police detective. I'm sorry—I've forgotten your name."

"Phillip Bethancourt," said Bethancourt. "I heard about your uncle—I'm very sorry for your loss."

"Thank you," replied Grandidge automatically. He looked more baffled than grief-stricken, however, as he held a hand out to Cerberus. "It's been quite a shock. I don't know quite what to think about it. I mean, you don't expect people you know to get murdered, do you? First Jody, and now my uncle . . ." He shook his head.

"It helps sometimes to keep your mind occupied with mundane things," suggested Bethancourt, gesturing to the boxes stacked all around them.

"That's what I thought," said Grandidge. "And it's not as if they don't desperately need me—it's amazing how quickly things back up. All this," he waved around, "should have been out in the shop days ago, not to mention all those special orders. I mean, I know old Mittlesdon and Gareth would have taken on the receiving and sorting, but to tell you the truth, I'd really rather do it myself."

"Because you'd have to clear up after them when you did come back?" asked Bethancourt, his lips quirking in amusement.

"Too right," agreed Grandidge. He returned his attention to Bethancourt. "But you haven't come to have me tell you how to run a bookshop."

"No," said Bethancourt. "I came to ask about your uncle and Jody. Did they know each other?"

"They'd met," replied Grandidge. "I mean, they didn't know each other particularly well or anything, but Uncle Brian met her when she and I were going round together, and then of course they often saw each other here, in the shop." He paused, then added, "Jody loved to talk about books, and so did my uncle. They got on rather well, really."

Bethancourt nodded, absorbing the information.

"Why do you ask?" said Grandidge. "Do you think there's some connection between them?"

"I don't know," said Bethancourt honestly. "It doesn't look like it on the face of it, and yet, on the other hand . . ."

"It's quite a coincidence," finished Grandidge. "Here," he asked, almost desperately, "is there anything you can tell me? The police are being very closemouthed, and my aunt Amy is laid out. All we know is she came home last night and found him dead. And apparently there was no robbery or anything."

"So far as I know," said Bethancourt, "the police haven't yet settled on a theory. I'm afraid it's often like that, despite what one sees on the telly. But I think they believe it was a premeditated murder, which means they'll want to know about anyone who had it in for Mr. Sanderson."

Grandidge shrugged. "Then they'll have plenty to choose from," he said. "Uncle Brian was good at offending people. Although, if you're looking for someone who wanted Jody dead as well, then you're in for a struggle. As I told you before, I can't think of anyone who would have wanted to harm her."

"Which makes a connection even less likely," said Bethancourt. He hesitated. "Look here, I don't mean to be offensive or anything, but is there any possibility at all that your uncle and Jody, er, well, knew each other rather better than you were aware of?"

At first Grandidge looked merely blank, but then realization dawned and he laughed. "No offense taken," he said, "but no. Jody wasn't my uncle's type—he liked petite women. Her taste was more eclectic, but I never saw any evidence she fancied him."

"Oh, well," said Bethancourt, "it was only an idea."

And apparently not a very good one, he thought as he bade goodbye to Grandidge and wandered back out into the shop proper. He wondered if he was engaging in mental gymnastics, trying to connect the two cases merely because he really had no role to play in the investigation of Ashdon's crimes.

"Hello." Mittlesdon blinked up at him through his spectacles. "Mr. Bethancourt, isn't it?"

"Yes," admitted Bethancourt. "How are you, sir?"

"Very well, thank you," replied Mittlesdon automatically. "It's a great relief to have the shop open again."

"I imagine it is," said Bethancourt. "And business seems quite brisk."

"Well, people have been waiting for their orders, you see," said Mittlesdon. He hesitated. "Have there been any developments?" he asked. "I mean, in the, er, the—"

"The case," Bethancourt finished for him. "Yes, I think you could say there have been, but I'm afraid I can't discuss any of it. Police business and all that."

"Of course, of course," agreed Mittlesdon, but he asked anyway, "Do you think there's any chance of its being cleared up anytime soon?"

He looked so anxious that Bethancourt longed to be able to tell him they were on the verge of an arrest.

"I don't know," he said. "These things are hard to estimate. There's no doubt the police are a lot forwarder, but that doesn't mean they're ready to wrap the case up yet."

"I suppose these things take time," said Mittlesdon despondently.

"A bit," said Bethancourt. "But not forever. And there has been progress. You'll be able to put it behind you soon enough."

"Well, thank you for all you've done," said Mittlesdon vaguely, since he had no idea what exactly Bethancourt did do.

"Not at all," said Bethancourt, and they parted, Mittlesdon moving on to the stockroom and Bethancourt heading for the door lest he be stopped by anyone else and subjected to another awkward conversation.

But at the door he met Alice, just pulling on her gloves. She looked up as he approached and smiled brightly.

"Are you leaving?" she asked. "Me, too. I'll walk you up to the Stonebow."

Bethancourt accepted this suggestion politely and they set out. The morning rain had turned to sleety drizzle and they both tucked their scarves more tightly about their necks as they went.

"You don't think Jody was having an affair with Brian Sanderson, do you, Alice?" asked Bethancourt.

Alice seemed to find the idea amusing. "No," she answered. "Whatever put that into your head?"

"I'm just looking for any connection there might be between the two murders," answered Bethancourt.

"But why should there be one?" asked Alice. "Sanderson was a wealthy man with—according to Tony—quite a few enemies. Jody was just an assistant in a bookshop, and very well liked."

"When you put it like that, I don't suppose there's any reason a connection should exist," said Bethancourt. "And yet . . ."

"And yet you think there is one," finished Alice.

"I don't know about 'think,'" replied Bethancourt. "Maybe I'm just hoping that if such a connection exists, it might shed some light on Jody's murder."

Alice looked concerned. "It's not going to be one of those unsolved cases one hears about, is it?" she asked. "Because although we're all getting on with business so to speak, things will start to fall apart eventually if the truth never comes out."

"No," said Bethancourt slowly, considering. "I believe Jack will solve it in the end. Only just at the moment, he's been called off to other duties and I'm left feeling as if I'm holding the ends of too many threads, if that makes any sense."

They had reached the Stonebow and stopped on the corner, both of them turned with their backs to the wind whilst Cerberus sniffed at a lamppost. Alice had paused thoughtfully, and now looked up at him.

"There's something you haven't told me about Sanderson's murder, isn't there?" she asked.

"Lots of things," Bethancourt assured her. "It's not that I don't trust you, Alice—I'm simply not allowed to discuss it. If I did, there would soon be an end of my involvement with the police."

"No, I understand that," she replied. Suddenly she grinned. "I'll give you odds your parents keep urging you to join the force."

Bethancourt laughed. "You'd win that bet," he said. "Here, do you have time for a cuppa? I'd like to hear anything you think about Sanderson—you must have known him, didn't you?"

Alice nodded. "Not very well," she said as they turned to cross the street. "But he did turn up now and again. I know one shouldn't speak ill of the dead, but he really was the most frightful person."

"I gathered that from Daphne Stearn," said Bethancourt. "She was at the Heywoods' the night I met him."

"Yes, she keeps up with everything," agreed Alice with a laugh. "Ever since her husband died, she's had time to sit back and play the grand dame, and I must say it suits her very well. She has the most marvelous time at it."

"She seems to have developed a very mordant kind of wit," said Bethancourt.

"Oh, she always had that," said Alice. "She just didn't allow it full rein while Rory was still alive—no doubt he found it unlady-like."

They dodged around tourists who were snapping pictures of Whip-Ma-Whop-Ma-Gate and turned into St. Saviourgate.

"Was Mrs. Stearn's attitude towards Sanderson the prevailing one?" asked Bethancourt.

"More or less," said Alice. "There were some people who were impressed with him—he did have money, you know, and a certain kind of business savvy. But on the whole the old crowd found him rather vulgar. People like the Heywoods put up with him because he contributed handsomely to their charities, but they hadn't much use for him else."

"What about his wife?" asked Bethancourt.

"Nice county girl," replied Alice. "Amy Hugill. It's generally thought that she married him for his money, although of course he hadn't very much at the time. On the other hand, the Hugills had even less."

"I know what you mean," agreed Bethancourt. "That genera-tion of impoverished gentleman farmers encouraged their chil-dren to marry where there was a bit of brass, as the saying went."

"Exactly," said Alice. "Anyway, she hasn't done badly out of it, considering Sanderson went on to make a small fortune. I don't know how happy they were together, but the children seem to have turned out reasonably well."

"Here we are," said Bethancourt, fishing his keys out of his pocket. Then he remembered that the house might be occupied, and said, "I forgot to say, my aunt Evelyn may be here. I do hope you don't mind."

"Evelyn," repeated Alice thoughtfully. "Was that Neil's mother?"

"That's right," said Bethancourt, letting them in and shutting out the rain.

"I remember her," said Alice.

They had just removed their coats and Bethancourt was hanging them up when there was a knock at the door. "And that's probably my aunt now," he said resignedly, and reached to open the door.

But it was not Evelyn. Instead a vision stood there, a tall, willowy creature with a cloud of coppery hair and a creamy complexion.

For a moment, Bethancourt simply stared, stunned.

"Marla!" he said.

Wide, jade-green eyes went from him to Alice and back again, and then narrowed.

"Oh my God," said Marla.

"What are you doing here?" asked Bethancourt.

"You left me for *her*?" demanded Marla incredulously.

"What?" said Bethancourt, struggling to come to grips with the situation. "Who—oh, no . . . Wait a bloody minute, did you say—"

"Fine," said Marla icily. "I hope you're very happy with *her*."

And she turned on her heel and strode off. Bethancourt stared after her for an instant, looking decidedly perplexed and rather dazed, and then slammed the door shut.

"Who was that?" asked Alice, sounding almost awed.

"That," said Bethancourt grimly, "was my ex-girlfriend. And, just for the record, I did not leave her. It was quite the opposite way round. Here, let's get that tea."

"She looked a little familiar," said Alice, following him down the hall.

"You've probably seen her picture in some rag or other," said Bethancourt. "She's a fashion model."

"Oh!" said Alice, and subsided while Bethancourt seized the kettle and held it under the tap. He was quite consumed with fury and occupied himself with getting out the tea things until he had his temper under control.

"I'm very sorry for the interruption," he said, belatedly realizing an apology was due. "You mustn't mind Marla—she has a devilish temper."

"Oh, that's all right," said Alice rather feebly.

"Very good of you," said Bethancourt. "Now, where were we?"

"I really haven't the faintest idea," said Alice.

Neither had Bethancourt, but he was determined to soldier on.

"We were talking about Sanderson, weren't we?" he said, adding hot water to the pot. "What else do you know about him?"

Alice made a visible effort to drag her mind back to the topic at hand.

"The thing is," she said, "I only know him from the shop and from the occasional party. And however often he put a foot wrong socially, well, it's not the kind of thing one kills for, is it? Isn't the man you want far more likely to be an enemy Brian made on the business side?"

"You never can tell," answered Bethancourt thoughtfully. "It would seem so on the surface, certainly, but I've known things to turn out very differently to the way logic would seem to dictate. Anyway, I imagine the police have all that side of things in hand. Unless you know something yourself?"

Alice shook her head. She still seemed distracted. "No, nothing," she said.

Bethancourt poured the tea, but they appeared to have reached the end of the subject, and Alice seemed more interested in Marla than in murder. But Marla was not a topic Bethancourt was willing to discuss, so the conversation limped along until Evelyn returned with the children from a shopping expedition. She and Alice renewed their acquaintance and shortly afterward Alice excused herself. Bethancourt saw her out with some relief.

In his new role as liaison between Scotland Yard and the Yorkshire constabulary, Gibbons had been elected to accompany MacDonald to interview Sanderson's widow while Constable Redfern remained at the beck and call of Brumby. Privately, Gibbons thought he had the better part of the deal, though his abdomen was aching and getting out of the car without grunting was a real effort.

Amy Sanderson, after her gory discovery the night before, had retreated to her sister's house in Westlands Grove, where she had spent the night heavily sedated. She still looked drugged as she sat on the couch in the drawing room with her sister, Sylvia Grandidge, on one side and her daughter on the other. Jessica Sanderson, a second-year student at university, wore a frightened, vulnerable expression that made her look far younger, and her swollen, red-rimmed eyes betrayed the tears she had recently shed. Indeed, all three women clutched already-sodden handkerchiefs, twisting them unconsciously in their hands.

Gibbons, looking at them, wondered, as he often did, what the murderer would feel if he could be faced with this collateral damage. Had his hatred of Sanderson been so great that it enveloped even these pitifully grieving people? Or had they just not figured into his calculations at all?

MacDonald was gentle with them, more gentle than Gibbons would have believed him capable of. Amy Sanderson responded to his questions in a low voice as he took her step-by-step through the evening, all of it confirmed by her daughter. No, she had noticed nothing unusual before leaving the house, and her husband had seemed just as usual. In good spirits, actually.

"He's been in very good spirits lately," added Jessica. "I thought he seemed a bit anxious just around Christmas, but then he cheered up."

"He wasn't sleeping well," murmured Amy. "The night before Christmas, I mean. But you're right, he'd been back to his old self the last few days."

"Did you know of any reason he was uneasy at Christmas?" asked MacDonald. "A little concerned about money matters, perhaps?"

"Oh, no." Amy shook her head. "If anything, I spent a bit less this year than most. And the business was doing very well, I believe. No, I don't think it could have been money."

"But he didn't mention anything else?" said MacDonald. "An argument with a friend? Or maybe just the winter blues? It's been a very grey season."

Amy looked blank, and after a moment her sister answered, "I don't believe Brian was ever much bothered by the weather, was he, Amy? He wasn't that sort."

"And arguments never troubled Daddy," put in Jessica. "He liked to argue."

"Yes," said Amy. "Yes, he did. But I don't remember there being any particular difficulty with anyone lately. I've been busy, of course, with all the entertaining. . . ."

"So nothing out of the ordinary occurred lately?" said MacDonald.

Amy just shook her head.

"Now, about last night," continued MacDonald. "You and Miss Sanderson had theatre tickets, I understand?"

"That's right," said the sister. "We all did. It was sort of a girls' night out."

"I get you," said MacDonald genially. "So Mr. Sanderson never planned on joining you? I had misunderstood—thought you had taken his ticket when he decided not to come."

"No, it was always planned to be just the three of us," replied Mrs. Grandidge.

"How long ago did you purchase the tickets?" asked Mac-Donald.

Mrs. Grandidge looked at her sister. "When was it, Amy, do you remember? I know we talked about it while we were Christmas shopping that day in Coppergate."

"Yes," said Amy slowly. "I think I got them the next day. Yes, that's right. I finished up some shopping and bought the tickets before I headed back to Poppleton."

"And when was that?" pressed MacDonald.

"About a fortnight before Christmas," replied Sylvia. "I can't be more exact, I'm afraid—oh, but yes, I can. I kept all the receipts."

"It would be very helpful, ma'am," said MacDonald.

Mrs. Grandidge nodded and, with a reassuring pat on her sister's shoulder, rose and left the room. Amy Sanderson shivered as she left.

"So I expect," said MacDonald, "that anyone could have known you and your daughter would be absent from the house last night?"

"Yes, I suppose so."

"But they couldn't have known where Daddy would be," said Jessica. "He might have been here in town, or out somewhere. Or even had friends in."

"Yes, we believe it to have been a crime of opportunity," said MacDonald. "Was he planning to do anything in particular whilst you were gone?"

"He was going to watch the last Manchester United game," replied Amy. "He had it recorded—it was a very good match, you know."

And this recollection started her tears again, silent but copious. Jessica put an arm about her mother.

"I'm very sorry, ma'am," said MacDonald. "I didn't mean to upset you further."

Amy nodded her acceptance of this while she buried her face

in her handkerchief and her shoulders began to shake. Sylvia, coming back in at that moment, hastened to her side.

"I think I've got everything I need for the moment," said Mac-Donald quietly, as Amy's tears continued to fall.

"Yes, thank you, Superintendent," said Sylvia. "I think it might be best if she and Jessica went back upstairs. You know where the pills are, Jessie?"

Jessica, who was also crying now, nodded and helped her mother to rise and together they left the room.

"We were shopping on the twelfth," Sylvia told them. "So Amy would have purchased the tickets on the thirteenth."

MacDonald nodded. "I wanted to be sure," he said. "Almost anybody could have found out about your plans in the course of a fortnight."

"Well, yes. There wasn't any secret about them."

"Now, one last thing," said MacDonald. "Can you think of anyone who would have wanted to kill your brother-in-law?"

Sylvia made a helpless little gesture. "There were a lot of people who disliked Brian," she said. "But to go so far as to murder him? No, I can't think of anyone who would do that."

"How did you feel about him yourself?" asked MacDonald.

Sylvia hesitated. "He could be a bit abrasive sometimes, and he was generally not very sensitive to any kind of nuance—Brian was the sort you had to hit over the head with something to make him notice. But he was a good husband to Amy, and a good fa-ther, too. I can't say he was my favorite person, but, well, he was family."

"Of course," said MacDonald. "And family's something you don't get to choose. I understand completely. Thank you, Mrs. Grandidge," he added. "We appreciate your cooperation at such a difficult time."

"We want you to find who did this terrible thing, Superinten-dent," replied Sylvia. "Anything we can do to help, anything at all—don't hesitate to call on us."

After Alice had left, Bethancourt was free to let his rage with Marla run free. He spent a little time trying for dignity and resolutely ignoring her sudden appearance, but gave it up in the end.

It was clear to him that Trudy Fielding had tattled about his flirtation with Catherine Stockton, and that Marla, coming upon him in the company of a blonde woman, had assumed that Alice was she. But why Marla should care enough to come running up to York from her holiday in Kent, he could not imagine.

"It's no good," he said to himself. "I have to have it out with her."

He tramped over to The Dean Court Hotel in a fury, barely noticing the rain, and rang Marla's mobile once he was there. Since Trudy was staying in the hotel, he was relatively certain Marla would be there as well.

She answered at once in an angry tone, but he cut her off.

"I'm in the lobby," he said curtly.

There was a brief pause, and then she said, "Room 212," and rang off.

He took the stairs, mounting them two at a time, and paused when he emerged on the second floor to get his bearings. Almost immediately he saw Trudy coming down the hallway toward him.

She held up her hands in a gesture of peace. "I'm decamping to leave you two alone," she said. "Look, I'm sorry, Phillip, but I had to tell her. She's my friend."

"In which case," said Bethancourt coolly, "I would have thought it incumbent on her to inform you that she had broken up with me just before Christmas."

Trudy raised her eyebrows. "Wow," she said. "You two really do need to talk. Marla doesn't think you've broken up—or at least she didn't until today. Look," she added, forestalling any further comment from him, "you go on along and get it all sorted, right?"

She moved past him, and Bethancourt let her go, continuing on to room 212, where he rapped smartly on the door.

It swung open at once and Marla stepped back to let him in. Her jade-green eyes were snapping, but he was surprised to see that they were also reddened with tears. It took him aback and gave her the opening move.

"I don't know what you could possibly want," she said, swinging the door closed behind him with unnecessary force. "First you don't ring me on Christmas, then you won't answer my calls, and then I hear you're up here cavorting about with some blonde. My God, Phillip, she's not even attractive."

"Well, now you know how it feels," retorted Bethancourt. "I see you don't like hearing third-hand about my goings-on any better than I did about yours."

Marla's eyes narrowed. "Is that it?" she demanded. "Have you been conducting an affair with that woman just to pay me back?"

"Certainly not," said Bethancourt. "Whatever I've been doing has nothing whatever to do with you. I don't owe you any kind of accounting because you broke up with me. If you've come up here to try to reconcile, I must say you're going about it in a very bizarre manner."

Marla stared at him for a moment. "You're mad," she said. "I never called things off. Why the hell would I?"

"I had the impression it was because I had the temerity to demand that you be more discreet about your infidelities," said Bethancourt. "But you would know best."

They glared at each other.

"So this is still about that stupid thing with Jason," said Marla at last. "I was right—you're trying to get back at me."

"No, I'm not," contradicted Bethancourt. "I'm trying to move on without you."

"I apologized for the Jason business," Marla shouted at him.

"You did no such thing," said Bethancourt. "You called me an offensive bounder and said you hoped you never set eyes on me again. I remember it quite distinctly. There was no apology involved, unless your definition of the word includes calling people names."

"I may have said that," Marla admitted, "but you know perfectly well I never meant it."

Bethancourt raised a brow. "And how, exactly, do I know that? Look here, Marla, this situation is entirely of your own making and I refuse to either take the blame for it or jolly you out of your temper."

"Oh, so now it's my fault you wouldn't answer your bloody phone?" she demanded.

At this, Bethancourt lost his temper altogether. "Let's recap, shall we?" he said with an edge in his voice. "Not only did you sleep with that photographer, you went off with him in full view of the rest of the shoot, thereby making sure everyone would be gossiping about it. Then, instead of coming to me and explaining what had happened, you let me hear about it from some woman whose name I can't even remember. And when I asked you—quite politely, I think—to have a little more care for my feelings, you told me you never wanted to see me again. Until you're ready to take some responsibility for all that, I don't think I want anything more to do with you."

Marla had tried at several points to interrupt this narrative, but Bethancourt had shouted her down, and now, while she was continuing to argue, he simply turned and left the room. He heard her shouting something after him as he strode down the hall, but he ignored her and went down the stairs.

He was still furious as he returned to the house, never even noticing that the rain had picked up and he was getting drenched. He was even ready to take on his aunt if she should cross his path, but thankfully she had taken the children back out for more shopping, and the house was empty. He stormed upstairs and discarded his wet things, abruptly feeling very chilled and tired. Once he was dry and dressed in a pair of jeans and a heavy jumper, he sought out the kitchen and made a coffee, his temper now spent but his mind still turning the argument with Marla over and over, even though another part of him was thoroughly sick of it.

He suddenly wished he were at home, in London, where distractions beckoned at every corner and where he had a large collection of friends, as well as a local pub, a favorite bookshop, and a club.

"This really won't do," he told himself. "The point of being in York is to solve this murder, and you're no forwarder with that than you were this morning."

But there were now two murders, or three, if one counted Ashdon's latest victim. Or, if Ashdon had killed Sanderson as well as the girl in the accessory shop, there would only be two cases, though of course there would still be three deaths. It all made Bethancourt's head hurt. He took off his glasses and rubbed his eyes and remembered that he had had a bare three hours' sleep the night before. Perhaps his thinking would be clearer if he had a nap, not to mention that being unconscious would no doubt do away with troubling thoughts of temperamental redheads.

He was just heading for the bedroom when he heard the front door. Expecting it was Evelyn and the children, he was hastening his pace when he realized it was a single pair of heavy footsteps on the stairs. He peered over the landing.

"Jack!" he said, surprised. "I didn't think you'd be back yet."

Gibbons raised a pale face and gave him a weak smile. "I've been sent off home," he said. "Apparently, I look like death, and MacDonald rather abruptly remembered I'd been shot recently."

"Good man," said Bethancourt, looking a trifle anxiously at the labored way in which Gibbons was climbing the stairs. "Do you want anything? I'll make some lunch or bring something in if you like."

Gibbons shook his head as he finally stepped off the stairs. "I don't think I could stay awake long enough to eat it," he confessed. "I'm all in, Phillip."

"You look it," said Bethancourt frankly. "I'll let you rest then. In fact, I was about ready for a nap myself."

Still, he hovered in the hallway after Gibbons had gone in and closed his door, just to be sure his friend did not discover some need to be fulfilled. But, as all in the bedroom remained quiet, eventually his own weariness got the better of him, and he sought his bed.

It was early evening when he woke again, and already dark outside. The darkness confused him momentarily, but he sorted himself out soon enough and switched on the bedside lamp while he sat up and shook his head in an effort to banish the heavy, dull feeling a long afternoon nap sometimes leaves behind. From downstairs, he heard voices and sounds of activity—Evelyn and the children had returned, then.

He yawned hugely and then rolled out of bed, squinting as he felt for his glasses on the nightstand. As he splashed water on his face in the bathroom, he found that things had fallen into place in his mind while he'd slept. Or perhaps, he admitted ruefully, he had just been too tired to think productively.

In any case, it was now clear to him that if Sanderson had not been killed by Ashdon, then the usual rules applied: i.e., the first and most obvious suspect would be the spouse. Amy Sanderson, however, had been out in public with her daughter and her sister when her husband had died, leaving the second-most-obvious suspects: either a mistress or someone who would benefit monetarily from Sanderson's death. Bethancourt could hardly hope to discover anything pertinent about the man's finances, but gossip was easy to come by.

Downstairs, he found his aunt trying to make dinner whilst simultaneously arbitrating a dispute that had arisen between the boys. Bethancourt lent a hand and was rewarded with dinner, a portion of which was set aside for Gibbons. After he had helped Evelyn clear up after the meal, he returned upstairs to check on his friend, opening the bedroom door very quietly and peeking in. Gibbons, however, was still sound asleep, so Bethancourt retreated again.

After some deliberation, he decided he might venture out without shirking his duty as friend to the injured. Still, he wrote a note to let Gibbons know about the food left for him before he departed.

The Heywoods were not holding open house tonight, but Bethancourt doubted they would be alone. He was proved right when he rang the bell and was ushered into the drawing room to find a small gathering of the Heywoods' more intimate friends.

"Here's Phillip," announced Donald Heywood to the rest of the company. "Now we shall get some answers to our questions. What are you drinking, my lad? Scotch? Right you are then."

"Come sit by me," commanded Daphne Stearn, waving him over. "Just pull up that chair there. My hearing isn't so good as it once was, you know, and I don't want to miss anything."

Bethancourt obeyed good-humoredly, pushing the chair into position and saying, "I expect you want to know about the Sanderson murder?"

Daphne snorted, while on his other side Pamela Rimmington said, "Yes, we've all been talking about it. And Peter says you've been working with the police?"

She sounded a bit dubious, as if it passed all understanding that he should engage in police work, so Bethancourt smiled deprecatingly.

"I've a friend in the detective branch," he explained. "He likes to talk things over with me, get a civilian view point and all that."

"Here you are, Phillip," said Heywood, handing him his drink. "I've topped it up nicely, the better to loosen your tongue."

Bethancourt grinned and sipped.

"But seriously," said David Rimmington, leaning forward around his wife, "what do you know? It's quite the most shocking news I've heard all year, but nobody seems to know a thing about it. Was it a robbery gone bad?"

"The police don't believe so," answered Bethancourt, mindful of what he could and couldn't give away. "But, of course, there's been no inventory taken as yet, so that hasn't been ruled out altogether. At the moment, they're taking the view that it was a deliberate crime."

"He was a most detestable man," said Daphne, "but that's hardly reason to murder someone. Goodness, if I were to go about murdering all the unpleasant people I encounter, why, the population of York would drop by half."

Everyone chuckled.

"Only half?" asked Bethancourt, and she winked at him.

"Well," said Heywood, resuming his seat, "I expect poor Sanderson had more enemies than most. Not that he seemed to mind, I must say."

"So I hear," said Bethancourt. "But who and why exactly?"

"Oh, Lord, I don't know," said Heywood.

"I know Harry Wellbourne wouldn't have anything to do with him," said Mary Heywood. "Don't you remember, dear? There was that charity event when Mrs. Crowley put them at the same table."

"Oh, yes, quite a dust-up, that," said Heywood. "Very bad form."

"I believe," put in Peter Heywood, in an attempt to answer Bethancourt's question, "that was over some property. Wellbourne felt he'd been cheated, though I don't know the details."

"There was some bad blood in the city council, too," said Daphne. "Rory used to tell me about it. He said Sanderson took advantage wherever he could."

"He pushed Dora Heald out of her tea shop when he wanted to expand the carvery in Stonegate," said Pamela. "I did think he might at least have helped her relocate—she'd been there for years, after all."

Bethancourt nodded, making a mental note of all these incidents to report to Gibbons later.

"Surely," said Heywood with a laugh, "you're not suggesting poor Dora Heald murdered the man—she wasn't half his size."

"Well, Harry Wellbourne wouldn't hurt a fly," retorted Pamela.

"What about his personal life?" asked Bethancourt. "Any jealous husbands or angry fathers about?"

Daphne Stearn gave a peal of laughter. "Good heavens, no," she said. "You'd met the man—what woman would have him?"

"His wife, I imagine, for one," said Heywood dryly. "He wasn't so very bad-looking a chap, Daphne."

She shrugged to show her disagreement.

"I always liked Amy Sanderson," said Mary. "I can't say I know her well, but from all I ever heard, they were happy enough together."

"He wasn't known as a womanizer, one has to give him that," said Rimmington.

"If he was, he was damned discreet about it," said Peter. "There was a lot of talk about him, but I never heard anything of that nature."

"But, here, Phillip," said Heywood, "you've hardly told us anything. What on earth happened?"

"Is it true he was killed in the house?" chimed in Mary.

"Quite true," answered Bethancourt.

"But didn't the servants hear anything?" asked Pamela.

"It was their night out, I gather," said Bethancourt. "The last of the Sandersons' Christmas guests had left the day before, you see. Amy Sanderson and her daughter had gone to a show, so Sanderson was alone in the house. The police are working on the theory that the murderer saw his chance and took it."

"And a rare chance it was," said Daphne. "From all I could make out, the man was perennially incapable of spending time by himself. I'm surprised he didn't take himself off to the nearest pub."

"Now, Daphne," chided Mary, "that's not fair. Lots of people go out a lot."

Daphne sighed. "I didn't like him," she said. "I suppose I rather resent having to feel sorry for him now he's been murdered. I much preferred poking fun at him."

"I don't know as your sorrow has been very noticeable," said Heywood with a grin to take the sting out of the words.

"Ah, well." Daphne shrugged.

They had a great many more questions, but Bethancourt, having revealed as much as he dared, managed to fend these off successfully and steer them back to gossip about Sanderson.

At least, he thought, as he wound his way home—once again feeling rather tipsy—he had managed to find a few nuggets that Gibbons might find useful in his investigations.

The rest of the house was asleep when he arrived back in St. Saviourgate. Gibbons's portion of dinner remained uneaten in the refrigerator, and when he checked on his friend upstairs, he found him still fast asleep, with no sign he had awakened during his host's absence. So Bethancourt removed the note he had written earlier and substituted one containing the gossip he had gathered at the Heywoods'. That done, he let Cerberus into the garden and smoked a cigarette while the great dog attended to business. The night sky was dark and there was a gusty northwest wind which blew splatterings of rain on him, the harbinger, he was sure, of more to come.

11

In Which the Investigation Becomes Waterlogged

*G*ibbons slept through the night, logging a solid fourteen hours' sleep and waking more or less refreshed. He arose feeling enormously hungry and very eager to discover what progress had been made in the investigation during the night. Bethancourt was still abed, and Evelyn was getting the children up and ready for their return to school, so after he had washed and dressed, Gibbons escaped the chaos of the house and went out to breakfast. He took with him a note he had found on the dresser from Bethancourt and read it over his meal, committing most of the sketchy details to memory.

He was among the first to arrive at the station, where he typed up the gist of Bethancourt's note for the case file while he waited for everyone else to arrive. Detective Inspector Trimble wandered in first, holding tightly to a take-away coffee; he mumbled good morning and slid into a chair in front of his computer monitor.

Redfern came in soon after, with MacDonald in his wake, both of them puffy-eyed and not quite awake.

"Brumby not here yet?" MacDonald grunted. "Well, no matter. What have you got there, Gibbons?"

"Just some gossip from some of the local worthies, sir," he answered. "I don't know if any of it's worth checking out or not."

"Let's have a look," said MacDonald. He took the sheet and ran his eyes down it while he sipped at his coffee. "Mm, yes, we've got some of these names already. But add the other ones on, by all means. In fact, you and Redfern here can get busy collecting alibis from all these fellows. You have the list, Redfern?"

"Yes, sir," said Redfern. "I'll have to find addresses for these new ones, though."

But MacDonald waved him off. "You'd best get started," he said. "Rowett can dig the addresses out when he gets here—that man's a bloody marvel at the computer. Call in when you've finished with the first lot and I'll have the rest for you. Or somebody will—Brumby and I are off to see Sanderson's solicitors as soon as their offices open."

"Right you are, sir," said Redfern, yawning. "Should have known," he muttered to Gibbons as they turned and left the incident room. "Nasty, raw morning—I would get sent back out in it."

"I'm not looking forward to tramping about all day in the rain," agreed Gibbons.

Redfern glanced at him. "How are you feeling?" he asked. "You looked pretty ragged yesterday."

"I'm fine," Gibbons assured him. "All I needed was a bit of rest. What're these alibis we're supposed to be collecting?"

Redfern took his notebook from his breast pocket and pulled a sheet of paper out of it.

"Here you go," he said. "It's a list of Sanderson's enemies—we spent most of yesterday evening putting it together. Not," he added, "that anyone thinks it's complete. And if your Brumby is right, and Ashdon killed the fellow, then it's all for naught in any case."

"You never can tell," said Gibbons, pausing and looking at the list. In a moment, he handed it back. "I've no idea where most of these places are," he said. "Shall I drive, and you can direct?"

"Sounds fine to me," replied Redfern. "I'd be grateful for the rest. Good God," he added as they came up to the outside door. "I think it's actually raining harder, if that's possible."

"Here's for it," said Gibbons, turning up his collar. "Where's the car?"

"Over there," answered Redfern, pointing.

And with that, the two young men dashed out into the rain.

It was still raining when at last they returned that afternoon, having interviewed not only everyone on their list but several other people suggested by those they had spoken with, plus a few added on when they rang in to the incident room.

"Do you suppose," said Redfern longingly as they emerged from the police panda and hunched against the cold, sleety rain, "that they'll at least let us have lunch before they send us back out?"

"I certainly hope so," said Gibbons. "I can't think how it got so late."

"I don't know either," said Redfern as they came up to the door. "It all seemed to go quickly enough—in and out, collecting alibis and moving on."

Inside, the hallways were awash with activity, and Gibbons and Redfern, breathing a sigh of relief as they were enveloped in the warmth of the central heating, were swept up in it as they made their way to the Sanderson incident room.

"Hullo, Henry," said Gibbons to a middle-aged man who was walking in their direction, frowning over a sheaf of papers as he went. "How's it going at your end?"

"Eh?" Henry paused and peered over the tops of his glasses. "Oh, Jack, is it? It's going well enough, I suppose. At least, it's a bit confusing just at the moment."

Gibbons was intrigued. Henry Collins was the Yard's financial man and he was not normally confused. More often he was to be found clucking his tongue over the nefarious financial activities of those he was investigating.

"Sanderson not paying his taxes?" asked Gibbons.

"Oh, no, I think he was," answered Collins. "No, it's not that. The accounting all looks quite aboveboard really. It's just that there's not quite enough of it."

Gibbons exchanged glances with Redfern, who only raised his brows and shrugged.

"How do you mean, Henry?" he asked.

"Not sure yet," said Collins, looking back at his papers. "But there's income, and then there's the outgoings. And the bills have been paid, but the accounts don't seem to have been debited. Or at least not in all cases. I'll work it out eventually, though."

"I never doubted it," said Gibbons.

They had reached the door of the incident room, and Gibbons reached to hold it for the older man, who nodded absently in return.

"What do you make of that?" Redfern asked Gibbons as Collins veered off to a computer terminal in one corner while they made their way to the back of the room where Brumby and Mac-Donald were conferring.

"He suspects Sanderson may have had an outside source of income," replied Gibbons. "Of course, it may be perfectly legitimate, just something Sanderson kept apart from his regular finances. But if it's not, if it's unexplained cash . . ." Gibbons trailed off, a thoughtful expression on his face.

Redfern looked doubtful. "I really don't think Brian Sanderson was a secret drug baron," he said.

"Hmm?" said Gibbons, recalling himself. "Oh, now there's an idea. I was actually thinking of blackmail."

Redfern considered this for a moment. "I would have thought," he offered, "that Sanderson was more likely to be blackmailed than to extort it from someone else."

"But would he be capable of blackmail?" asked Gibbons.

"I can't say no," said Redfern. "Although of course I didn't know him well."

"Blackmail?" echoed MacDonald, looking up as the two young men approached. "You think Sanderson was a blackmailer?"

"We were only speculating on possible sources of extra income," replied Gibbons. "Henry thought Sanderson might have been making a bit on the side—he's not sure yet, though."

"Was Sanderson the type who would blackmail someone?" asked Brumby.

"Sure," answered MacDonald. "So long as he could work out a reason it was justified, I can't see him balking at a bit of extortion. But that leaves your Ashdon out in the cold—Sanderson didn't have very high principles, but I don't think he'd have kept quiet about a murder."

Brumby sighed. "It's hell, not knowing where we are. I wish forensics would get a move on."

"Well," said Gibbons, "whether he was a blackmailer or not, I don't think any of the people we talked to this morning killed him. Some of their alibis will need checking, of course, but they seem pretty straightforward. Only this Louis Orgill doesn't have one worth mentioning."

"Orgill?" said Brumby. "Which one was he?"

"He's an estate agent," supplied Redfern. "There was bad blood between him and Sanderson over a couple of deals back in 2003."

"Doesn't seem very immediate." Brumby grunted.

"It's early days," said MacDonald. "We'll put Orgill in the 'maybe' column. What does he say he was doing last night, by the way?"

"Spent the night at home alone, watching telly," answered

Gibbons. "His wife and daughters are off visiting her mother in Essex, and they have no live-in servants."

"Well, and he probably did do," said MacDonald, shaking his head. "Never mind—the most obvious suspects had to be looked at." He cocked his head at Brumby. "If I'm to interview the sister, shall I take the sergeant here with me, in the spirit of joint cooperation and brotherly love? I'll leave you Redfern in turn."

Brumby's lips twitched in a smile. "By all means, Superintendent," he said.

"Come along then, lad," said MacDonald, clapping Gibbons on the shoulder.

Gibbons hid a sigh, thinking of the coffee he would not now have time for, and fell in behind MacDonald.

"Who are we going to see, sir?" he asked.

"Sanderson's sister," replied MacDonald. "Name of Lydia—she lives alone out in Nun Monkton. Bit of an oddball, so I understand, and just the opposite of her brother—reticent where he was expansive and so on."

"I see," said Gibbons. "Is she a suspect?"

MacDonald snorted. "Everybody's a suspect, lad." He glanced back at Gibbons, who was frowning as he went through his pockets. "Lose summat?"

"I think Redfern must have the panda keys," answered Gibbons, drawing up. "I'll run back and fetch them."

"Nay, don't bother." MacDonald looked amused. "I'm not riding around in that little bit of a thing in this weather—we'll take my Land Rover. And I'll be doing the driving, Sergeant—it takes a countryman to get along on these roads. Let's make a dash for it then."

Bethancourt had planned to have a lie-in that morning, but was thwarted by his aunt, who saw no reason why he should not help her install the children at St. Peter's.

He had not slept well, having been plagued with visions of Marla, and did not wake well, having something of a hangover from the scotch at the Heywoods'. He was thus impatient with his charges as he tried to settle the two girls into their house, earning him disapproving looks from the housemistress.

"Did you say Mrs. Keems would be checking in as well?" she asked with steely politeness.

"That's right," said Bethancourt, who was carting in a large trunk and not inclined to stop. "She's just seeing to the boys over the way."

The housemistress's eyebrows rose. "Boys?" she asked. "I was not aware the Keems had any boys at school here at this time."

"They're not hers," retorted Bethancourt, and turned his back on her to heave the trunk up the stairs.

He escaped as rapidly as he could, electing to have Bernadette tell Evelyn he had left rather than telling his aunt himself, and set out to walk back to St. Saviourgate. It was a walk often undertaken in his youth and still tolerably familiar, but one that was just long enough to leave him completely drenched by the time he reached his front door.

He had planned to go back to bed, but a glance at the bags assembled in the hall told him his aunt would be returning before setting out for Ilkley, and he knew she would be in no very good temper with him. The better part of valor, he decided, would be to be absent when she arrived. So he changed into dry things, collected a large umbrella from the assortment in the hall stand, and set out for Mittlesdon's. He did not actually expect to garner any information there, but it had the advantage of being close-by and provided a convenient excuse for his absconding from his aunt at St. Peter's.

It was still raining in earnest, so he left Cerberus at home since otherwise the big dog's first act on entering the bookshop would be to give a mighty shake, liberally coating everyone and everything with a spray of water. Cerberus, having poked his nose outside, did not seem to mind.

The bookshop was quiet. Libby Alston was ringing up a customer's order at the counter while Rod Bemis shelved books in the narrow hallway beyond. It seemed unbelievably peaceful to Bethancourt, who propped his umbrella by the door, nodded to Libby, who smiled back, and then wandered in past the bestseller displays in search of nothing more than idle diversion. He turned toward the stairs that led to the children's section and Catherine's office above, pausing to examine the framed photographs that were clustered on either side of the doorjamb. He had looked at them, he remembered, on that first day in the shop with Gibbons, but at that time he had not known any of the principals, other than the more famous authors represented. Or at least he hadn't thought he knew any of them. Catherine Stockton was very prominent in a photograph with Brian Jacques, and Alice was pictured in two of the others, though he did not blame himself for failing to recognize her with only his memory of an eighteen-year-old girl to go on.

"Jody isn't in any of them, you know," said Libby Alston softly from behind him.

He turned to smile down at her.

"No," he said, "I don't see her. There's you there, though."

He pointed to an older photograph, in which several members of the staff were pictured with an upright middle-aged man Bethancourt did not recognize.

"That's Malcolm Neesam," said Libby, "the Harrogate historian. It's funny you should pick that photograph—if I remember aright, it was Jody who took it."

Bethancourt looked back at the picture with renewed interest.

"And I remember the occasion rather well," continued Libby with a laugh. "You can't see it because Veronica's sitting in front of me, but I was pregnant with my youngest at the time."

Bethancourt froze, struck for the third time by the old-fashioned name, and this time he remembered where he had encountered it before. He pushed his glasses back up on the bridge of his nose and peered at the very ordinary English girl seated in front of Libby Alston in the photograph.

"That's Veronica?" he asked. "Didn't Alice tell me something had happened to her?"

"Yes, it was very sad," said Libby. "She had been gone from here for some time by then, of course. Oh, excuse me—there's a customer waiting."

"Wait—" yelped Bethancourt, swiveling around, but she was already bustling off. "Damn," he muttered. He thought for a minute and then went off in search of Alice.

After scouring most of the endless rooms, he found her on the top floor, shelving a carton of used books. The room was rather dim, giving it a musty air, and the rain beat against the old-fashioned mullions in a steady tattoo. Alice sat near one corner on a footstool with the box of books beside her on the floor. She looked up from her work as he came in, but when she saw who it was, she smiled with a distinct lack of enthusiasm.

"Hullo," he said. "I've been looking for you."

"Oh, hello," she said, and looked back at the book in her hands.

Undaunted, he squatted beside her in one smooth movement.

"I need to ask you something, Alice," he said.

She gave a little laugh, but it had a desperate sound to it, and her eyes as she looked at him were tinged with sadness.

"I can't do that anymore, you know," she said.

"Eh?" he asked, taken aback. "Do what?"

"Get down on the floor so easily like you just did," she answered. "How did you stay so young while I got so old?"

"What?" he said, feeling completely at sea. "Alice, what are you talking about? We're exactly the same age—we always have been."

"No." She shook her head. "No, we're not, not in the ways that matter. I realized that when I met your Marla."

"I told you not to take any notice of her," said Bethancourt.

"She has atrocious manners. Look here, Alice, can we talk about this later? I really need to know something."

Alice waved a hand. "Oh, don't mind me," she said unconvincingly. "What did you need?"

"This Veronica girl who used to work here," said Bethancourt. "What exactly happened to her?"

It was Alice's turn to be surprised. "She was murdered," she answered. "Didn't I tell you that?"

"I think you did, but I wasn't paying proper attention," said Bethancourt. "Tell me again."

"I don't really know that much about it," said Alice. "Veronica worked here for a year or so, maybe less, and then she moved south to take care of her mother or aunt—some elderly relation at any rate who needed someone to live in. She'd been gone for some months when we heard she'd been murdered. They thought it was by a boyfriend at first, but then it turned out to be a random crime."

"Do you remember any other details?" asked Bethancourt.

"I'm afraid not," answered Alice. "None of us had kept up with her after she left the area—we were all shocked to hear she was dead, but all I remember now is that it was a very gory killing. Why is it important?"

"I'm not sure that it is yet," said Bethancourt. "I've got two more questions. When was she killed?"

"Oh, two or three years ago now," said Alice, who had been drawn out of her funk and was now evincing curiosity. "What's the other question?"

"What was Veronica's surname?"

"Oh dear." Alice frowned in an effort to remember. "Matthews, I think," she said in a moment. "Something like that at any rate. Phillip, what's this all about?"

"I don't know what it all means yet," said Bethancourt. "But I think your Veronica was Ashdon's first victim. That's not for publication, though."

Alice's eyes had widened. "No," she said. "No, of course not. I understand."

Bethancourt leaned forward and kissed her cheek.

"Thank you, Alice," he said. "I promise we'll talk later. Right now, I have to ring the police."

He rose and strode swiftly out of the room and in a moment she heard him clattering down the stairs.

Gibbons was at that moment sitting in the Land Rover with an extremely frustrated MacDonald. Nun Monkton, the small village to the northwest of York where Brian Sanderson's sister lived, lay at the confluence of the Nidd and Ouse rivers, neither of which was cooperating with MacDonald's plans. The torrential rains which had begun yesterday had continued throughout the night and were still pouring down, causing the rivers to flood their banks and, indeed, making rivers out of any low-lying bit of roadway. If there was a way through at one place, it was blocked farther on, and MacDonald, who knew his patch intimately, was aggravated by the fact that even he could not find a water-free route to Nun Monkton. He and Gibbons had now spent quite some time in driving this way and that, trying to come at the place from different angles, but MacDonald had at last had to admit defeat. It had not put him in a good temper.

"What the bloody hell is that?" he demanded, as Gibbons's mobile began beeping. His tone was that of a man who suspected that someone else had found a way to get to Nun Monkton.

"It's just my phone," replied Gibbons, who had decided the best way to deal with MacDonald in a temper was to say as little as possible in a calm, even tone. "It's only my friend Bethancourt," he added, closing the phone again.

"Well, you might as well answer it," said MacDonald. "For all you know, he's sitting in Nun Monkton having tea with Lydia Sanderson."

"I'm pretty sure he's stuck in York with the rest of us," said Gibbons genially, but he obediently flipped the phone open and scrolled down to Bethancourt's name.

"Are you alone?" asked Bethancourt when he answered.

"No," said Gibbons. "Superintendent MacDonald and I are on our way back to headquarters."

"Oh," said Bethancourt.

"You aren't by any chance in Nun Monkton having tea with Lydia Sanderson, are you?" asked Gibbons.

MacDonald snorted loudly.

"What?" demanded Bethancourt. "Why on earth would I be in Nun Monkton? And who is Lydia Sanderson?"

Gibbons sighed. "I thought not," he said.

"Then why did you ask?"

"Just to eliminate a possibility," said Gibbons. "What did you want?"

"I've got news," said Bethancourt, a little hesitantly. MacDonald was, to him, an unknown factor, and he didn't like to have the distinction made between what he came up with and what Gibbons discovered himself.

But Gibbons was impatient. "Well?" he demanded. "Are you going to tell me what it is, or am I supposed to guess?"

Bethancourt threw caution to the wind. "It's about Veronica Matthews," he said, "Ashdon's first victim."

"Right," said Gibbons. "I'd forgotten the name. What about her?"

"She used to work at Mittlesdon's," Bethancourt told him.

There was a moment's stunned silence before Gibbons said sharply, "What?"

"I know," said Bethancourt, answering the feeling rather than the sense of the question. "I don't know what to make of it either. But surely it's too fantastic to be a coincidence."

"No," said Gibbons flatly, "it can't possibly be coincidence. How did you find out?"

Bethancourt briefly ran through the events that had led up to his discovery, ending with, "So Veronica had been living down there for less than a year before she was killed."

"Yes," said Gibbons. "I remember that. But it was assumed her killer—they weren't calling him Ashdon yet, then—had stalked her there, in Essex. The Yorkshire angle was never investigated to my knowledge, though I'll have to check with Brumby about that. I don't think his team was brought in until after the second murder."

"But Ashdon doesn't kill his victims in situ," said Bethancourt. "And Jody was definitely killed in the bookshop."

"I know," said Gibbons, who was as perplexed as Bethancourt at this piece of news. He was also acutely aware of MacDonald's growing impatience beside him. "Let me pass this on," he said, "and we'll talk later."

"Right," said Bethancourt at once. "Ring me when you can."

"That friend of yours seems to make himself very useful," said MacDonald as Gibbons rang off.

"He likes to take an interest," said Gibbons distractedly. "Sir, he's just found out that Ashdon's first victim worked at Mittlesdon's."

MacDonald squinted at him. "I think I would have remembered if a serial killer had struck on my patch," he said.

"No, not here," said Gibbons. "She had left Mittlesdon's and gone to live in Essex before she was killed. I don't remember exactly, but I think the case file said she had been living with her grandmother there for about five or six months when she was murdered."

MacDonald was silent as he guided the Rover through the rain.

"But Brumby—and you yourself, Sergeant—were sure that Jody Farraday hadn't been killed by Ashdon."

Gibbons spread his hands. "I know, sir."

"Good Lord, but it's a lot of killing for a respectable bookshop," said MacDonald. "I'm beginning to suspect Mittlesdon is running an assassin's agency on the side. All right, Gibbons, you had better ring Brumby. Tell him we're coming into town now—it won't be long before we're back at the station."

They were already embroiled in the city's traffic, coming off the A59 and poking along Nunnery Lane on their way to Skeldergate Bridge.

"Always providing the damn bridge isn't under water," added MacDonald glumly.

But although the Ouse was running high, it had not yet swamped the bridge, and they crossed safely over and turned south for the station.

There was a lull in the constant hum of activity in the Sanderson incident room. At the back of the room, to one side of the whiteboard, Brumby set the phone gently in its cradle and stared thoughtfully out into space.

The first results of the forensics tests were beginning to come in, and, according to his experts, the crime scene was remarkably clean. The phrase was one he had come to dread, since it accompanied every confirmed killing by the Ashdon serial murderer.

But the Sanderson murder was not part of the pattern. Brumby had been profiling and investigating serial killers for most of his career, and although he had learned to expect the unexpected, he had never before come across such a break in a killer's pattern. This murder, if it had indeed been committed by Ashdon, was special. And Brumby was excited by it, because it gave them a connection to Ashdon apart from his psychosis; it was a part of Ashdon's regular existence, the one filled with co-workers and neighbors and perhaps even friends who knew nothing about the man who stalked women, selected his victims, and then, after judicious torture, murdered them.

While MacDonald looked for more ordinary motives for Brian Sanderson's murder, Brumby had been on the lookout for anyone connected with the dead man who would fit the profile he had developed for Ashdon: a very bright man, mostly a loner but with a need at times to show off his cleverness to other people, a true psychopath who probably was truly unaware that he was not close to anyone. But so far there had been no one.

All the men (and for that matter, the women) on whom suspicion had thus far fallen were well-established people with families. None of them, in Brumby's opinion, showed much sign of psychopathy, nor did they appear to have another significant trait of Ashdon's: a strong creative streak.

From the very first, the way Ashdon arranged his victims had struck Brumby as artistic; the man had the same kind of visual sensibility and awareness of spatial relationships as a stage director. He certainly had a flair for dramatics. Brumby believed he was looking for someone who could not repress the creative spark, even if his day-to-day job was a humdrum one.

But psychopaths did not have ordinary motives for murder. Ashdon might have killed Sanderson over something anyone else would consider quite trivial. If, of course, Ashdon was the murderer. And there was Brumby's problem in a nutshell: did he spend time, men, and money on what could very well turn out to be a dead end, or did he concentrate his resources on the crime that he was certain Ashdon had committed?

It was, in the end, a gut decision. And Brumby's gut told him he had just stumbled onto the greatest piece of luck possible.

He tapped his fingers absently on the desk and then jerked to attention as his mobile rang. Frowning a little at being interrupted, he answered it rather brusquely.

Halfway down the room, DI Howard was collecting faxes. He didn't know why, in the midst of skimming over the pages as they came off the machine, he looked up at Brumby. But when he saw the look of intensity on his superior's face, he knew what it meant. He was already moving toward the superintendent by the time Brumby clicked off his mobile and called for his second in command.

12

In Which Aunt Evelyn Graciously Contributes

*M*acDonald and Gibbons were borne into the station on a great gust of wind and rain, leaving puddles in their wake as they hurried down the hall. MacDonald was accosted by several underlings almost as soon as he was in the door, but he did not pause in his march down the corridors, merely gathering them to him like a pied piper of police detectives. He seemed to pay scant heed to what they said, however.

"You there, Brummet," he said, picking one out from the crowd. "There'll be a fellow called Phillip Bethancourt arriving in a few minutes. Go nab him when he comes and bring him to the Sanderson incident room."

"Yes, sir," said Brummet. "Er, sir, I did want—"

"Later, Brummet, later. Fetch Bethancourt first."

"Yes, sir."

Brummet ceded the argument and dropped behind. One by one MacDonald deflected the others until, by the time they reached the Sanderson incident room, he and Gibbons were again alone.

They walked into an almost silent room in which the intensity was palpable. Everyone sat hunched over the long tables, so fiercely focused on case files and computer monitors that no one even looked up at their entrance. Brumby alone seemed to notice their presence; he beckoned to them impatiently from the far end of the room.

"Good work, good work," he said as they came up, but there was a perfunctory quality to his tone. He was like a hound who had found a scent, only he was keeping himself tightly leashed, narrowing his focus down to laser sharpness.

"No work of mine." MacDonald grunted.

"Or mine," chimed in Gibbons hastily before Brumby could make the assumption. "My friend Bethancourt found out about it while he was at Mittlesdon's."

Brumby's eyebrows rose. "Is that the fair chap who was at the crime scene the other night?"

"Yes, sir," said Gibbons, trying not to sound defensive.

Brumby's glance was calculating, as if he was debating the necessity of delivering a lecture about communicating privileged information to civilians.

But MacDonald stepped into the breach. "I've told him to get himself down here right smartly," he said. "He should be along any minute now."

Brumby nodded briskly. "Good, good," he said. He indicated the reports laying open on the table in front of him. "This is the original case file on Veronica Matthews," he told them. "There's no mention of Mittlesdon's at all—just," and he selected a sheet of paper, tilting his head back to focus through his reading glasses, "that she held 'a series of retail jobs in York.' But it's the same woman," he added, setting down the paper. "It only took Andy about five minutes at his computer to verify that."

"Was she from this area?" asked MacDonald.

"No," responded Brumby. "She lived here less than a year. She was just one of those ordinary, feckless young people who are out to have a good time before they settle down to producing a family. She was brighter than most, which meant she never wanted for work, but there was nothing else special about her. She came to York with a boyfriend—one Ben Williams—who told the original investigator that she first got a job at Evans in Coppergate Walk. Their relationship didn't last, though, and he didn't know where she went after she left there."

MacDonald had raised an eyebrow. "I take it this Williams was looked into?" he asked.

"Oh, yes." Brumby gave him a wry smile. "Probably had the life scared out of him, but there was nothing to find. Most of the investigation focused on Essex, where she was living when she was killed and where she was originally from." He gestured around the room. "I've got everyone looking back through the Ashdon file to see if any of his other victims had a York connection, but there's nothing so far."

"It's a surprise, that's for sure," said MacDonald. "I can't recollect the last time I was this flummoxed by a turn in a case." He reached for one of the chairs tucked neatly beneath the table and dragged it over to face Brumby's seat. "Ah, that's better," he said, settling himself in. "Get yourself a seat, Sergeant, and we'll hammer this thing out."

Gibbons obeyed with alacrity, before anyone could suggest that he should be given some routine parcel of background work to do. It was not often, he thought, that a mere sergeant got to sit in on a brainstorming session with two superintendents.

And, it turned out, an inspector. DI Howard, seeing that a conclave was beginning, came over from where he was working at one of the computer terminals to join them, taking the empty chair next to Brumby's.

"So," said MacDonald to Brumby, "what are you thinking? Were all these murders committed by Ashdon?"

"It's possible," answered Brumby. "The Accessorize murder is most definitely Ashdon's work. The Sanderson murder—well, we haven't all the forensics back yet, but from what has come in, it looks very like an Ashdon crime scene. But the Mittlesdon murder doesn't seem to fit in."

"Not that we're ruling it out altogether," put in Howard. "Unlike any of the other murders, the one at Mittlesdon's appears to be totally unpremeditated, which might account for the difference."

Gibbons was glad to hear that Jody's case was still being considered, although he said nothing. In this sudden spate of serial murders and everyone's attendant focus on the famous killer, he was beginning to feel as if the Mittlesdon case had been almost abandoned, like an orphan whom no one wanted the trouble of caring for. But Gibbons still did care: he wanted badly to solve the case, even if it was not one that would be splashed across the national press.

"Exactly," Brumby was saying. "What we have here in York is, first, another in a series of multiple murders, remarkable only in its location; then an impulsive, perhaps even unintended, murder; and lastly the premeditated murder of a leading York citizen. We need to discover if there truly is a connection between all three, or only between two, or possibly no connection at all."

MacDonald grinned broadly. "If none of them are connected, I'll swear off beer for a month."

Brumby's return smile was dryly amused. "Yes, I think it very unlikely, too," he said.

"Excuse me, sir," said a new voice, and Gibbons swiveled round to see Bethancourt, looking about him with some trepidation and accompanied by Brummet. "Here's Mr. Bethancourt."

Bethancourt gave the assembled company a hesitant smile.

"Ah, Mr. Bethancourt," said Brumby. "I hear we have you to thank for this break in our case."

"Is it a break then?" asked Bethancourt hopefully.

MacDonald snorted. "Butter wouldn't melt in your mouth, would it, lad? Yes, it's a bloody break. How did you come by it?"

Brumby said nothing, but his look was expectant.

If this made Bethancourt nervous, he did not show it.

"Pure luck, really," he said, with charming frankness. "I was looking at the photographs on the wall at Mittlesdon's, and Libby Alsop came up and was pointing out the people in them to me. One of them was Veronica." He shrugged. "It's an odd enough name that I remembered Jack here having mentioned it in connection with the Ashdon case."

Brumby seemed willing to take this story at face value, though Gibbons was willing to bet that his desire to move on had more to do with that than his faith in Bethancourt's words.

But even MacDonald appeared ready to let the explanation pass muster, and Gibbons was grateful for his friend's facile account of the matter.

"I think a brief overview would be useful," Howard said. "Just to put the superintendent and Mr. Bethancourt here in the picture."

"I could do with a refresher course," said MacDonald. "I can't say as I was paying much attention when you lot first arrived. Pull up a chair, Mr. Bethancourt."

"Thanks very much," murmured Bethancourt, stepping around to pull out another chair and position it off to one side and just behind Gibbons's seat.

Brumby took off his reading glasses and laid them aside, pausing for a moment to muster his thoughts before saying, "What we've got is a series of murders of young women over the past two years. We believe that our killer stalks his victims to determine their habits, but probably strikes whenever he sees a possibility open up."

"We've had two cases where the victim was abducted in a place she didn't ordinarily frequent," put in Howard.

"He uses a Taser to capture them," continued Brumby, "and then ties them up and tortures them for a brief period before killing them—our average estimate is that they die within twenty-four hours of being taken. His signature, as you all know, is his expertise with alarm systems and his arrangements of the bodies in various shops, as if they were merchandise for sale."

MacDonald looked intrigued by this remark, as if he had not considered the positioning of the victims in that light before, but he said nothing, and Brumby went on without interruption.

"One departure from the norm—so far as serial killings can be said to have a norm—is that instead of being grouped in a specific area, Ashdon's victims turn up all over the south of England. They began in Essex, with the first two murders, and then moved into nearby Hertfordshire, but after that, they're all over the map. One in Bath, and then another three months later in Buckinghamshire. That was why," he added to MacDonald, "when we got your call, I didn't think at first it could be Ashdon."

"I wasn't sure myself," agreed MacDonald. "But it just rang a bell."

"Thank God it did," said Brumby. "But it begs the question: why the departure? Did Ashdon relocate? Does he travel a great deal and just kills whenever he finds a suitable victim, wherever he is? Is this merely his first trip north?"

MacDonald quirked a dubious eyebrow. "And?" he asked.

Brumby gave him a tight smile and a shrug. "We don't know, of course. But the Sanderson murder makes me think this is Ashdon's home territory. And the fact that both Ashdon's first victim and Sanderson were connected to Mittlesdon's Bookshop makes me think Ashdon also knows the place. And that brings us to the Farraday murder." He turned to Gibbons. "You're the one to give the overview on that case, Sergeant," he said.

"Yes, sir," said Gibbons, taken thoroughly by surprise, but rising to the occasion. He succinctly outlined the investigation to date, ending with, "So Veronica's brief tenure at Mittlesdon's would have coincided with Jody's time there—they would have known each other."

"It's a very thin connection," said Howard doubtfully.

"It's what we've got," said Brumby, "so let's see what we can make of it. Now, any number of Sanderson's enemies also patronized the shop, but I'd like to also look at Mittlesdon's itself. Sergeant," he said, turning to Gibbons, "you investigated all the Mittlesdon employees pretty thoroughly. Let's take another look at them with Ashdon in mind."

Gibbons was doubtful. "I don't think any of them could be Ashdon," he said. "I mean, I don't think they could have been down south when all the murders were committed."

"Perhaps not," said Brumby, a little impatiently. "But you never know. And in any case, they probably know him, perhaps only as a customer, but possibly as a friend or even a relation. I'd like to go over everything you've uncovered about these people."

"Of course, sir," said Gibbons, feeling rather chastised.

MacDonald fixed a stern gaze on Bethancourt. "And you," he said, "you chime in as we go through this. I'm getting the impression that you've been making your own study of these people."

"Glad to be of help," murmured Bethancourt obediently.

"Well," said Gibbons, "let's start with Mittlesdon then."

For the next two hours they discussed the minutiae of the bookshop employees' lives, trying to find the interstices where a mysterious killer might lurk. Since Gibbons's investigation had focused on ruling them either out or in as potential suspects in Jody's murder, there were many gaps in his knowledge of their friends and relations, all of which were noted down for further inspection.

"There's a connection to that bookshop somewhere," declared Brumby, though Howard seemed less convinced.

"But is there a connection to Jody's murder?" asked Gibbons, and there Brumby seemed less sure.

"I don't know," he said. "It would seem so on the face of it, but so far there's nothing concrete, is there?"

Despite MacDonald's admonition, Bethancourt was largely silent, speaking up only when appealed to. It was not that he felt uncomfortable in his admittedly unusual surroundings, or that he found the police detectives intimidating, but he was acutely aware that Gibbons would be judged by his words far more than he himself would, and he was loath to make any kind of unfavorable impression.

But he found the discussion fascinating, and he was gratified to learn some of the details of the profile Brumby had constructed of the killer he searched for. The mania of serial killers still held no particular interest for him, but Brumby himself he found a fascinating study, in much the same way Gibbons had when he first encountered the superintendent.

Eventually, the long meeting broke up and they were dismissed to go and have some supper before heading out to reinterview the Mittlesdon employees, this time with a view to discovering what, if any, connections they might have to a multiple murderer. Bethancourt, who had had very little to eat so far that day, eagerly led Gibbons off to a restaurant.

"So what do you think?" asked Gibbons as they sat at a cramped table in a little bistro, waiting for their meals.

Bethancourt shrugged. "I like motives," he said. "Serial killers don't have them—or at least not ones that ordinary people can understand. I don't think I'll be much help in this kind of case."

Gibbons considered this for a moment, sipping his beer. "There's other things besides motive," he said. "Opportunity, method, that sort of thing. Surely all the facts we've accumulated about these cases suggest something to you."

"Oh, I'm an inventive sort of chap." Bethancourt grinned at him. "I can make all kinds of stories out of the facts at hand. But without a personality to tie them together, well, it's hard to choose between them."

"But neither Sanderson's murder nor Jody's was part of Ashdon's pattern," objected Gibbons. "He didn't kill them to satisfy whatever twisted pleasure he gets out of killing—he killed them for more ordinary, garden-variety reasons."

"Well, yes and no," said Bethancourt. "The first part may be true enough, but from what Brumby said, someone as drunk on murder as Ashdon could have killed either one of them for some imagined slight. And the connection to Mittlesdon's could be purest coincidence."

"We're more or less agreed on that," said Gibbons. "But I still can't help feeling that if we could ferret out the coincidence, it would tell us something. Although I find it incredible that any of the Mittlesdon employees could be Ashdon."

"Well, and what would they want to kill Sanderson for if it were one of them?" said Bethancourt. "I'm sure he was a very tedious customer, but he can hardly have been the only one, and I should have thought anyone working in a shop would become accustomed to dealing with that sort of thing."

"I should have thought so, too," agreed Gibbons. "And as improbable as it may be that the Mittlesdon connection is coincidence, well, odder things have happened."

"True," said Bethancourt thoughtfully. "So what if it is nothing but coincidence? Where does that leave us then?"

"No place very good," said Gibbons glumly.

The waitress arrived then with their plates, lavishing attention on them since they were her only customers. They smiled back at her, giving their assurances that they wanted for nothing, and eventually she took herself off.

"I should ring Alice," said Bethancourt once the waitress had gone, and felt in his pocket for his mobile.

"What?" Gibbons looked up from his contemplation of his meal, startled.

Bethancourt paused. "Aren't we going on to interview her first?" he asked. "I thought that was the plan."

"It is," said Gibbons. "I just don't see why you think it a good idea to warn the witness of our intentions."

"But it's Alice," said Bethancourt. "She'll be thrilled at the idea of you coming to talk to her again, and if I let her know now, she'll spend the intervening time dredging up all manner of things in order to be helpful. You'll get far more out of her than if we show up unexpectedly. That only works with people who have something to hide. You don't think Alice does, do you?"

"Not really." Gibbons sighed. "Go ahead then."

"Right," said Bethancourt, producing his phone.

He had a sudden qualm, however, as he searched through his contacts for Alice's number. Their last conversation, he remembered, had been rather odd and he had promised to return to it; he hoped she did not assume his call now was for that purpose.

But in fact, she sounded quite like her usual self when she answered, and their conversation was not long.

"All set," he said, returning the phone to his pocket and gazing with anticipatory pleasure at his meal.

"Was she thrilled?" asked Gibbons dryly, but his sarcasm failed to hit its mark.

"Naturally," replied Bethancourt, the larger part of his attention on his food. "I told you she would be. I don't think, Jack, that you properly appreciate what a thrill it is for the innocent bystander when Scotland Yard comes calling. It's like a telly program come to life for them."

"I can't see how you would know," retorted Gibbons. "You never watch television."

"I know because they tell me so," retorted Bethancourt, scooping up a bite of pork. "And I do watch the occasional program. You seem very cross all of a sudden."

"I am not—" began Gibbons, but then he broke off with a sigh. "I expect it's because deep down I don't think any of this is going to solve Jody's murder."

Bethancourt looked up, alert at once. "But you started off by saying you thought working out how Mittlesdon's was connected would tell us something," he said.

"I think I let myself get carried away by Brumby's enthusiasm," said Gibbons. "He badly wants there to be a connection because that would give him more possible evidence against Ashdon. But when I consider it more objectively, it just doesn't make sense to me. Ashdon is a clever, careful killer. Jody's murder was neither. Even if he had reason to kill her on the spot like that, I don't think that's how he would have done it. And if he somehow did, then I don't think he'd have rushed out without cleaning up the scene. It's just totally out of character."

Bethancourt chewed and thought about this. "I have to admit," he said at last, "your reasoning strikes me as sound. I also recollect that Brumby was somewhat reluctant to come out and declare Ashdon her killer, which makes me think he secretly shares your opinion."

"There you are then."

They fell into a contemplative silence while they devoured their dinner, the rain drumming against the plate-glass window, beads of water glistening with reflected light in the dark.

When at length they left the restaurant, they found the rain had not abated in the slightest, and they were soaked by the time they retraced their steps to the Jaguar.

"God, I'm tired of this," said Bethancourt, settling himself behind the wheel and banging the car door closed against the elements. "Will it never stop raining in this benighted town? You do realize, don't you, that even if we solve the case tonight, we'll never be able to leave until the water recedes?"

"I'm more concerned about making it out to Mrs. Knowles' house," replied Gibbons.

"Oh, that shouldn't be a problem," said Bethancourt, starting up the car. "She only lives over in Heworth. It's not far."

So they crept along the rain-soaked streets, moving out of the city's center and into a more residential area.

"It'll be along here somewhere," said Bethancourt, peering out the windscreen. "Number seventy."

"Perhaps," suggested Gibbons, "we should just find a place to park and walk from there."

"I was hoping there would happen to be a spot out in front," said Bethancourt, "but I expect you're right. Yes, you are—there's number seventy now. Well, it was worth a try."

"I think I see a space a little farther on," said Gibbons. "Down past that tree."

In the end, they had less than a hundred yards to walk, though, as Bethancourt pointed out, since they hadn't dried out from their previous immersion, it hardly mattered.

Alice's home belonged to a row of well-kept-up Regency houses; hers was on the end with a black door and a shiny brass doorbell. She welcomed them in eagerly, but insisted they divest themselves of their dripping coats and boots in the entrance hall before allowing them further into the house. Then she led them to a back sitting room where two young boys were lying on a rug, watching television.

"These are my sons," Alice said proudly. "Boys, say hello to Mr. Bethancourt and Sergeant Gibbons."

The three-year-old was shy, but the five-year-old stood up politely and said, "How do you do?" in a credible manner.

"We'll be next door in the front room," Alice told her children. "Try to be good while I speak to these gentlemen."

She ushered her guests into a well-appointed reception room with a real fire burning in the grate and offered them drinks.

"Nonsense," she said when Gibbons tried to decline, "it's a cold, miserable night and you must be chilled to the bone. Do you drink scotch?"

Gibbons admitted that he did.

He produced his notebook while Alice brought the drinks over from the liquor cabinet, and, the pleasantries out of the way, they got down to business. Alice, as Bethancourt had predicted, was quite eager to help, and readily answered Gibbons's questions, while Bethancourt settled in one corner of the large sofa, sipping his drink and watching the fire. By subtle observation, he was trying to discover whatever it was that had been bothering

Alice that afternoon, but there seemed no trace of her earlier melancholy tone. If anything, she seemed a little brighter than usual, which he had certainly not expected. He mulled over their conversation in the bookshop that afternoon, but could still make neither head nor tail of it. With a sigh, he gave up on this particular mystery and returned his attention to what the others were saying.

Alice knew no more of Veronica Matthews than she had already told them, but she was able to tell them of other employees—since gone—who had worked at Mittlesdon's during Jody's time, and gave them a list of regular customers who would have known her.

And she was the only member of Mittlesdon's staff who knew anything at all about Brian Sanderson's milieu, and where she really shone was in associating him with other bookshop patrons, or, in many cases, eliminating a connection.

"Of course, I'm mostly there in the mornings while the boys are in playschool," she said. "There are a lot of other regular customers whom I wouldn't know."

"But you might recognize their names if they were acquainted with Mr. Sanderson?"

Alice nodded. "I might," she said. "At least some of them."

Gibbons smiled at her. "Then I may be back to pester you, Mrs. Knowles," he said. "My colleagues will be gathering names from your fellow employees, and I'd like to run them by you, if I may."

"By all means," she said. "I'm glad to help. It's rather exciting, really, although it's a bit scary as well. The thought of that man, roaming about York . . ."

"Hopefully we'll put an end to that soon," Gibbons told her, rising. "Thanks very much again for your assistance."

Reluctantly, they donned their still-wet coats and ventured back out into the rain. Bethancourt grumbled over the weather during almost the entire drive out to the university neighborhood where Catherine Stockton lived, and Gibbons humored him, aware that the real source of his bad temper was the fact that he would have to wait in the car while Gibbons spoke with Catherine. In fact, it was Bethancourt himself who had suggested it.

"It was good of you to nab the interview with Catherine," he had said as they left the police station. "I do appreciate your covering up my indiscretion."

Gibbons had merely grinned at him.

"But you'd better interview her without me," Bethancourt had continued, and Gibbons had been surprised.

"You don't want to sit in?" he had asked.

"It's not that I don't *want* to," Bethancourt replied. "It just that things are going to go a lot smoother if I'm not there. She thinks I'm pretty awful, really."

"But she asked you out," protested Gibbons. "She can't hate you that much."

"She still thinks I only chatted her up in order to get information about Mittlesdon's," said Bethancourt gloomily. "I haven't been able to convince her otherwise, though God knows I've tried."

So, when they reached Catherine's flat, Bethancourt left Gibbons off at the door and then drove idly round the block. There was no parking, so he stopped the Jaguar in the road outside the door, keeping one eye on the rearview mirror, and lit a cigarette.

Gibbons, meanwhile, having announced himself and been buzzed in, climbed the stairs to the second floor and found Catherine standing in her open doorway. Unlike Alice Knowles, she did not look thrilled to be receiving this visit. Perhaps, thought Gibbons as he greeted her and was ushered in, Catherine did not watch enough television. At least, there was not a set in evidence in her sitting room.

"I don't know," she said, once he had acquainted her with the reason for his visit. "Brian Sanderson wasn't a particular client of mine—I got him one or two things for his niece. I know he liked a lot of attention whenever he was in the shop because Gareth would complain about it, but I didn't know him very well myself. I can certainly give you a list of my regular clients, but half of them rarely come into the store and the other half are usually there with their children. I'm not saying none of them knew Mr. Sanderson, but I doubt they knew him through time spent at Mittlesdon's."

"I understand," said Gibbons. "I'd still appreciate having the list."

She nodded. "I'll print it out for you tomorrow morning—unless you need it tonight? I'd have to go back to the shop. . . ."

"No, no, tomorrow will be fine," said Gibbons. He produced a card from an inner pocket. "If you could fax the list to this number?"

"Yes, of course." She took the card, examining the number before laying it on the coffee table in front of her.

"Thank you," said Gibbons. "Now I want to ask you about a girl named Veronica Matthews. She used to work at Mittlesdon's about two years ago."

"Yes, I remember her," said Catherine. "She was a nice enough girl and she was very good with children. She used to help me occasionally when I had a big crowd for story time."

"Do you remember any customers she was particularly friendly with?" asked Gibbons.

Catherine shrugged and reached for a packet of cigarettes. "Not really," she answered. "Honestly, I don't see that much of the rest of the staff since I'm always upstairs in the children's section. And Veronica wasn't with us for long."

She lit a cigarette while Gibbons said, "Are you aware of what happened to Veronica once she left Mittlesdon's?"

Catherine frowned. "I think she moved away?" she suggested. "I'm sorry, I'm sure I knew at one time, but I simply don't remember anymore."

Gibbons let this stand without bothering to elaborate.

"Then I think we're done," he said. "Thank you for your time, Miss Stockton."

"You're quite welcome, Sergeant."

She rose with him and followed him back to the door to let him out. As he said good night, he paused and then added impulsively, "I know it's none of my business, but I'd just like to go on the record as saying my colleague Bethancourt really didn't know you worked at Mittlesdon's when he first met you."

A slow smile spread across her face. "I'm beginning to believe the same thing," she said.

"Ah," said Gibbons, rather at a loss.

"And you want to know why I haven't forgiven him," she said.

"I'm curious," admitted Gibbons, "though, as I say, it's none of my business."

"No, it's not," she agreed, but she was still smiling. "The truth is that your friend is quite charming when he apologizes. I thought I'd let him do it another time or two before I gave in."

"Oh!" said Gibbons. "I see."

"But you're not to tell him that, mind," she said, opening the door and holding it for him.

"My lips are sealed," Gibbons promised. "Good night, Miss Stockton."

"Good night," she echoed.

Downstairs, he peered through the vestibule window in search of the Jaguar and was relieved to see Bethancourt double-parked directly in front of the building. He fastened his coat and dashed out into the storm.

"It's remarkable how wet one can get in just a few feet," he said as he settled into the car.

"Isn't it?" agreed Bethancourt. "Are we for home, then?"

"We are."

Bethancourt let in the clutch and guided the Jaguar down the narrow street, starting up the wipers again with a flick of his wrist.

"So how did it go?"

"You're right," said Gibbons, "she really hates you."

"You needn't rub it in," said Bethancourt, shooting him an annoyed glance. "Did she tell you anything else, or was your conversation confined to her romantic troubles?"

"She hadn't much else to tell," admitted Gibbons. "She's faxing me a list of her clients in the morning, but I doubt it will be much help. Most of them have children, for one thing, and it's difficult to conceive of Ashdon with a family."

"That serial killer in America had one," said Bethancourt. "Though I can't imagine how one could live day in and day out with a monster and not know something was wrong."

"Oh, I know who you mean," said Gibbons. "Yes, that was an unusual case, but I don't think we have that sort of thing to worry about with Ashdon. At least we don't if Brumby's profile is anywhere close to being on target."

"No," said Bethancourt reflectively, "no, I don't suppose we do."

It was not a long drive back to St. Saviourgate, and both men were glad to reach their destination, having thoroughly tired of the discomfort of soggy clothing. But as Bethancourt brought the Jaguar into the bay behind the house, he stepped sharply on the brake and said, "Oh hell."

Gibbons looked out the windscreen at the mud-splattered Volvo 4×4 and said, "I thought your aunt was going home to Ilkley today?"

"So did I," said Bethancourt glumly. "She probably couldn't get through because of the flooding. And she's going to be cross with me for running out on her at St. Peter's today. Oh, well, there's nothing for it."

They were already so wet that they did not even bother to quicken their pace as they walked up the length of the garden to the back door. They removed their dripping outer things in the boot room and then entered the kitchen quietly.

"She's here all right," said Bethancourt in a low tone, indicating the diet book open on the kitchen table, the place marked with a scrap of paper.

"She's been cooking," remarked Gibbons, sniffing the air and bending to read the recipe in the book.

"I could do with a snack myself," said Bethancourt. "But first, dry clothes."

"Definitely," agreed Gibbons, still reading.

"Let's nip out into hall—" began Bethancourt, when two things happened simultaneously: his aunt called out from the dining room, and Gibbons drew in a sharp breath of surprise.

"Phillip, is that you?" asked Evelyn.

"Yes," answered Bethancourt as Gibbons seized him by the sleeve and held up the scrap of paper that had marked the recipe's place in the book.

"Is that your aunt's handwriting?" he demanded.

Evelyn was calling to them to stop lurking in the kitchen and come in to say a proper good evening, but Bethancourt was transfixed by his friend's intensity.

"Looks like it," he answered, peering at the telephone number jotted on the paper. "It's her book after all."

"Why would your aunt have Tony Grandidge's mobile number?" asked Gibbons.

"Is it really?" asked Bethancourt, taking another look. "I thought the number seemed familiar."

"Is he a friend of the family?" asked Gibbons.

"Not that I know of," answered Bethancourt. "It's easy enough to find out— Yes, we're coming, Aunt Evelyn," he added, raising his voice. "Come along, Jack."

Evelyn was sitting at one corner of the dining-room table with her meal on a woven placemat in front of her and an open magazine to one side.

"There you are," she said. "I thought you were never coming in. Phillip, what did you mean by running off this morning? I thought I could at least depend on you to see the girls settled in."

"I did get them settled," protested Bethancourt. "They got their keys and signed in, and I carted every blessed piece of their luggage up to their room."

"Yes, but—" Evelyn was beginning when Gibbons gave Bethancourt a nudge.

"Right," he said. "I'm very sorry about this morning, Aunt Evelyn, but I need to know something."

Evelyn was taken aback by the apology; she had clearly been prepared for an argument. Having had the ground swept out from under her feet, she was at a loss for a new tack to take, so she merely asked, "Yes?"

"How do you know Tony Grandidge?" asked Bethancourt. "Is his mother a friend of yours or something?"

And for the first time in his life, his aunt looked back at him awkwardly, as if unsure of what to say. He had not expected it, and found himself nonplussed in response.

"I think I've met Mrs. Grandidge," said Evelyn uncertainly.

"I'm more interested in Tony, Mrs. Keams," said Gibbons, intervening. "As you may know, his uncle was murdered recently, and we've had cause to interview Mr. Grandidge in regard to another matter as well. Can you tell me what your connection with him is?"

Evelyn listened to this speech, her blue eyes going very wide as it was borne in on her that he was talking about a police matter. Gibbons was generally rather quiet around the other members of Bethancourt's family, feeling himself a little out of place in their solid county sphere, but here he was on firm ground and it showed.

"I—well, Tony's been getting some of the supplements for my diet," said Evelyn. "Some of them can be hard to find over here, you see—it's an American diet."

"And Tony Grandidge has set up shop selling diet supplements?" asked Bethancourt skeptically.

"It's ever so much less expensive than on the Internet," said Evelyn.

Gibbons was also looking unconvinced. "Just what kind of supplements are we talking about?" he asked.

"Well, there's Stevia," said Evelyn nervously. "And a vitamin supplement . . ."

Bethancourt was casting back in his mind to the afternoon he had spent at Mittlesdon's looking over the diet book, and suddenly it all clicked. He stared at his aunt, rather horrified.

"Good Lord, Aunt Evelyn," he said, "you haven't been taking human growth hormone, have you?"

And Evelyn blushed bright red.

"HGH?" said Gibbons, also seeing the light. "That's illegal. And you say Tony Grandidge was selling it to you?"

"I don't think it's really illegal," protested Evelyn. "I mean, you can get a prescription for it."

"Only in limited cases," said Gibbons severely. "Certainly not for dieting. And Mr. Grandidge, to the best of my knowledge, is not a licensed physician."

"But it's dangerous," said Bethancourt, more concerned with his aunt's health than her criminal behavior. "Really dangerous— not at all the sort of thing you want to play around with."

"That's a misconception," said Evelyn, turning defiant. "Dana Dugan explains that in the book. It's perfectly safe and does wonderful things—"

"Aunt Evelyn, Dana Dugan is an *actress*," said Bethancourt, "not a doctor. She doesn't even work in a health-related field—I'm not sure she even has a university degree."

"But she takes HGH herself," argued Evelyn, "and just look at her! She's lost weight and looks ten years younger than her age."

"Probably genetics," observed Gibbons tersely. "Do you have any of this stuff Grandidge's sold you?"

But Evelyn shook her head. "I was going to pick some up while I was here," she answered. "But when I rang, Tony said there had been a delay in his shipments and he wouldn't have any until later."

"Oh, good grief," said Bethancourt. He looked at Gibbons. "The bookshop shipments. That's how they're moving the stuff—that's why Grandidge's involved. I knew he wasn't the entrepreneurial type."

Gibbons nodded. "Yes, that must be right," he said. "Look here, Phillip, I'll have to go back out after all."

"Yes, yes, I'll come with you," said Bethancourt. "Aunt Evelyn, I will e-mail you links to credible HGH research. Read them."

And he followed Gibbons back out to the kitchen, leaving his aunt spluttering in their wake.

It was getting late by this time, and it was later still when they arrived at Tony Grandidge's flat in St. Mary's Street. But Grandidge was still up, and seemed not to mind the hour, though his uncle's death had clearly left its mark on him. His first words upon recognizing them was, "Is everyone all right?"

"Yes," answered Gibbons. "We're here on another matter, not with news."

"Thank God," muttered Grandidge, stepping back to allow them entry. He tried for a deprecating smile, and partially succeeded. "I'm nervous as a cat," he said. "There's been so much upset, well, I don't know what's coming next."

"That's very understandable," said Gibbons, as Grandidge closed the door and led the way into the sitting room. Grandidge waved a hand at the sofa while he himself dropped into an armchair and looked at them expectantly.

"We understand," said Gibbons, settling himself on the couch, "that you've gone into business for yourself in a small way."

Grandidge's expression was quizzical. "I don't know what you mean," he said, and he appeared sincere.

"Don't you?" asked Gibbons. "Well, perhaps I've misunderstood the situation."

"*What* situation?" said Grandidge, exasperated.

"I'm sorry," said Gibbons. "I'll try to be clear. I was talking about your little business in selling dietary supplements to ladies who wish to lose weight."

Grandidge's expression changed at once: from tired and confused he became alarmed and wary.

"Oh," he said, and Gibbons could almost see his mind racing as he tried to decide whether to deny it or not. In another moment he realized he had passed the point where a denial would hold water. It was then that Gibbons said, "Would you care to tell us about it?"

Grandidge snorted. "I might as well," he said, "but you're the day after the fair, you know. It was my uncle's gig."

Bethancourt's eyebrows shot up, but Gibbons was remembering Henry Collins telling him that Sanderson had had an extra source of income. Still, he had no desire to let Grandidge get away with none of the blame, so he said, "It's convenient that your uncle is no longer able to confirm that."

"It's true all the same," said Grandidge, shrugging. He took a sip from a half-empty beer bottle on the table at his elbow, and shook out a cigarette from the packet there. Both Bethancourt and Gibbons noticed that his fingers trembled as he brought the cigarette to his lips and lit it. "I don't even know where Uncle Brian came up with the idea," said Grandidge. "But I think he'd been running the business for a little while before it occurred to him to involve me. At least, I know he'd been making a lot of trips to London and that he stopped after I started receiving the stuff at the bookshop."

"Let's start at the beginning," said Gibbons. "How and when did you come to know about this sideline of your uncle's?"

Grandidge took a deep breath. "All right," he said, thinking briefly. "There was a family party about two years ago now. I apparently talked about my job at Mittlesdon's, because later on

Uncle Brian took me aside and asked me the details of how the books came in and all that sort of thing. It seemed an odd thing for him to be interested in, but I told him and didn't think much more about it."

"No," murmured Bethancourt, "why would you?"

"Exactly." Grandidge puffed at his cigarette. "It was maybe a month later that Uncle Brian came back to me and asked if I would like to make a bit of extra money. I said sure, and that's when he told me about the whole thing, and how he had figured a way to ship his supplements through the book-supply chain. All I had to do was separate his packages out from the books when they arrived and set them aside." He gave a wry half smile. "That didn't last long, of course. Uncle Brian wasn't one to do the work himself if he could get someone else to do it for him. Before long, I was packaging the stuff up and dealing with all the ladies who wanted it. The one rule was that I never used the mail—Uncle Brian didn't fancy the kind of charges that would come from misusing Her Majesty's Royal Mail."

"Very wise of him," said Gibbons dryly.

"But how did you get your shipments out of the shop?" asked Bethancourt. "Didn't they notice you carrying boxes out?"

"No; I was careful," answered Grandidge. "And the boxes were small—it was easy to take them out to my car when I stepped out to smoke. Besides, there was no reason for anyone to suspect anything since I wasn't stealing from the shop."

"True," said Bethancourt thoughtfully.

Gibbons was eyeing Grandidge with disapproval. "You don't seem," he said, "to have had any misgivings about engaging in a criminal activity."

"Oh, come now," said Grandidge, looking irritated. "I suppose technically it wasn't legal, but let's be honest here: it was more on the lines of exceeding the speed limit than it was dealing cocaine or something."

Gibbons seemed to find this droll. "I'm curious," he said. "Exactly where do you draw the line on banned substances? Hashish perhaps?"

"What banned substances?" demanded Grandidge, sitting up a bit. "There wasn't any of that kind of thing. I admit, Uncle Brian was cheating the Exchequer out of the import taxes, but none of the stuff was illegal, just hard to find over here."

Gibbons just looked at him for a long moment. Then he said, "I almost believe you didn't know."

Grandidge was looking from one to the other of them, alarmed.

"Know what?" he said. "Look, I swear—there's no illegal drugs involved." He started to rise. "I'll show you—I've got a package in the bedroom right now."

Gibbons let him go without a word and then turned to Bethancourt and raised a brow.

Bethancourt shrugged and took off his glasses to polish the lenses. "I almost believe him, too," he said.

Grandidge returned, carrying a cardboard box.

"Look," he said, pulling out a package labeled STEVIA. "Artificial sweetener. And this," he produced a plastic bottle, "this is just some special kind of multivitamin." He dropped the bottle on the chair and pulled out a small vial. "And this is some injection," he said. He squinted at the bottle. "'Somatropin,'" he read. "I don't know exactly what that is, but I know what it's not: heroin or cocaine or even hash."

"I know what it is," said Bethancourt. "It's mentioned in Dana Dugan's book. It's synthetic human growth hormone."

"Which," said Gibbons, "is quite illegal."

Grandidge was gaping at them, so Gibbons added, "Did you really think your uncle would worry that much about import taxes? He was a successful businessman after all."

"Well, Uncle Brian was known as a warm man," said Grandidge weakly. He set down the box and dropped into the chair, half rising again to pull the bottle of vitamins out from under him before collapsing again. "And this was his way of making an extra bit on the side—I figured he looked on it more in the way of a windfall than a business."

He seemed quite dumbfounded at this revelation of the character of his uncle's sideline. He picked up his bottle of beer and finished it in three gulps.

"So how did you deliver the goods to the customers?" asked Gibbons. "They couldn't have all come to the bookshop."

"God, no," said Grandidge. "That *would* have aroused suspicions. No, I'd drop the packets round their places if they lived in York, or else I'd arrange for them to come here or to meet them somewhere, depending."

"And these ladies paid you cash?" asked Gibbons.

"Mostly," answered Grandidge. He ran his hands through his hair, shoving it out of his eyes. "Sometimes they'd give me a check—I never minded. Hell, I've put myself right in it, haven't I? I should have kept quiet and got a solicitor."

"It might not turn out so badly," Gibbons told him. "Provided your claim that you didn't know the substances were contraband holds up, the prosecutor will probably go easy on you if you help them find the people responsible."

"But I don't know who's responsible," protested Grandidge. "I tell you, it was my uncle's show, not mine. All I know is there's a fellow named Nate who works at TBS and packages the stuff up in the boxes he ships up to us."

"What's TBS?" asked Gibbons.

"The Book Service—they're major distributors," said Grandidge. "But that's all I know—I don't know where Nate gets it from—I don't even know Nate's last name. I've got his number, though. . . ."

Grandidge pulled his mobile from a pocket and began searching through his contacts.

Gibbons took down the number when he found it. "This isn't

really my bailiwick," he told Grandidge. "But I'll mention how helpful you've been when I hand it over."

Bethancourt had been silent for some time, only half listening to the details of the arrangement. Now he said suddenly, "Jody Farraday knew about it, didn't she?"

Grandidge looked at him, startled. "Yes, she found out," he said. "But she didn't make any trouble over it—in fact, she'd had it figured out for a while before I realized she knew."

"Who else knew?" asked Gibbons.

"Nobody," answered Grandidge. "Not unless Jody told someone, and she wasn't a talker. I really don't think she did."

"What about your aunt or your cousins?" suggested Gibbons. "Or someone else in your family."

Grandidge shook his head vigorously. "I never told anyone," he said. "Not even my sister. I mean, why should I? I was making a pretty penny out of the deal, and Uncle Brian had been quite clear that he'd shut the whole thing down if so much as a whisper got out. So I kept it to myself. I suppose he might have told Aunt Amy, though I wouldn't have thought so. I mean, I don't think he usually discussed his business affairs with her."

"And you're certain," said Gibbons, "that he never approached anyone else at the bookshop about it? Not Mittlesdon or perhaps Rhys-Jones?"

"God, no." Grandidge looked scornful. "They'd never have gone along—especially not Mr. Mittlesdon."

"But Jody knew," said Bethancourt, returning to his point. "Was your uncle aware of that?"

Gibbons looked startled for a moment, then turned to look at his friend, a thoughtful frown on his face.

"He found out," admitted Grandidge. "We had quite a row about it, actually. I'd never seen Uncle Brian so upset—he wouldn't take my word for it that Jody would never tell. But he didn't find out until Jody was on the verge of leaving York anyway, and he calmed down about it after that."

"I see," said Gibbons neutrally. "Well, Mr. Grandidge, you've been very helpful. There will have to be an investigation into this matter, but I'll do what I can for you. And I'm afraid I'm going to have to confiscate that box."

Grandidge seemed almost eager to give it to him, as if by thus disposing of the evidence he could make the entire problem go away.

They took their leave, but as soon as Grandidge's door closed behind them, Gibbons turned to Bethancourt and said, "Sanderson? You really think so?"

"It fits," said Bethancourt in a low tone, mindful that Grandidge might overhear them. "Remember what kind of man he was, Jack: somebody who thought quite a lot of himself, and wanted everybody else to share that opinion. Any threat to his standing in the community would probably have made him see red."

Gibbons nodded; then gestured toward the stairs, wanting to remove this conversation further from Grandidge's front door.

"But was it really a threat to his standing?" he asked as they made their way down to the vestibule. "It is, after all, a very white-collar sort of crime."

"Making money under the table implies that your aboveboard earnings are lacking," said Bethancourt. "Since money was how Sanderson reached his standing, I think this news would have put a pretty good dent in it. Not to mention that he was dealing ladies' dietary supplements—he'd have been a laughingstock."

"Yes, I see your point." Gibbons paused at the bottom of the stairs, resting the box he carried against the banister. "Still, from everything we know of her, Jody would have kept his secret—he was in no danger at all from her."

"He may not have realized that, though," said Bethancourt. "It's one thing when your nephew who's trying to avoid your wrath and keep his extra income swears Jody is reliable—it's another to actually trust that information. Sanderson likely saw

247

Jody as one of those odd bookshop people: interesting, no doubt, but not reliable."

"But how did he come to know she was back in town when even her old friends hadn't heard yet?"

"That I don't know," admitted Bethancourt. "She certainly wouldn't have contacted him. Coincidence, I guess?"

"It could be," said Gibbons. "It bears thinking about, anyway." He peered out the window. "It's coming down in buckets," he announced.

"No, really, is it?" said Bethancourt sarcastically.

But Gibbons was still thoughtful. "Phillip," he said, with a new note in his voice, "if you're right, and Sanderson did murder Jody, then *who killed Sanderson?*"

They looked at each other in the dim light of the vestibule sconce, realization dawning.

"Ashdon," breathed Bethancourt.

"And it follows then, doesn't it," said Gibbons excitedly, "that his motive was revenge for Jody's death? Ashdon may not have known Sanderson at all—he was part of Jody's world, not Sanderson's."

"God, you're right," said Bethancourt. He sank down to sit perched on the stairs. "We've been looking in the wrong place for him. Hell, Jack, you've probably spoken with him—you interviewed all of Jody's friends you could find."

Gibbons's mind was already racing through those interviews, as well as those who had been mentioned but whom he had not been able to find.

"The age is right, according to Brumby's profile," he said. "I'll have to look through my notes and see which of them could have been absent from York at the time of the murders. Damn, it could even be one of the bookstore crowd after all."

"It ought to be fairly easy to narrow it down," said Bethancourt. "What else did Brumby say?"

"About Ashdon? There's a whole file's worth of stuff," said Gibbons. He thought for a moment. "Very smart," he said. "A thorough and deliberate planner, but someone who can also react quickly when the unexpected arises. Obviously, someone with either . . ."

"With what?" demanded Bethancourt impatiently, recognizing a breakthrough of some kind. "What are you thinking, Jack?"

Gibbons turned back to him, a faint smile on his lips. "I was going to say, someone with either a van or an isolated house, or both."

He expected Bethancourt to demand the answer, but the words had barely left his mouth when his friend's eyes lit up and he said at once, "Jenks. Wilfrid Jenks. That's who you're thinking of, isn't it?"

"It's positively annoying, how quick you are sometimes," said Gibbons. "Yes, that's who I'm thinking of. He was the only one who knew Jody was in town, so he was the only one who might have known where she went that night, might even have known if she ran into Sanderson."

"What does he do for work?" asked Bethancourt. "Could he have done the other murders?"

Gibbons shook his head, frustrated. "I don't remember," he said. "I'm not sure I ever knew—something in Leeds, I think."

"Right," said Bethancourt. "He mentioned that when we spoke."

There was a clattering of footsteps on the stairs above them. Bethancourt rose hastily, and Gibbons shifted the box back into his arms as Grandidge pelted into view, drawing up abruptly when he saw them.

"What're you still doing here?" he asked.

"Hoping the rain will let up," said Bethancourt, gesturing toward the door.

Grandidge snorted and came the rest of the way down to join them.

"Fat chance," he opined, peering out at the deluge.

"And where are you off to on such an inclement night?" asked Gibbons.

Grandidge grinned sheepishly. "I'm off to make a clean breast of everything to Mummy and Daddy," he said. "Best to get it over with, I think. I'm hoping I can make points on being led astray by Uncle Brian."

"Good luck to it," said Bethancourt, who sympathized with the plight of having to explain difficult things to one's parents.

"Thanks," returned Grandidge. "I'm going to need it. You might as well brave the elements with me—I don't think it's going to let up."

Bethancourt sighed. "It never does," he said, and opened the door.

13

In Which the Detective Superintendents Take a Break for a Good Meal and Are Served a Solution Instead

*B*rumby and MacDonald were enjoying a late and well-deserved supper. The evening now being too advanced to go knocking up witnesses, they had sent their interviewers home to get some rest, left their researchers intent at their computers, and had slipped out for some food.

The two men did not have much in common beyond their jobs, but respectful admiration of each other's professional abilities gave them a reason to make an effort to find some small talk—something that neither man was particularly good at. MacDonald, being the more voluble of the two, had already introduced several topics, only to find that Brumby knew little about sports, or the merits of various beers, or the onerous aspects of home-ownership, so they had fallen back on the beauty of the Yorkshire countryside and the current miserable weather. Both of them, however, remained determined to avoid shop talk during this brief recess.

Until, of course, they should be called back to it. MacDonald was in the middle of consuming "the best fish and chips in York" with great gusto, while Brumby was eating his portion with neat efficiency when his phone rang.

"There we go," said MacDonald, checking his watch. "Well, we got a whole forty-five minutes away from it—not bad, considering."

Brumby smiled, acknowledging the truth of this, while he examined his mobile.

"Gibbons," he announced, answering it.

MacDonald returned his attention to his meal, but pricked up his ears when he heard Brumby say, "Hold on a minute, Sergeant. *What* did you say?"

MacDonald looked up and found Brumby's eyes fastened on him in an effort to communicate silently. That something was up was clear, and MacDonald found himself somehow unsurprised that it was the young sergeant who had produced whatever information was currently giving color to his colleague's pale cheeks.

"I see," said Brumby. "I think you and your friend had better join the superintendent and me over here, Sergeant."

His brows raised in question and MacDonald nodded eagerly.

"We're at a fish-and-chips place near the station," said Brumby. "It's—hell, I don't know where it is. Here, MacDonald, you talk to the lad."

The directions were sorted out quickly and MacDonald rang off and handed Brumby back his phone.

"Gibbons has come up with new information," Brumby told him. "It throws a whole new light on both crimes, I'll give him that, though I'm not sure if he's really found Ashdon or not."

His tone was cautious and yet there was an underlying thread of hope.

"He thinks he's found Ashdon?" asked MacDonald, a little startled.

"No proof," said Brumby quickly, "just a theory. That's why I asked him to come over. No reason for us not to finish our meal if this is just a flight of fancy on the sergeant's part."

MacDonald nodded. "Do you think it is?" he asked.

Brumby hesitated for a moment. "No," he said at last. "No, I don't think it is. Tell me, did you ever suspect Sanderson of dealing drugs?"

MacDonald, on the verge of biting into a chip, froze. "Can't say that I did," he answered skeptically. He took the bite, chewed thoughtfully, and then shook his head. "No," he said, "I still don't. It doesn't fit."

"Gibbons says he has evidence," said Brumby neutrally, and MacDonald's eyebrows went up.

"Does he now?" he said. "I'll be most interested to see it. But how do drugs tie in to the Ashdon case?"

"They don't, not directly," answered Brumby. "Gibbons apparently thinks Sanderson killed Jody Farraday because she found out about his drug dealing."

"Ah," said MacDonald. "Now that I can believe—Sanderson was an egomaniac, and they'll do anything to protect themselves. But that still doesn't explain how Ashdon fits in."

"It does if he was a friend of Miss Farraday's," replied Brumby, frowning thoughtfully.

"Ah!" said MacDonald.

They ate silently for a few minutes, both contemplating the possibilities, until the door of the tiny establishment opened to admit two very wet young men.

They did not seem to mind their waterlogged state, striding rapidly across to the older men's table with eager faces, leaving a trail of puddles behind them.

"Hello, sir," said Gibbons, allowing the greeting to encompass both officers and unintentionally splattering them as he came up.

Brumby looked at his dripping subordinate.

"Perhaps, Sergeant," he suggested gently, "you might want to divest yourself of your rain gear before you sit down."

"Oh, are we sitting down?" said Gibbons. "Thanks, sir."

"Give me your gear and I'll put it away," offered Bethancourt, who was vainly trying to wipe his glasses dry.

There was a few minutes of bustling about while Gibbons and Bethancourt got themselves sorted, but as soon as they had settled into the two spare chairs at the table, MacDonald demanded, "What's this I hear about Sanderson being a drug dealer?"

"Not the kind of drugs you're thinking of," said Gibbons.

"Good Lord, what other kind are there?"

"Ladies' diet supplements, including human growth hormone," replied Gibbons.

Both superintendents' eyebrows shot up toward their hairlines.

"I've just finished putting it into evidence," continued Gibbons. "It'll have to be tested to confirm what Grandidge told us, but I have no doubt it's true."

"Diet supplements?" said MacDonald, starting to laugh. "Well, I can easily see how he'd kill to keep that a secret."

"But how did you come to suspect such a thing?" asked Brumby, eager to have the story start at the beginning. "I've seen no hint so far in Sanderson's history of anything like this."

Gibbons looked at Bethancourt, who said, "It was my aunt. She's been on the diet and has been getting her supplies from Tony Grandidge."

"Ah, yes, the nephew," said MacDonald.

"And you've spoken with him?" asked Brumby, sticking to the point.

"Yes, sir." Gibbons went through the night's events, giving an orderly report of their discoveries and conclusions.

"It's all just theory right now," he ended up. "I don't even know where Sanderson was on Christmas Eve when Jody was killed—he may turn out to have been in full view of his loving family the whole time."

"But it's sound reasoning nonetheless," said MacDonald. "I'll put forensics onto looking through the trace evidence from the Farraday crime scene for anything connected to Sanderson."

"Yes, it's a clever solution," said Brumby impatiently. "But who's this Jenks person you mentioned on the phone?"

"A friend of Jody Farraday's," replied Gibbons. "She was actually staying with him over the holiday. He lives in an isolated bungalow in Appleton Roebuck and drives a white panel van."

There was silence for a moment.

"Wait a minute," said MacDonald. "Are you trying to tell me that the bloody serial killer has *friends?*"

"That's not unknown," murmured Brumby, never taking his eyes from Gibbons. "Were they more than friends?"

Gibbon shook his head. "No, I don't believe so."

"Even so," said Brumby, "it's a powerful motive for murder. And it does tie the Mittlesdon and Sanderson cases in with Ashdon's crimes."

"It takes a bunch of disparate facts and makes sense of them," admitted MacDonald. "It's just—I truly never thought of Ashdon having a Christmas party. Are you sure he didn't mean to murder Jody, too?"

"I don't think so," said Gibbons. "I mean, he'd known her for years—they were childhood friends."

"In that case, no," said Brumby, his lips twitching in a half smile. "It's not likely he was planning to make her one of his victims. But let's get all our facts straight before we go any farther—at this point, Ashdon's identity is still just a theory. Andy can work on digging out Jenks' records tonight, and by morning we may have a notion as to whether this man even had the opportunity or not. Then we can go from there."

"If he checks out, you'll want a search warrant then?" asked MacDonald.

"Eventually," said Brumby. "Hopefully, we'll turn up something that will give us cause."

He had entirely abandoned the food left on his plate and his eyes had an abstracted look as he mentally cataloged the possible ways to come at this suspect. "I think I'd like to meet Wilfrid Jenks," he said. "Where's this place of his again?"

"Appleton Roebuck," answered Gibbons.

"And you'll not be getting there tonight," said MacDonald. "I doubt there's a country lane in all the district that's passable by now. We'll have to hope the rain stops before morning, then we might have a chance."

Brumby nodded reluctantly.

"Meanwhile," said MacDonald, taking his last bite of fish, "I think I'd better start looking into this bit of contraband that's been making the rounds right under my nose." He shook his head. "Illicit diet drugs," he muttered. "What will they think of next?"

Andy Rowett did not seem much bothered by the crowd gathered around his computer terminal as Gibbons, standing over Rowett's left shoulder, read off Wilfrid Jenks's name and address. Rowett's stubby fingers moved rapidly over the computer keys, and in a moment the home-sale record for the bungalow in Appleton Roebuck appeared on the screen.

"Here we are," said Rowett, adjusting his glasses. "He banks at Barclays and is employed by Revetment Limited in Leeds."

"And what's Revetment Limited when it's at home?" asked Brumby.

"Good question," said Rowett, but his fingers were already dancing over the keyboard again. A page of dense prose came up and everyone unconsciously leaned forward to decipher it.

"They install alarm systems and security gates for small businesses," announced Rowett, a note of triumph in his voice.

"Ah." Brumby breathed. "Do they indeed?" He grinned at Howard, who grinned back, elated.

In fact, with those few words, the tension in the room eased and was replaced by an air of excitement.

"Looks like they started as a local company," continued Rowett, scrolling down the page before anyone else was ready. "They've grown slowly into a national concern, but they've got a very small footprint outside of the north."

"Nothing in the home counties?" Brumby squinted at the monitor.

"Hmm, hmm," said Rowett, abruptly switching to a different screen and typing in the name of the company. "A lot of business in Lincolnshire," he murmured to himself as the page on the screen shifted rapidly at his command. "Ah, yes, here we go—Revetment has been trying to expand its business to the south. Over the last four years—let's see here—they've acquired clients in Buckinghamshire, Essex, Surrey; all the counties around London. Oddly, they haven't done so well in the Midlands. I wonder why . . ."

Brumby breathed again.

"Jenks looks like your chappie, right enough," said MacDonald. "So what's next?"

"We have to be sure of our ground," said Brumby. "Before I go after Jenks, I want a talk with Revetment. We have to find out if and where Jenks has been traveling for them, and exactly what his job is."

"Getting to Leeds tomorrow could be dicey," said MacDonald doubtfully.

"A phone call first would be in order," replied Brumby. "If Jenks is in the office tomorrow, we don't want to spook him. Andy here will ferret out a number to reach someone in authority."

Rowett, his gaze still fastened on the screen, nodded automatically.

"Didn't you say you had the name of the school he went to?" he asked Gibbons, who had been dividing his attention between the computer monitor and Brumby.

Gibbons flipped over a page of his notebook. "Not the name of the school, I'm afraid," he said, looking for the information and turning another page. "Just the name of the village. Rachel, Jody, and Jenks were all in year three there together. Here it is: Haxby."

Rowett nodded and went to work.

Bethancourt had not returned to the station with the others; he tended to be impatient with any kind of drudgery and he knew Gibbons would ring him as soon as there was news.

He was oddly tired, and was not looking forward to a discussion of HGH with his aunt, so he was greatly relieved, when at last he got home, to find she had gone to bed. Or at least she had gone to her room; perhaps, he thought, she was no more in the mood for the discussion than he was. Still, he felt some responsibility to his promise to provide her with objective data, so he got himself a drink and settled in on the couch with his laptop.

He was still there two hours later when Gibbons returned, looking rather weary but pleased with the night's events.

"Still up, eh?" he said as he looked into the room.

"Still," agreed Bethancourt. "Get yourself a drink and tell me how it all went."

"Very smoothly," answered Gibbons, pouring himself a healthy tot of scotch. "Andy did his magic with the public records, and Jenks is looking very like our man so far—of course, there's still a good deal to be sorted." He dropped into an armchair, stretched out his legs, and pulled a sheaf of papers from his briefcase. "I've got it all here," he continued, "although I think I remember most of it. You know that job in Leeds that Jenks referred to?"

Bethancourt nodded.

"Well, it's with a security company—they do alarms and gates, that sort of thing."

"Brumby must have been delighted with that," said Bethancourt, smiling.

"He was indeed," said Gibbons. He sipped his drink, savoring both the taste of the whisky and the memory of the moment. "They've looked into that angle before, you know, only of course they were concentrating on companies headquartered in the south."

"Seems like a rather monumental task," said Bethancourt. "There are dozens of such companies—not to mention all the one-man shops."

"It was early days then," said Gibbons. "They thought they were dealing with someone in Essex, in the Saffron Walden area. Once the crimes started cropping up in different places, they had to abandon that direction. Anyway, it still remains to be seen what exactly Jenks' job is with this company, not to mention whether he travels for them or not."

"You don't seem to have much doubt about the outcome," remarked Bethancourt.

Gibbons grinned at him. "I think we're right about this one," he said. "You know the feeling, when everything just starts to fall into place and all the little details you couldn't fit in before suddenly resolve themselves into a whole picture."

"Yes," said Bethancourt. "I know the feeling—almost godlike for just a moment."

"Still," said Gibbons, "it doesn't do to be sloppy on that account. Police annals are full of cops who were absolutely certain they were right and who turned out to be wrong in the end."

"Thus tomorrow's program," said Bethancourt. "I take it you'll be off to Leeds bright and early?"

But Gibbons shook his head. "Brumby and Howard are going," he said. "No need for a whole troop of us, much as I'd like to see it through. No, I'm to report in to see what else Andy Rowett has come up with—he's still researching over there. He's already tracked down Jenks' parents and siblings."

"That's quick work," said Bethancourt. "Anything interesting there?"

"Yes and no." Gibbons took another sip of his whisky while he marshaled his thoughts. "Jenks' mother was a drug addict—she was declared an unfit mother and he went into foster care when he was just a few months old. Eventually, she cleaned herself up and reclaimed him, but by then he was nearly four."

"Quite a sea change for a toddler," said Bethancourt, raising an eyebrow. "I mean, he couldn't have remembered her."

"Very likely not," agreed Gibbons. "But we're not too sure about the foster home he was in, either. One of his fellows grew up to be a pedophile, and another became a thief. You've got to wonder what those foster parents were up to. Anyway, his mother had married his father by then and they went off to become one big happy family. The father'd had some drug problems himself, but he and his wife were AA members and attended regular meetings and Jenks Senior had got himself a job in a warehouse."

"And they all lived happily ever after?" asked Bethancourt, though he could tell from his friend's tone that this was not the case.

"They dropped off the radar for a few years, so presumably everything went all right," answered Gibbons. "The next thing Andy turned up was a death certificate for the mother about four years later. She'd overdosed on heroin."

"Oh, dear. What about all those AA meetings?"

Gibbons shrugged. "You know how it is—some people make it, some don't. Jenks' father remarried about a year later, and Jenks' half-sister was born about a year after that. Then the family apparently moved, but Andy hadn't got farther than that when I left. I expect by morning he'll know what color socks Jenks wore in the sixth form."

Bethancourt lit a meditative cigarette, then said, "It does make one wonder if a more favorable upbringing would have changed anything. Or was he destined to be a sociopath no matter what?"

"You never can tell," said Gibbons. These days they seem to think it's all in the genes."

"Yes, but genetic predispositions don't translate into unavoidable traits," said Bethancourt. "If his problems had been identified early and he had been receiving treatment all this time, would some or all of the deaths have been prevented?"

"Impossible to say," replied Gibbons. "One would like to think so, but there's no real evidence. Until someone actually kills, it's very difficult to determine whether they're capable of the act or not. So if we were looking at a psychoanalyzed, medicated Jenks who had never killed anyone, we'd never be sure he would have killed if he hadn't been psychoanalyzed and medicated."

"Very true." Bethancourt's lips twitched. "And of course in all this, we're presuming guilt. It's all right for me, but you're an officer of the law and are supposed to be impartial."

"Ah, well, it's only speculation," said Gibbons. He tossed off the last of the whisky in his glass. "I'm all in," he confessed. "All the excitement buoyed me up, but I'm knackered now. I'm going up to bed."

"Sleep well," said Bethancourt. "I probably won't be far behind you."

"Good night then."

Gibbons got to his feet, but Bethancourt stopped him just as he got to the door.

"Jack," he said, "if Jenks *is* Ashdon, and you catch him, do you think he'll shed any light on Jody's murder?"

"I don't know," replied Gibbons. "According to Brumby, most serial killers can't help but talk about their crimes. But he may not like to admit to Sanderson's murder, in which case we might not get anything out of him about Jody. But we'll see. Brumby has a great deal of experience with these kinds of criminals—I've seen some of the transcripts." He cocked his head. "Feeling a bit anticlimactic?" he asked.

"A bit," admitted Bethancourt. "Jody's case was the one I found interesting, you see. And although we've found the answer, well, there's no way to prove it with Sanderson dead."

"We can't take it to court," corrected Gibbons. "But in order to close the case, the forensics will be gone over pretty carefully. I think in the end we'll find evidence. But you're right—it will never have the satisfaction of an arrest and a conviction."

Bethancourt nodded and let his friend go.

But as he sat in the quiet drawing room and listened to the rain, he reflected that what bothered him most was the lack of surety. He very much hoped that when Jenks was arrested, he would tell what he knew about Jody's death.

14

In Which Brumby Gets a Good Night's Sleep

*I*n the early hours of the morning the rain ceased at last. When the early winter sun came up it was clearly visible in the pale blue sky for the first time in a week.

It took several hours, however, for the waters to recede, and it was nearly eleven o'clock before Brumby could start for Leeds, having ascertained by phone that Jenks was still on holiday and not expected at the office. Gibbons, with the rest of the team, poured over the data Andy Rowett had uncovered during the night, but once again he felt superfluous: Brumby's team were experts at this kind of thing and they had it well in hand.

The most important new piece of information was that Jenks's stepmother had been American, and when the family left the York area, they had apparently relocated to Indiana. This had Rowett searching United States databases of unsolved crimes in the Indianapolis area and collecting the telephone numbers of various police departments to ring later, when it would no longer be the middle of the night across the Atlantic.

Gibbons, who felt himself rather outclassed among these research specialists, helped where he could and kept one eye on Rowett, guessing that if any further discoveries were to be made, they would come from him.

Thus he alone was close enough to hear Rowett murmur to himself, "Now that's a bit of interesting."

"What's up?" he asked, scooting his chair over.

"This report here," answered Rowett, never taking his eyes from the screen. "Four years ago in Marion County—that's where Indianapolis is," he added, and Gibbons nodded. "A homicide— young woman, fits our profile, bore the marks of having been tasered before she was killed, cause of death was a massive blow to the left temple, body left displayed by the side of the road."

Rowett's voice was almost chanting as he ticked off the salient points.

"That sounds right," said Gibbons encouragingly.

"She was last seen in a shopping mall marketing lot," continued Rowett, "the afternoon before her body was found."

Gibbons was peering over his shoulder. "She doesn't seem to have been tortured at all," he remarked.

"No, and she wasn't killed with a skewer to the brain, but if this was an early attempt, you wouldn't expect all the elements to be in place yet. Let's see, this was eighteen months before the first murder here. If this is our man, there has to be more somewhere."

"When did Jenks return to this country?" asked Gibbons.

"Two years ago last June," replied Rowett. "Veronica Matthews was murdered that September. Fits well enough, though that's nothing to go on by itself—I could come up with hundreds of people who fit that bill."

He was continuing his search of the American databases as he spoke, scrolling through lists of unsolved homicides. Gibbons watched quietly for a moment, then left him to it.

At two, Gibbons volunteered to go out for sandwiches, and

when he returned, he found that Brumby was back and holding court at the long conference table.

"Ah, good," he said when he saw Gibbons. "We can all eat while we discuss developments. And I have a special job for you, Sergeant," he added.

Gibbons felt himself suddenly grinning.

"I bought a couple of extra sarnies," he said. "Have you eaten, sir?"

Brumby had not, although he seemed surprised to remember it, and took a sandwich gratefully.

"I was just telling the others," he said to Gibbons as he unwrapped his food, "that Jenks most definitely had opportunity. Howard is still at Revetment, getting all the details, but according to Jenks' supervisor, Jenks is one of the technicians they send off to oversee installations, and most of his jobs have been down south. The company has a couple of sales representatives who live down there, but everything else is run out of the Leeds offices."

"What do they think of him there?" asked one of the researchers.

"Much as you'd expect," answered Brumby. "Quiet, works very well, but is the odd man out. Mind you, we didn't canvass the entire staff—we didn't want word getting back to Jenks that we'd been there."

"Of course not."

"And I've got a titbit for you, Andy," continued Brumby. "Revetment dug out his application—I've got it in my bag—and he came to them with a wealth of experience in the States. There's a list of American references, as well as one from England. Before he got the job at Revetment, he'd been working as a jobbing electrician in Portsmouth."

"That'll be helpful," said Rowett, munching industriously. "I've got a titbit for you, too. I've found a murder in the Indianapolis area that might be Ashdon's early work. Investigating officer was a Lieutenant Roy Baker."

"Just one?" asked Brumby quickly.

"One so far," corrected Rowett. "I reckoned you should ring this Lieutenant Baker—those Yanks love a posh accent."

The rest of the table tittered around their food while Brumby smiled deprecatingly.

"Very well, Andy," he said. "If you think it best."

Gibbons, who had been champing at the bit to know what his own job was to be, took the opportunity, after the laughter had died down, to ask, "And what did you have in mind for me, sir?"

"Ah," said Brumby, turning to him. "I want you to reel in the fish, Sergeant. When we're ready for him, I want you to ring Jenks and tell him we've found a bag we think belonged to Jody Farraday. Ask him to come up and identify it."

"Yes, sir," said Gibbons. "I take it you're not ready for him yet?"

"Not yet," said Brumby. There was a speculative look in his eye. "But soon, Sergeant, soon."

Bethancourt had a lie-in that morning. If he had been hoping by this stratagem to avoid his aunt, he was doomed to be disappointed: she, like Brumby, had to put off her start time until the water had cleared from the roads. So they spent an awkward morning together, both avoiding the topics of HGH, diets, criminal investigations, Mittlesdon's Bookshop in general, and Tony Grandidge in particular.

Some balance was restored when at last Evelyn was ready to leave and they fell back into their usual roles: Bethancourt carried her bags out to the car for her and installed them while she directed their arrangement. A quick peck on the cheek, an admonishment to drive carefully and give his regards to his uncle, and she was gone, leaving Bethancourt feeling much relieved.

He returned to the empty house and immediately went in search of his mobile to ring Gibbons and find out what was happening in the Jenks investigation.

"Did you just get up?" asked Gibbons suspiciously.

"It's after lunchtime," protested Bethancourt. "Even I'm not that slothful. No, I just got rid of Aunt Evelyn, so this is first chance I've had to ring. Have there been any developments?"

"Jenks is looking very much like our man," reported Gibbons. "Brumby confirmed that he had opportunity, and now they're engaged in putting brick on brick, so to speak. I'm more or less kicking my heels at this point," he added, lowering his voice. "Howard's off nailing down exactly when Jenks was where over the past two years, Andy Rowett's investigating unsolved murders in Indiana, and Brumby is making arrangements to speak with a detective over there, while everybody else is putting things together for a search warrant for Jenks' bungalow and van."

"When will you interview Jenks?" asked Bethancourt.

"Brumby wants to have a go this evening," answered Gibbons, "but he wants everything in place beforehand. His idea is to get Jenks here, and have the search warrants executed while Jenks is out of the way."

"So an arrest is imminent?" said Bethancourt.

"Depending on what happens," said Gibbons. "But, yes, I think it likely."

"Well, I never thought you and I would end up finding Ashdon when we started the Mittlesdon case," said Bethancourt, who could still hardly believe that this in fact was the case.

"Neither did I," admitted Gibbons cheerfully. "But it's worked out very well. I'll let you know if anything surprising turns up."

"Yes, do," said Bethancourt. "Oh, there's the doorbell—I'll speak to you later then."

Cerberus, who had had an energetic run in the garden that morning and had thus been sound asleep on the drawing room carpet, roused at the sound of the bell, and the way his tail was wagging as he stood at the front door gave Bethancourt a very good idea of whom he would find when he opened it. He took a moment to steel himself and reached for the latch.

Marla did not smile when he greeted her, although she did automatically bend down to fondle Cerberus's ears. Instead, she looked almost hesitant, not a quality normally associated with her.

Bethancourt decided to help her out. "Did you come to talk?" he asked, striving to keep his tone neutral.

"Yes."

She nodded soberly and he responded by swinging the door open and motioning her in. She shed her heavy coat in the hallway, revealing well-worn jeans and a clinging cashmere sweater that immediately made Bethancourt want to touch it, despite his current conflicted feelings about its wearer. Manfully, he refrained, and led the way into the drawing room instead. He gestured toward the couch, but Marla had abruptly screwed up her courage. She turned to face him.

"Look, Phillip, you have to know I never meant any of it to happen. Not the thing with Jason, not your finding out about it, not that stupid argument we had," she said, all in a rush.

She paused for breath and Bethancourt had time to think that thoughtlessness was not much of an excuse for all that had happened.

"I only blew up because you didn't seem to care that I'd been to bed with someone else, only that I wasn't more discreet about it," she continued, her voice rising. She seemed to realize this and stopped herself, taking another breath. "Anyway, I'm sorry for all of it," she finished.

Bethancourt noticed that she did not promise amendment. Still, it was a much greater admission of guilt than he had been expecting, taking into consideration the fact that Marla generally considered the best defense was a good offense. And he still wanted to touch the sweater.

"I cared like bloody hell," he said, but even as he said it, he knew his pride had suffered more than anything else. And what did that say about his feelings for her? He was suddenly nonplussed by his own emotions.

Marla sensed his hesitation. "I know I sometimes let my temper get the better of me," she admitted, "and I honestly don't remember what I said. But I certainly never meant to break up with you. You're the only boyfriend I've ever had that's lasted more than a few months."

That hardly seemed a decent basis for a long-term relationship, but Bethancourt was nonetheless comforted by the compliment.

"So you do want to make up?" he asked.

"I'm here, aren't I?" she said, a trifle impatiently, and then paused. "Only I'm not sure you do anymore," she added in a lower tone.

Bethancourt wasn't sure he did, either. On the other hand, he wasn't sure he didn't. This was turning into a much more serious discussion than he had been prepared for. He realized all at once that he had believed the relationship was over largely because he had had no intention of wooing her back this time. Even with her arrival in York, he had not anticipated that she would take on the role of wooer.

"I hadn't thought it was a possibility, frankly," he told her.

She shrugged, though it was a rather forced gesture. Unstated but understood was the fact that Marla would never stay anywhere she was not wanted.

"If you'd rather not bother," she said, turning a little away from him but still waiting for his answer.

"I didn't say that," protested Bethancourt, rather flattered by her obvious desire to have him back, and she turned at once. "If you want to try, then I'm willing to give it a go," he said with a crooked half smile. He was unaware that the quirky smile made his hazel eyes gleam, and that it was one of the things that made him so attractive to women.

The look in Marla's eyes grew warm in response.

"Yes," she said, holding out her hands. "Let's."

He took her hands, drawing her to him and bending to kiss her. And at last he was free to explore the cashmere sweater.

Gibbons's big moment, for which he had waited all day, turned out to be anticlimactic.

By tea time Howard had returned from Leeds with Jenks's itinerary for the past two years; it showed him as having been in the south when every single Ashdon killing had occurred. Moreover, there was some correlation of the place of the murders with the place of Jenks's previous job. In May, for example, he had been installing an alarm system in Bedfordshire, and had gone on from there to a job in Surrey. Toward the end of his work in Surrey, an Ashdon killing had occurred near Stevenage in Bedfordshire. Moreover, research had shown that several of the small shops the bodies had been placed in had had their alarm systems installed by Revetment, Ltd., though not all by any means. Still, as Howard had said, it was significant.

By five o'clock, the search warrants had been expedited, forensics was standing ready, Rowett had found a possible connection to another murder in Indiana, and Brumby had finally been cleared to talk with Lieutenant Roy Baker.

Baker, once contact had been established, sounded rather bemused to be speaking to Scotland Yard.

"I remember the case quite well," he told Brumby in a broad American accent. "I never did find motive, and we decided it must be a random killing. I went through our records and found a couple of cases where girls had been tasered and abducted, although in both of those, the girls were let go—they just woke up after a few hours, one in a house under construction, and the other in a back alley. Then I heard they had a similar case over in Hendricks County, so we turned it over to the FBI. I think they found another case to tie in, but so far as I know, the crimes simply stopped after that."

Baker really had little more to add; he had never had any suspects in the case, and the only clue he had was some grainy footage from the mall car park security camera, and that showed only a blurred figure, face turned from the camera, escorting the victim out of camera range.

"The guy was medium," he said. "Medium height, medium hair, medium weight. There was just nothing to go on."

After a bit of searching, he came up with the name and number of the FBI agent who had been given charge of the case, and Brumby, noting the information down, thanked Baker for his trouble and promised to let him know if the case turned out to be connected to the Ashdon serial murderer.

Brumby immediately dialed the FBI office and asked for Special Agent Mancuso. Mancuso was out in the field, so Brumby left a message with a secretary who promised to relay it.

When he had rung off, he sat silently for a moment, mulling over what he had heard. Then he turned decisively to his team, his grey eyes searching out Gibbons.

"I'm not going to wait for the FBI," he said. "We've got enough to go on. Make the call, Sergeant."

Gibbons nodded smartly and turned to the phone. He dialed Jenks's number, his story of a bag needing identification fully formed and ready, and listened to the rings with increasing dismay. After the sixth ring, voice mail picked up, and Gibbons left a brief message. Then he rang off and turned to look at Brumby helplessly.

Brumby was frowning. "He may simply be out for the evening," he said, but not as if he believed it. He hesitated for a moment more, then turned to two of his people.

"Take an unmarked car," he said, "and run down to his place. Park somewhere inconspicuous and ring me the moment you have sight of Jenks returning—or if he's already in residence. It's not unknown," he added dryly, "for people to screen their calls. Gibbons here can give you the lay of the land."

Gibbons, feeling slightly crestfallen that he had missed his mark, turned to make a sketch of the area. He was pleased, however, that he was not the one being sent to wait in the car on what was rapidly becoming a very cold night. He had always hated surveillance.

Bethancourt woke from a pleasant doze to the sound of his mobile ringing. The ring was faint, since the phone was across the room in his trousers pocket, but he came to with a start nonetheless and tried to answer it. Since his limbs were thoroughly tangled up in Marla's as well as in the sheets and blankets, the effort was somewhat abortive, and ended with him halfway out of the bed, with one foot still firmly entangled amid the sheets, and his phone still well out of reach.

"Good Lord, hang on half a mo, can't you?" said Marla sleepily, trying to unwrap his foot.

"It's probably nothing," said Bethancourt, falling back on the bed with his leg bent under him at a rather uncomfortable angle. "I don't know why I lunged for it."

In their newly amicable state, he did not want to mention that it was likely Gibbons, reporting progress on the Ashdon case: Marla had never cared for his sleuthing hobby. But in the next minute, he remembered that it could well be his father, heralding the imminent arrival of another family member or, even worse, of the parental units themselves. Considering their reaction over Christmas to the mere suggestion of his liaison with a fashion model, he was not an eager for any members of his family to meet Marla in the flesh, much less in her present location and state of undress. Groaning, he disentangled himself and went to retrieve the phone, shivering in the sudden cold of the room.

The caller ID showed that it had been Gibbons after all.

"I'd better ring him back," he told Marla, picking his trousers up from the floor and hastily drawing them on. "He might be coming home."

"We should get up anyway," she answered, sitting up and

searching amid the bedclothes for her underwear. "Don't you think it's time for dinner? I'm starving."

Bethancourt agreed, while privately hoping Gibbons was not ringing to suggest the same thing.

Gibbons was not.

"There's been a bit of a hitch in the plans," he told Bethancourt. "Jenks is apparently away. When he didn't answer my call, Brumby sent Susan and Doug off to do surveillance in Appleton Roebuck. They spoke to a neighbor who told them Jenks had been gone since yesterday—the neighbor assumed he was off on one of his business trips."

"But I thought you said he was still on his Christmas vacation," said Bethancourt.

"He is," answered Gibbons. "Which just means we have no idea where he might be. It could be a perfectly innocent holiday trip, or he could be stalking another victim. Needless to say, we're hoping it's the former."

"Not likely though, is it?" said Bethancourt.

Gibbons sighed. "No, not terribly likely," he said. "So Brumby's decided to put off the search of the bungalow and concentrate on finding the van instead. He's put out an alert for it in connection with Jody's murder. The thinking being that mention of that case should alarm him less, since I've already spoken to him about it."

"And he's therefore more likely to come along to the nick voluntarily," said Bethancourt.

"That's right," said Gibbons. "Although Brumby believes Jenks would come along anyway, thinking he's smarter than any policeman. Anyway, I should get back to the others—I just wanted to tell you what was happening and let you know I'm stuck here until there are further developments."

"Right," said Bethancourt. "Ring me back when there's news."

"Will do," promised Gibbons, and rang off.

Bethancourt set down the phone and turned to find Marla already struggling into her sweater.

"Is Jack up here for that serial killer?" she asked, her head emerging from the cashmere.

"That's right," said Bethancourt, pulling a shirt over his head.

Marla shuddered. "I hope he catches the bugger soon," she said.

"I've no doubt he will," answered Bethancourt. "They seem to be making progress in the case. Shall we go? Dinner awaits."

There was a very practical side to Brumby. When no reports of Jenks had come in by ten o'clock, he returned to the hotel to get a good night's sleep.

"Bastard probably will, too," muttered Howard.

A couple of the others followed Brumby's example, but for the most part the rest of them found it impossible to leave, somehow certain that the break would come the moment they did so.

Gibbons, however, had pushed himself over the last few days and found that his recently wounded body was beginning to rebel. Though he was as convinced as anyone that news would come the minute he was out the door, he found himself at about midnight having to give in and call it a day. Extracting a promise from his fellow officers to ring his mobile if anything should develop, he rang for a taxi and was transported back to St. Saviourgate.

The house was quiet when he let himself in, and if he was surprised to find Bethancourt already abed, he did not bother overmuch about it. The coffee he had drunk in the course of the evening was beginning to churn in his stomach, so he headed to the kitchen to get a glass of milk to take up with him.

He was just replacing the milk jug in the refrigerator when he heard the sound of dog nails on the parquet and Cerberus trotted in, his feathered tail waving a welcome. He was momentarily followed by his master, who was wrapped in a quilted dressing gown and was engaged in putting on his glasses.

"You're back," he said. "I thought I heard you come in. Is there any news?"

Gibbons shook his head. "We're all just waiting around for some report of Jenks or his van to surface," he said. "Until he does, not a lot more will happen."

"That's tedious," said Bethancourt frankly.

"Yes," agreed Gibbons. "It is rather." He took a sip of his milk and then sank into one of the kitchen chairs with a sigh.

Bethancourt fished in the pockets of his dressing gown and eventually found his cigarette case. He lit one and went to join Gibbons at the table.

"So you just cool your heels here until Jenks is found?" he asked.

"I don't know," answered Gibbons. "I'm superfluous at this point—there's nothing going forward that Brumby's team can't handle. But I think the superintendent is giving me a chance to stick around to see the end."

"Good of him," said Bethancourt. "How do you feel about it?"

"Oh, I'd like to see Brumby wrap it up," said Gibbons. "On the other hand, I don't much fancy sitting around the York police station with nothing to do. So I suppose it all depends on how long it takes them to find Jenks."

Bethancourt nodded. "Would you mind awfully if I went ahead home then?" he asked. "You're welcome to stay here, of course."

Gibbons looked a little startled, but he agreed at once. "I can see there's even less for you to do here than there is for me," he said.

"There isn't really," said Bethancourt. "And, well, there's been a development of sorts here."

Gibbons raised his brows. "Let me guess," he said. "Alice has begun to stalk you."

Bethancourt laughed. "No," he answered, "though, now you mention it, I did promise to have a talk with her before I left." He scowled. "I hate talks," he added. "There can't be four other words in the English language more designed to strike one cold as a woman telling you, 'we need to talk.'"

It was Gibbons's turn to laugh. "But what's the development then?" he asked.

"Well," said Bethancourt, feeling rather sheepish, "Marla came round this afternoon and apologized."

"Ah!" said Gibbons. "The light dawns—that's why you were in bed so early. I take it you've made it up?"

"We have," said Bethancourt. "But even before she turned up, I was thinking I'd like to be getting home. Jody's murder is as solved as it's likely to be, and the Ashdon case seems well on its way to being solved as well. And I'd rather like to get home."

"I wouldn't mind that myself," said Gibbons. "I'd barely seen my flat before they sent me up here, and I was weeks and weeks at my parents' house before that. It would be nice to feel like I lived in London again."

"It'll come," said Bethancourt. "Jenks is bound to turn up sooner or later, and then you'll be home and regaling me with the details of how it all went while we drink scotch in my living room."

Gibbons smiled, a little wearily. "That would be nice," he said. "Well, I'm for bed. You'll ring me tomorrow before you leave?"

"Oh, yes," said Bethancourt, rising and leading the way to the stairs. "I haven't even put it up to Marla yet, though I doubt she'll have any objections."

Gibbons nodded and yawned as they climbed the stairs. On the landing they bade each other good night and turned to their respective rooms.

Throughout the night, while Bethancourt and Gibbons slept, all across Britain, white Volvo panel vans were having their license plates scrutinized by various members of law enforcement. But none of them was Jenks's van.

15

In Which Gibbons Watches the Snow Fall

*T*he air in the incident room the next morning was one of dogged weariness. They were all painstakingly placing one brick atop another, all the while waiting to see if their work would be needed.

Brumby apparently had had a very good night's rest; he was clear-eyed and energetic, but there was unfortunately little for him to do. He spent his time ringing up his forensics team, who were very busy back in the lab, sorting out the wheat from the chaff. Thus far, however, there had been considerably more chaff than wheat, and there did not appear to be much promise of more to work on until Jenks and his van were found.

Rowett had discovered that prior to buying the bungalow in Appleton Roebuck, Jenks had rented a series of inexpensive flats in and around Leeds. Howard was out interviewing some of Jenks's erstwhile neighbors, but it seemed incredible that he would have held, tortured, or murdered his victims in a studio flat. The van, Brumby had decided, must have been the scene of the crime. But so far it had remained elusive.

With so little to be done, Brumby turned to updating Ashdon's profile, checking their work off against what was thus far known of Jenks. Gibbons, who had been left quite at loose ends, was roped into this discussion so that they might pick his brain of any little nugget of information he might have garnered about Jenks from his encounter with him. He did not in fact have much to contribute, but he found the conversation interesting and felt that at least he was learning a good deal about human psychology.

So he was there when Rowett, whose eyes were developing a permanently glazed look from the endless hours at the computer, suddenly let out a whoop.

Brumby's head jerked around. "Andy?" he said.

"I've got it, guv," said Rowett triumphantly. "I've found the place. The bugger's been renting a cottage in Buckinghamshire."

"What?" Brumby shot out of his chair and crossed the room with long strides to stand behind Rowett, who blinked up at him, grinning broadly.

"A place in Little Horwood called Bluebell Close," he said. "Look, there it is on the satellite picture—nice and isolated."

He pointed at his monitor and Brumby leaned forward to peer at it.

"My god," he said, clapping Rowett on the shoulder. "You're bloody brilliant, Andy." He straightened and addressed the rest of the room. "Let's get started on a search warrant for this place. Andy, do you have a landlord?"

"Of course," said Rowett scornfully.

"Well, give Bradley there the lowdown on him so he can get a warrant," said Brumby. "Bill, ring up the locals to let them know we'll be invading their patch, and have them do a drive-by to see if the van's in evidence. . . ." He continued to hand out assignments as they occurred to him, one bit of business after the other, and the machine that was his team shifted into high gear once again.

Bethancourt had thought about getting an early start back to London—providing Marla agreed—but they slept late and then he found that although Marla agreed in principle with the idea of leaving as soon as might be, in fact it was likely to take some time before she was ready to go.

"I've only got to pack my things up and say good-bye to Trudy," she told him. "We'll probably just get something to eat."

Bethancourt accurately summed this up as an extended conversation between the two women, the details of which he would likely prefer not to know. Not to mention the "packing up." He had traveled with Marla before and knew all too well that she inevitably had difficulty fitting everything she had got out of her suitcase back into it. At least, he thought, he would not be called upon to help in the present instance.

And it occurred to him that he, too, had an errand to run. Thinking it over, he reluctantly decided that conscience mandated he let Alice have her say rather than slinking off out of town before she was aware of his departure.

He packed up his own things and then, with both resignation and a touch of anxiety, rang the bookshop, only to be informed that Alice was not there. Hoping that she was out for the day, he called her house, ready with an apologetic message. But she was in and answered the call.

"I was wondering if we might have that talk," he said, once the pleasantries were out of the way. "I know it's short notice, but I've decided to drive back to London today—last-minute decision and all that."

"Oh," she said, sounding a little taken aback. "Well, how good of you," she went on, recovering. "Would it be at all possible for you to drop by now? I've plans for later this afternoon, you see."

"Of course," said Bethancourt. "That would fit in very well. I'll see you shortly, then."

He rang off and sighed. He had really been hoping he would not have to go through with it.

"Come along, Cerberus, old boy," he said. "Time for a walk."

Cerberus, at least, greatly enjoyed the walk over to Heworth, trotting briskly in the cold, though his master could well have done without it. He took the last puff of a cigarette, pitching the butt into the gutter before turning and ringing the brass bell beside Alice's front door.

She opened it with a smile.

"Perfect timing," she said. "My nanny is just giving the boys their lunch."

Bethancourt stepped in. "Then perhaps you'd allow me to take you to lunch while they're busy?" he asked politely.

Alice shook her head. "Thank you, but George is coming to take me to lunch in half an hour," she said. "And once we're done, we're taking the boys on an outing, since it's the first day in weeks it hasn't been raining."

"Cold, though," said Bethancourt, shrugging out of his coat.

"Oh, the boys won't mind that," she said. "They'll run around and get warm in no time. Don't you remember how it was when you were young?"

"I remember having to go for freezing-cold swims in prep school," said Bethancourt, shuddering. "I can't say I enjoyed it."

Alice laughed, leading the way into the drawing room.

And Bethancourt again remarked the change in her tone since yesterday afternoon. There was also something different in her manner, a certain joie de vivre, that he had never noticed before. Putting two and two together, he drew a bow at venture and asked, "I don't think you've mentioned George before—that's not your ex-husband, is it?"

"Oh, no," said Alice, motioning him to a seat. "No, George is a new acquaintance. He's the father of one of my son's friends, but we only met the other day. He and little Frank's mother are divorced, you see, so I usually see her when the boys get together. But last week, she came down with the flu and George stepped in to take the boys on their outing."

"But the boys aren't going to lunch with you today," said Bethancourt.

And Alice colored slightly as she replied, "Well, no. George rang quite unexpectedly yesterday afternoon to ask me to lunch."

Bethancourt beamed at her. "And you said yes," he said. "I take it you were impressed with him on the boys' outing the other day?"

"Well, yes, rather," Alice admitted with a laugh. "I never dreamed he would ask me out, though. And then I found out from my son that he'd seen quite a bit of George and liked him—he'd never mentioned that before."

"So he's a good father, too," said Bethancourt.

Alice nodded and then cocked her head. "Haven't you ever thought of having children yourself?" she asked.

"I've thought of it," said Bethancourt. Then he grinned unrepentantly. "I don't think I'm enough of a grown-up yet," he said.

Alice laughed. "Well," she said, "we all grow up at different rates. One never understands that when one's a child, but it's clear as day once you're a parent."

And Bethancourt, thinking this over, saw how true it was and suddenly began to understand what she had been speaking about the day before. But looking at her now, he rather doubted she wanted to have that conversation anymore.

"I'm glad you came by before you left," she continued, growing serious. "I know you're not to talk about the case, but I was hoping you might give me some kind of information. Because, what with Brian Sanderson's murder and the Ashdon case, Jody seems to have got lost. And, well, we're still walking on eggshells over at the bookshop."

Bethancourt considered this. "It's rather awkward just now," he confessed. "As you've so cleverly intuited, I'm heading home because the cases are all but solved. On the other hand, the police are at a very delicate moment, and if I were to let the cat out of the bag . . ."

"Of course, I understand," said Alice. "But surely it couldn't hurt to just tell *me*. I do promise not to say anything until you give me permission, or it becomes public knowledge."

Bethancourt knew perfectly well that he should say nothing, but he had never held himself to the standards required of Her Majesty's officers of the law. And he really didn't feel it was fair to leave Alice in the dark.

"All right," he said abruptly. "I'll tell you what I know—in general outline. But it must go no farther until after Superintendent Brumby has made an arrest in the Ashdon murders. If anyone else gets wind of it before then, it could jeopardize his case and result in a serial killer going on about his business."

Alice nodded, frowning a little in puzzlement over the connection between Jody Farraday and the Ashdon killer. But she seemed to take his point.

"I would hate to be responsible for anything like that," she said.

"Well, then," said Bethancourt, "where to start?"

The question was addressed to himself, but Alice answered it.

"Start with Jody, if you can," she said.

"All right," said Bethancourt. "It's as good a place as any. Did you know that Jody had rather a habit of picking up bits and pieces of other people's secrets?"

Alice looked appalled, and opened her mouth to reply, but then a thought struck her and she said thoughtfully, "I'm not certain I know what you mean by that. Jody was very discreet, but, well, I did sometimes get the feeling that she knew more than she let on about some things."

"That's it," said Bethancourt. "Well, through her involvement with Tony Grandidge, Jody became aware of a secret he knew about his uncle. She had," he added, "no intention of using the information or telling anyone else about it—it was just something she happened to know."

"Yes," said Alice. "That sounds like the Jody I remember. I take it I'm not to know what the secret was?"

Bethancourt smiled apologetically. "I'm afraid not," he said. "Suffice it to say that it was something which, if revealed, might have harmed Sanderson's standing in the community."

Alice's mouth made a little O, and then a horrified look came into her eyes.

"You don't mean . . ." she said.

"It's not proven," answered Bethancourt. "It may never be, although Jack assures me forensics will do their best. But, yes, we think that Sanderson killed her. Tony confirmed that his uncle was aware that Jody knew his secret, but he only found it out just before she left York. As best we can piece things together, Sanderson must have encountered Jody on her return. We don't know what she might have said to provoke him, but the idea that she was back in York and in possession of his secret was untenable to him."

"But if Sanderson was the murderer," said Alice, bewildered, "then who killed him? We've all been thinking it was the same person."

"We believe it was Ashdon," replied Bethancourt. "And there is some evidence for that. If Superintendent Brumby is right, Ashdon was actually a friend of Jody's—not that she knew anything about his, er, recreational activities. He would have killed Sanderson in revenge."

"Well," said Alice, sitting back to think it through, "at least that makes some kind of sense."

"A lot of it is supposition, however," Bethancourt warned her. "The police haven't yet picked up this friend of Jody's, and it may be that when they do, they'll find they were mistaken. You can see how crucial it is that nothing should come out about this until the police have completed their investigation."

"Yes, of course," said Alice. "I do assure you I won't breathe a word."

"I trust you, Alice," said Bethancourt, hoping that he did. "And I did want to thank you for all the help you've been in this case. Really, I don't think we'd have figured it out without you."

"Oh, I didn't do much," said Alice. "Just passed along gossip, really. Women are always better at that sort of thing than men, I think. But it was delightful to see you again, Phillip."

"And you," said Bethancourt, taking this as a dismissal and rising. "Wonderful, really, to run into you like that."

Alice had risen as well; it had nearly been half an hour since his arrival, and she no doubt wanted to be rid of him before her date came by.

They bade each other good-bye while Bethancourt donned his coat and bent to kiss her on either cheek.

"You're off today then?" she asked as she opened the door to a blast of arctic air.

"That's right," said Bethancourt, wrapping his scarf more firmly about his neck. "Or at least sometime tonight," he amended, remembering his original plan to get an early start, which had slowly dissolved upon contact with Marla and the real world.

"Better go earlier rather than later," Alice advised, "else you'll find yourself snowed in."

"Snow?" demanded Bethancourt, swiveling round to look at the clear blue sky.

"Yes, they're expecting the storm to come in sometime this evening," Alice told him. "By this time tomorrow, we should be a foot deep in it." She sighed. "We really have had the worst weather this season."

But Bethancourt was now thoroughly alarmed by the prospect of being snowed in and forced to extend his stay. He took his leave of her politely enough, but he was already pulling his phone from his pocket as he walked down the street.

"Marla?" he said when she answered. "We're going to have to speed things up—there's a snowstorm on the way and God knows when we'll be able to get away if we don't go before it hits. Yes, I'll pick you up at the hotel."

Everything was set in motion. Inspector Howard had been called back from Leeds in preparation for a departure for Buckinghamshire, and the local police had been alerted to keep an eye on the M1 north of Milton Keynes. The search warrant was in the works, and Brumby hoped to have it in hand by the time he reached Little Horwood. The uniformed branch had already reported back that there was no van or vehicle of any kind parked at Bluebottle Close. The nearest neighbor had been interviewed, but had been able to say only that the cottage's tenant was there infrequently, and that she had not noticed him in the last day or two. But she had no direct view of the property because of the trees, and so would have been likely to see Jenks only as he came and went.

"He'll show up at one place or the other," predicted Brumby. "And I want a look at this cottage—it's far more likely to be the scene of the crimes than the bungalow here is."

Gibbons, having waited all day for an assignment, had in the end drawn the short straw and been sent to relieve the team presently watching the house in Appleton Roebuck. He would much have preferred to drive south with Brumby and Howard, but he supposed it was only reasonable of them to choose one of their regular team members as a driver. So he made a quick stop back at the house for his warmest things, hoping to find Bethancourt there, but finding instead only a hastily scribbled note with the caretaker's phone number and the news that Bethancourt had headed back to town with Marla.

He provided himself with a thermos of hot coffee and his iPod and then climbed back into the police Rover and drove off to Appleton Roebuck as the sun was dipping toward the rooftops and clouds were gathering to the northwest.

Since Jenks's bungalow was the last house on the road, the detectives had only to watch the intersection with the larger way, and to this end they had simply parked in the village school car park, which handily overlooked the main road and the lane that branched off from it, leading to Jenks's bungalow.

Gibbons eased his Rover in beside his cohort's, glad to see that there were still other vehicles in the car park as well.

"Glad you've come," said DS Ford. "It's not so bad here, but it's deadly dull—hardly a car goes by."

"Won't I rather stand out once the car park empties out?" asked Gibbons, trying to judge how it would look from the road.

"Doubt anyone'd even notice," returned Ford. "There's no lights here, and apparently it's not unknown for some of the staff to leave their cars here and walk up the road to the pub. I think you're safe enough."

Gibbons nodded. "All right then," he said. "Don't forget to have someone relieve me."

Ford laughed. "Never fear. Got your mobile? Good, then. I'll see you back at the station."

He reversed out of the parking space and Gibbons watched him drive off. Then he made himself as comfortable in his seat as he could, and turned on his iPod. He had bought an audio book to listen to on the train ride up, but had never got further with it than that; this, he reckoned, would be a good time to catch up on it. He left one earbud dangling so as to be able to hear any traffic that came past and settled in for a long wait.

It was full dark by the time Bethancourt and Marla reached Leicester and pulled off the M1 for a break. As he guided the Jaguar into the service area, Bethancourt could make out the flashing lights of police pandas, several of them, all gathered in front of the refreshment center.

"I wonder what's up," said Marla, shading her eyes from the glare.

"I don't know," said Bethancourt, slowing the car. "But I don't think here is the best place to stop—there wouldn't be that many police unless they've got a serious situation."

Marla nodded. "Next one, then," she said.

Bethancourt agreed, and angled the Jaguar away from the restaurant and toward the petrol station, heading for the exit and the ramp leading back to the M1. Marla craned in her seat, releasing her safety belt so she could boost herself up for a better look at the commotion.

"Looks like they've surrounded a white van," she said as they passed by. "There doesn't seem to be much action, though—they're all just standing about."

"A white van?" said Bethancourt, pausing for just a moment and glancing back. But he had driven too far and could make out nothing beyond the ring of police cars. "Well, well," he said, returning his attention to the road. "I think, Marla, they may have just caught the Ashdon serial killer."

"Thank God for that," said Marla, settling back and reaching to relock her belt. "It's creepy, having one of those on the loose."

"We'll ring Jack from the next service area," said Bethancourt, "and see what the news is."

If it had not been for the cold, and the feeling that more-exciting things were going on elsewhere, Gibbons would not have been unhappy with his lot. He was comfortable enough in the car, and the audio book was continuing to hold his attention. He could see, however, why Ford had complained: he was two hours into his watch and had counted a grand total of three cars passing by.

He was contemplating starting the car up again to run the heat for a bit when he saw the first snowflake, pale against the dark sky. He leaned forward to gaze up through the windscreen and saw a full snowfall in the making.

"No wonder I'm cold," he muttered, and switched on the engine. He poured himself a cup of the coffee he had brought and watched the snow drift steadily down until there was a light frosting on the railings of the car park.

He had finished the coffee and was turning off the engine again when his mobile rang. He reached for it eagerly, but it was only Bethancourt.

"Ringing to cheer my lonely hours are you?" he asked.

"Are you lonely?" replied Bethancourt. "I thought you were in an incident room full of people. Or is this one of those existential situations where you are never more alone than when surrounded by other people?"

"No," said Gibbons. "I am, in fact, alone in a car in Appleton Roebuck, waiting in case Jenks should return to his bungalow."

"You might be in for a long wait," said Bethancourt. "I was actually ringing because Marla and I just saw a bevy of police cars surrounding a white van in the M1 service area near Leicester. I take it you haven't heard anything yet?"

"No, but that would be good news," said Gibbons. "Those would be the local lads—they may not have called it in to the Yard yet. Or," he added, as another thought occurred to him, "it may be the wrong van. I gather there have been a lot of those."

"Oh." Bethancourt sounded crestfallen. "I hadn't thought of that," he said.

"But Leicester makes sense," said Gibbons. "What is it, an

hour north of Milton Keynes? Because Andy Rowett found another property Jenks has been renting west of there."

"He did?" said Bethancourt. "Well, I expect Jenks would have needed someplace to stay in the south—I assumed he'd been putting up at an hotel."

"I don't know," confessed Gibbons. "I never heard all the details, but I would have assumed the same."

"Well, ring me if you hear anything," said Bethancourt. "I've got to go—Marla's coming back."

"All right," said Gibbons. "I'll talk to you later."

He set the phone aside, greatly wondering if Jenks had indeed been found and, if so, how long it would take somebody to call him off his wait here. He would give it another half hour, he decided, before he rang the station to check in. In the meantime, the snow was very pretty. He much preferred it to the endless rain.

It had been something under a half hour when he heard the sound of an engine and saw the beams of headlamps approaching. He waited, squinting, till the vehicle was passing and he could identify it as a white panel van.

His heart skipped a beat and he snatched up his mobile even while he watched the van slow and make the turn into the lane. He could not see the number plate in the dark, but he had no doubt it was Jenks.

Detective Inspector Trimble answered the phone in the incident room.

"Jenks is back, sir," reported Gibbons. "The van just passed me."

"Damn it," said Trimble. "And Brumby's halfway to Milton Keynes. Well, there's no help for it. Hang on, Sergeant— Bill! Ring Brumby at once and tell him we've got Jenks up here. Gibbons, you there?"

"Yes," said Gibbons. "What do you want me to do?"

"Sit tight," replied Trimble. "If Jenks leaves again, ring me and follow him. But I don't want you going in there without backup. Ford and I are on our way."

"Right," said Gibbons. "I'll be here."

It did not take them long. In fifteen minutes, another police Rover sped into the car park and slid into the space beside Gibbons. Trimble got out and switched cars, joining Gibbons.

"All serene, Sergeant?" he asked as he climbed into the passenger seat.

"Yes, sir," answered Gibbons. "Jenks hasn't moved, not unless he's taken a walk across the fields."

Trimble grunted. "Not likely in this weather," he said. "I've spoken to Brumby and he and Howard are on their way back. They think they can make it in a little over an hour—they hadn't got farther than Nottingham."

"Are we to wait then?" asked Gibbons doubtfully.

"No, no." Trimble shook his head. "We're to take Jenks back to York for questioning and execute the search warrants for the bungalow and the van. The SOCKOs are following on. I'm going to leave Ford at the scene to head up the search while you and I take Jenks back."

Gibbons nodded. "Very well," he said. "Shall we start then?"

"If you please," said Trimble. "I think," he added as Gibbons started up the car and began to back out, "I'll let you take the lead when we get there, since you've already spoken to Jenks. That way he'll see this as being connected to your earlier visit and your investigation of the Farraday case."

"I'll do my best," said Gibbons.

He led the way, following the trail of the van's tire tracks in the snow, down the narrow lane and around the curve to where the bungalow was situated. This time, knowing what might have taken place here, the setting looked sinister to Gibbons. He parked the Rover carefully behind the white van, and he and Trimble got out, making their way toward the front door while Ford, in the second car, pulled in behind them.

Gibbons rang the bell and waited, feeling unusually nervous and hoping it did not show. There was the sound of footsteps and then the door opened to reveal Jenks, looking much as he had on their previous encounter.

Gibbons smiled. "Hello, Mr. Jenks," he said. "I've been trying to get in touch with you. Been out of town, have you?"

"Sergeant Gibbons, isn't it?" said Jenks. "Here, come in. Yes, that's right—I've only just come back, as a matter of fact. What was it you wanted?"

Gibbons and Trimble stepped into the little hallway and Jenks closed the door behind them. As on the last occasion, though, he did not invite them farther into his domain, but turned politely to await their pleasure. He did not seem to Gibbons to be overly suspicious.

"It was a matter of helping us in the Jody Farraday case," said Gibbons. "This is my colleague, by the way, Detective Inspector Trimble."

"Hello, sir," said Trimble, shaking hands.

Jenks raised an eyebrow. "What happened to the other fellow?" he asked.

For a moment, Gibbons did not know whom he meant, but then the light dawned. "Mr. Bethancourt had to return to London," he answered. "But the inspector and I are managing to get along without him. In fact, there have been some developments in the case since I last spoke with you, Mr. Jenks. It's one reason I've been so anxious to get hold of you. I'd very much like to have you come back to the station with me to go over it all."

"What, now?" Jenks seemed surprised. "I'm afraid it's not a very good time—I'm in the middle of cooking a fry-up for my supper, you see."

"Thought I could smell cooking," said Gibbons genially. "Well, sir, I'd be glad to have a sandwich or something brought in for you if you wouldn't mind helping us with our inquiries. It's really become quite urgent—I've been trying to get in touch with you for two days."

Jenks looked from one to the other of them, sizing up the situation, and a faint smile appeared on his lips.

"I see," he said. "You think I did away with Jody, don't you? Well, I don't mind coming along to put you straight on that account. But I'll hold you to that promise of a sandwich, Sergeant. Just let me switch off the hob."

Both policemen tensed as Jenks turned away, retracing his steps down the hall to what was presumably the kitchen door. He disappeared through it and Gibbons listened intently to the sound of his footsteps. To his great relief, he heard them returning in a moment, and then Jenks reappeared.

"Here I am then," he said, rejoining them and reaching for his coat, which was hanging from a peg on the wall behind the door. "How does this work? Will you bring me back, or do I follow you in my car?"

"We'll give you a ride," said Gibbons.

"It wouldn't be possible for you to take your vehicle anyway, sir," said Trimble, producing some papers from his breast pocket. "I have a search warrant for it and the house."

For the first time, Jenks looked angry. He pressed his lips together as he took the papers Trimble offered him and opened them, holding the pages under the sconce while he scanned them.

"You didn't need to do this," he said. "I never killed Jody, and these won't help you prove something that isn't true. But I don't suppose I've any choice."

"No, sir," said Gibbons. "It's standard operating procedure, I'm afraid."

Jenks still did not look happy. He thrust the documents into his coat pocket and zipped the garment up.

"I hate having my things mucked about," he muttered. "All right then, Sergeant, let's have this over with."

And he pushed past the policemen to open the front door and lead the way out into the snow.

Gibbons, feeling greatly relieved and not a little proud of himself, followed his suspect out to the car.

Wilfrid Jenks sat alone in the small grey interview room. He seemed quite at ease, sitting up at the table and munching his way steadily through a sandwich and a packet of crisps.

The gathered detectives watched him intently on the monitors in the crowded control room, all of them juggling for the best viewing position, all of them tense and impatient.

"Is Brumby back yet?" asked someone.

"Been back for half an hour," replied Howard. "He's getting himself sorted."

"Look at the blighter, eating his sandwich as if he hadn't a care in the world," said Rowett, at Gibbons's shoulder. "You should have poisoned it, Jack."

Gibbons smiled at the jest but did not shift his focus from the monitor in front of him. He opened his mouth to reply, then cut himself off to point at the screen and say, "There he is."

Instant quiet fell as they all watched Brumby enter the room. Brumby's manner was quiet and contained, but even in the grainy image on the monitor his eyes betrayed a laser-sharp focus.

Jenks looked up as he came in, and Brumby inclined his head.

"Mr. Jenks?" he said. "I'm Detective Superintendent Brumby. Thank you for coming in to help us."

"You're welcome," said Jenks.

"Was the sandwich to your liking?" asked Brumby, settling himself at the table and opening the thick file he had brought with him.

"It was very nice," said Jenks politely. "Sergeant Gibbons has been most accommodating."

Brumby nodded, put on his reading glasses, and peered at the first page of the file. Jenks, too, was staring at it, but Brumby had positioned it in such a way that it would be difficult for Jenks to make out.

"Good, good," said Brumby. "Well, shall we start?" He cleared his throat before rapidly repeating the date and time and enumerating those present for the camera.

Then he proceeded to take Jenks meticulously through the day of Jody's arrival in York—what train she had come in on, how crowded the station had been, where Jenks had parked his van, how much luggage Jody had brought with her; Brumby covered every detail. Jenks responded to all these questions amiably, leaning back in his chair with his arms crossed over his chest, a hint of a smile at the corners of his mouth, like a parent indulging a small child. Gibbons, watching him, thought that the man truly had no inkling he might be suspected of more than Jody's murder.

And then Brumby changed the subject.

"What about the day before?" he asked, and Jenks looked startled.

"The day before?" he echoed.

"Yes, the twenty-second," said Brumby. "What did you do on the twenty-second?"

"Lord, I don't remember," said Jenks with a laugh.

"Don't you?" asked Brumby. "Did you go to work, perhaps?"

"No." Jenks shook his head. "No, my holiday began on the Monday. Let's see." He paused, thinking. "Well, I suppose I must have tidied up a bit," he said. "Yes, I remember putting fresh sheets on the bed in the guest room, and hoovering the lounge, that sort of thing."

Brumby nodded. "Of course," he said. "You wanted to have everything ready for Miss Farraday on the morrow."

"Yes, of course," said Jenks, a little impatiently. "That's normal when one's expecting guests, isn't it?"

"Quite," said Brumby. "So you got everything ready. Yes, I see. And then what did you do?"

"When?" asked Jenks.

"After you'd finished tidying up," said Brumby. "That evening, the evening before Miss Farraday arrived. Did you go out, perhaps? Take a run into York?"

Jenks's eyes had narrowed. "No," he answered. "I spent the evening at home."

"Finishing up a few last-minute things?" suggested Brumby.

"I already told you I tidied up the bungalow."

"Of course, but I thought there might have been other business you wanted out of the way, so as to be able to give all your attention to your guest."

"No," said Jenks. "There was nothing else."

"Very well then," said Brumby. He put his glasses on and looked down at the file, turning over several pages.

"You do a lot of work down south, don't you, Mr. Jenks?" he asked.

Jenks was wary now and seemed more engaged than he had at the start of the interview; all trace of condescension had left his manner.

"Yes," he replied. "My company sends me all over England."

"But mostly to the south," said Brumby, still focused on the papers in front of him. "For example, last August you were working in Wiltshire."

"I may have been," said Jenks. "I'd have to check my diary to be sure."

"But you recollect doing a job in Wiltshire last year?" asked Brumby, looking up.

"Yes, of course," replied Jenks. "In Warminster, it was. I put in a security system at a little shop there—I don't remember the name of it now, but they sold antiques."

Brumby nodded and returned to the file in front of him. "Muckle's Antiques, it says here," he read. "You were there a fortnight."

"That sounds about right," said Jenks.

"But you never made plans to see Miss Farraday while you were there," said Brumby.

Jenks relaxed again. "I rang her," he said. "But she couldn't get away and I didn't want to drive all the way out to Cornwall. It's not like it's next door to Wiltshire, you know."

"No, but it's considerably nearer it than Yorkshire," said Brumby. "I just wondered, was all. It seemed a little strange, with you and she being so close, that you hadn't made the effort to meet up."

Jenks said nothing.

Brumby continued on, dancing around the Ashdon murders, but always somehow tying his questions back in to the Farraday case. Gibbons watched as Jenks grew suspicious, was reassured he still held the upper hand, and then had his suspicions rearoused by a new tack from Brumby. Gibbons couldn't have said when exactly it happened, but there came a point at which Jenks's attitude underwent a subtle change, and Gibbons was sure he knew they were talking, however obliquely, about the serial killings and no longer about Jody. Jenks's confidence seemed undiminished, but his attention sharpened, and he watched Brumby with a new look in his eyes.

Why at that point Brumby continued to avoid any direct mention of Ashdon, Gibbons didn't know, but he was convinced that Jenks did. It was as if the two men were playing a game only they understood the rules of, and as it went back and forth, the tension ratcheted up.

Brumby brought up the cottage in Buckinghamshire; Jenks admitted his use of the place freely.

"As you've pointed out, Superintendent," he said, "I work a great deal down south. It makes more sense for me to rent a place than to stay in hotels all the time."

"Yes, it certainly would, from your employer's point of view," agreed Brumby. "Far less expensive. And yet, they didn't seem to know you had such a place. They were under the impression that you stayed with a cousin when you were working in the south."

"I did stay with my cousin on the first couple of jobs, before I found the cottage," countered Jenks. "My boss must have remembered that, although I'm sure I told him about renting my own place."

"No doubt, no doubt," said Brumby.

Brumby accepted nearly all of Jenks's explanations, and to the uninitiated it might have sounded as if Jenks was indeed innocent. But innocent people protest when the police show too close an interest in their private affairs. To Gibbons's mind, the very fact that Jenks had not once asked what all this had to do with Jody's death gave him away.

"I understand," said Brumby, "that you were living in the United States until the last few years."

"Yes," answered Jenks. "I finished school there, in fact."

"And you learned your trade there, too, didn't you?" asked Brumby.

Jenks nodded. "Yes, I did. I picked it up working summers while I was still in school."

Brumby picked up a sheet of paper from the file and looked at it. "There was a crime in Indianapolis almost three years ago. I believe you were still living there at the time?"

"Three years ago?" asked Jenks, thinking it over. "Yes, I would have been there then. I didn't leave Indiana until June of that year."

"They recovered DNA evidence in that case," continued Brumby.

"That must have helped the prosecution at trial," said Jenks.

"No doubt it would have, had there been a trial," said Brumby. "Unfortunately, they had no suspect to compare the DNA to."

"A pity," said Jenks. "What was the case about?"

"Didn't I say?" asked Brumby. "A young girl, name of Brenda Turner. She was killed with a blow to the head. They found her body displayed on the side of a road. The—let me see—Rockville Road," he read from the report, and then set it down and looked at Jenks over his glasses.

"I'm familiar with it," said Jenks. "US thirty-six it's called."

"Do you remember the murder?"

"No." Jenks shrugged. "I may have heard about it at the time, but it doesn't ring a bell now."

"It's a funny thing about it, though," said Brumby. "I was talking to my counterpart at the FBI recently, and he said there was another case, over in Hendricks County, that he thought might have been tied to the Brenda Turner case. They were quite similar, another girl abducted and then found dead some miles away, again killed with a stab to the head."

"Did they find the same DNA evidence?" asked Jenks.

"No," replied Brumby. "There was very little trace evidence in that case. The FBI agent I spoke to seemed to think the killer had learned from his mistakes the first time."

"Then it would be difficult to tie the two cases together," said Jenks. "Unless, of course, there was some connection between the girls?"

Brumby shook his head. "Not that anyone could find."

"Too bad, that."

"Hmm, yes," said Brumby, looking back down at the file. "They had a few other cases they thought they could tie in to the Turner murder, too. In fact, I gather they thought they had a serial killer on their hands. But then the killings stopped."

"Perhaps the killer went to prison for some other crime," suggested Jenks. "It happened that way in a movie I saw once."

"That's not unknown," said Brumby. "Or he might have moved—that's also been known to happen."

"Of course," said Jenks politely.

Brumby turned over pages in the file, almost idly. "The thing is," he said, "those killings in Indiana stopped just before the Ashdon killings started over here. I expect you've heard of the case?"

In the control room, everyone held their breath, staring at the monitor.

An odd light had come into Jenks's eyes, but he replied casually, "It's been in the papers."

Brumby nodded. "And there are a remarkable number of similarities in the cases," he continued, still examining the papers in the file, as if picking out the similarities as he spoke.

"Are there?" said Jenks, but not as if he was interested.

"Yes, quite a few," answered Brumby. "It occurred to me, you see, that if we were to find a suspect in the Ashdon cases, it might be useful to compare his DNA to that found over in the States, in the Turner case."

"And do you have a suspect?" asked Jenks.

Brumby raised his eyes to meet Jenks's.

"I think I do," he said.

And then, at last, Gibbons saw that all that had gone before was merely preamble. The game in earnest began now. Brumby completely discarded his glasses and the file on the table in front of him; Jenks abandoned his pose of indifference and leaned forward on his elbows. Their eyes met and did not flinch away, but held each other mercilessly as Brumby went on the offense and Jenks parried. Gibbons, watching Brumby at work, thought it was as if he were burrowing into Jenks's brain and staking out a place to live there. There was something frightening in his intensity.

"Do you really think," asked Brumby at one point, "that there's absolutely no trace left of your victims in either that van or in Bluebell Close?"

"Trying to plant seeds of doubt, are you?" returned Jenks.

"We all have doubts," answered Brumby. "I imagine you used a tarp to torture your victims on and then tossed it in the bin afterwards. You're too clever to keep something like that, not even if you doused it with bleach ten times over. And those tarps are probably long gone. Except for the last one. That one would still be in the system, still traceable from the tip back to your bin."

"Throwing out a tarp is not a crime," pointed out Jenks.

Gibbons had watched many interrogations over the years and had seen many suspects broken, or boxed into a corner they could not escape from. He had seen them persuaded that it was in their best interests to confess, and he had seen them stolidly demand their lawyers. But this one did not end in any of those ways. It ended differently.

Jenks was still maintaining his innocence when Brumby changed tacks and said, "I'll be honest with you here, Mr. Jenks. I would probably never have suspected you if it hadn't been for the Sanderson murder. It was so clearly your work, and yet it broke from the pattern completely. I had to ask myself why you'd done it."

There was a subtle change in Jenks's countenance when he heard this. "And what did you think the reason might be?" he asked. His tone was light and conversational, but it was belied by his expression, which for the first time evinced emotion.

"Because he murdered Jody Farraday," said Brumby simply, "and she was your friend."

For the first time in a long while there was silence. Jenks was staring at Brumby as if trying to read the detective's mind. Then he smiled and inclined his head, in the manner of a chess player conceding the game before checkmate is reached.

"Yes, he did," said Jenks. "And you would never have caught me if he hadn't."

A collective sigh of relief went through the control room, but if Brumby felt it, too, he gave no sign. He was not yet done.

"You handled it very cleverly," he said. "I've never seen such clean crime scenes."

And that introduced an entirely new phase of the interview. Gibbons watched with a growing sense of revulsion as Brumby became the admiring student, with Jenks as the arrogant instructor. Brumby played it perfectly, never making himself out to be too much of a dullard, but nevertheless appearing ignorant enough to encourage Jenks's boasts. He coaxed every detail out of the monster in front of him, and did it all as if the two of them were somehow in collusion.

When at last it was over, when Jenks was officially charged and Brumby had let him be escorted out by uniformed officers, chatter broke out in the control room, everyone wanting to comment on various points. But Gibbons felt only the need for some fresh air. He was still feeling quite sick from some of the descriptions he had listened to, so, while the others fell into a discussion of the case, he slipped out, making his way through the empty halls of the station to the side door.

Outside, it was still snowing and everything looked clean and white. Gibbons took deep breaths of the frosty air, as if by doing so he could cleanse his mind.

He had not been there long when the door opened and Brumby appeared, alone.

"Hello, Sergeant," he said, joining Gibbons under the eaves.

"Hello, sir," said Gibbons, and watched while Brumby pulled out a packet of cigarettes and lit one, inhaling deeply and then blowing the smoke back out in a long stream. Gibbons would have expected him to be jubilant, if a bit weary, but Brumby appeared quite calm and neither tired nor worn out, but instead almost eviscerated, empty. Some of his usual intensity had faded from his grey eyes and the hollowness lurking in their depths was more evident.

"Very well done, sir," ventured Gibbons. "I've never seen an interview so masterfully conducted."

"Thank you, Sergeant," said Brumby. A slight smile touched his lips. "Do you know," he said, and his tone was nearly regretful, "the first time I did one of those I had to come out and be sick afterwards?"

"I'm feeling a bit queasy myself, and I didn't have to face up to him," admitted Gibbons, knowing this was the reason why the insight had been vouchsafed to him.

Brumby only nodded, looking out at the snow as he smoked. The silence between them was not uncomfortable, but Gibbons felt the need to express the sentiment growing within him as he watched the superintendent.

"We're all lucky to have someone like you," he said. "Most people may not know what you have to do to put someone like Jenks away, but they're grateful for the results anyway. I hope you know that."

Brumby glanced at him then. "Thank you for saying it," he said quietly. "In my position, one often forgets."

Epilogue

In Which a Familiar Setting Is Encountered

*I*t was more than a week before Gibbons at last returned to London. He got in late on a Friday, had a lie-in on the Saturday, and turned up at Bethancourt's Chelsea flat that evening for drinks and dinner. He had endeavored to keep his friend abreast of developments with frequent phone calls, but these often had to be cut short; and Bethancourt, back in his milieu, had been busy and not always available to chat.

"I want to hear it all, from beginning to end, in a coherent manner," said Bethancourt, handing Gibbons a glass of single-malt scotch. "The bits and pieces you've given me lately have me more muddled than informed."

"That's hardly my fault," said Gibbons. "I've barely been able to get through to you this last week."

He took his drink and settled himself in his favorite armchair, a deep, overstuffed one upholstered in green and beige stripes. Bethancourt took his usual place at the end of the couch, propping his feet up on one of his many coffee tables. Cerberus was curled up on the hearth rug, his nose tucked under his tail, while on the mantel above, the ship's clock quietly ticked away the minutes. Altogether it was a very comforting and relaxing atmosphere.

Bethancourt raised his glass. "Here's to your promotion," he said. "That's really splendid news, old man."

"Well, it's not certain yet," warned Gibbons. "Brumby only said he was recommending I take the inspector's exam—but what I didn't tell you is that he got MacDonald to endorse it, too."

"Did he?" said Bethancourt, enormously pleased for his friend. "That ought to cinch it—you'll be an inspector by February."

Gibbons laughed. "Hardly that quickly, if it happens at all," he said. "But I admit I've got my hopes up."

"Here's to it," said Bethancourt, raising his glass again, and this time Gibbons joined in the toast.

Then he paused, sniffing. "Something smells good," he said.

"I've made a daube," said Bethancourt. "It'll be ready about eight or so—I thought it would taste good on a cold night."

"It will," said Gibbons with a satisfied sigh. "All right then, where shall I start?"

"You were telling me about Brumby's interview with Jenks," said Bethancourt. "You had just got to the part where he told you about Jody—you said he confirmed what we thought?"

"Yes, it was pretty much as we'd figured it," said Gibbons. "According to Jenks, Jody ran into Sanderson as soon as she arrived, getting off the train. He was there to meet some guests and they bumped into each other. That was the single thing Jenks seemed sorry about—that he hadn't realized Sanderson was any kind of threat. Anyway, Sanderson must have been considerably startled to see Jody, but he was fast on his feet, and got her number. He called her the next day, and when he found out she and Jenks were planning on attending Christmas Eve midnight Mass at the Minster, he suggested they meet beforehand. He implied he might have a job for her."

"Which was probably being paid for keeping her mouth shut," said Bethancourt.

"Yes, well, Jenks didn't know about that," said Gibbons. "Jody never told him anything about Sanderson's sideline. He thought it all a bit odd, but, as he said himself, so much was odd about Jody that he didn't pay it much mind. They went into York together that evening and had dinner and then she went off to see Sanderson. She was to meet Jenks at the Minster in time for the service, but of course she never arrived."

"Then how did Jenks find out what happened?" asked Bethancourt.

"Well, he knew where she was meeting Sanderson," said Gibbons. "Apparently Mittlesdon's was Jody's own idea—Jenks said she seemed to find it amusing, though he couldn't see why. When she didn't turn up to midnight service, Jenks went along inside anyway, thinking she was just late, and then waited by the door for her after it was over. When he realized she'd never arrived at all, he walked over to Mittlesdon's to search for her. The back door was still unlocked—he found her keys and locked it when he left—so he just slipped inside and looked around for her."

"And found her dead, of course," said Bethancourt quietly. "I can almost feel sorry for him there."

Gibbons nodded. "He seemed the most, well, the most like a normal person when he was telling Brumby about the events on Christmas Eve."

"He seemed normal enough to me the one time I met him," said Bethancourt. "You know, so many people are a little odd in one way or another—I never thought Jenks was any different. It seems strange to me now, that I could have talked to a madman and never had a clue, not even a frisson up the spine."

"But you should have seen him after he admitted to being Ashdon," said Gibbons. "He was so proud of himself, and there was a gleam in his eyes—I don't know, I found it eerie."

"How far do you think his version of events is to be trusted?" asked Bethancourt.

"You mean about what Sanderson told him?" asked Gibbons. "Oh, I think he was honest about that. Sanderson was terrified and at the last was willing to tell him anything he wanted. And the story Jenks got from him makes sense—he offered Jody money to keep what she knew quiet, and she took offense. She told him to stick his money and he took that to mean she would tell anybody she pleased. They argued about it, she laughed at him, and he grabbed her and shook her. She fought back and pushed him away, but slipped and fell in doing so and hit her head. That dazed her, and Sanderson, now more frightened than ever, strangled her to death and then fled. He claimed to Jenks that he never meant to kill her, that the fight had simply got out of hand, but I'm not sure I believe that, and Jenks certainly didn't."

"Didn't he? You never told me that."

"He told Brumby that you know when you're killing someone. He actually laughed, and said, 'Do you think I would do it if I couldn't tell when it was happening? It only feels good when you can see the death in their eyes.'"

"Ugh." Bethancourt shuddered.

"Exactly," said Gibbons, and took a healthy swallow of scotch.

Bethancourt sipped his drink, too, as if the whisky were an anodyne to the uglier things in the world.

"So," he said, setting his glass down carefully, and reaching for his cigarette case, "now that you've got a full confession, does that mean all the other evidence is for naught?"

"Oh, no," said Gibbons. "They like to have a fully rounded-out case. They collected tons of trace evidence from the van, and more from the Buckinghamshire cottage. Oh, and they found Jody's missing bags in the bungalow, stowed away in the guest room, where she must have left them."

"I'd forgotten about the bags," admitted Bethancourt.

"So had everyone else," said Gibbons with a chuckle. "The

SOCKOs were most perplexed when they found them—at first they thought they'd got Jenks' souvenir trove from his murders, but the deeper they got into the bags, the less that seemed to fit. Nobody could figure it out until Howard happened to mention them to Brumby in front of me."

"Did Jenks have a souvenir trove?" asked Bethancourt curiously.

"Oh, yes," said Gibbons. "According to Brumby, they always do. But it was in the Buckinghamshire cottage, not in Yorkshire. He kept an earring from each of them, which Brumby says is pretty mild compared to other collections he's seen. I didn't ask further."

"No, neither would I," said Bethancourt. "There are some things I don't want to know."

"And I hope I never have to," said Gibbons. He paused, then said slowly, "Brumby, well, he's an odd case. He knows what delving into the brains of these people is doing to him, but he does it anyway because he's the one who can. One's got to admire that, but I don't think it's something I could do."

"No shame in that," said Bethancourt. " 'From each according to his abilities,' you know, and we can't all be Brumbys."

"No," said Gibbons.

"By the by," added Bethancourt, "I do appreciate you not going into great detail over Jenks' confession. The version the papers get is as much of that as I want."

"It's as much as I want, too," said Gibbons. "I'll be happy to leave the criminally insane to Brumby and his team—it's not a place I want to visit again."

"I'm quite selfishly glad of that," said Bethancourt. "It would mean the end of my hobby if you were to join Brumby's team permanently. Give me a nice, ordinary murder any day of the week."

"Hopefully, I'll be back to that shortly," said Gibbons. "Anyway, Carmichael is due back from his holidays on Monday, and I'm to report to him."

"A new case?" asked Bethancourt.

Gibbons shrugged. "Maybe," he said. "If so, I won't find out till Monday."

Softly the clock began to chime.

"That means dinner should be done," said Bethancourt. "Shall we adjourn to the dining room?"

"By all means," said Gibbons, finishing his scotch and rising. He stretched a bit and then started as the sound of a car alarm began wailing outside.

"All right?" asked Bethancourt, misinterpreting the start as a wince.

Gibbons grinned. "It's wonderful to be back in London," he said.

ACKNOWLEDGMENTS

First and foremost I must thank Kelley Ragland and Matt Martz for their extraordinary patience in the seemingly endless wait for this book. And also my thanks to any readers out there who were feeling the same way.

Jack and Mary Dodge made delightful traveling companions on my research trip to Yorkshire—I really don't know what I would have done without them. Our days in the Dales are some of my fondest memories.

Linda Pankhurst once again proved herself willing to discuss all aspects of British vernacular and to correct me where I went wrong. Plus she came all the way up to Yorkshire to visit. And Beth Knoche again volunteered her eagle eye for proofing. Thank you, ladies.

Jennifer Jackson is the best agent anyone ever had. Nuf said.

I love my cover art—thank you, Sergio Baradat.

I must also acknowledge the enormous role played by Mark Alicea in the writing of this book. I'm not sure exactly what he did, but his contribution was huge—I know this because he has assured me of it several times. (I think mostly he made me laugh at work.)

And Luis Cruz: your turn is next.